AUGUST
PEOPLE

Books by Ralph Graves

AUGUST PEOPLE

THE LOST EAGLES

THANKS FOR THE RIDE

Ralph Graves

AUGUST PEOPLE

DOUBLEDAY & COMPANY, INC., GARDEN CITY, NEW YORK

1985

All characters in this book are fictional
and any resemblance to actual persons,
living or dead, is entirely coincidental.

Library of Congress Cataloging in Publication Data
Graves, Ralph.
    August people.
    I. Title.
PS3557.R2887A95   1985   813'.54
ISBN: 0-385-19476-5
Library of Congress Catalog Card Number: 84-24661

For Eleanor

Without her, I would never have noticed, appreciated or understood many things in this book. More important, it would be impossible to imagine the last thirty years without her.

AUGUST
PEOPLE

August. This was the time when the entire Winderman family, all sixteen of them, assembled at the Island.

Last summer Ellen, as a brand-new Winderman, had been nervous about August. There were just too many Windermans, all in a swarm, all of them on a single piece of land, bound together not just by the land and the family name but by the fact that they all had to be there in August.

Lawrence had warned her, before they were married, not quite as a condition to their marriage but not quite as an option, either.

"Look," Lawrence had said, after they were already sure of each other, "there's something you have to put up with. I'll take you with me on bank trips, especially when I go to Europe, and we'll get other pieces of time here and there. But one thing you have to accept. Vacation comes in August, and we will spend it with my family. All of them. At the Island."

Ellen had already spent two surreptitious weekends there with Lawrence and had loved it. "I accept," she said. As an only child, she liked the idea of a large family gathering. And in the Winderman family there was even a certified patriarch, Lawrence's father, known affectionately to all by the preposterous patriarchal nickname of Ah-boo. "What's the problem?"

"Well," Lawrence said. He thought about it, then laughed. Although he often smiled, he seldom laughed. Ellen did not know whether this was his nature or his banker training. The first principle of banking, Lawrence said, is that banking is never a laughing matter.

"Why does it have to be August?" Ellen asked. "What's wrong with July? Or the fall? Or June?"

"Oh, those are all very nice," Lawrence said. "We can go there for weekends any of those times. Actually, there's less fog in July—or so the July people claim. They say the weather's generally better in July and not quite so hot, and of course the Island's less crowded then. Rents are lower, too, by a third. But we just happen to be August people. It's Ah-boo's pick, of course, and he picked August. It's *the* summer month. That's what you get when you get me."

"Since I've got you, I'll be an August people."

"The islanders, the year-round natives, have some opinions about us, not all flattering. They say July people are nicer, less demanding. And more informal. They say August people are always in a big hurry and want everything done yesterday, and that we are, I regret to say, a much bigger pain in the ass. But there's one area where August people win hands down. Care to guess?"

Ellen shook her head.

"Money," Lawrence said with his smile. "August is the month for the big spenders. The Island folks may not like us as much, but they definitely appreciate the way August people spend their money."

"Does that mean I get to spend more? I'm going to love being August people."

"Ready or not," Lawrence said, "it comes with the franchise."

Deck Day

Deck Day. Always the first clear morning in August.

Last summer Ellen had been so new to the Winderman family, so busy trying to be accepted and to remember all their names, including those of her own sudden stepchildren, that Deck Day had seemed total confusion. This summer, with all the names and faces memorized, Ellen could see Deck Day for what it was: a highly organized family ritual, like the tennis tournament or putting out the boats or Ah-boo's birthday party. Since she had grown up in a tiny family, these rituals took some getting used to. Deck Day was an Event.

Her brother-in-law, Brad, had called this morning at seven o'clock to confirm and to remind her that the order of houses today was Martha's, Brad's, then hers for cocktails and finally Ah-boo's. Since this program had been discussed in detail yesterday afternoon when the good-weather prediction came over the radio, Ellen didn't need a reminder; but Bradford still thought of her as the new girl who needed instruction in family ways. He meant to be helpful, not condescending, so she did not really mind. Besides, sometimes she needed the instruction, which Lawrence did not always provide.

She plugged in the coffee and woke Lawrence before

knocking on the children's doors and calling "Deck Day!" A predictable groan from Bryan, a deep sleeper who would have to be roused again in five minutes—and perhaps again after that. She did not enjoy waking Bryan—or, to be more honest, she did not enjoy Bryan, who seemed determined to make the stepmother-stepson relationship as difficult as possible. Not that he was hard to like. He got along well with the rest of the family and with all his cousins and aunts and uncles, and he had loyal friends outside the family. Ellen herself was his problem.

She knocked on the door of Howard, older stepson and also oldest of the nine Winderman grandchildren. He answered promptly and courteously, as though he had been awake for hours. She wished he wouldn't always be so courteous to her. A more natural tone of voice, some touch of warmth, would be so welcome. Lawrence's explanation was, "That *is* Howard's natural tone of voice," but he could not convince her. Howard, like Bryan, just didn't accept her, but he was more subtle about it. He kept a cool distance, while Bryan jabbed at her.

Only Nancy's voice was quickly cheerful. "Okay," she answered, and then almost in the same breath, "what a gorgeous day."

That's the way to wake up, Ellen thought as she walked back to the kitchen, past the living-room picture window and the sliding glass doors. And it was indeed a gorgeous day. She looked out over the field of wild grass, huckleberry and viburnum, past the big blue spruce and the tennis court, down to the bright ocean, the shallow waves breaking gently on the sandy beach. Offshore the sailboat and the Whaler bobbed on their moorings in the sparkling blue water. Yes, the first clear morning in August. A light breeze off the water, enough to ruffle the wild grass.

She put out juice, a loaf of Portuguese sweet bread and a loaf of sourdough. No one, not even Bryan, would want eggs and bacon this morning, since there would be food and drink at each house, although Bryan was capable of asking why there weren't any eggs, just to be pesky, just to see if he could get a rise.

This summer she and Lawrence would be supplying cocktails, right before the swim break and the lunch at Ah-boo's. Last August Lawrence's house had been second in rotation, which had made her assignment Kool-Aid and cookies. Ellen could smile about it now, but last August she had worried and wondered about how many packets of Kool-Aid and how many dozens of cookies were needed to serve all the Windermans. "And besides," she had asked Lawrence, "shouldn't I get some Cokes for people who don't like Kool-Aid?" Lawrence had disposed of that idea: "Cokes come at the third house with the cocktails. Second house is always Kool-Aid."

The Windermans always remembered where their traditions came from, and if anyone forgot, he could look it up in Ah-boo's notebooks, which ran all the way back to the day he bought the property thirty-eight years ago. Kool-Aid on Deck Day came from the time when Lawrence, Brad and Martha were children, and only the main house existed. "But it took much longer to paint the deck then," Ah-boo explained to her. "We didn't have Cuprinol, so we had to measure and mix linseed oil and turpentine and paint dryer. We used paint brushes then instead of rollers, and there were only five of us. It took all day to do this one deck. Anne and I used Kool-Aid as a midmorning bribe. It still works with the grandchildren, at least the younger ones."

Nancy came bouncing out barefoot and wearing her old one-piece red bathing suit and a tattered blue shirt of Bryan's, too big for her and rolled back at the sleeves. She was patting her short light brown hair roughly into place with both hands. She walked straight to Ellen, her wide blue eyes full of cheer, and gave her a friendly kiss on the cheek. "Good morning, Big Mommy," she said, then patted Ellen's belly through the full maternity skirt. "How's Old Seventeen today?"

The forthcoming baby, due one month from now, had been nicknamed by Nancy because, whatever its eventual name and sex, it would be the seventeenth member of the family—if you counted Ah-boo's housekeeper, Mary Benjamin, as everyone did.

"Just fine," Ellen said. She wondered if she could possibly like her new baby as much as she did this twenty-year-old stepdaughter. Nancy confounded all the rules about stepchildren. Supposedly the daughter was the one to resent most strongly the father's new wife, the female interloper who suddenly took the daughter's place in the father's affections. It had not been that way at all. Nancy and Ellen had been quickly at ease with each other, and friends soon after that. Nancy was glad to have another woman in what had been for many years a very male household. Now they had moved beyond friendship, although not quite to mother-daughter standing. That might never happen, since they were only a dozen years apart, but Nancy made Ellen feel completely welcome. Bryan and Howard were the ones who made Ellen feel the interloper. So much for psychology.

"Want some toast?" Ellen asked.

"Only juice," Nancy said. She put ice cubes in a tall glass and filled it with orange juice. One of the things that had astonished Ellen last summer was the amount of orange juice her new family consumed. Two quarts a day, minimum. That and the milk and the beer. She had solved her shopping problem by putting a second refrigerator in the basement for juice, beer, white wine, Coke and milk. Even so it was possible to run out if she didn't check on the supply.

Lawrence joined them, still a little sleepy, rubbing a hand over his face to persuade himself that perhaps he didn't have to shave today—or at least not yet.

"Hi, Pops." Nancy stood on tiptoe to kiss her father good morning. "Happy Deck Day."

Lawrence growled something and held out his hand for the mug of black coffee Ellen had poured for him. As he was fond of saying, all he wanted before his morning coffee was silence —and damn little of that.

"Too much sunburn, Daddy," Nancy said, reaching up to touch his pink, balding forehead. "Better wear a hat today."

Lawrence simply ignored this and sipped his coffee. He was the only Winderman to have lost any hair. Brad's was thick and brown, and Ah-boo's, though almost pure white, was also full. Lawrence's was soft and thin and now almost two inches back from the original hairline. Ellen thought it gave him great distinction, with his height and his long, bony Winderman face. But, she had to admit, it was more distinguished in New York than when he was wearing his Island garb. He was dressed in his ragged khaki shorts, green polo shirt and old white sneakers without socks. A handsome man, a little too heavy. She was still pleasantly surprised, a year and a half after marriage, that he was hers. His first wife, whom she had never met and would surely never meet, must have been insane to leave. Whatever the reason, and Lawrence would not talk about it, Ellen was grateful.

"Nancy," she said, "go get Bryan and Howard, will you? We're supposed to be at the barn in fifteen minutes."

Instead of walking back across the living room to the boys' bedrooms, Nancy put her fingers in her mouth and whistled. "Bryan! Howard!"

A snarl from Lawrence.

"Oops. Sorry, Dad." She put her empty juice glass on the counter and went to get the boys.

Ellen left Lawrence alone with his coffee and returned to their bedroom to take her heartburn pill. Actually she had almost no heartburn, just as in the early months she had had almost no morning sickness: a disgustingly healthy pregnancy. But because she was thirty-two and because this was her first, she believed in preventive measures. She popped the yellow pill into her mouth and chewed it.

Howard was standing at the kitchen counter, even taller than his father but with the extreme lankiness of young manhood. He was slicing a piece of Portuguese bread with the precision and neatness that characterized not only his actions but even his thoughts and speech. He paused to say good morning, then completed cutting the perfect slice. As Lawrence said, Howard was going to be very good at the bank. He placed the slice in the center of the toaster-oven rack and pushed down the switch. Age twenty-two, going on forty.

Bryan shuffled across the living room to join them. He was even less a morning person than Lawrence. Lawrence was fine after a cup of coffee and would even help make the bed after two cups, but Bryan was simply out of it. He could, and on vacation often did, sleep through to lunch. He was now on his feet but just barely. He leaned back against the counter and folded his arms across his bare chest. He wore only shorts, which he had neglected to zip up.

"Hey, good-lookin'," Nancy said, "your fly's open."

Bryan uncrossed his arms and looked down. "So it is." He crossed his arms again. "Why do we have to start so early?"

"Because it's so much *fun,*" Nancy said. She ruffled her younger brother's tangled curly hair. He tried to shake her off but didn't quite have the energy.

Lawrence finished his second mug of coffee and looked at his watch. "Time to go," he said. He was now himself: a man of pleasant, quiet authority. He took Nancy's sunburn advice and put on his floppy white tennis hat. "Come on, Bryan. And zip that fly."

Ellen unplugged the coffee. Howard brought along his piece of toast. They all followed Lawrence out the living room door into the bright August sunshine.

Lawrence led them single file down the sandy path that

would take them past the tennis court to the lower bridge. Ah-boo insisted that each household keep all its paths clear of blackberry vines, bull vine, poison ivy and huckleberry so that everyone could walk barefoot to all four houses. The grandchildren usually went barefoot from morning till night except when playing tennis. The court they were passing was empty now because of Deck Day, but normally it was in use all day long.

In spite of the hot sun, Ellen felt comfortable with the breeze fresh off the ocean a few yards away. The soil underfoot was soft and sandy this close to the beach, but then as the path curved away toward the stream and the blue spruce, it hardened into a mixture of clay and sand. In the back part of the property around Brad's and Martha's houses, the soil was dark brown loam.

Great variety existed in these fifty acres—actually only 49.3 acres, as every Winderman well knew. Near the shoreline behind the fine sandy beach the land was almost flat, gently rising away from the water, covered with beach grass and wild roses and patches of huckleberry. This was the area of Ah-boo's house, the barn, the tennis court. Lawrence and Ellen's house was farther back, where the land really began to rise and pines and scrub oak took over from the beach grass. Still farther away from the shore and on still higher land stood the last two houses. There the land had had to be cleared of thick old oaks before the houses could be built. All four houses had a view of the ocean but, because of the way they had been placed and the way certain trees had been left standing, no view of each other.

Through the middle of the property flowed the stream shown grandly on old Island maps as the Quatchum River. The Quatchum was never more than four or five feet wide until it came down to the beach, where it broke up, spread into small channels and trickled into the ocean. "The Quatchum Delta," the family called it. At its upper end the

Quatchum was beautiful: clear, fresh water flowing over and around dark gray rocks. The sandy bottom was never more than six or eight inches below the surface except after heavy rain. In midsummer the streamers of grass were brilliant yellow-green in the water, and on the banks grew thick ferns and pepper bushes.

They came, still in single file led by Lawrence, to the lower bridge. It had been built by hand more than thirty years ago, and looked it. Ah-boo, the designer and chief builder, claimed it was the true "rude bridge that arched the flood." He had seen drawings of the one in Concord and pronounced it, by comparison, a marvel of modern engineering. Lawrence waited to give Ellen a hand up the two plank steps that rested somewhat uncertainly on rough concrete slabs. Then came "the center span," wide two-inch-thick boards nailed to rough posts sunk in the Quatchum's banks. No railing was necessary, not even for pregnant women. If someone fell off the bridge, it would be only a three-foot drop. The boards, the posts and the steps had to be replaced every few years because of rot, but no one thought of changing the design. It had, Ah-boo said, a certain outrageous integrity.

Just across the bridge stood Ellen's favorite tree—everyone's favorite tree, the blue spruce. The Windermans planted it soon after they had bought the property almost forty years before. Perhaps because of its location near the stream, perhaps because no nearby trees interfered with its sunlight, perhaps because of some secret genetic strength, it was a giant. The trunk was barrel-thick and the foliage spread across almost forty feet. The path wound past the outer edge of the branches so that you could look underneath into the cool shadow and the floor of fallen needles.

Then they were in the open. Ah-boo's grand old shingled house with its steep roof and row of old-fashioned white-trimmed dormer windows stood gray and sturdy and huge in the sun, beach grass waving all around it in the morning breeze. Behind the house was the barn, the same weathered gray as the house but built of vertical planks rather than shingles. Here was the starting point of Deck Day.

A dozen figures in front of the barn were loading equipment into the green pickup truck. Brad's Volkswagen van was parked at the corner of the barn to help move the family from one house to another. Ellen could pick out Brad's bright red swordfisherman's cap with the long black visor and Ah-boo's white hair as he stood beside the truck, directing his grandchildren. Nancy shouted hello. The figures looked up and waved, and Nancy ran ahead toward them. Howard and Bryan followed more slowly, Howard in dignity, Bryan in morning fatigue.

Lawrence looked down at her. "Ready to face it?"

She smiled up at him and hugged his arm. He didn't realize how much she enjoyed the Winderman festivals. As they approached the group around the truck, she ran through her catechism from left to right, just as she always did, just to make sure. Charlie, Brad Junior, Amy, Sue, her own Nancy, Anne, Ah-boo, Brad, her own Howard, Alice, Martha, Martha's latest "friend"—what was his name? yes, Richie— her own Bryan and poor, angry Christopher. Herself and Lawrence. All accounted for except Bonjy, Ah-boo's housekeeper, who would be up at the house working on lunch for the entire crew. Ellen was glad she hadn't had to do lunch last summer, when it was all new to her, and rather glad not to have to do it this year. However, next year would be her inexorable turn, baby and all.

Ah-boo walked up to her in his unfailingly polite way to say good morning. The finest-looking of all the Winderman men, he carried his seventy years with great style. Although not as tall as Lawrence or Brad, he stood straight and trim with none of Lawrence's slouch nor Brad's hulkiness. He still played tennis—doubles only, he would say deprecatingly— and swam every day. He had given up smoking years ago, an accomplishment of which he still boasted to his grandchildren, urging them to follow his lead. His eyebrows were iron gray above the warm, welcoming, very direct blue eyes. They always looked straight into the eyes of the person he was speaking to. He bent forward now and kissed Ellen lightly on the cheek.

"This is very nice, my dear. I wasn't sure you would feel up to it."

"I wouldn't dare miss it. I feel wonderful. How are you?"

"If you don't pry too much," he said with a smile, "I'm fine too. Ah there, Lawrence. Now then, everybody, let's finish loading up."

All the grandchildren from nine-year-old Alice to twenty-two-year-old Howard handed into the truck the paint trays, the long-handled paint rollers with their fluffy new sponges, the rolls of masking tape, the big, gray five-gallon cans of wood preservative, can after can, enough to cover the decks of four houses. This would keep the wood from drying and splintering. The last step was for everyone, grandchildren and parents alike, to follow Ah-boo into the barn and pick out a pair of work gloves from the mammoth collection hanging on the back wall. Ah-boo bought work gloves of all sizes every summer by catalogue, just as he bought dozens of tennis sneakers to keep in the wooden bin down by the court.

"Okay, all set," Brad told Ah-boo. He tapped the visor of his swordfishing cap with two fingers, almost a salute. "Want me to drive the truck with the kids? Sue can take all the grown-ups in the van."

Ellen noticed an almost deliberate hesitation in Ah-boo's reply, not as though he were thinking it over but as though he were drawing Brad's attention to the fact that he hadn't simply said yes. Only a few seconds.

Then, in his always courteous voice: "No, Bradford, I think I'll drive the truck. Why don't you go with Sue and the others? Or you can ride with me. Now, Ellen, where will you be most comfortable?"

She wanted to answer that it didn't matter, but because he was being thoughtful, she asked to ride in the front seat of the van. Ah-boo handed her in himself, then climbed into the cab of the pickup. The grandchildren were scrambling into the truck bed behind him.

In the driver's seat of the van, Brad's wife, Sue, looked around at her passengers and announced with her customary enthusiasm, "Ready to roll."

"So roll," came Martha's voice from the back seat. She seemed slightly amused by Sue's cheerleader phrasing and also slightly disdainful. Sue and Martha managed to rub against each other on many subjects.

Sue reversed into the curve of the driveway, braked, then shifted smoothly forward into the dirt road that would take them out to State Road. She was an expert driver, honed by years of delivering her four children and their friends to all the social, educational, athletic and medical centers of suburban New York. Ellen, who let Lawrence do most of their family driving, was not in Sue's class.

This year's schedule started with Martha's house. You could not get from Ah-boo's barn to Martha's house without going out to State Road and then turning in the far driveway on the other side of the Quatchum. Then, after Martha's, it would be back to State Road and back down this same driveway to Brad and Sue's. Then later back once again to the far driveway to Lawrence and Ellen's house, and finally back once more to finish at Ah-boo's. Each time it was better than a mile's drive with all the equipment and people, and it made no logical sense. "Yes it does," Lawrence had explained. "You're just using the wrong logic. We do the houses in reverse order of their age, and each year each house moves up one notch in the order. Ah-boo's logic. We're all taking turns being first, but always in order." Ellen still found it ridiculous.

As the land rose toward State Road, the dirt drive changed to macadam tracks with thank-you-ma'am bumps to guide the rainwater off to the side. Sue had to shift gears at each bump but did so with almost no loss of momentum. Now they were among the oak trees, passing Brad and Sue's house with its wide expanse of deck waiting its orderly turn for the Cuprinol preservative. A few hundred yards brought them to the twin granite pillars marking the entrance to the property. Then down macadam-topped State Road, passing over the Quatchum to reach the matching granite pillars marking the far driveway. At Martha's house Sue parked on one side of the crushed-gravel circle, and they all got out. All the houses were weathered shingle with various combinations of picture windows and sliding glass doors. Martha's was both the newest and the smallest.

The pickup came right behind them, two of the boys riding on the front fenders. Ah-boo had barely stopped before grandchildren began hopping out and passing down equipment from the truck bed.

Years of organization and practice now took effect. Brad and Lawrence moved quickly along the house-side perimeter of the deck with their three-inch rolls of masking tape, covering the bottom edge of the cedar shingles so that the preservative would not splatter them. Under Ah-boo's direction the aluminum paint trays were placed on three different areas of the fir decking. With screwdrivers the older boys pried open the tops of the five-gallon cans and filled the trays with the clear, oily, brown-gold Cuprinol. Alice, who was Brad and Sue's youngest, had the job of bringing the paint rollers from the truck and placing two beside each tray. By the time Lawrence and Brad had finished masking, the trays and rollers were ready.

"All right, Bradford," Ah-boo said. "Got your watch? Let's begin."

Brad already had his stopwatch in hand. Everybody was smiling and eager. "Twenty-minute shifts as usual. Team One. That's Lawrence, Charlie, Anne, Bryan, Brad Junior and Sue. Everybody got a roller? Martha, you ready with the eats? Team Two, inside for coffee and doughnuts and stay off the deck. Here we go, and remember, spread it even. No pools and no sloshing. Go!"

Ellen, who had refused an exemption for eighth-month pregnancy, was on the second team, so she went indoors with her group. The big tray of fresh doughnuts from the Island Bakeshop looked luscious: glazed, chocolate, plain, cinnamon-sugared and jelly. She took her mug of coffee from Martha and moved away from temptation. But temptation followed her in the form of little Alice, chocolate doughnut in one hand and jelly doughnut in the other.

"Aunt Ellen," she said during glorious bites, "don't you think it's unfair that I can't be a roller?"

Ellen knew this appeal was addressed to her only because she was the newest member of the family and therefore might be sympathetic. Indeed, she was completely sympathetic. However, she was well-informed on this particular rule. "How old are you now?"

A pause. Another fierce bite. Ellen could see that the jelly was strawberry, her absolute favorite. Alice had her mother Sue's small brown eyes which now narrowed defensively. "Practically ten," Alice said.

"That's not quite ten, is it?"

"Yanh-yanh on Alice." It was the mocking voice of Christopher, who had come up behind them. Christopher often turned up unexpectedly, seeming to wander everywhere alone.

Ellen was sure he meant to be funny, pretending to talk at Alice's age level, but it didn't come out that way. Christopher was Martha's son by her second marriage. Very few things seemed to come out right for him. Sixteen years old, he had the long, thin Winderman face and long, loose blond hair. Alice squeezed her lips together hard and turned away without answering.

"That wasn't very nice," Ellen said. "It's hard to be the youngest."

Christopher's mouth twisted. He had a nicely shaped mouth, but it was constantly doing something or saying something to make it less attractive. "Not all *that* hard. Besides, I didn't make the rule. Grandfather did."

Alone of the grandchildren, Christopher sometimes referred to Ah-boo as Grandfather. This was particularly odd because it was Christopher who had invented his grandfather's nickname. Ellen had not only heard the legend from Lawrence; she had seen the proof of it, framed and hanging on the wall of Ah-boo's living room next to the fireplace.

Charles Winderman had always believed in Family Occasions, one of which was reading aloud to his children and grandchildren on Christmas Eve. One of the poems he always read was Leigh Hunt's "Abou Ben Adhem," a poem for which he had limited respect but which sounded well on Christmas Eve. It was also an easy poem for the young children to understand and could, in any event, do no serious harm. He believed it was important to reach children early, on their level. Improvements could be made later.

After several years of Christmas Eve readings, Christopher, then one of the youngest and perhaps the brightest of all the grandchildren, wrote a Christmas card for his grandfather that cited the opening line of the poem. With a five-year-old's misspelling it said: "Ah-boo Ben Adam, may his tribe increes." Since the Winderman tribe was already large and definitely increasing, and since Christopher's card was original and entirely his own creation, it instantly achieved family status. Within a year, Charles Winderman was Ah-boo to everyone—to in-laws, grandchildren, close family friends, even his own children, who switched back and forth between Ah-boo and Father. Quite a triumph for young Christopher, who had not enjoyed many triumphs since. He had been expelled from two schools, so far, and there had been police trouble for speeding while driving without a license, being under age and "borrowing" someone else's car. Martha made it clear to everyone, including Christopher, that Christopher was a trial. Each year she announced with pleasure that he would be spending the month of July with his father. Nobody knew how Christopher's father felt about this event, but when Christopher rejoined the family at the Island in August, he was in no better spirits than before he left. The situation was not helped, Ellen felt sure, by the fact that Martha usually had a new "friend" as her "house guest." This year it was Richie Miller, a New York City personnel consultant—whatever that was. Last year it had been that tennis coach, Will Something. Ellen had been amazed that Ah-boo would permit such a flagrant arrangement, but Lawrence explained that Ah-boo thought it better to keep Martha on the Island, even with a houseguest, than to have her running off to the Berkshires or to Newport. In any case, the "friend" and Christopher never got along, but then neither did Christopher with most of his cousins. Bryan thought Christopher was a pill, and while Howard would not say such a thing aloud, Bryan usually thought what Howard thought. Nancy, however, stood up for Christopher, and not just because she was naturally generous. "He's much nicer than he lets on," Nancy said, "and besides, everybody's always judging him." Because of Nancy, Ellen tried to see the best in Christopher, but sometimes it was difficult.

A buzzing sound. Brad pulled out his fancy stopwatch, shut off the warning signal and said, "Okay, Team Two. Everybody outside for the next shift. That's Ellen, Howard, Amy, Christopher, Nancy and me. Fifteen seconds."

Team Two trooped through the sliding glass doors to take over the rollers from the first shift. Three large sections of the deck were already finished, dark and damp. Ah-boo and Martha's friend, Richie, were pouring fresh supplies of Cuprinol into the paint trays. Ellen took Sue's four-foot-long roller, dipped the spongy end into the tray, pressed out the excess liquid and attacked a new deck area. She loved the oily scent of the preservative. The wide roller covered the dry fir boards easily and smoothly, and she did not have to bend over to do the work. Unlike, say, weeding or dusting, one could see the results instantly. She was teamed with Howard. He dipped and rolled in concentrated silence, covering the boards rapidly with his long reach. He did not speak to her, which she did not mind, except on principle. Down the deck Brad was working with Martha's daughter, Amy. Still farther along were Nancy and Christopher, Nancy chattering away and Christopher making low-voiced answers. It was hot in the bright sun but not unpleasant.

Standing on the steps out of the way of the rollers, Alice was repeating her complaint to Ah-boo. "I'd be *such* a good roller," she said. "I'm the only one who's not allowed."

"Everyone else is ten or older." Ah-boo explained what Alice already knew.

The kindly patience in his voice annoyed Ellen. Much as she admired and liked the old man, she thought he imposed far too many rules and regulations on his large family. Everything was done his way. Surely it would do no harm to let Alice wield a roller, as she was dying to do, but Ah-boo's rule, established years ago, forbade this. Like the fine teacher he had once been, Ah-boo was now treating Alice's complaint with thoughtful attention. Ellen had never heard him be impatient or abrupt with the grandchildren, but she knew this was an argument that Alice could not win.

"Besides," Ah-boo went on, "you have your own important work to do. Handing out and collecting the rollers. Stripping the masking tape after we finish. Keeping your eyes on the trays to make certain no one runs out."

Alice kicked at the step railing with one bare foot. "But I could do all those things when I was five. It's not fair."

"No, it's very fair," Ah-boo said. "You may not like it, Alice, but it's fair because it's the same for everybody. Everyone in the family has been through the same apprenticeship. Even your father when he was little had to wait till he was ten. He was impatient, too."

"But that was with paintbrushes," said Alice, who knew her family history. "That was much harder, you always say. Rolling is *easy*."

"We'll see how you do next year. I'm sure you'll be very good because you've been watching how it's done."

A terrible thought occurred to Alice. "Who's going to do my jobs next year? There aren't any younger kids."

"That's certainly going to be a problem, isn't it? But actually there will be someone younger. What about it, Ellen? Do you think your baby will be ready for Alice's jobs?"

"Oh, Ah-boo!" Alice said, giggling. "The baby won't even be a year old."

"But you said your jobs were so easy."

"Not *that* easy."

"I never thought they were. I guess we will just have to split them up until the baby grows up to the responsibility."

Ellen stopped rolling and turned to look at Ah-boo. There he was, manipulating little Alice to the hilt, just as he did everyone in the family. He had been doing it so long, in most cases since birth, that they were used to it, perhaps did not even realize what was being done to them. But it was easy for Ellen, a newcomer, to recognize. Alice, for example, had just been taught several lessons, she had been made to feel happy and important, but at the same time her reasonable request had been refused. Ah-boo returned Ellen's look with a benign smile and walked off to see how the other rollers were getting along. Absolute self-satisfaction.

It was too much for Ellen. "Alice," she said, loudly enough for Ah-boo to hear, "my back is stiff this early in the morning. How about finishing my shift for me?"

"Yow!" Alice said. She jumped forward to take Ellen's roller.

Ah-boo turned slowly and stared at Ellen. No anger, no resentment, just a long, steady appraisal. Ellen returned the look as she said to Alice, "Do a good job now." And then for Ah-boo's benefit, "I'll be all right for my next shift."

Another shift and a half were enough to finish Martha's house. What remained in the trays was poured into a large bucket so that it would not spill during the transfer. Trays and rollers were stacked in the truck. Alice pulled the masking tape off the shingles and threw it in the kitchen wastebasket. Everyone piled into the truck and the van to drive to Brad and Sue's house, which had the biggest deck of all. The team on duty when Martha's deck had been completed now served a final eleven minutes by Brad's stopwatch. Martha took Sue's place on Team One so that Sue was free to dispense Kool-Aid and cookies. Sue did not just dispense; she hustled, urging everyone to have another glass. "You had grape last time. You haven't lived till you've tried the orange. Better take two of the raisin cookies. They're great with the orange."

It was past eleven when they reached Ellen's house. Now she was excused from rolling to handle the Cokes and cocktails. Richie took Lawrence's place on the rolling crew so that Lawrence could help her. Everyone knew the rules, which remained the same no matter which house had the cocktail duty. For those under sixteen, only Coke or Pepsi. That was Alice, Brad Junior and Anne. From sixteen to eighteen, which meant Christopher, wine and beer were permissible. Eighteen and over, anything goes. In the olden days before Ellen's time, the rule had been only wine and beer from eighteen to twenty-one, but after several years of consultation and pleading, Ah-boo had agreed to the liberalization. Whenever anyone accused him of inflexibility, as everyone did now and then, he always cited his change in the Deck Day liquor laws.

As Ellen had noted last year and had prepared for this year, the overwhelming favorite was icy white wine. She had stocked her drinks refrigerator with magnums of Soave and kept filling and refilling plastic glasses as the shifts came in from the deck. Lawrence, of course, had his martini instead of wine, and Martha—of course, of course—had Scotch on the rocks, one for each twenty-minute break.

Martha did, indeed, drink a lot but with little effect on her speech, her walk or her intelligence. If there was any difference to be detected, it was a seeming increase in her sensuality. There was, Ellen thought, a more direct, more speculative way that Martha looked at men and something that was almost a sexual swagger, although nothing so overt as that word implied. It was more atmospheric than physical. Martha had been fortunate: her face was not as long as her brothers', and her mouth was soft and well curved. Her eyes were big but almost without lashes, so that they looked wide open and slightly vulnerable. She was deeply interested in men, an interest she conveyed not so much by word or movement as by aura. She never flaunted herself, but it was there to be read. Few men missed it. As Lawrence said: "In my experience, money causes far more trouble between men and women than sex does. Far more. But in Martha's case I have to make an exception."

Martha had to make a few concessions now to being forty, but not too many and not too serious. Her breasts, shoulders and legs were still good, but Ellen noticed that this year all Martha's bathing suits had skirts to disguise the spreading

hips. Martha's favorite summer jewelry had been big, costumey necklaces pointing the way to the nice cleavage, but
the necklaces had surrendered to the deterioration of
Martha's neckline. Big, costumey earrings had taken their
place.

Ellen saw that Martha's glass of Scotch was going to run
out before the twenty-minute break ended. Martha saw it too,
interrupted her conversation and came back to Lawrence for
a refill. Lawrence crammed her glass with ice cubes before
pouring the Scotch. Martha walked away happy.

"Have to look out for little sister," Lawrence said.

Five minutes later, when Brad announced the change in
shifts, Martha took her glass out on the deck. She was soon
back, however.

She grinned at Lawrence and Ellen. "Thought I might get
away with it in the confusion," she said, "but Ah-boo caught
me."

"What did he say?" Ellen asked.

"What do you mean, what did he say? He said 'Martha.'
That was the entire conversation. 'Naughty girl' was only
implied."

Ellen laughed. Martha mocked herself as much as she did
anyone else. "I'll save your drink for you."

"Don't bother. It'll be water by then. But save the bottle."

This proved unnecessary, for their deck was finished during Martha's shift. Brad stuck his head in the door to say they
would be moving on to Ah-boo's house for swimming and
lunch and that Ellen and Lawrence could shut down the bar.

"Going to swim?" Lawrence asked her.

"Certainly. Let's clean up and change."

Ellen collected plastic glasses and cans from all over their
living room while Lawrence put away bottles and sponged
the bar table. Most of the others had been in bathing suits all
morning, and the few exceptions could borrow suits from the
spare supply at Ah-boo's house. There would be no maternity

suits, however, so Ellen went into her own bedroom to change. She had all her clothes off and was admiring her huge bulge in the full-length bathroom mirror when Lawrence came in behind her. He patted her ass as he did whenever she was nude, then cupped her breasts in his hands. They looked at each other in the mirror, both smiling. His chin rested on the top of her head.

"If it weren't for Deck Day," Lawrence said.

"There's always Deck Night. Hurry up, put your suit on."

He pretended a deep sigh of despair and gave her a final squeeze. "It's hard to get any satisfaction around here."

"Ho ho," Ellen said. "Let me get dressed."

Why were all maternity bathing suits made of flowered prints, Ellen wondered, as she tied herself into the pink and green pants and then wriggled into the dress portion. It made her feel like an overstuffed easy chair.

By the time they had their suits on, the family was loading the green pickup for the last time. They drove back to the barn where they had started early this morning. Ah-boo told them to leave everything in the truck and get to the beach. He himself walked to the house to make sure that Bonjy had lunch under control, even though everybody knew she did.

When Ellen and Lawrence and Martha and Richie reached the sand, the nine grandchildren and Brad and Sue were already in the water. The waves today were too small for surfing, so they had swum out to the two boats, the sailboat and the Whaler hitched to their moorings. The rest of the Winderman fleet lay pulled up on the beach far above the high-water mark, their bows touching the beach grass. This was another of Ah-boo's rules: whoever used the smaller boats—the catamaran, the two Sunfish, the dinghy—had to drag them to the edge of the grass. This was higher than necessary for safety, except in the biggest storms, but Ah-boo believed that rules should be clear and not subject to interpretation.

Failure to drag a boat to the grass meant a loss of boat privileges for three days.

Colored shirts lay scattered on the sand near the pile of towels. This was a remarkable stretch of beach. The clean sand ran ten yards deep before the grass started. The Island had become such a popular resort in the last twenty years that waterfront property, even as little as fifty feet of it, brought an extraordinary price. Very little such land ever came on the market. The best that most new homeowners could hope for was water-view property—no land touching the water but a view of the water. Even that was expensive. Yet here Ellen stood on five hundred beautiful sandy yards of Winderman beach, interrupted only by the area in the center where the Quatchum emptied into the ocean. No season passed without real estate agents asking if by any chance some of the Winderman beach front might be for sale.

Ellen and Lawrence waded into the ocean a little distance down the beach from where the rest of the family whooped and cavorted. The ocean water was chill at first in spite of the August sun. They swam out together, Lawrence swimming slowly to keep even with her.

Twenty yards out Ellen said, "Far enough for young mothers. You go ahead." She stopped, treading water, and Lawrence then swam out at his normal speed.

The grandchildren were playing boat tag, a game that Lawrence and Brad had invented when they were little and whose rules grew more elaborate every summer. It involved climbing up on the sailboat and the Whaler and performing various rituals in a precise order before leaping back into the sea. A complex subset of rules dealt with the two mooring lines. Ellen had never bothered to get the game straight in her head, but she was sure that her baby would.

She looked back toward the long stretch of beach. Down to her right at the far end of the Winderman property, beyond the blue spruce and the tennis court, she could see the stone wall marking the boundary between their land and the state land. There the shore curved out to form a small, scrub-covered bluff where the white concrete lighthouse stood. She could see the roof of her own house behind the tennis court. Almost directly in front of her, Ah-boo's wide, old-fashioned house loomed authoritatively above the sand. The second stone wall marking the near boundary of the property came down to the water at a sharp slant, and over to her left was the Smollett house, smaller than Ah-boo's but built in the same style, with the same second-floor dormer windows cut into the roof line.

Ah-boo was not interested in selling property. He was interested only in buying. For years he had been trying to persuade Smollett to sell him that triangle of land alongside the slant of the stone wall, but Jack Smollett was stubborn. He liked his land the way it was, and he did not need money. According to Lawrence, Ah-boo would never give up trying to get that piece of land.

When Ah-boo first bought his property from the Benbow estate back in 1946, both he and the Benbows' lawyer had understood that it was a fifty-acre tract. The Benbow family had owned the land for generations going back more than a hundred years, and everybody "knew" it was fifty acres. This was not part of the deed, which simply described the property's borders: State Road, the two stone walls and the ocean. Only when the land was surveyed for title registration did Ah-boo learn that instead of owning fifty acres he owned 49.3 acres. Lawrence had no memory of the uproar that followed, but his mother had told him that Ah-boo was furious. He paid for two additional independent surveys, but it still came out 49.3. Since the land was bounded on three sides by State Road, by the unpurchasable state land where the lighthouse stood and by the Atlantic Ocean, the only possibility for expansion, the only chance to get back to that nice, round, substantial total of fifty acres was the Smollett property. And

Jack Smollett continued to say no—no at any price, no for any part of his land, and especially no for that acre of water-front land by the slanting stone wall. Ellen had met Smollett, an otherwise reasonable and pleasant gentleman with a good sense of humor. He and Ah-boo managed to be civil to each other, and Smollett acted like a man who would be willing to go further, to become a good neighbor and even a friend. But of course this was impossible.

There, across the water, came the three mournful notes of the foghorn mounted on Ah-boo's deck post. That meant fif-teen minutes to lunch. Ellen began to swim toward the beach, knowing that Lawrence would catch up by the time she reached shore. All the Windermans were, understandably, splendid swimmers. The grandchildren and the others were wading in. Nancy came running down the sand with a yel-low beach towel. She waved to Ellen, waved the towel and dropped it on the sand for her and Lawrence to use.

She and Lawrence were drying off hands and faces, each using one end of the towel, when the single long note from the foghorn announced lunch in five minutes. They walked to the house together, the last to arrive but still on time.

Two long trestle tables stood in the yard. Bonjy was di-recting traffic so that the family moved down both sides of both tables, loading their bright-colored plastic plates with deviled eggs, cucumber sandwiches trimmed of crusts and Bonjy's fried chicken. At the end of each table were glasses of iced tea with lemon wedges on a platter beside them.

"Anything left for us?" Lawrence asked.

"Lawrence!" Bonjy said, beaming as though she hadn't seen him in weeks instead of just last evening. "Ellen, come right here and get some nourishment for that baby. There might be a scrap of chicken left. I fried eight of them."

Mary Benjamin had been Ah-boo's housekeeper since his wife's death nearly twenty years ago. She was still house-keeper by occupation but accepted by all as a full family member. Except that in this clan of people with long bony faces and lanky bodies, Mary Benjamin plainly came from different stock. She was round-faced, round-cheeked, cheerful, bustling and easy to be with. Her eyes, behind rimless spectacles, were bright and twinkling. Her body, always in a dress, never in slacks, was matronly. She had straight light brown hair now turning white. She wore it pulled back into a bun "to keep it out of the way." She was a born provider. An opportunity like this to serve lunch for sixteen people with big appetites was enough to keep her happily excited for days ahead. Everyone called her Bonjy except Ah-boo, who used Bonjy and Mary and Mrs. Benjamin interchangeably, depending on mood or circumstance. Although she was devoted to him, she always addressed him as Mr. Winderman. There was nothing formal about her, but it reminded everyone, perhaps including herself, that Ah-boo was, after all, her employer.

Ellen had a hard time convincing Bonjy that one piece of chicken was all her weight permitted. Ellen loved fried chicken but did not dare make it in her own home or even let her cook make it. Fried chicken with spices and homemade biscuits started from scratch, without the help of any prepared biscuit mix, had been the specialty of Cecilia, Lawrence's cook for fifteen years. Cecilia had retired when Ellen and Lawrence got married. She had been beloved by the children, especially Bryan, and her departure had been a serious, unforgiven strike against Ellen. Ellen had risked fried chicken only once, but Bryan had been so contemptuous that she did not repeat it. She never risked biscuits at all. She was proud of her skill in the kitchen, but some things were beyond skill—fried chicken and Bryan, to name two.

The grandchildren and Brad and Sue all ate sitting crosslegged on the grass, circled by Ah-boo's old airedale, Lionel, who was looking for handouts. This position was more than Ellen could manage without a derrick. She sat with Martha and Richie on the broad steps leading up to the veranda, balancing her plate on her crowded lap. Ah-boo and Lawrence ate apart on one of the veranda benches. Ellen guessed from the serious murmur of their conversation that they were discussing bank business. Both would have to fly to New York next Tuesday for the monthly board meeting of the Winderman Trust Company. Lawrence must be filling in his father on some current problem.

Ah-boo had great respect for Lawrence's business abilities, which he had described to Ellen with pride. "Lawrence is the perfect banker," Ah-boo had said, "conservative, skeptical, discreet." The Winderman Trust had not invested any of its assets in foreign loans, even when every other bank was rushing to get some part of the action. "Lawrence said no," Ah-boo had told her, "and we went along with him, even though some of the board thought we were missing out on the interest rates. As a result, we don't own the slightest portion of the Mexican problem or the Brazilian problem or the Polish problem. Our customers appreciate that, and it's all Lawrence's doing."

Ellen was no expert on banking, but her eight years in the retail fashion business had given her a lively interest in money and an awareness of profit and loss as an unforgiving system of measurement. She liked listening to Lawrence talk about his work, even though some of its subtleties and intricacies were impossible to follow. Because she had worked herself and enjoyed it, she always wanted to know about other people's work. In fact, as he often reminded her, the first thing she had asked Lawrence when they met at a dinner party was what kind of work he did. He had answered that he was in a bank but one she had never heard of, the Winderman Trust. "You're right," Ellen said. "What does it do?" Lawrence had looked at her for a moment, judging the extent of her interest, and also, as he admitted later, thinking how attractive she was—attractive but perhaps a bit nosy. Then he answered: "We specialize in the affairs and concerns of the rich. Especially the very rich." Ellen had laughed aloud, delighted both by his candor and by his willingness to outrage a stranger. She wished she could hear what Ah-boo and Lawrence were saying now.

Nancy came around with a platter of fried chicken. Richie took a piece, Martha said no. Ellen was about to say no thanks, but Nancy simply put a breast on her plate. "Old Seventeen is starving," she said. "Besides, you're going to say no to dessert, which is chocolate cake, and this will make Bonjy feel better. And you too."

Quite true, Ellen thought. "You're a bad influence," she said, and then gratefully took a crunchy bite.

Nancy moved on to peddle the chicken to others. What a nice girl, and what a pretty figure. Not too bosomy, wonderful long slim legs. Ellen would have loved to look like that at twenty. It gave one such a head start.

Only after the chicken platters were reduced to a few wings did Bonjy bring from the kitchen her chocolate cakes with thick fudge icing. This and blueberry pie were her dessert specialties, but it would be another week before the blueberries were ripe. They were always ready in time for Ah-boo's birthday party. Lobster and corn and blueberry pie on the beach, another family ritual, the grandest event in August. And this year especially, because Ah-boo would be seventy. That reminded her: she had to start thinking about her poem. No presents were allowed, because Ah-boo believed that the young should not give presents to the old. Only speeches or original poems, no matter how brief, were acceptable gifts. Ellen knew vaguely what she wanted to say, a message from Old Seventeen complaining about all the missed birthday parties of the past but looking forward to catching up next summer. This would be the last of Ah-boo's grandchildren. Sue, in her mid-forties, was presumably (even if not technically) beyond breeding age. Martha might well marry again but would never have another child. And Ellen and Lawrence simply wanted to have one child together. Old Seventeen would be the last of the generation. Then would come the great-grandchildren.

She would not have minded staying on the steps in the sun, or even going home for a nap, but the final deck remained. As soon as the last slice of cake had vanished, Brad herded the grandchildren to the truck to get the equipment. Ah-boo and Lawrence finished their talk and took the benches off the deck. Ellen tried to help Bonjy clear the trestle tables but was shooed away.

Ah-boo's house, built in the twenties, did not have a modern deck. A veranda ran across the front of the house and then wrapped around the two sides. Its entire length was covered, as though the Benbow family had wanted to insure that anyone sitting here was protected against sunburn. The veranda roof, supported by pillars, became the underflooring of the second story. In the years he had owned the house Ah-boo had made many improvements—a modern kitchen, an electric baseboard heating system, a washer and dryer and freezer—but no one could persuade him to change the veranda or any other aspect of the exterior. He wanted all the family to see and remember how they had started.

On Deck Day everyone was grateful for his resistance. Although the veranda seemed interminable in length, it was narrow compared to all the decks they had rolled this morning. The teams worked quickly, leapfrogging ahead of each other as patch after patch was finished. When the last team came to the last patch of the last deck, the entire family gathered around. Ah-boo sent Alice to bring Bonjy from the kitchen.

Howard stopped rolling before the final two boards. "Ah-boo?" he said. "Want to finish up, sir?"

Again Ellen could feel the deliberate pause before the old man answered. A manipulative pause, she felt sure, designed to add a little extra weight, a touch of solemnity to the moment. Or was he, perhaps, actually tempted? She did not think so.

"No, thank you," he said at last. He smiled around at all his family, at this full gathering of the Winderman clan that had successfully completed another tribal rite. "Your privilege, Howard."

Howard swooped his roller down the two final boards and then brandished it in the air. Everybody cheered. Ah-boo then shook hands with each member of his family, thanking every one.

When he came to Ellen, he made no direct reference to Ellen's defiance in letting Alice have a chance to roll the deck, but Ellen could feel it in the steady blue eyes. "So, Ellen," he said, shaking her hand.

Another Deck Day passed into family history.

Showing an Interest

Ellen was just making family conversation with her stepchildren, showing an interest. She had not intended to start anything.

"Who are you all inviting to Ah-boo's party?" she asked.

She and Nancy were seated on stools at the kitchen work counter to shell peas for dinner. Ellen kept a cook in New York, but at the Island she preferred to run her own kitchen, especially since Nancy always helped. Howard was stretched out, long and lanky, in his father's easy chair, reading a paperback. Bryan lay on the couch almost upside down, his legs draped over the back of the couch, his tousled head hanging over the front. He lay limp but comfortable, like a snoozing cat.

"Well, that's when Sam's going to be visiting," Howard reminded her about his college roommate. Although his voice was polite, as always, Ellen could hear the note of patience. How could she possibly, he was implying, have forgotten about Sam? "I already cleared him with Ah-boo."

This custom was of ancient origin. As a boy, Lawrence had once had a houseguest in late August, and obviously no houseguest could be excluded from the birthday party. Brad and Martha complained that this wasn't fair to them: if Lawrence's friend was invited, why couldn't each of them ask a friend? Ah-boo and Anne, still alive then, agreed this was reasonable, but Ah-boo reserved the right to approve each invitation. The added guests would make the occasion even more festive but, as he said, he didn't want his party to become "a rout."

Ever since that year's party the custom had continued, even after Lawrence and Brad and Martha were grown and married. Each family member could invite one guest. Now the privilege extended to the grandchildren. This made for very large parties, although not every grandchild always asked a friend. Christopher, for instance, never invited anyone. The guests were other summer people or friends from school.

"A great big surprise from me," Bryan said, not moving from his position of perfect indolence. "Angie, of course."

The sarcastic tone was not quite rude enough to deserve comment from Ellen. A dozen or more times a day she had to decide whether or not to respond to something Bryan threw at her. Although her instinct was always to throw something right back, she was not willing to let Bryan have the constant satisfaction of provoking her. Sometimes, when Bryan went too far, Lawrence would interfere in her behalf, but usually he seemed not to notice—or pretended not to. He did not relish embroilments. So it was left to Ellen to choose her own moments for taking on Bryan. This was not one of them. After all, if she had given it a second's thought, she would have known that Bryan would invite Angie.

Angie Dunlap had been Bryan's closest summer friend for thirteen years. They never saw each other during the winter because the Dunlaps lived in Richmond, but their summer home was just across State Road within ten minutes' walking distance. Each August, Bryan and Angie were together every day, sailing, playing tennis on the Winderman court, sleeping out in Angie's tenthouse. Angie was eighteen and one month

older than Bryan. Lawrence said it was remarkable that as the
two boys had grown up, they managed to pick up every summer just where they had left off. Ellen liked Angie, a big,
redheaded boy with countless freckles, but because he was on
Bryan's team, he did not have much to say to her.

Nancy had stopped shelling peas and had lighted a cigarette. It was unlike Nancy to be the last to speak. When she
still didn't say anything, Ellen looked at her and raised an
eyebrow.

"Aren't you asking anybody?"

"Oh yes," Nancy said airily. She blew out a jet of smoke. "I
thought I'd ask Anthony."

"Who's Anthony?"

"Nancy's big enchilada," Bryan said, still upside down on
the couch.

"Oh, shut up, Bryan," Nancy said.

Ellen noticed that Howard had put down his book and was
studying Nancy in a slightly curious way.

"Have I met him?" Ellen asked.

"No, I don't think so," Nancy said in a tone that meant
definitely not.

"Well," Ellen said, "I'm glad somebody in the family is
asking a member of the opposite sex, whoever he is."

"He's an islander," Nancy said, as though that explained
whatever there was to explain.

"Oh? Good. It's about time we had somebody besides other
summer people."

"I think so too. I met him at the Purple Grape." This was
the Island disco, immensely popular with all the young people. "You'll like him, Ellen."

"I'm sure I will."

"But that isn't the question," Howard said, courteously
pointing out that Ellen's opinion did not matter. "The question is, will Ah-boo? You sure this is a good idea, Nance?"

Nancy banged out her cigarette. "Sure I'm sure. Don't you like him?" She reached for another one.

"I don't really know him."

"Well I do, and I like him a lot."

That was becoming obvious. And Nancy was growing defensive. Ellen wondered what this was all about.

"Okay, out with it," she said. "What's wrong with Anthony?"

Bryan at last swung his legs around and sat up. In that special mocking voice he reserved for Ellen, he said, "Twenty Questions! Is he a cripple? No. Is he gay? Not if he's Nancy's date, certainly not. Is he—from outer space?"

Howard laughed. When even Nancy laughed, Ellen decided to let this one go, too. But don't push me anymore, Bryan.

Nancy turned back to Ellen and said, with a certain defiance, "Anthony is Anthony Balto."

"Then I know I haven't met him. Balto? As in Balto's Hardware?"

"Yes," Howard said. Then, to educate Ellen about what really mattered here, he added, "And also as in Tony Balto, selectman."

"The one who . . . ? You mean the one that your father says practically runs Summertown? This is his son?"

"Zabba-dabba-doo!" Bryan said. "She actually got it."

Crack! Ellen hit the counter top hard with the flat of her hand. Nancy jumped. Bryan's eyes opened wide.

"That's enough," Ellen told Bryan in her hardest, toughest voice.

"Enough what?" Bryan tried to look innocent.

"Enough snottiness."

"Who's being—?"

"You are. Stop it."

Bryan tried to match her stare but could not hold it. He

looked away. Then he folded his hands and shrugged. "Sorry," he said, his voice sullen.

Ellen decided that that was, under the circumstances, acceptable. At any rate, it would have to do.

Ellen knew a lot about Tony Balto, as did everyone on the Island, summer visitor or native.

Like many members of the Island's large Italian community, Tony Balto was in the construction business. But that was not where he had started. The Balto family had long been one of four or five small Island firms that handled plumbing and heating, but Tony Balto brought two new elements to the family business: vision and energy. First he persuaded Caglieri & Sons to join forces with Balto, making the new group the largest plumbing and heating contractors on the Island. He was an indefatigable salesman. From the newspaper, from hearsay, from building contractors, from the bank, he learned about every commercial or residential building project that was about to happen. He got in touch with the owner as far in advance as possible. Sometimes by phone, more often by a personal visit, he learned details and then made an early bid.

Often he got the job. He never gave any thought to whether or not he had the manpower to execute all the bids he made. If he did not have the men, he hired them away from other plumbers. If he was desperate, he hired inexperienced teenagers. If projects fell behind schedule, as they frequently did, he made do with promises and charm. The Island was used to things being behind schedule. Two years after merging with Caglieri, Balto absorbed still another plumbing business. Now Balto & Company was so large that it was difficult to consider anyone else for plumbing and heating on a major construction.

But there were building contractors on the Island who did

not like Tony Balto's aggression or the quality of his work. Even he had to admit that with so many jobs in progress there was bound to be occasional sloppiness, a pump that did not function, a bathtub that refused to drain, a thermostat that did not deliver its message to a furnace. What did people expect? But he did not like being at the mercy of contractors, so he expanded into the construction business. This was not popular. By custom, plumbers did plumbing, electricians did wiring, builders did building. This made it possible for everyone to get a slice of the summer people's business. Tony Balto did not believe in yesterday.

He soon learned that, as he had suspected, much more money could be made from building houses than from installing toilets. He put his brother in charge of plumbing and his brother-in-law in charge of heating while he concentrated on building houses. Fortunately he also had a still younger brother so that when he later expanded into electrical work, a family member was available to run that part of the business.

The hardware store was a recent addition. He had watched with dismay the continuous rise in prices for even the simpler tools he needed, hammers and screwdrivers. The growing complexity and popularity of power tools led to prices still more outrageous. Since he saw no reason for these profits to go elsewhere, he started his own hardware business outside of town in a structure built, wired and heated by Balto & Company. Everybody admitted that it had more stock and more convenient parking than the old hardware stores in Summertown and Bel Harbor.

Politics was almost an accident. Tony Balto had been racing so fast for so many years that he had given no thought to anything but business. But as the Island became an increasingly popular summer resort with more and more building, and as the environmental movement began to be heard from more and more loudly, Tony Balto found himself harassed by all kinds of bothersome creatures. Building codes. Building permits. Zoning regulations. Planning commissions. Conservation groups. Variances. Water-table analyses, for Christ sake. Each of the Island's two towns and three villages had its own selectmen, its own boards, committees and tax assessors, and it sometimes seemed to Tony Balto that each was trying to outdo the other in red tape and complexity. Since he was doing business in every corner of the Island, he was badgered everywhere.

Still, it had never occurred to him to do anything but protest and, if possible, evade. Then he lost an especially lucrative job, a summer palace for a wealthy New Yorker, because the Summertown selectmen refused to grant a perfectly reasonable zoning variance. He was driven to action—but only because his youngest brother, the electrical contractor, suggested that Tony run for office himself. If you can't beat them, replace them.

Many summer people would never have voted for Tony Balto under any circumstances, but they did not have the vote. Only permanent residents of Summertown could vote, so his campaign was concentrated. While he had enemies in this group too, he had advantages. He was the most important member of the Italian community. He had more employees than anyone else on the Island. He was well-known, reasonably popular and rich. Besides, many people agreed with him that no one should interfere with the main business of the Island, getting money out of summer people.

His opponents for selectman revived the story from his early plumbing days that had led to the nickname of Tony Circulari. On a job to convert an old farmhouse into a modern summer home, he had had the task of putting new piping in the basement, along with a furnace and heating ducts. It was a long job, and the owner was impatient and critical, even for a summer visitor. When the job was finished, Tony Balto submitted a huge bill. The owner complained, of course, but Tony Balto had the work records and the receipts for materials to back it up.

Several years later, when a different plumber was doing repairs in the basement, he made a discovery. In the course of trying to track down a block in the system, the plumber began to follow a section of half-inch copper pipe that he thought might be the source of the trouble. He followed the pipe all around the basement as it turned up, then down, then detoured past supporting pillars, then returned mysteriously on itself before changing direction yet again. Several times the plumber almost lost his way when the pipe threaded between other pipes. But with great care and with the aid of a flashlight, he finally traced the full course of the copper tubing. But that can't be right, he said to himself. I made a mistake.

So he did it all over again, all the way around the basement, even more carefully this time, keeping his hand on the pipe so that he didn't confuse it with any of the other pipes. He had not made a mistake after all. That enormous length of copper pipe (and the expensive labor to install it) traveled all over the basement in a convoluted path only to return to itself. It did not carry water because it wasn't connected to anything. It had no function except cost.

Being an islander, the plumber did not announce his discovery to the owner, but after making the necessary repair, he did ask who had been the plumbing contractor. By nightfall everyone in the plumbing trade had heard the story, and by the following night it was all over the Italian community. Someone christened him Tony Circulari. Naturally no one told summer people.

But that had been long ago. Everybody had forgotten it until the story was spitefully revived during the election campaign as evidence of Tony Balto's dishonesty. It was even printed in the *Island Chronicle*, which is how the summer people finally learned of it. Fortunately for the candidate, the owner of the circular copper pipe was no longer alive. The new owner was so proud of his landmark plumbing that he showed it to all his guests.

As it turned out, the story did no harm in the election. It might even have helped. Tony Balto got the highest vote of the three winners. He became a hard-working, popular select-man, who pursued the best commercial interests of Sum-mertown. Everybody prospered, especially Tony Balto, and he had been reelected twice.

Yes, everyone knew about Tony Balto, though Ellen had never met him or even seen him.

"What's he like?"

Nancy thought she was asking about Anthony. "Very nice," she said. "He's a real good dancer, and he has a great sense of humor. He's very funny. And to tell you the truth, he's quite sexy."

"Hubba hubba," Bryan said. He and Angie Dunlap col-lected scraps of ancient slang and used them repeatedly in conversation. Another of their favorites was "Twenty-three skidoo," which they amended at very special moments to "Twenty-seven skidoo." They were also fond of "the bee's knees" as an accolade, which they diminished, as lesser praise, to "the bee's elbows." Ellen would have found it more amus-ing if she got along better with Bryan.

"What's his father like?" she asked.

"Oh, I've never met Papa," Nancy said. "You know, that family's as big as ours. Maybe bigger. Anthony's got aunts and uncles and cousins and brothers and sisters. Even two nieces. He says he stopped counting years ago."

"Just the same," Howard said, "you better think twice about asking him."

"Too late. I asked him last night and he's coming."

"Want to bet?"

"Now, Howard, don't tease," Ellen said.

Howard gave her a blank stare before answering. "I'm not."

"Ah-boo's never said no to a guest," Nancy said. "Besides, he'll like Anthony."

"I hope you're right," Howard said.

"I'm sure you are," Ellen said. "Now help me with these peas."

Lawrence came in from his tennis game with Brad just as they were finishing. After he showered, he made drinks for himself and Ellen. They took them out on the deck to watch the sunset light on the ocean. Lawrence was in a good mood. Although he had lost to Brad, as he almost always did, his first serve had been going in all afternoon.

"This is the nicest time I know," he said, "in the nicest place I know." He was looking out at the lovely light on the water. The blue spruce now shone silvery gray. "God really hit the target when He invented sunset and martinis. I'll bet He invented them at the same time. On the seventh day, when He was resting."

Ellen liked seeing him so relaxed and peaceful. In New York, work was usually on his mind or not far away.

"What did you and the kids do while I was being an athlete?"

"Nothing much. We just talked. Oh, guess who Nancy invited to Ah-boo's birthday party. Tony Balto's son."

He turned from the water to stare at her. The line between his straight eyebrows went deeper. "The hell she did. Are you serious?"

"She says he's very nice."

"That's not the point."

"So what is the point? Drink your nice drink."

"She can't do that. How did she get to know him?"

"She met him at a dance. At the Purple Grape. My impression is that she likes him quite a bit."

"Oh, Christ. Well, she can't ask him. That's all there is to it."

"Of course she can ask him. She already has. It's all settled."

"My dear wife, one thing I can promise you is that it is not all settled. She's just going to have to disinvite him."

Ellen felt herself get angry. Not only was she irritated by "my dear wife" used in that condescending tone, but sometimes Lawrence was just too sure of himself, especially about family affairs. "Lawrence, that's silly," she said. "You and Howard both. What business is it of yours? What do you have against him? And besides, you don't even know the boy."

"No, and I very much doubt that I ever will. We better get her out here."

He opened the sliding screen door and called for Nancy. No use: the children were playing music. Lawrence had to go to their end of the house to summon Nancy. They came back together, Nancy looking pretty in blue jeans and a pink halter top. Pretty but slightly nervous, running her fingers through her short brown hair.

"Sit down," Lawrence said.

Ellen was relieved that it was his friendly voice, not his stern one. Nancy pulled up one of the green canvas director's chairs. Lawrence sat down again and took a sip of his drink. Ellen could tell from his expression that he was organizing his thoughts the way he did when he was about to explain a complicated banking process to her.

"The first thing," he said to Nancy, "is that this is nothing personal. As Ellen says, she and I don't even know your friend. I never heard his name until five minutes ago."

"So why—?" Nancy began, then stopped at the look on her father's face.

"You have to listen for a minute to some economic facts that have social consequences. The Island, as you well know, is divided in two. Summer people and islanders. There are many more of us than there are of them. Almost ten times as many. But most of us are here only a short time: July people or August people, seldom more than a month. Lots of summer people are actually here less time than that, as little as a week or just a weekend. A few summer people can stay longer, retired people like Ah-boo, teachers with long summer vacations. But there aren't many of those, and even they stay only the summer months. Then everybody goes home, and a large part of the Island simply closes down. Remember what it was like that year when we came up for Thanksgiving? Restaurants closed. Hotels closed. Movie theaters and stores closed. No boats in the harbors. A completely different world—and that's what it's like from Labor Day till next Memorial Day. Closed down for almost nine months, and during those nine months it's difficult for the islanders to make much money. Many of them have nothing to do economically except collect unemployment checks. Therefore they have to concentrate on those three fat months when the summer people are here. That's why summer prices are so steep, higher than in Manhattan. Get it from the summer people while the getting is good."

"But, Daddy, Anthony isn't—"

"Hang on a second. They count on us. We're their meal ticket, all of us summer people. And while we're here, we count on them. This whole Island community is designed around a single economic principle: cash in on the summer people while they're here. And there's not much we can do about it. We can't bother to go back and forth to the mainland to shop more cheaply, especially since the ferry prices for cars and passengers are jacked up fifty percent during the summer months. We're pretty much at their mercy, and don't think they don't know it. Summer people pay more than ninety percent of the taxes here because they own the most land and the nicest houses, but they have no say in how things are run. You remember from your American history that taxation without representation is tyranny? Way back in the eighteenth century? Well, that system is alive and well on the Island today."

Ellen could tell that he was coming to the end of his lecture, because he had that summing-up look on his face.

"All right. So you have two communities, each totally dependent on the other, one for income, the other for goods and services. They are basically antithetical."

"Daddy, you make it sound like we're enemies."

"I don't mean to, except economically. Ellen, you want another drink? Nancy, you want a beer?"

He came back with another martini for himself and a beer for Nancy. The sun had set. The light was now pale and soft.

"Sometimes we're enemies. Summer people can be arrogant and too demanding, and some islanders try to gouge too deeply. But mostly both sides try to get along with each other. My point is that there are two sides, and their goals are totally opposite. Now of all the permanent residents in Summertown—and maybe on the whole Island—the purest, most successful proponent of 'Get it from the summer people' is Tony Balto. It's Us and Them, Nancy, and he's the biggest Them of all. We have no business socializing with each other. If we are going to tolerate each other, we do it at arm's length. Now that's why I think your invitation is a mistake."

A stubborn look had been growing on Nancy's face. She did not seem confused, it had all been clear to her, but Ellen could see that she did not accept her father's argument. During Lawrence's last speech she had been swinging one bare foot back and forth, waiting to have her say. Ellen hoped she would not overdo it.

"Can I say something now?" Nancy asked in a slightly exasperated voice.

Lawrence caught the tone but let it pass. "Of course." He was good at knowing when not to be formidable.

"All that sounds kind of snobby to me. I mean, we all love

the Island or we wouldn't be here, so why shouldn't we try to be friends with each other? Anthony and I are friends, we like each other. That's not some kind of sin, is it?"

"Certainly not."

There was not going to be a crisis, so Ellen said, "I'm going to start cooking. I can hear from the kitchen."

"I'll set the table," Nancy said, "in just a minute. Daddy, look. You see this as a banker with your economic principles and everything. But I see it as a woman who's met a terrific man. I just want to have him to a big family party. Why don't we leave it like that? It isn't going to do any harm. Anthony isn't going to gouge anybody at the party. Really."

From the kitchen Ellen heard Lawrence say, "It's not my birthday party. It's Ah-boo's, and he's not going to like it."

Ellen was trying to make herself comfortable so she could read. She was stretched out on their blue sailcloth-covered couch, but no matter which way she arranged the half-dozen white and blue cushions, she felt bulky and lumpy. One of the mysteries of pregnancy was that she could manage all the active events—walking, swimming, driving, cooking—but had difficulty sitting or sleeping.

Lawrence sat formally in his easy chair, deep in the monthly Trust Report from the bank. When it was banking business, Lawrence unconsciously sat behind an imaginary desk, his face solemn as though customers were sitting right here in this white-walled, wood-beamed living room. Ellen smiled to herself at the sight of this solemn banker in his polo shirt, chino pants and bare feet, sitting up so straight in his blue-and-white striped easy chair as he turned each page of the report. A peaceful moment. The kids out for the evening, Lawrence deep in his work. She tried another rearrangement of the pillows before turning back to Henry James, whom Ah-boo had told her she must read at least once. She felt she needed ideal conditions to meet Mr. James toe to toe. Now then, Strether was just about to aver—

The screen door of the deck clattered open. Nancy.

At first Ellen didn't notice anything wrong. "I thought you were going over to Bel Harbor with everybody else. What happened?" Then Nancy came forward into the light and Ellen could see that she was close to tears. "What's the matter?"

"I decided not to go," Nancy said in much too bright a voice. "I decided I better go talk to Ah-boo and get his permission. About Anthony."

Lawrence put down his report but said nothing.

"He was sweet," Nancy said, now with a catch in her voice. "Very sweet, the way he always is. I mean, he listened to me. He treated me like an adult, not a grandchild. He was—he was so interested in hearing about Anthony that I just knew it was going to be fine. And then he said—" Nancy stopped. Her eyes were so shiny it was painful. "He said he hoped it wouldn't hurt my feelings, but he couldn't invite—he preferred not to have any member of 'those families' in his house. And then he said, he actually said, I shouldn't smoke so much. I should give it up the way he had. Honest." The tears broke. "What am I going to say to Anthony? How can I tell him?"

Ellen got her bulk to her feet and put her arms around Nancy, who now began to cry hard. Ellen looked over Nancy's shoulder at Lawrence. His expression was torn between sympathy for his daughter and embarrassment at this public emotion. Lawrence didn't think people should give way. He never did himself. Ellen had to handle it.

She hugged Nancy and then patted her head while she thought what to say. "You probably just caught him by surprise. He's going to need a little time to get used to the idea." She thought Ah-boo's decision was outrageous, but then he didn't understand how much it meant to Nancy. Anthony

Balto was clearly more important than a casual summer acquaintance.

Nancy shook her head against Ellen's shoulder. "No, he meant it." She drew back and wiped at her tear streaks. "I'm sorry. I promised myself I wasn't going to cry about it, but I can't help it. It's so—it wouldn't have hurt *anybody.*"

"Of course it wouldn't." Ellen was angry. Angry at Ah-boo for doing this to Nancy. Angry at Lawrence for not helping. But first she had to help Nancy recover, give her some reason to feel better. "I'm sure Ah-boo didn't realize how much it meant to you. Your father and I didn't either." She wondered if Lawrence was going to say anything. She gave him the opportunity, but when he still didn't speak, she went on. "Now go wash your face and then we'll talk about what to do. Don't forget, Ah-boo's going to be seventy this month. He's an old man. We have to be patient and get him to change his mind." Ellen herself did not feel the least bit patient.

This led Lawrence to contribute at last. "Don't get your hopes up," he said. "For all that sweetness you talk about, Ah-boo can be very stubborn."

Nancy nodded sadly.

Ellen glared at her husband. "I can be stubborn too, in case you hadn't noticed. Now go wash," she repeated to Nancy. "We can't make a sensible plan if you're all streaked up."

Nancy managed a smile. "Thanks." She gave Ellen a quick kiss on the cheek. "You're not such a cruel stepmother, you know."

Ellen felt a flash of warmth in her own eyes. Ah-boo had no right to do this to this girl. She patted Nancy's shoulder. "We'll think of something. I'll talk to Ah-boo myself. We'll make him understand."

Only after Nancy had left the room did Lawrence comment. "Ah-boo doesn't change his mind very easily. Or very often."

"I don't care," Ellen snapped. "He's going to change it this time. He thinks he can do anything he wants to, and everybody else is just supposed to fall in line. I am not going to let him hurt Nancy. And that young man, too."

"After all," Lawrence explained in his patient voice, "he is the head of the family."

"That's exactly the trouble."

"Well," Lawrence said as he picked up his report, "good luck."

The Blue Spruce

Charles Winderman was used to surprise visits from his children and grandchildren. He encouraged them. Even in the years when he was teaching—doing research, correcting exams, organizing courses, writing—even during the days of the Bernstein trial, when he was preparing for his appearance as an expert witness, he had always been willing to be interrupted. As he told them all, family comes first.

Now, of course, he had far more time available. But he knew that if he had not established the principle in those early years, they would not be coming to him now with their problems and requests, great and small. It had been well worth it. A major part of life in a large family was the existence of habits and customs and traditions.

Deck Day, for example, was an important occasion because it involved the entire family. He could easily have paid someone to roll his deck, and so could the three children. Doing it all themselves took a lot of trouble and preparation. But it was such a family tradition that he had never considered giving it up.

Besides, he did not pay islanders to do any work the family could do for itself. Not to save money, although he believed in prudence, but because he wanted his family to be as independent as possible. In the early years he and Anne had been hostage to expensive native labor. Now he held that to a minimum. Deck Day brought the entire family together for a useful endeavor, which he had always tried to make pleasant for everyone. On Deck Day he still drank a ceremonial glass of Kool-Aid—well, part of one glass—just so that all the grandchildren realized he was part of everything. He did not, however, pretend to smack his lips over Kool-Aid the way Brad and Sue did.

This evening he was reading a book of chess problems in an effort to improve his chances against Roger Bernstein, when he heard the steps on his deck. Lionel, the nine-year-old airedale asleep on the rug in front of his chair, did not react until the knock on the screen door woke him into a short bark.

"It's Nancy. Can I come in for a minute?"

"Of course." He closed the book and laid it on the end table. He was always glad to see Nancy, for whom he had a special fondness. He recognized special qualities in each of his grandchildren and nurtured them, so in that sense he had a special fondness for each one but especially for Nancy, whose sunny love of life and capacity for enjoyment were unusually high. She was so full of good cheer and family spirit that sometimes she did not show good sense, but that would come. He believed in Nancy.

He could see she was nervous tonight, as family members often were when bringing him a problem. When she began to talk about inviting her young man, or at least the moment she spoke his name, he guessed the cause of her nervousness. This was going to be awkward—perhaps painful for her. She was an impulsive girl. If this invitation were mere impulse, it would be easier to deal with. He drew her out, asking interested questions about this Anthony. He needed time to gauge the extent of her involvement. Besides, it was always important to create the impression of a full and fair hearing. If he had to deliver an unwelcome decision, as he certainly did in this case, Nancy should at least feel that her position had been sympathetically understood.

Finally, of course, he had to say no. He started to explain why, but she was no longer concentrating. He was sorry to see her hurt. The kindest act was to stop talking and let her go, saving explanations for another day. Better to change the subject, give her something else to fret about. He delivered a brief lecture about her smoking and told her good night. Even on another day she might not understand. There was, after all, a long, complicated background.

When he and Anne had bought the Benbow property soon after the war, even the Benbow lawyer conceded that the house was run-down and the land badly overgrown. Old Mrs. Benbow and her companion had done minimum housekeeping during their last years. He remembered how this living room had looked when he and Anne first saw it: windows smudged, holes in several screens, ragged straw mats and unraveling hooked rugs on the painted pine floor, the dirty plaster ceiling flaking in one corner from an upstairs leak. Black horsehair furniture was scattered around the room so that wherever one's eye rested there was a specimen of black, uncomfortable ugliness.

And yet when he and Anne walked through the sagging screen door onto the long veranda, the ocean sparkled only a few yards away. And when they walked out the dirt driveway all the way back to State Road, and then took the even longer walk along State Road to the stone wall that the lawyer said marked the far boundary of the property, they marveled at the extent and variety of the land. Fifty acres, as they thought then, formed a huge bloc.

That same afternoon, they returned in old clothes, intending to walk the length of the stream from State Road to the beach. The vegetation stopped them. Viburnum and elderberry and ferns and pepper bushes stood thick along the

banks. Bright yellow-green bull vine with sharp thorns en-
twined dead trees and bushes that it had strangled. They
tried walking in the stream bed itself, but in many places the
vegetation had grown across the stream in a dense mat. They
had to give up, but that afternoon Charles Winderman made
up his mind that if he bought this ramshackle property, he
would clear the stream so that he and Anne and the children
could walk along its entire length. After growing up in New
York City, he was overwhelmed by the prospect of a beautiful
stream with a strange Indian name running through his own
land. And having a big house, no matter how dilapidated,
right on the beach. And owning fifty acres, no matter how
widespread the bull vine. Truly an estate.

Anne felt the same. She had introduced the family to the
Island just before the war, having remembered a pleasant
weekend there during her college days. They had rented
twice, in the summers of 1940 and 1941, and they had an
option for a third summer until Charles decided to enlist in
the Army. During the war years they wrote letters about
going back to the Island, and by the end of the war they knew
they wanted to own a house there. They had not, to be sure,
imagined buying such a broken-down house or so much land.
They had been thinking along the lines of the house they had
rented, right in Summertown where they could benefit from
city water and electricity and telephone service and have use
of the town beach. But the real estate agent insisted they look
at the Benbow place, which was a steal because it had none of
these conveniences and was three miles out of town. It was
indeed a steal, well within the limit of the money Charles had
inherited from his mother. As the real estate agent predicted
—quite accurately for a real estate agent—"Someday the
town is going to grow out to here. This place could be worth
a lot of money."

Someday. Meantime they would have to live with kerosene
lanterns, bottled gas for the stove and refrigerator, a gasoline

pump for the well water. They would have to drive to town for mail and shopping or just to use a telephone. The shabby old house, the tumbledown barn (was it worth saving?) and all that bull vine. But also the long, lovely stretch of beach, all those acres of land and their own private stream. Next morning they made the down payment. They were thirty-two, the war was behind them, their last child, Martha, had just been born, the adventure was irresistible.

After the signing in the lawyer's second-story office on Main Street, Charles Winderman bought a blue spiral notebook in the stationery shop next door and made the first entry in his diary record of the house. Eleven of these blue notebooks now lined a shelf in his living room bookcase. They were consulted more often than the dictionary and by all members of the family, although no one was permitted to take a notebook out of this room. The notebooks were a complete family history of their life on the Island. Thirty-eight years now, three additional houses, nine grandchildren, with a tenth due next month. And ever since 1951, as celebrated in the third notebook, you could walk along the stream from State Road all the way to the beach.

But the early notebooks contained many entries of anger and discouragement. They might be amusing now, sometimes hilarious—the grandchildren often read 1947 and 1948 aloud to each other—but Charles had written them in outrage. He and Anne were eager to work, and they enlisted their children for simple chores as soon as they were old enough to help. They could all clear brush with saws and clippers, shears and loppers, and deliver it to the town dump. But for all the major repairs to the house and barn, for painting and carpentering and new shingles and the replacement of rotten floorboards, for everything that really mattered, they had to depend on Island workmen.

Most materials and equipment had to be ordered off-Island and shipped over by ferry. A single long-delayed part could postpone a project for weeks. When the refrigerator collapsed and had to be replaced, Anne ordered a new one from the mainland. When it arrived, two weeks overdue, it was the wrong model, much too small for their needs, and had to be sent back. For six weeks that summer Charles drove to the ice house at Bel Harbor every day to bring back a block of ice to put in the rented ancient ice chest that leaked on Anne's new kitchen floor.

Nothing arrived on time except trouble. Workmen failed to appear because an emergency erupted somewhere else on the Island or because, he frequently suspected, it looked like a grand day for bluefishing. Charles and Anne would take turns driving to town to use the pay phone to try to reach the plumber or carpenter or painter who had promised to be there that morning and who was now not answering his phone.

At the end of the second full summer Charles promulgated Winderman's Law, entered in the notebook on August 29, 1948:

> All work will take longer than promised.
> All work will cost more than estimated.
> All work will be unsatisfactory in at least one essential respect.
> All complaints will be rejected as either 1) unjustified, 2) unfixable or 3) incomprehensible but in any case "not my fault."

The money was not central, although the costs were venomous. His share of income from the Winderman Trust Company was more than adequate—enough, as his father often observed, to permit Charles the luxury of being a professor of literature. Anne had some money as well and could contribute when necessary. No, it was not the money. The delays in getting things done, and done right, offended his sense of order and efficiency, especially since his and Anne's eagerness to improve the property consumed them. Worse yet, he felt that all these people he depended on really did not care, just as long as he paid the bills. He was convinced, although without evidence, that they were secretly laughing at him. It did not matter what their names were—Balto, Palucci, Ramsdell, Harper, Stark, Conigliari. At one time or another he employed them all, every firm listed in the slim Island phone book, and he imagined them all laughing at him from their impenetrable bastions of indifference. Laughing at other summer people as well, no doubt.

He could remember only one improvement that had gone well from the start, and that was mostly a gift of nature. That first summer when the tractor and heavy brush cutter had cleared all the land behind the barn and the lower end of the stream, he and Anne bought from Browning's Nursery a four-foot-high blue spruce, its root ball wrapped in burlap and twine. The nursery's instructions were simple: use plenty of peat moss and give it plenty of water. They planted it near the stream where it could be seen from the house.

To their amazement it thrived. In a few years its top was visible from the beach. Each June when they arrived to open the house after the college year ended, he and Anne and the three children rushed to see how the blue spruce had grown over the winter months. In the early years they measured it and recorded the growth in the notebooks, but soon it was too tall for anything but a rough estimate. He treasured it for its beauty in every kind of light and later for its grandeur and finally for its dominance, towering over them all. One summer, at Martha's suggestion, they discussed the possibility of naming the whole property Blue Spruce but decided they did not approve of tacking names on summer houses. They planted another blue spruce, but that same winter some thrifty islander with good taste cut it down for a Christmas tree. The original tree was, however, now far too large for such depredation. It became lasting proof to Charles Winderman that it was possible on this Island to select, buy and install something perfect. It gave him hope, if not faith, that he could undertake other projects and that with patience, endurance, money and persistence they could be compelled to succeed.

So he had continued, in spite of the Baltos and Starks and all the rest, to commit himself again and again to whatever would bind the family closer to this place and therefore to each other: the tennis court, originally clay surface but since replaced by dark green composition; Lawrence's house, undertaken when Howard, the first grandchild, was born. That had meant more than just one house. He and Anne and a surveyor and an architect planned the eventual placement of three houses, because Bradford and Martha must also have their own homes. That meant access roads and a second driveway entrance to the property at the far end of their land. And because by then the town had indeed grown out to the Windermans just as the real estate agent predicted, it also meant trenches to carry pipelines and underground telephone lines and electricity. It meant building permits, approval of proposed septic-tank locations, and fair notice to abutters for all structures and roadways.

He was neither so naïve nor so optimistic as in the early years. He even considered giving the work to off-Island contractors, but quite aside from the expense of bringing them to the Island, he realized that this kind of subversion would create serious problems. If he took that much money away from the Island economy and gave it to outsiders, he would be punished later on when he needed repairs and maintenance. If he took away the islanders' God-given right to make money from the summer people, they would ignore every plea to repair a stove or replace a window.

He stayed subservient to the Island but put every aspect of the work up for bids. He hired an Island lawyer to draw up contracts that would stand up in the Island court. The contracts specified step-by-step payments, and he negotiated fiercely for low contingency allowances. Wherever possible he inserted penalty clauses for failure to complete work on schedule, although this was such a revolutionary notion that he had little success. He was careful to include in the contracts descriptions of materials to be used that could not be changed without his written approval, hoping to insure against the ingenious substitution of lower-grade pipe or lumber because the agreed-on grade was "unavailable." Finally his lawyer said, "You know, Mr. Winderman, we don't usually do things this way here." Then he knew he was on the right track. He even tried to take out insurance against excessive delays, but no Island insurance agency would touch such a policy.

In spite of the contracts, when it came to work done right there on the property, many things went wrong. He had expected that. His only intent had been to instill some sense of concern among the contractors and to protect himself against extreme aberrations. But there were loopholes he had not foreseen. When the Summertown expert arrived to test drainage standards for the septic tank at Lawrence's house, he drilled in the wrong spot and cut the new power line, shutting off all electricity for power tools until the repair could be made. Charles Winderman found himself giving his written approval to changes in specifications to prevent long delays in obtaining the right kind of tile or lighting fixtures. He had no idea how many other specifications were changed without his knowledge. Most of the work was done in the off season when he and Anne were away. No telling how many lurid secrets lay hidden underground or within the foundations or behind completed walls. A good many, he felt sure, and he imagined his contractors still sharing laughter at his expense. But not so much as in the early years.

Anne lived to see Lawrence's house finished and to go over the plans for Bradford's and Martha's houses. He often wondered if she would have agreed with the decision he made about ownership. Probably not, but he made it deliberately. Lawrence and Bradford and Martha would not own their houses. He kept the property intact, all 49.3 acres, in his own name. He left it to them in his will but still as a single unit, no part of which could be sold, inside or outside the family. His explanation, which was partly true, was that he and Anne had bought it as a single property for the family and that he wanted it to stay that way. He also explained, and this was totally true, that he still hoped to persuade his neighbor Jack Smollett—or Smollett's heirs, if necessary—to part with the plot that would bring his land to fifty full acres.

What he did not explain was that only by keeping the entire property in his name could he control everything that happened to it. This policy had peril. When Bradford and Sue married and had their first child, they considered building elsewhere. Sue's own family was North Shore Long Island, and Bradford's work in advertising made that appealing. He could commute to New York, have the year-round use of his house and be close to the golf-tennis-country-club life that was so important to his business. And, as Sue pointedly said, "We'd own our own house."

A serious threat to the family. There had only been a few: Anne's death, the flight of Lawrence's first wife, Martha's two divorces. Charles performed every maneuver he could think of to persuade Bradford and Sue to stay. Fortunately Bradford had a strong sense of family, stronger actually than either Lawrence or Martha, and a deep attachment to the Island, where he had spent almost every summer of his life. Bradford had been torn from the beginning, so it was Sue that Charles Winderman had to work on, with charm, affection, special attention and considerable generosity. He had won, and on his terms: the property remained intact in his name.

He had been lucky. Bradford and Sue did not have the idea

of building a swimming pool until long after their house was completed. Then it was easy enough to say no, to insist that the ocean was the key to the character of the Winderman property and that a pool would be inappropriate so close to the water. Sue didn't like it, but Bradford didn't really care, and the pool idea eventually fell of its own damp weight. It might have gone differently if Sue had proposed the pool while the year-round North Shore house was still under consideration. He supposed he would have had to give in.

His control endured, and he kept it benign. No large problems threatened. Sooner or later Martha would want to marry again—every new man was a potential threat—and that had to be watched closely. Most of the grandchildren seemed fine, except Christopher, of course. He didn't know quite what to do about Christopher other than to remain friendly and open to him. He wished Martha would do the same. The boy had so much in him but was so dangerously miserable and lonely—lonely even in this large family.

The most difficult thing to foresee and to manage would be what happened after his death. He had no intimations of mortality. His health was excellent and his spirits were good. His heart was sound, his hearing and eyesight good, and he could swim and play tennis every day. His doctor was extremely pleased with him, almost boastful. He wished he could say the same for his dentist. For perhaps a dozen years now he had been enduring the indignities of periodontia, which must surely be as dreadful as the heartbreak of psoriasis. All that disgusting paraphernalia that he and his dentist employed to protect his teeth and gums from the depredations of plaque: the Cavitron, the scraping and curettage, the slimy bandages capped by aluminum foil, the dental floss (unwaxed), the brush that had to be slithered back and forth between the teeth, the round toothpicks jammed into the holes of the Perio-Aid and then snapped off at the base so that the teeth could be jabbed at one by one, the miniature hypodermic syringe for squirting disinfectant under the gums, the hydrogen peroxide rinses (you, too, can foam at the mouth). Much of this equipment came from the John O. Butler Company of Chicago, and Charles Winderman had often thought of telephoning Mr. Butler to tell him exactly what he thought of him and all his jolly products. Still, if one thought about it dispassionately, which was not easy to do, prolonged periodontal treatment was a relatively small price for a man of his age to pay. It could be much worse. He really should not complain, except now and then.

But a man who was only a few days less than seventy had to make provisions. He was willing enough but not sure what those provisions for the future should be. Control of the family in the grandchildren's generation did not concern him. Not only was that years away, but the pool of talent was large enough to provide promise. No, it was his own children who constituted the problem. To whom would the power pass?

Lawrence had the natural authority and good judgment, but there was an aloofness about him, a privacy, a tendency not to get involved. It was remarkable that his new wife, Ellen, had been able to break through that protective shell. Charles Winderman had given up hope that Lawrence would marry again after that first disaster, but Ellen had managed it, and in the process she had made Lawrence more human. She was a good addition to the family, though she would certainly bear watching. That business on Deck Day, letting Alice use her roller immediately after he had explained his age rule. Too much independence there for the family's good, but there was no question she had helped Lawrence. But even with Ellen's influence, it was hard to imagine Lawrence taking a keen interest in all his nephews and nieces, hard to believe that he would actively preserve old traditions and create new ones. Under Lawrence the family would be like a holding company, each part functioning separately but not closely bound together. Charles Winderman knew how beneficial it was for every family member to recognize himself as part of a larger whole. It provided confidence, security, an awareness of the importance of helping each other, of belonging to the tribe. Love was the key, and the leader must carry the responsibility. Hardly Lawrence's cup of tea.

Bradford was just the opposite. Bradford loved the sheer size of the family. He threw himself into rituals such as Deck Day, stopwatch at the ready. He loved to organize happenings of every kind. A born participant and an enthusiastic one, he had energy and a broad if somewhat shallow affection for all family members. However, his judgment was no match for Lawrence's, nor was his authority. Bradford would manage the family more like a scoutmaster than a patriarch, taking his troop on glorious three-day hikes that might end in a swamp. Everyone would have fun, until the expedition ran out of food. Lawrence would know where the swamp was and avoid it.

As for Martha, she was bright enough, but she did not focus well or long on other people's difficulties. Her own son, Christopher, was a striking example. Martha had probably lost more through Anne's death than any of the others, although Anne herself hadn't always been able to manage Martha. It would be interesting to see how Martha changed, as he felt sure she would, when she was no longer so preoccupied with her own glandular propensities. He continued to have hopes for her in spite of the men, in spite of the drinking, but his hopes did not include managing this property and this family.

Probably the answer was some combination of Lawrence and Bradford, sharing control in awkward alliance. This did not suit Charles's sense of fitness. He believed in clear lines of authority, in a family, in the army, at college, at the bank. Makeshift always had drawbacks.

Lionel lifted his head and barked again, then got to his feet and trotted to the screen door. That would be Mary Benja-

min coming home from her bridge game. He had missed the
sound of the car arriving at the barn. One for Lionel.

"Hello there, Lionel," her voice came from the deck, and
then she walked in, looking pleased. That didn't mean she
had won. She always looked pleased. It made her a nice companion as well as a fine housekeeper. Bonjy never brought
trouble.

"How did you do?"

"Just fine." Lionel had finally been trained not to jump up
on people, not even his favorites, but he compromised by
lifting his front paws a few inches off the floor and bouncing.
She untied the sweater sleeves from around her neck and
gave Lionel a quick pat. "I won enough for two packs of
cigarettes."

"You ought to play for higher stakes."

"Oh," she said, beaming, "that's more than enough."

Love Is the Key

Ellen supposed that, as everybody on the Island said constantly, the fog would burn off by noon. Sometimes the fog
lasted several days, usually while weekend guests were visiting, but the prediction remained the same.

She must deal with Ah-boo this morning before he grew
too comfortable with last night's decision. Older people
tended to crystallize their thinking, and she wanted to reach
him before that could happen. Her own household was still
asleep, but Ah-boo and Bonjy were early risers. She took her
coffee out on the deck to watch the rolling fog. The good
thing about being here an entire month was that a few foggy
or rainy days did not matter. She could still remember the
year of her week's vacation in the Bahamas when the weather
was overcast for eight days. That was when a week's vacation
was all she got, and when a week in the Bahamas was a great
slice of her salary. She had cried on the flight home. Now she
could enjoy the soft, damp fog as she thought about what to
say.

A few minutes after eight she phoned the main house and
got Bonjy. "I'm taking my early morning exercise walk," she
said. "Is Ah-boo going to be around? I'd like to see him."

"Come on by," Bonjy said. "Mr. Winderman's going to be here most of the morning. I'll keep the coffee hot."

Not to wake Lawrence, Ellen used the small lavatory off the living room to comb out her dark hair, which the damp fog had turned even curlier. She was pleased by the way her face was surviving pregnancy. She had been afraid of looking old, bloated and blotchy, a look she had been noticing all too frequently on other pregnant women during the last six months of observation. Instead she thought she looked happy and healthy. Her face was fuller, of course, costing her the shape lines of her cheekbones but on the other hand softening the line of her jaw, which she had always thought a bit too definite for a woman. Her skin was already well tanned—a side benefit of not owning an alabaster complexion—and here on the Island she had stopped wearing lipstick except when they went out in the evening. Not gorgeous, she told herself, but not bad. She wished her hazel eyes were as big as Nancy's, but at least they were much bigger than Sue's bright little mongoose eyes. How mean of me, she thought, but how true. She stuck the comb in the pocket of her blue denim maternity skirt; she would want to comb again after the walk to Ah-boo's.

On the path she turned to look back at her house, all pale gray in the softening light of the fog. Weathered gray cedar shingles, slightly darker weathered gray fir of the deck, still darker gray of the asphalt tile roof, all accented by the deep charcoal-gray trim that she had persuaded Lawrence to change from white, and, darkest of all, the black panes of window and door glass. The orange day lilies blooming along the front edge of the deck and the bright green director's chairs jumped out from all the cool shades of gray and black. There was not a sound to break the perfect stillness imposed by the fog.

Well, time to go to work for Nancy.

Walking up to Ah-boo's house, she thought how different it

looked in different kinds of weather. In bright sunlight it seemed almost quaint in spite of its size. Here in darker weather it could be the neighborhood haunted house, the three big dormer windows staring at the ocean like great blank eyes.

Bonjy and Lionel met her at the door. "Come in out of the fog," Bonjy said, as though fog might be hazardous to an expectant mother. "Coffee's all ready for you. Black with sugar, right? Mr. Winderman's in the study."

"I don't want to interrupt him."

"Oh, pooh, he's not studying. Go on back. He's expecting you, and I'll bring the coffee."

When Bonjy turned to the kitchen, Ellen quickly ran the comb through her long, damp hair, then walked through the dining room to the study. This was where Ah-boo had worked during his college teaching career, a small, quiet room away from the noise of household traffic. Now it was known as the setting for private family conferences. Ah-boo would be seated at his ancient mahogany desk and the conferee sat beside the desk like a student, in a straight-backed Windsor armchair. A second chair could be brought from the dining room if two people were in trouble. But I'm not in trouble, Ellen reminded herself.

"Good morning," she said.

He came to his feet, this handsome, courtly man with the style and manners of an earlier time. He smiled his warm greeting and bent down to kiss her lightly on the cheek. "You're out early," he said, which was plainly meant as a compliment. He had once worn a mustache, Ellen knew, a full mustache that made him look like Oliver Wendell Holmes, as everyone had pointed out. In fact, his friend Roger Bernstein had been merciless about the resemblance, constantly addressing him as "Wendell" or "Mr. Justice" or even "Ollie." When, in exasperation, Ah-boo had finally shaved it off, Roger Bernstein took one look and said, "You look just like Oliver Wendell Holmes the day after he shaved off his mustache."

Ah-boo was wearing his Island uniform: wash-faded but spotless khaki trousers, a white polo shirt—bare of any animal emblem—that matched his neatly combed coarse white hair. Old moccasins and white cotton socks, as white as his shirt and hair. The tan of his arms and face was a leathery burnish against all the white. Ellen had spent enough years in the fashion business to know that the effect was not accidental.

"It's nice to have you visit me," he said. "Sit down, sit down."

Ellen settled herself in the Windsor chair. "Until now," she said with a smile, "I never knew the meaning of that awful expression, 'take the load off your feet.' Now I appreciate it."

Bonjy, trailed by Lionel wagging his stumpy tail, brought in the cup of coffee and a bowl of sugar, placing them on the edge of the desk beside Ellen. "There," she said. "Now I'll leave you two alone."

"Don't go," Ellen said, hoping to indicate that this was not to be a solemn conference.

Bonjy would have none of it. "Housework," she said. "You and Mr. Winderman have a nice talk. Come on, Lionel." She took the dog out and closed the door.

So there they were in a Family Conference, her first alone with Ah-boo since Lawrence had introduced her as his fiancée and they had had a private get-to-know-you talk, seated just like this. This morning she had hoped for something less formal.

"I'd like to talk about Nancy," she plunged right in. "She came home in tears last night."

"Hm. What's the matter? Anything serious?"

She looked at him while stirring sugar into her coffee. His face showed only interest and mild concern, and yet she was certain that a man of his sensitivity had made the connection between Nancy's tears and her visit to Ah-boo. All right, Ellen said to herself, if you want to make me spell it out. "This was right after she came to see you," she said. "About the birthday party."

"Oh? You mean about the young man she wanted to invite?" He shook his head. "Dear me."

"She's more serious about him than I thought at first. I don't yet know how serious, but I think he's quite important to her. I'm very fond of Nancy. I don't want to see her hurt."

"No, of course not. Nancy's very attached to you, Ellen. She needed a woman to look after her and to look up to. It's a great pleasure for me to see you together. Just the right mixture of affection and humor and feminine friendship."

He did notice everything, as Lawrence always said. She was tempted to bask in Ah-boo's approval. "Yes, it's exactly that between us. She's wonderful about the baby, you know. Both solicitous and full of jokes. Did you know she calls it Old Seventeen, the seventeenth member of the family?"

"I think of it as Old Ten, my tenth grandchild." Then he said nothing, waiting for her to go on.

Ellen sipped her coffee and thought about how best to attack this. "Nancy's a very emotional young woman. Her feelings are close to the surface and easily touched. Little things can make her extremely happy, but they can also hurt her just as easily. It's part of being twenty years old, but it's more than that."

Ah-boo looked out the window for a moment, although there was nothing to be seen except the fog and the Russian olive tree that grew close to the house. He turned back to ask, "Do you think she is having an affair?"

Ellen had already asked herself this question and decided that the answer was a highly probable yes. All the signs, including Nancy's own warm nature, pointed that way. "I don't know," she said coldly. "I haven't asked her." She was surprised that Ah-boo would come out with it. He was not as old-fashioned as he seemed.

"That would be most unfortunate." His face was serious, the wise blue eyes looking directly into hers. Then a little smile. "Don't misunderstand me. I'm aware that virginity is a rare condition these days, even among those we love best. Perhaps especially among those we love best." Then he grew serious again. "Have you met this—Anthony?"

"No, but I intend to. Howard and Bryan know him and seem to have no complaints. Besides, I trust Nancy's taste. I'm going to ask her to bring him around."

The straight iron-gray eyebrows rose skeptically. "I would not encourage this, Ellen. It will end with the summer if we don't nurture it."

The manipulation again, but she decided to treat this as lightly as possible. "Oh, Ah-boo," she said with a laugh that sounded girlish even to her, "you've never been a lovely twenty-year-old woman just beginning to discover herself. A summer romance is the most important thing in the world."

He laughed with her. "I won't pretend to be an expert on that. I'll have to take your word for it."

"Then take my word for something else, Ah-boo. I hope you'll see it from Nancy's view and mine, and let her bring Anthony to the party. It's only for one evening, and it will mean so much to her. And to me."

His laugh ended, but his eyes remained kind and friendly. "True, it's only for one evening, but it's a very important evening for the family. And for me."

Ellen instantly regretted the way she had put it. She had made it sound as though Ah-boo's own feelings were not significant, or at least that they mattered less than Nancy's. A foolish mistake. "Of course. I can imagine what it's like to be seventy and to have your birthday in this beautiful place, with all your children and grandchildren around you. I'm truly pleased for you and so glad to be a part of it. It's a wonderful occasion. I don't mean to take away from that. But you've never been selfish about your birthday. You've always shared it with your family's friends so that even more people could enjoy it. That's all I'm asking. Please let Nancy share this too. It will make her so happy. Making your own family happy is the nicest thing I know."

He stared at her for a long moment that stretched out in silence. She could read the depth of approval in his eyes. Then he sighed. "My dear, you're very eloquent. And I love the way you feel about Nancy and this family. Love is the key."

Ellen and everyone else had heard that countless times. He said it so often, in fact, that the grandchildren could sometimes anticipate it and chant it with him: "Love—is—the key." To general laughter, including Ah-boo's. She thought she had won.

His voice changed. "I tried to explain to Nancy last night, but she was not in a mood to listen. Perhaps I can explain it to you. One has to stand by what one has learned. By experience. I've spent almost forty summers here, and I know from that very long experience that there are two cultures on this Island. They don't mix. I don't believe they ever will. They are best kept apart."

Ellen interrupted him. "Lawrence was saying the same thing last night. The summer people and the Island people. But he called them two different economies, not cultures."

"Lawrence is a banker. It's more than just economies."

"Oh, Ah-boo," she said, holding back her exasperation, "I've read your blue notebooks. All the way through. I understand what a difficult time you and your wife had with the islanders. But that was so long ago."

"Some experiences and the emotions they evoke last a very long time, my dear. Especially when you reach my age, you have to depend on what your heart has learned, and live by it. I am a part of all that I have met, as Ulysses said. Yes, I will do business with the islanders when I must, as I always have, but I cannot invite one of the Baltos to my home on a major family occasion. Any more than Selectman Tony Balto would think of inviting me to his home to celebrate his wedding anniversary. Given the past, either event is unthinkable."

"But it isn't you and Tony Balto. It's Nancy and Anthony. And it isn't the past, it's the present."

For a moment she thought she had gone too far, that he was angry. But she was mistaken.

"Then Nancy should invite him to her home—your home. Although I certainly do not recommend it."

"She's already invited him to your party, you know. And he accepted. Do you realize what it would cost her to cancel the invitation? Twenty years old, in love, and she has to tell him, 'Sorry, my grandfather says you can't come.' "

He was sympathetic. "Some things are very hard to do. If she had been less impulsive, if she had come to talk to me before inviting him, then any embarrassment could have been avoided. Anyway, I wouldn't be surprised if Mr. Balto has already told his son he couldn't come."

"Suppose he hasn't."

"Well, Ellen, I don't think I will base any decision of mine on anything Mr. Balto does or doesn't do."

Impasse. Ellen tried to think of other arguments, but nothing occurred to her. "Will you at least please think about it? Think about what I've said? This hurts Nancy."

"Of course I'll think about it," he said. "I couldn't do less for you and Nancy."

Ellen suspected this was merely a tactic on his part, but she had no other ideas. She pushed herself to her feet. "Thank you anyway for listening," she said, without much conviction. "The fog seems to be lifting."

He was on his feet with her. "It will burn off by noon," he promised.

When he stayed behind in the study to pay bills, she went

to look for Bonjy. The family often called on Bonjy to soften up Ah-boo. While her loyalty was first to Ah-boo and only then to other family members, she was believed to be an effective if gentle persuader. She had a casual access completely different from the kind of formal meeting Ellen had just had in the study. Besides, Bonjy was practical. She did not get tangled up in high principles, nor did she construct impregnable positions for herself or others. If it sounded all right and did no harm, that was usually good enough for Bonjy. I need allies, Ellen thought. Although she could understand Ah-boo's point of view, she thought it selfish. This whole Nancy thing was a perfect example of Ah-boo simply issuing a patriarchal directive, and then they were all supposed to tug their forelocks and obey. Well, not this time. And not just because of Nancy.

Ellen found Bonjy in the workroom off the kitchen, doing her ironing. This old house still had so many rooms, even though Ah-boo and his wife had knocked down many walls to enlarge the little postage-stamp cells that had been the custom when the house was built. Ellen knew that behind this workroom there had once been four storage rooms for food and firewood and washtubs. Anne Winderman had persuaded her husband to convert them into a large bedroom-sitting-room-bath area that would become their downstairs living quarters when they grew too old to climb stairs. Originally used as an extra guest room, this had become Bonjy's domain.

While Bonjy ironed with a cheerfulness that Ellen could never bring to this particular household chore, Ellen balanced on a kitchen stool and explained Nancy's predicament. Bonjy looked up from time to time as she raced through a stack of napkins, then started on a pair of Ah-boo's khaki trousers.

"He promised to think about it," Ellen finished. "I just wanted to fill you in so that you could give Nancy some help. If you get a chance."

"Well, the poor child," Bonjy said. Her eyes behind the rimless spectacles were all sympathy. "They're practically my children, you know. I hate to see any of them suffer. Poor little Nancy. Mr. Winderman didn't say a word about this last evening."

"I hope you can help. Use your influence."

A pleasant smile brought creases into her round cheeks. "Oh, influence, pooh. I don't have any influence with Mr. Winderman. That gentleman makes up his own mind. But I'll talk to him. Why, with twenty-five or more people at the party, what difference will one more make? Nobody will even notice what's-his-name."

"Anthony."

"Yes, Anthony." Her round, smiling face did not change expression, but increased emphasis came into her voice. "I hope he's a *nice* young man."

"I'll let you know when I've met him, but I'm sure he is. However, Bonjy, that isn't the point."

"What is?"

Ellen could not say what came into her mind: that people in this family had to have some freedom, sometime, to choose for themselves. That was no way to enlist Bonjy's help. Instead, she said, "Love is the point." And then with a smile, "Love is the key."

Matching Camels

Ellen's true family had been her dolls. Her father, her mother and the grandmother who lived with them were less important figures, except when her grandmother was sewing new dresses for the dolls. Eventually thirteen dolls filled her bedroom because that was what Ellen requested for each birthday and Christmas. They appeared to be scattered haphazardly about her room, as her mother frequently complained, but each had an assigned place—on the bed, on the windowsill, on the bureau—and Ellen could tell at once if her mother had moved anybody. Ellen gave them what she considered romantic names—Tabitha, Agatha, Louisa, Beatrice, Hortense—perhaps to compensate for the ordinary names of her parents, Harry and Mary, and her grandmother, for whom Ellen had been named.

Ellen Lane. What could be more ordinary than that? It was as ordinary as her home and her daily life, growing up in Elmira, New York, where her father owned a very ordinary but successful grocery store. As soon as she was old enough, Ellen worked in the grocery after school and in the summers. She did not mind. She was a tall, awkward, lonely girl with more aptitude for business than for making close friends.

Even her schoolwork set her apart; her high grades made her classmates uncomfortable. Her real friends were at home in her bedroom.

Each new doll was given a complete personal history. Most of them were only children like herself, and several were orphans or foundlings. One was a princess who would have been a queen today if she had stayed at home in Tasmania instead of eloping with a pirate. All had led adventurous lives in faraway places bearing no resemblance to Elmira, and they told each other stories about their desperate experiences. Ellen could remember details from these stories years after she had given up inventing them.

Although each doll was admirable in some special way, her favorite was Hortense, who had wavy dark hair like her own. Hortense was rebellious and extremely independent. She did not take orders from anyone, and she thought rules were made to be broken. She encouraged the other dolls to take chances, to go their own ways. She even gave Ellen advice. Whenever Ellen's grandmother produced a new doll dress, it usually went to Hortense. Hortense was generous. After wearing a new dress for several weeks, she often passed it on to one of the other dolls.

Ellen's grandmother sewed prolifically. From any scrap of cloth, from any discarded dress or blouse or scarf, she ran up doll clothes on her sewing machine. Ellen herself never mastered the sewing machine, but she was fascinated by clothes: what worked best with what, which color combinations were daring but successful and which were impossible, which styles conveyed which effects. With thirteen dolls and a small trunkful of clothes, she could try everything. She never tired of exchanging and experimenting. At a very early age she learned the connection between clothes and personality.

By the time she was a teenager, Ellen had begun to choose and wear her own clothes with imagination. Although she was still tall for her age, she no longer towered over her classmates, and when her body filled out, she realized that her case was far from hopeless. She learned to walk with pride and grace. In her senior year, despite her continuing high grades, she became almost popular. She had no time now for those long evenings of doll stories and doll clothes, but she still kept all thirteen in her room, and she still consulted Hortense on important matters. Hortense continued to push her in new directions. Be yourself, Hortense always said.

Her father hoped that after graduation she would work full time at the grocery, where she had become his most valuable employee. He even offered her a small piece of his considerable profits—but canned tuna fish and frozen broccoli had lost their charm. Ellen chose Mount Holyoke College instead. During the summers, instead of returning to Elmira, she wormed her way onto the staff of New York City fashion magazines, working without pay for the chance to learn more and more about clothes. She was so busy and excited during these summers that she had no time to fall in love, although she managed to fit it into her college schedule, once very seriously as a junior and casually as both a sophomore and senior. It was the time when everyone was discovering that promiscuity could be called freedom, and that a meaningful relationship could begin on the first date. She survived this philosophy and graduated with honors, writing her final art history paper on the influence of fashion on art.

One of the fashion magazines she had worked for offered her a permanent job. The salary was tiny, but at least she was no longer expected to work for nothing. She turned it down because she was able to get what she really wanted, a spot in Bloomingdale's training program. Not only did Bloomingdale's pay more, but Ellen already knew she wanted to be in the business end of fashion, buying and selling clothes rather than preparing stories about them for magazines. Go where the action is, Hortense said.

Ellen and a Holyoke classmate named Sally Aikens found a

cheap walk-up apartment in the Eighties off Third Avenue, and every morning, even on rainy days, Ellen walked briskly down to the Fifty-ninth Street department store to learn her profession. At first she didn't mind that she was learning more about merchandizing, logistics, administration and computers than about selecting clothes. She was eager to learn everything, and the supervisors she worked for told her she was very good. Everything was exciting, including New York City itself.

She and Sally Aikens, who worked for a publishing house as a junior editorial assistant, seldom had much money. If Ellen had not been able to buy from Bloomingdale's at an employee discount, clothes would scarcely have fitted into the budget. Too many other expenses: restaurants, movies, occasional but invariably costly visits to Angelo's Alley, the neighborhood singles bar, and of course white wine, the obligatory drink of the seventies, which they bought in big green gallon jugs that occupied a large portion of their tiny refrigerator. To make up for the restaurant dinners—who could bear to be young and single in Manhattan without enjoying restaurants?—Ellen and Sally Aikens lived at home on pasta and English muffins. Their rent check was always late.

Fortunately for their economy, they met four young men who lived together in a huge apartment on their block. Not only did it have a wide wooden deck, useful for parties and sunbathing, but two of the young men were associates in a major law firm, and the other two worked for Kidder Peabody in Wall Street. All had money to spend. Whenever they held a cocktail party or a grilled dinner on their deck, Ellen and Sally were invited. Once the girls tried to return the hospitality by inviting the four young men to dinner at their apartment, but the six of them were so ludicrously cramped that they all agreed never to repeat it. "Let's just use our place," one of the lawyers said at the end of the evening.

At one time or another Ellen thought she was falling in

love with one or another of the four young men, but she turned out to be mistaken. No one minded. They were all good friends and could enjoy their times together without having to be active lovers. Sally did have a serious affair with the younger of the two lawyers, but both went on to other things, and the friendship continued. It all seemed easy and convivial in those cheerful days.

When Ellen completed her training program, she at last became a department manager, and that meant more money and more prestige. She and Sally moved to an elevator apartment with more space and better security. But it did not bring her closer to clothes; it brought her closer to computers and to administration. She knew she had a quick eye and a strong sense of style—everybody she worked with had told her so—but these talents lay fallow while she had to concentrate on inventories, reorders and personnel problems. She was an outstanding success in the wrong job. Then change it, Hortense advised. Go somewhere where you can be yourself.

She heard about the opening at Bendel's through the network and applied for it. Although the people who interviewed her at Bendel's did not let her know it, they had heard of her too through the same network. They knew she was both hot and frustrated. The vice-president of fashion, who everybody knew was the clothes conscience of Bendel's, took her through half-a-dozen talks, first at her fifth-floor office in the West Fifty-seventh Street building, then on long tours of the five sales floors. They visited everything: the beauty floor, furs, brides, lingerie, nightwear, at home, the forest of first-floor boutiques, from "Scentements" to bags and belts, from "Shoe Biz" to jewelry and the "Gilded Cage."

Although the executive seemed merely to be pointing things out—this from Italian ready-to-wear, that from Japan —Ellen knew that her own reactions and comments were being measured. Since she had never suffered from indecision about fashion, she responded to everything straight out, no weaseling. If the vice-president didn't like her opinions, at least she would know what those opinions were.

When the vice-president took her to lunch, word got back to Bloomingdale's, as Ellen had half feared—and as the vice-president must surely have known. Ellen was encouraged. They would not expose her if they were not serious. She was encouraged again when she had a long, thorough interview with Bendel's business conscience, a tough-minded man who was not interested in her fashion views but who cared very much about her grasp of costs, markups and profits. They even talked about the grocery back in Elmira and the markup on canned soup, which was substantially lower than Bendel's. Ellen thought she had done well. That evening she celebrated by taking Sally Aikens to dinner at the French restaurant they had agreed they still could not quite afford.

Then nothing for three weeks. As she learned later, Bendel's was checking her out with every possible source in the marketplace, inside and outside Bloomingdale's, but Ellen assumed she had failed. She consoled herself with the thought that she had told no one except Sally about being "virtually certain" of the job, but that turned out to be false consolation. Sally had told the lawyers and brokers, and next time Ellen went there for a chicken cookout, all four congratulated her. They even produced two bottles of champagne at the end of dinner. The evening was so difficult that next day Ellen could not bear to remember it.

But the champagne was lucky after all. Two nights later the vice-president of Bendel's called her at home and asked if she could "come in to see Gerry." The meeting was pleasant because now, indeed, it was all settled. Gerry, who had introduced the boutique concept more than a decade before and forced all the big department stores to copy her, was bright, fast and easy to talk to. She said three things that Ellen took to be guiding principles:

"Bendel's is a very personal business with lots of personal attention and a strong character."

"We don't have branch stores or big volume, so we have to compete in other ways, by being different and being first."

"We aim for the high end of the low-price scale up to the low end of very high prices. We don't do his-and-her matching camels."

Nothing could have delighted Ellen more than her new role as one of a dozen Bendel's buyers. Looking always for something new, something original, looking for clothes that might be expensive or funky or *outré* but always distinctive and strong, she managed to stay away from "matching camels," leaving that temptation to Neiman-Marcus. When Sally Aikens moved in with the man she would eventually marry, Ellen could afford to keep the apartment alone. For the first time, she had her own home all to herself, along with the most exciting job she could ask for. Everything would have been perfect if she had not met James Carvel.

James Carvel, designer of expensive casual clothes for men, had his own store on Madison Avenue. It was excessive in every way, as was he. Very tall, very slim, he might have been created to wear the clothes he designed: open-neck shirts with his flamboyant monogram on the left cuff, tight cut slacks, leather boots so soft that he sold them under the name of Gooferfeathers, the old Two Black Crows' term for the fuzz of peaches. He never wore a tie or jacket, able to convince even the most rigid restaurant maître d' that a James Carvel shirt was already the final word in being perfectly dressed. His hair, which he wore long and blown dry, was a soft, light blond. He was the most glamorous man Ellen had ever met, and she was grateful and flattered when he took her up. The first week they spent together she appeared in two gossip columns which, in spite of her personal pleasure, she decided not to send to her parents. Elmira would not appreciate James Carvel.

It turned into the worst six months of her life. James Carvel warned her that his success demanded that he maintain a
particular image, that he must be seen in certain places and
not seen in others. His was a late-night world of private
clubs, the most current discos, large but exclusive parties in
private townhouses and luxury apartments where the avail-
ability of cocaine was mandatory. Ellen could avoid the cocaine, even though it made her seem a bit quaint to this society, but she could do little about the late hours if she wanted
to be with him. If she had not been strong and healthy, her
work would have suffered, but she could survive on very little
sleep. Being known as James Carvel's girl helped her in the
fashion world.

However, being James Carvel's girl was a nonexclusive
role. Within three months she realized that he was scrupu-
lously unfaithful, not just now and then but whenever it occurred to him. In another month she discovered that he was
broad-minded enough to include men in his system of infidel-
ity. He never apologized or even discussed his transgressions.
Her last two months with him were months of the most painful withdrawal. Only pride pulled her out of it. James Carvel
himself would have been willing to continue. She was a suit-
able adornment and good company, provided that she did not
make scenes or objections. It was a hard time before she at
last broke free, but she walked away with the determination
never again to be subservient to any man. No, and not to any
woman either, for that matter. Be yourself, as Hortense had
always said.

Later on, after she had met Lawrence Winderman, she regretted the way she set about proving her total independence.
She was a substantial rising star in the world of her choice,
but she was almost thirty, and she was convinced that she
would never marry. Although she enjoyed men, she had
never considered herself promiscuous and she disapproved of
those who were. But now, after the Carvel fiasco, she told

herself, the hell with such moldy principles. She would take men and use men as indifferently as Carvel had treated her. Men were not important. She was above them. She was Ellen Lane.

She did not realize how false and wasteful this was until she met Lawrence. An unlikely meeting, for it was hard to imagine that they had any mutual friends. Indeed, the host of that dinner party was not actually a friend to either of them. William Cowan was a leading manufacturer of quality clothing who had made a superb line of expensive blouses to Ellen's specifications. The workmanship was meticulous, to the satisfaction and benefit of both, but while they looked forward to future projects, they were strictly business associates. And the Winderman Trust Company handled William Cowan's financial affairs, which were substantial enough to warrant a dinner appearance from the Trust Company's president. Ellen and Lawrence, seated next to each other, were the only single people at Cowan's sedate but perfect dinner party for twelve. Knowing Cowan's conservative reputation, Ellen wore her severe black dress. And Lawrence, as they would joke about it later, naturally wore his severe black banker's suit. Matching camels.

William Cowan would probably not invite either of them again, Ellen decided, because she and Lawrence talked almost exclusively to each other. Coming from such different worlds as banking and high fashion, they interviewed each other exhaustively. He was impressed not only by what she had accomplished but by how and why she had made her choices. He told her much later how he admired her achievement— and how lively and pretty she was. She liked the way he talked about his own work, which he plainly enjoyed. "You're unusual," he told her, even before dessert. "Most women aren't interested in banking, although they are interested in money." "Oh, I'm interested in money!" Ellen admitted. "Good," he said with a smile.

I'm going to like this man a lot, Ellen told herself, so I'm not going to go to bed with him. At least not yet. And I'll bet he doesn't ask me. At least not yet.

Although he took her home at the end of the evening, she did not invite him up for a drink. They shook hands at her door. "That was a pleasure," he said. "I hope I can call you."

"I hope you do."

They went to dinner the next week. Then to the opera— "To impress you with how good my seats are," Lawrence explained many weeks later. Then to dinner again. Although they found everything to talk about—conversation would never be one of their problems—Lawrence said nothing about his personal life or his family. Ellen forbore to ask. He had a privacy, a reserve, that she felt she absolutely must respect. When he wanted to tell her, that would be soon enough. "It was one of the extraordinary things about you," he said later. "Most women want to know everything right away, preferably yesterday." "Oh, I wanted to know all right," Ellen said with a laugh. "I just didn't want to spook you."

He did not even kiss her good-night until their sixth evening together. She had known exactly how it would feel, because she had watched his mouth and his hands and the way he moved. A very masculine man behind that steady, reliable banking façade. She could feel it in his kiss, and she wanted to take him straight upstairs to find out all the rest of it. But, she reminded herself, I don't do that kind of thing anymore.

The next time he called her he asked, in his careful voice, if she would like to have dinner at his apartment, then quickly added that he had quite a good cook and that one or two of his children might be around. Was he trying to reassure her that this was not an attempted seduction? That wasn't necessary. She decided that his mention of children permitted a personal inquiry. "How many do you have?" she asked. "Three," he said, "two in college." "Does that make five altogether?" She could hear the smile in his voice as he said, "No, no, just three. That seems like enough."

That was what Ellen thought too, both before and after she met them.

Ellen had known, of course, even before she saw Lawrence's apartment for the first time, that he was rich. Those dinners with exceptional wines at Cote Basque and Le Cygne, the Metropolitan Opera subscription with his name in the program as a Sponsor Patron, the Mercedes and driver, the dull but expensive clothes, the mere fact that he was president of a trust company with his own family name on it. But she had not realized how rich until she walked into his marble-floored foyer, which was as large as her living room, and then on into his living room, which seemed the size of her apartment, although actually it was smaller. The high ceiling with full-length beams and the picture windows overlooking the Central Park reservoir made it feel bigger than it was. As an art-history major she knew that the five paintings in the room were extraordinary, although knowing Lawrence, she was not surprised that none of them was modern. (Surely that was not a Sargent? Yes, it was.) How could a man who lived like this dress like that? He was still wearing his banker's suit, although since this one was dark blue with pinstripes instead of his more customary dark gray or black, perhaps he had changed suits after all and this represented his jolly at-home costume for an intimate dinner. At least he was not wearing a vest.

He mixed her drink at a green marble-top bar in the corner, then said, "This room is too large for two people. Let's sit in the library."

The library was a true library, cozy and comfortable, even though it too had a picture window. They sat together on a small couch, drank their cocktails and talked about their respective workdays. No sign of children, and Ellen did not ask about them. She felt more relaxed than she had expected, curious but not nervous. She could not tell about Lawrence. She already knew how skilled he was at not letting things show.

When they were halfway through a second drink—Campari and soda for Ellen, a martini for Lawrence—a tall, majestic black woman appeared in the library doorway. She wore a formal maid's uniform, black dress with starched white apron. Her long braided hair was wound tightly around her head, coronet style. Her skin was deep black. Her features had an almost Indian cast, high cheekbones and a wide straight mouth. Even before she spoke, Ellen was struck by the woman's dignity.

"Dinner is ready at your convenience, Mr. Winderman." The accent was faintly British, just a bit clipped.

"Thank you, Cecilia," Lawrence said. And then he introduced them. "This is Miss Lane, Cecilia. Cecilia Jones, Ellen. She's been with us for many years."

"How do you do, Miss Lane," the woman said, formal but not unfriendly. "I hope you enjoy your dinner."

"We'll be in in a few minutes," Lawrence said.

As soon as she left the room, Ellen said in a low voice, "What a marvelous-looking woman."

Lawrence nodded. "Care to guess how old she is?"

"I couldn't. Maybe forty? Forty-five?"

"She's just over sixty. She's done more to raise the children than I have. Considerably more."

"Is she from Jamaica?"

"Antigua. Come on, let's have dinner."

Serving a complicated crabmeat dish in large scallop shells, followed by tournedos with a light herb sauce, Cecilia was silent. She spoke only when Lawrence asked her, "Where's Bryan?"

"He's doing his homework," she said. And then, with a slight, affectionate smile, "Supposedly."

"Well, ask him to come in and say hello. He can have a cup of coffee with us in the library."

As they walked back to the library, Ellen said, "Which one is Bryan?"

"The youngest." At first that seemed to be all he was going to say. Ellen had decided to accept this solitary morsel when Lawrence added, "He can be a bit of a handful, except with Cecilia. Then comes Nancy and then Howard. Both off at college."

For Lawrence, this was almost an effusion of private family information. Maybe he's beginning to trust me, Ellen thought fondly. She poured their coffee from the silver service already in place on the library table. They had almost finished when Lawrence's son entered the room.

He was a tall, athletic-looking boy with strong shoulders. The family resemblance between father and son was pronounced, but as she would learn later, that Winderman look —long, bony faces and hands, straight noses, bright blue eyes —ran through almost all the males in the Winderman clan. The boy's face still had some of the softness of youth—he was about sixteen, Ellen guessed—but the principal differences between father and son were hair and clothes. Bryan's brown hair was tousled and curly, almost matted, while Lawrence's was thin and receding. And Bryan's attire was extremely casual: a bright red sweater without either shirt or undershirt, floppy brown corduroy pants and white tennis sneakers. Plainly there had been no dressing up to meet his father's guest.

"Hello, Bryan. I want you to meet Miss Ellen Lane."

"How do you do, Bryan."

The boy stared at her with suspicion. Then his left eyebrow went up in what Ellen would later recognize as his characteristic Bryan-to-Ellen look that seemed to say, What's all this? "Hello," he said at last.

"Join us for some coffee?" Lawrence invited.

"No thanks. I got some in my room. I have a lot of work to do."

"Very conscientious," Lawrence said, with an edge of irony in his voice. Ellen gathered from the tone, and from Cecilia's earlier comment, that studiousness might not be one of Bryan's strengths.

"Well," Bryan said, looking briefly at Ellen, "it's nice to meet you. I better get back to work, Dad." He gave Ellen one more suspicious glance, then left them.

"He looks a lot like you," Ellen said.

"Wait till you see Howard."

If Howard were going to be as suspicious of her as his younger brother, Ellen could hardly wait. And then a daughter besides.

They had a second cup of coffee, and Lawrence put on a tape of *La Gioconda*, an opera Ellen didn't know. Later they had brandy. Lawrence kept his jacket on but was otherwise companionable.

"Let me ask you something," Ellen said.

While his expression did not turn wary—she could read nothing from his eyes—Ellen sensed rather than saw a sudden reserve. He thought she was going to invade his precious privacy. Well, she was, but not in a way he would mind. "I'd like to be kissed again."

He looked at her gravely before he smiled. "That's funny," he said. "I was just thinking the same thing."

This time only confirmed what she had felt before, a powerful physical attraction, mixed with a lovely warmth and affection and—no, she would not use that word yet. His hands, those long hard hands, made her restless with pleasure.

When they stopped to look at each other, she could finally

read his eyes. They were glowing. She knew hers must be. There was something extra she had never felt before.

"I think," he said, "that you are going to be a serious problem."

"I hope so. I'll try to be."

"We have to be quiet," he said softly. He nodded his head toward the door. Cecilia and Bryan.

"I don't want us to be quiet," she said. "Let's go to my apartment. Besides"—her laugh was shaky—"I don't like this opera."

When she walked to work next morning, she was all but dancing with happiness. She told herself, but did not quite believe, that all her behavior of the past year had only prepared her to appreciate Lawrence Winderman. True or not, she did appreciate him. She could not help being nervous—in fact, squeamish—about all that money, with which she had no experience, and those children, of whom she had met only one unpromising sample, and Cecilia, who had run that household for many years. And Lawrence's own propriety and correctness, which bordered on stuffiness (though not in bed). None of it mattered. She was going to marry this man if he asked her. And if he didn't ask her? But he will, he will. He has to. During the day three people told her how well she looked.

He did ask her, although not for five months. She was in no hurry. They got to know each other wonderfully well, although there were places in Lawrence's mind or heart that remained out of bounds, not to be pried into. He would not discuss his first wife at all, except to say that the marriage was all over very long ago when Bryan was a baby. He would not even tell what had happened. He also volunteered nothing about other women, although considering the kind of man he was, there surely must have been some, perhaps many. That was fine with Ellen. She had always believed that her sexual life, and anyone else's, was a private matter, not an occasion for telling war stories. Lawrence seemed to have no interest in her sexual past, although she did not know whether this was lack of curiosity or simply respect for privacy. Either way, she was grateful.

With alarm, but acknowledging the necessity, she met the other two children. Howard did indeed resemble his father even more than Bryan did, right down to the cool reserve. Ellen could coax Lawrence out of his, but Howard's reserve seemed impenetrable. At age twenty, he was polite, self-contained, very intelligent—and glacial, especially with her. On the surface, she could get along with Howard, each keeping a correct distance, unlike Bryan, whose suspicion of her blossomed into hostility with further meetings. Both boys were difficult in completely different ways. But then, to make up for it, there was Nancy.

The first time they met, in that imposing living room, Nancy walked straight up to her, a sunshine smile on her pretty face, and shook hands, almost eagerly. Ellen knew at once: with this one, it was going to be great. Nancy chattered about college and boys and clothes and even teased her father, which would be unthinkable for Howard and beyond Bryan's capability. Nancy Winderman had winner written all over her. Well, one out of three was not an impossible beginning.

From Nancy, Ellen learned more about the other parts of the Winderman family and about the Island than she had picked up from Lawrence. Nancy was, as she herself put it, "a family freak." She loved belonging to a big family with lots of cousins, and she looked forward to August as the best time of the year, "when we all get together and mix it up and share all these things." It was obvious that being part of a large family, almost a tribe, gave Nancy a wonderful confidence, a great sense of belonging. And it was all because of her grandfather, Nancy said. He was the one who made it possible.

"You ought to meet him," Nancy said.

Ellen intended to.

Cecilia also turned out to be helpful, though in a quite different way. Without surrendering any of her dignity, Cecilia managed to let Ellen know she was acceptable. On the fourth time Ellen came to the apartment for dinner, Cecilia changed her form of address from "Mr. Winderman" to "Mr. Lawrence," which was apparently what she used in the family when no formal guests were present. On their next dinner at home, Cecilia had given up the maid's uniform with the starched apron and was wearing a brown dress. But when Lawrence gave a small business dinner party to which Ellen was invited, Cecilia went back to the uniform and to "Mr. Winderman." Cecilia had none of Nancy's cheerful openness. While Ellen knew she had passed some of Cecilia's private standards, she remained "Miss Lane" until after she and Lawrence got engaged.

She learned from Nancy's chatter about the other Windermans, but for a long time she did not meet them. She knew Lawrence's father was still alive, a retired English professor who lived in New York City. And there was a younger brother, Brad, who was vice-president for advertising of a large oil company with headquarters in Manhattan and who lived within commuting distance somewhere on Long Island. And a still younger sister, Martha, who was "between divorces" and who, Nancy said, "doesn't do much of anything but has a good time not doing it." All of them were nearby and readily available, but Lawrence never suggested that she meet them, not even on the most casual basis. In fact, he did not talk about them, and Ellen knew enough not to ask. If Lawrence wanted to keep her separate, for whatever private reason, she refused to care. Anything else might have seemed like pressing or, worse yet, begging, and she would not beg any man, especially not Lawrence. Lawrence would have to

choose his own banker's timing, even if that meant the head-
long recklessness of a snail.

But that spring he did invite her to spend a weekend at the
Island. "We can fly up Friday evening and rent a car."

"I thought your house was closed until summer."

"Who told you that?" Lawrence asked, as though she had
acquired privileged information.

"Nancy did."

"Oh." That was all right then. "We'll stay at a hotel.
There's a nice one in Bel Harbor that stays open through the
year."

"Discreet?"

He smiled. "Nothing is discreet on the Island, especially
off-season when there's not much to talk about. We'll have to
stay in separate rooms, and even so . . ."

Ellen loved it. She had never been to the Island before,
although she had heard many people in her business talk
about it. The time was late April when the trees were still
budding pale green and the only strong colors were the yellow of forsythia and the white and yellow of daffodils. She
had guessed correctly that this was an occasion for quiet, informal clothes. But she brought a soft blue loose-knit Italian
sweater with floppy sleeves to set everything off. "That looks
pretty," Lawrence said the first time she wore it. "It better,"
she answered. "I bought ten dozen of them for the store."

He showed her the whole Island Saturday morning and
then took her to the Winderman property. He opened the
padlocked wooden gate, she drove through, and he locked the
gate behind them. They spent the afternoon looking through
the four Winderman houses, to which Lawrence had separate
keys, each one tagged on an enormous key ring. They also
walked along the beautiful Winderman beach, keeping back
from the heavy-breaking surf. They returned to Lawrence's
house and made "Island love—the best kind" in Lawrence's
bedroom and then had martinis, still cold from the thermos,

on Lawrence's living-room couch before driving back to the hotel for dinner.

Aside from the Island itself and the Winderman property, the weekend brought two revelations for Ellen. The first was Lawrence's clothes transformation. Long accustomed—even inured—to his city banking style, she now saw him in garments of an extraordinary scruffiness, as though he had only two options, both at the extreme ends of the spectrum with nothing in between. His shoes were long-unpolished Wallabees with their crepe soles worn down on the edges. His shapeless corduroy pants could have been borrowed from Bryan, although they were more rumpled than Bryan's. His shirt was a Navy blue wool CPO jacket, dating possibly from World War II if not World War I and dotted with ancient pieces of lint that resisted removal. He wore a red cotton hat that was best not described. So there *was* a second sartorial side to Lawrence, his Island side, which left lots of room for improvement in the middle.

The second revelation came on Sunday afternoon when they were again walking the Winderman beach toward the lighthouse and he asked her to marry him.

"You bet," Ellen said.

It was only then that Ellen began to meet other members of the Winderman clan, and perhaps only because Lawrence could not easily delay this until the small family wedding ceremony. Not that he was ashamed of her; he was actually proud and said so. But to the greatest extent possible, Lawrence liked to keep his own life in his own world, exposing the minimum even to his relatives.

The response of Lawrence's children was predictable, although she had hoped otherwise. Since the forthcoming marriage was an unavoidable, unmistakable fact, she had hoped that this reality, as opposed to a mere threat, would change everything, or at least signal the beginning of change. Not at all. Nancy was delighted, giving Ellen an enthusiastic hug three seconds after hearing the news. Howard was politely congratulatory, but not a single ounce more. Bryan was sullen. At least that was his initial reaction, and while it disappointed her, later she would have settled for it.

The problem was Cecilia. In her own way, Cecilia was pleased and let Ellen know it. They shook hands, Cecilia called her "Miss Ellen" for the first time and told her that she had been "good for Mr. Lawrence from the very start." That was the first talk. Two nights later when Ellen came to the apartment, Lawrence said that Cecilia had something she wanted to say to her. His face and voice were careful, completely level, so she knew something was wrong.

"What is it?"

"Cecilia prefers to tell you herself. I'll send her in."

Ellen waited in the library until Cecilia appeared alone. Despite Ellen's invitation, she would not sit down, so Ellen remained standing too. They stood side by side at the picture window overlooking the reservoir, the sunset light burnishing Cecilia's lustrous black skin.

Cecilia said what Ellen was afraid she would say. "Miss Ellen, this is in no way personal, but I am going to be leaving. It's something I have to do."

"There's no need for you to do that. I don't want you to go. Please stay, for all of us."

Cecilia shook her head. "I'm pleased that you want me. I do appreciate your saying that. But my time is over. It's your time now."

"But I don't want to be the cause of your leaving. Did Mr. Lawrence tell you I was going to go on working? We'll need you to run this big place, just like always."

"It wouldn't work," Cecilia said. She smiled, not sadly but just acknowledging a truth. "You would be deferring to me because you are a polite lady and wouldn't want to hurt my feelings. And I would start to do something the way I've always done it, and then I'd think, maybe I better ask Miss

Ellen to see if she wants it some different way. Neither of us would like that. No, it's better that I go. I'm going home. I'm an old lady now, you know, and I should be back home again, after all these years. And you will have your own home, the way you should. You'll be better off with someone new."

"Cecilia," Ellen said, "everybody loves you. You're going to break the children's hearts."

The black woman swallowed before she spoke, but that was the only show of emotion she permitted herself. "I brought them up to be stronger than that, I hope. Howard and Nancy, they will be fine, but take care of my Bryan. Your Bryan. He will need some special attention."

"He doesn't want any attention from me. He doesn't even want me here. He wants you."

Cecilia did not bother to deny any of this. "He'll change. He's a good boy, and I will talk to him. I wish you and Mr. Lawrence the best. And I'll stay to help through the wedding, if that's what you both want."

"I just wish you'd stay, period." The thought of taking over this apartment and these children without Cecilia's help was intimidating, even for Ellen. But she could also feel the truth of Cecilia's words.

"No, it's your time now."

That evening after she had served dinner, Cecilia told Bryan. Afterward, as Lawrence had requested, she came to the library to report.

"Well?" Lawrence asked.

"He's upset," Cecilia admitted in her faintly clipped voice. "He's gone to his room and closed the door."

"I better talk to him," Lawrence told Ellen.

"Best to leave him alone," Cecilia advised. "At least for a while. He has to get used to the idea."

"Can I do anything?" Ellen asked. "What should I do?"

Cecilia's expression was compassionate, but apparently she had no advice to give. "I'll be cleaning up now," she said.

"Mr. Lawrence, Miss Ellen, I'll help you find someone to take my place. You don't need to worry."

But both Lawrence and Ellen did worry, not about Cecilia's replacement but about Bryan. They spent a stiff, awkward hour in the library, waiting for Bryan to appear.

"We have to expect some of this," Lawrence said at one point, in the tone he might use to explain to a client an adverse fluctuation in the bond market. "It's hard for Bryan to adjust."

"I know," Ellen said, thinking but not saying that it was also difficult for Howard and Cecilia and Lawrence and Ellen, perhaps even for Nancy. She straightened her shoulders. Here now, Hortense used to say, no self-pity.

Lawrence gave Bryan an hour and fifteen minutes, occasionally checking his wristwatch against the library quartz clock. Finally he said, getting to his feet, "I think perhaps I should talk to him."

Ellen got up. "I'm coming too."

"I wonder if that's—"

"I'm his problem," Ellen said. "I have to know."

They walked together down the hall to the bedroom wing. Bryan's door was still closed. She and Lawrence looked at each other. Then he knocked. "Bryan?"

Silence. Another knock. "Bryan, I'd like to talk to you."

Another pause before they heard the creak of bedsprings. That's bad, Ellen thought. He's been lying down. Footsteps to the door.

"What?"

"I'm not going to talk through the door."

Another pause while Bryan thought that over. Then the door opened.

His eyes, red and puffy, widened when he saw Ellen standing there, but then he looked only at his father.

"We're all sorry about Cecilia," Lawrence said. "Ellen too. Come on out and let's talk it over."

"I don't want to. There's nothing to talk about."

"Sure there is."

"Bryan, I really am sorry," Ellen said. She might as well not have spoken.

Bryan's young voice was hoarse. "What's to say? She made Cecilia go."

"That's not true," Lawrence said, very calm and judicious. "It's Cecilia's own choice, as she must surely have explained to you. Ellen wants Cecilia to stay, just as you do."

"Yeah," Bryan said with teenage sarcasm. "Well, thanks a bunch."

"Bryan, don't use that tone with me."

"Or with me," Ellen said. She had to draw this line sometime. Might as well start.

Bryan's eyes did not shift from his father's face. He was both angry and hurt. "I wasn't talking to *her,*" he said.

Always Take Charge

When he was twenty-two, Charles Winderman made his most important decision, the one that led—eventually—to all the others. It came as a terrible shock to his father. In fact, Amos Winderman had at first been too flabbergasted to be furious.

That his second son, Charles, might not follow his older brother into the Winderman Trust Company was understandable. After all, Peter was seven years senior and already the most powerful vice-president. He would clearly become Amos's successor, so it was natural for Charles to want to try his wings somewhere else. Because of Charles's shares in the Winderman Trust and because the family virtually owned the bank, conflict of interest would prevent Charles from entering any other banking enterprise. Government banking regulations would see to that. But many fine businesses existed in New York, companies and corporations run by men with whom Amos was on first-name terms. Any of them would be glad, even proud, to give Amos Winderman's son a start in an interesting, challenging position. Charles could learn business from a different angle, find out how the system worked in the New York community, gain responsibility and then join the Winderman Trust later. Or, if he was successful in the new career, he could stay with it and serve only as a director of Winderman, where his outside experience and contacts would be useful. All that was possible, Amos thought. It even made good sense. But *this?*

Charles Winderman had braced for this talk for weeks, and it had gone every bit as badly as he had anticipated. Perhaps worse. His father took a full thirty minutes to work himself into a fury. He reminded Charles of the history of the Winderman Trust Company. How there had been twenty partners at the beginning, with the original Winderman brothers putting up a large share of the investment and doing most of the work. How the Winderman family, through energy and enterprise, had always dominated the business, buying out other partners whenever possible. How Amos Winderman's own father, the previous chairman, had finally consolidated almost ninety percent of the shares into family hands. How he had then forced the other stockholders to accept a closed corporation whose shares could not be sold on the open market but could only be sold back to the corporation itself. How Amos Winderman's father, with the support of the other Windermans of his time, concocted a plan that distributed shares *per stirpes* at age twenty-one only to direct descendants in each generation. This document was elaborate, ingenious and above all legal. Amos Winderman could recite its provisions from memory, and frequently did while Charles was growing up. Now here was a closed corporation, Amos Winderman said, his voice beginning to rise, a marvelous edifice that insured family control in perpetuity over this still-expanding and wonderfully profitable institution, but it all depended on one principle.

Charles knew perfectly well what that "one principle" was, because this too had been part of his earliest education. He was about to hear it again, but this time stated in anger rather than in paternal pride. *Family participation,* his father said. The Windermans are committed to this enterprise. They will serve the Trust, they will preserve it, they will, by God, slave for it and guarantee its ever-increasing prosperity. That is their heritage and their responsibility. And now *you* want to teach literature.

There was much more of this, all through that long evening and for weeks thereafter. Amos Winderman knew only one ruling style for both his bank and his family: fear and force. He exerted these now. He brought up artillery: Charles's older brother, Peter, and the other directors, most of them Windermans by blood. It was more than a campaign; it was war.

But Charles Winderman had been listening carefully all those years when his father had been explaining the structure of the Winderman Trust Company. He was of age, he was independent. And he was as determined as his father. He had worked his college summers at the bank and knew that he could not devote his life to it. The bank was in good hands, not only his father's and Peter's but those of younger Windermans and Winderman in-laws. When he became old enough, he would serve as a director, he would attend board meetings, he would vote his substantial bloc of shares. But he would also teach.

Amos Winderman never forgave him. He took no interest in his son's career. Although Charles kept him informed, he did not acknowledge the progress: Ph.D., instructor, then up the professorial ranks at Rutherford College to chairman of the English Department. Even at the time of the Bernstein trial when Charles was in all the newspapers and magazines and on television, his father gave no credit to what he called "this defense of filth." At board meetings he treated Charles with angry courtesy, never asking his opinion but listening when it was offered. Only during Amos Winderman's last years, when Charles's older son, Lawrence, appeared at the bank did the old man concede that Charles's branch of the family was at last contributing to society, and that was only because Lawrence showed such total aptitude for the profession Charles had rejected.

Charles did not hate his father, but he hated growing up in a family where the only acceptable behavior was abject obedience and the only ruling method intimidation. He knew that he would treat his own family very differently. A family had to be held together by a better glue than this. He would find it. Respect rather than fear. Persuasion, not intimidation. Affectionate concern instead of iron pronouncements. Love was the key. It could all be done.

After the original breach, Amos Winderman made only one serious effort to influence his son. That came in 1942 when Charles told his father that he planned to enlist at the end of the college year. Amos accepted this equably—everyone was going into the services—until he realized that Charles intended to be, literally, an enlisted man. Then he exploded. Charles was twenty-eight, wasn't he? He had a graduate degree, didn't he? And despite his bizarre choice of career, surely he realized that he had a special intelligence to contribute and a family name and position to maintain, didn't he? The absolute least he could do was become an officer, which could easily be arranged. And not just a lieutenant, either.

"Father," Charles said, "I've been an officer all my life. I was born an officer. I'd like to try something different."

"What does your wife think of this?"

"She says it's entirely up to me."

His father snorted. "Women. She's no smarter than you are. They'll probably make you an officer anyway."

Charles took steps to avoid it. While he did not actually lie on the Army's questionnaire, he omitted facts that the Army might like to have known. He listed his occupation as English teacher, not mentioning that he was an assistant professor. He gave his place of employment as Rutherford, not bothering to say that this was the college rather than a town school.

He did not inform the Army about his various degrees or his published papers. When he took the mechanical aptitude test, performing the battery of chores with screwdrivers and pliers, he did not have to conceal anything. His native inability with tools produced such a low score that he was automatically eliminated from any military activity involving the repair, maintenance or use of machinery or weaponry.

But he made a serious mistake on the written General Classification Test. He swiftly and accurately filled in all the answers, just the way he had been doing on tests all his life. His GCT score was so high that the Army invited him to apply to Officer Candidate School. Charles Winderman said he wasn't interested in OCS. The indifferent sergeant processing his papers let it pass, merely pointing out that this was the biggest fucking mistake Charles would ever make. After basic training he was assigned to cryptography school, four weeks of learning how to encode and decode messages.

Having had a narrow escape because of his GCT score, he was careful not to overdo at cryptography school. He did not want to be assigned to cryptanalysis, which he suspected would land him in Washington, D.C., tabulating and retabulating German or Japanese word clusters in some vast office building. He finished in the top quarter of his class but not so high as to attract dangerous attention. As he wrote Anne, since he was in the Army anyway, it would be far more interesting to get overseas.

He got his wish and, as with many granted wishes, did not at first care for the result. He spent the war in a series of indistinguishably dreary bases in New Guinea, working eight-hour shifts in the message center with a variety of codebooks and systems, deciphering incoming messages and enciphering outgoing ones. He spent the other sixteen hours a day trying to make them pass—playing cards, writing letters and reading more books than he had ever read in his life, four and five a week. He was awarded the inapt but inevitable

nickname of Windy. Partly because of his age and partly because the young first lieutenant in charge of the message
center liked and trusted him, he made sergeant and was put
in charge of the other cryptographers.

Lieutenant Burke soon liked him for a new reason. Every
so often a message came in with a three-letter "Q" signal at
the top which meant "to be decoded by an officer." The first
time this happened Charles Winderman called Lieutenant
Burke to tell him the bad news. Bad news because the lieutenant hadn't the slightest idea of how to use the codebooks. His
control of the message center was administrative, not func-
tional. Charles took him into a corner and helped him work
through the message. It required the use of the strip code, an
especially unwieldy code for someone not accustomed to it.
Charles showed Lieutenant Burke how to use the eraser tip of
a pencil to slide the strips of paper back and forth in their
slots, but there was no way to teach him how much pressure
to use. Like all messages transmitted over radio in dots and
dashes, this one had its share of garbles that could be cleared
up only if one were familiar with the codebook dictionary
and could guess what the originator of the message was probably trying to say. They spent two hours on what would
normally have been a fifteen-minute piece of work for
Charles. The message turned out to be a long list of supplies
that the battalion would be receiving next week. The only
conceivable information requiring the attention of an officer
was the time and date of shipment.

"Jesus," Lieutenant Burke said when they finished. "And
you have to do this twenty times a day?"

"Or more," Charles said. "I like it. It's like doing complicated crossword puzzles."

"Yeah," the lieutenant said, "and I never liked *them* either."
He looked across at the other three cryptographers and lowered his voice. "Listen, Windy. The next time you get one of
these 'officer' messages, you do it. Then you bring it to me, I

initial it and take it to the C.O. Hell of a lot faster and nobody needs to know."

The system worked perfectly and would have survived to the end of the war if Lieutenant Burke had kept his mouth shut. But he bragged to the communications officer of a nearby fighter control squadron about his nifty solution to the "officer" message problem. Sergeant Winderman, Burke boasted, was the soul of discretion and an accurate, high-speed decoder besides. The fighter control squadron officer thought this sounded wonderful. He begged Lieutenant Burke to provide him with the same discreet service. For a consideration of Scotch, shared equally with Charles, Lieutenant Burke agreed.

Everybody was happy, including Charles's fellow cryptographers, who asked no questions while they drank the only Scotch in the battalion that belonged to an enlisted man. Not too many messages had to be decoded by an officer, and Charles was reliable. He never talked about the content of a message, not even when it contained the most prized of all rumor information, the movement of troops from one base to another.

Lieutenant Burke was not only an enterprising officer with initiative; he also loved Scotch. After consultation with Charles, who agreed that he could handle more messages and more Scotch, Burke sounded out other communications officers on the base. When he encountered one who decoded his own messages without complaint, he terminated the discussion. There were few such officers. Most enthusiastically joined the Burke-Winderman network. Soon so much trade existed that Lieutenant Burke was able to vary the form of payment. Other liquors became acceptable, as well as cold beer, wristwatches and high-quality war souvenirs. More and more people were happy. Sergeant Winderman became Staff Sergeant Winderman.

The base commander, General Cummings, learned what

was going on in his command only by accident. A colonel mentioned the system at the officers club one night. Next morning General Cummings assigned two officers to look into it. By midafternoon he knew he was in grave danger. If MacArthur's Headquarters in Hollandia found out that virtually every supersensitive message to Cummings's base was being decoded by a noncommissioned officer, and for *pay*, Cummings would be shot out of a cannon. He was a career officer from West Point, and now some sergeant and first lieutenant were jeopardizing that career. And apparently had been doing it for months. Civilians! Court-martial and punishment were clearly deserved but out of the question. The last thing he wanted was a public record of what had been happening. That would make Headquarters leap for his throat.

"All right, get them over here," he ordered.

When they were standing at attention in front of him, the lieutenant in khakis, the sergeant in green fatigues, he took a minute to look them over. Neither man was what he had expected. The lieutenant was scared but not terrified. He was short, trim, with a rather young but intelligent face. In other circumstances General Cummings, who put great store by his first impression of a man's character, would have welcomed him on his own staff.

The sergeant was not terrified either. Unless General Cummings was mistaken, he was not even scared. The general had been prepared for a mafioso or at least some little rat-eyed rascal, the kind of smart-ass conniver who was always trying to beat the army system. Instead, here was—no other word for it in his West Point lexicon—a gentleman. Damned fine-looking one too. Tall, slim, a strong face, a steady, level gaze that met his own without fear.

Although the men were different from his expectation, he saw no reason not to proceed as he had planned. After a silence long enough to build maximum tension, he let them have it. Drawing on twenty-five years' experience with verbal abuse, all the way from helpless plebe to brigadier general, he told them what he thought of their behavior: dereliction of duty, disobedience, subversion of other United States Army officers, compromise of secret information, bribery, simple greed. The phrases came readily to mind, and he delivered them in a hard, pounding voice. He could see that some of his accusations came as new thoughts to the lieutenant, whose state of alarm rose perceptibly. Still, the lieutenant did not unravel. Good stuff there. He couldn't be sure about the sergeant. The man listened with strict and proper attention— but almost, if the general could trust his own perception, with approval. The sergeant seemed to be admiring his phraseology.

Although General Cummings could have gone on indefinitely, he believed short tirades were more effective than endless ones. He concluded with the threat of court-martial, which usually had a wonderful impact on civilian soldiers. They could not know that in this case the threat was empty.

Then, because of the two faces he had been studying, he asked the question that had been growing in his mind since they entered his office and stood at attention before his desk. "What in hell made you do this?" Because he knew it was something more than simple greed.

"No excuse, sir!" the lieutenant snapped out.

"You're not answering my question, Lieutenant. I know fucking well you don't have an excuse. I asked why."

"Yes, sir." The lieutenant visibly put his thoughts in order but did not lick his lips. He still wasn't terrified. "I'm afraid laziness, sir. I didn't know how to do the codes."

"Then you learn."

"Yes, sir. No excuse, sir."

"And what about your corruption of your fellow officers?"

"No excuse, sir."

"Lieutenant, if you say that once more, I'll see that your

punishment is doubled. Was it laziness that made you seek out other officers and get them to pay for your odious service?"

"No, sir. I'm—I can't explain it, sir."

General Cummings needed no explanation on this point. He knew how these little cancers expanded. He was much more interested in what the sergeant had to say. "Sergeant, what's your story?"

The sergeant hesitated a few seconds, then said, "Sir, do I have permission to give a full answer?"

An extraordinary request from a noncom to a general, but the general wanted to hear. He nodded.

"Sir, the Army gives its officers no training in cryptography. Lieutenant Burke and the other communications officers were designated only because someone has to be responsible for the message center, just the way somebody has to be mess officer. They have no decoding experience, and most of the time they don't need any. Only one out of several hundred messages calls for decoding by an officer. But when it does happen, the result is extreme inefficiency and delay in delivery of what is presumably an unusually important message. The mess officer is never asked to cook a meal. Even if a communications officer does learn the codes, he will be severely handicapped without constant, daily practice. In my message center sometimes two or three men will work together over a particularly difficult decoding job, trying to figure out which of a dozen possible errors was responsible for a mishmash of words. To ask an untrained officer to do this alone is impractical. Sir, this is not an excuse but an explanation. The system is inefficient. No matter what happens to me, it ought to be changed."

An arrogant answer but probably correct. For the first time General Cummings wondered how this problem was handled at other army bases. At Headquarters it would be different, with a fat supply of officers to encode and decode messages whenever somebody pushed a button. But what about all the commands like his own, scattered all over the Pacific? However, this man needed to be knocked down. "Sergeant, you are not in charge of army efficiency. You're supposed to run a message center by regulations, and you broke them right and left. And got paid for it besides."

"Yes, sir."

"Why do you suppose certain messages are specifically directed to be handled by an officer? This is not done at random. It's on purpose. Who gave you the right to ignore that?"

"No one, sir."

"I did, sir," Burke interrupted. "It was my suggestion."

"Don't interrupt. So why did you do it?"

"Sir, I was cleared for security when I became a cryptographer. I trusted myself."

Jesus, the general thought. Again, an arrogant answer but probably correct. "And how do you justify getting paid for it?"

The sergeant gave him an absolutely straight look. "Sir, it was like winning poker chips. It was fun."

Inwardly the general whooped with pleasure. A straight answer from a sergeant to a general. You don't get two of those a year. However, he banged the desk with the flat of his hand. "By God, you're not going to think it's fun anymore. The fun is over, Sergeant. If Headquarters ever hears what's been going on here, this whole base will have its ass in a sling. Every officer who participated and probably a lot of C.O.s who knew about it. But very especially you two. I haven't decided what I'm going to do about this, but for openers, Sergeant, you can take off those stripes, and you're relieved from message center duty. Lieutenant, you are confined to quarters until further notice."

And now Lieutenant Burke did lick his lips, but General Cummings could tell that it was because he had something radical to say. You didn't get many of those in a year either.

"Sir, with your permission, sir, could I make a—I'd like to

make a—a somewhat unusual suggestion. In the spirit of protecting the base?"

"What is it? Spit it out."

"Well, sir"—more licking of lips—"sir, you could make Sergeant Winderman an officer."

"Dismissed!" General Cummings hissed at them.

But it was the right solution. It cast a shroud of obfuscation over the recent past. It legitimized an efficient improvement to a cumbersome system. There might even be a way to take extra credit with Headquarters. True, it rewarded the sergeant instead of punishing him, but that couldn't be helped. It also let off the hook all those communications officers, especially Burke, but there was the even higher priority of getting the base and its commanding general off a larger and sharper hook.

General Cummings prepared a lengthy memorandum to the Chief Communications Officer at Hollandia. Unlike most of his memorandums, it went through several drafts before he was satisfied. Even then he was taking a risk, but that was why he was a general.

According to the memorandum, it had come to the attention of General Cummings that an inefficient and possibly dangerous condition existed in the area of messages to be decoded by an officer. He then lifted, virtually intact, Sergeant Winderman's attack on the old system, including the part about mess officers never being asked to cook meals. He described a hypothetical but plausible situation in which a message of genuine urgency was delayed two hours, causing severe disruption. Then came the risk: for the last several months his base had been conducting, in the very highest interests of the Pacific Theater, an unauthorized experiment. It had selected its most trusted and proficient message center chief and assigned him the duty of decoding all "officer" messages. Intense precautions were taken to preserve security during the experiment, and the results were carefully monitored. Gains in speed and accuracy were found to be significant.

Since the experiment had succeeded, General Cummings had decided to make it permanent. Sergeant Winderman was promoted to the rank of second lieutenant and was henceforth responsible for all messages to and from the base that required encoding or decoding by an officer. General Cummings closed by recommending that this system be considered for adoption throughout the Pacific Theater wherever the appropriate conditions pertained. Respectfully submitted.

In due course, when MacArthur's Headquarters issued the directive to all base commanders, neither General Cummings nor his base was credited by name, but his thinking and much of his phrasing were recognizable. Better still, a Letter of Commendation for initiative went into his file. The general conceded that all had turned out well.

Except that his conversation with Winderman was not totally satisfactory. The general had kept him dangling for a week in the rank of private before summoning him and promoting him to lieutenant.

Instead of being grateful and relieved, Winderman demurred. "Sir," he said, still with that level gaze, "I don't deserve this."

"You bet your ass you don't. But any time you are offered an undeserved reward, take it. There will be plenty of times when you do deserve a reward and don't get one."

Then Winderman actually said, "General Cummings, I *like* being an enlisted man."

"That's just too bad. Listen to me, Winderman. If you are competent to be in charge, then always take charge. Always. Because the other man almost certainly isn't competent."

"Yes, sir."

Charles Winderman never forgot the advice.

It's His Party

"Well, don't bring him here," Lawrence said.

"Why not? This is Nancy's home."

"Because Ah-boo said no."

"He only said no to the party. He even promised to think that over. And Bonjy's going to talk to him. He didn't say anything about not having Anthony here."

"He didn't have to."

"Lawrence, he practically suggested it."

"If he did, he didn't mean it. You said his phrase was he 'didn't recommend it.' "

"That's very different from forbidding it. Besides, whose house is it?"

"Technically it's Ah-boo's, but that has nothing to do with it. Listen, darling, let's not make waves."

"Waves!" Ellen said. "Inviting a friend of Nancy's to our own house for a drink?"

"Not this time," Lawrence said. "Take him out somewhere if you feel you have to meet him."

Ellen looked at her husband. He was rarely intransigent about social matters, usually leaving them to her. "It seems very odd to me, and it will probably seem odd to Anthony."

"Be that as it may," Lawrence said with finality. "And Ellen, for the same reason, please don't take him to the club."

She would never have thought of taking Anthony and Nancy to the North Point Beach Club, where the service was slow and the atmosphere creaking, but this prohibition was too much. "What dress do you want me to wear? How big a tip should I leave?"

"Now, Ellen—"

"Can I borrow the car? What time do I have to be home?"

"Ellen, stop it. My advice is for you to stay out of this. Nancy will get over it. After all, it's a very trivial matter."

Her anger grew, as it always did when Lawrence used the word *trivial* in an argument. "You can stay out of it," she said. "But count me in. And it isn't trivial to Nancy, or to me. I don't like being pushed around. Anyway, it's Ah-boo who's being trivial. He's allowed to be trivial or anything else, just as he pleases. Doesn't anybody around here ever blow the whistle?"

Lawrence got that closed look on his face. "It's his birthday party," he said in a stiff voice. "I think he's entitled to pick his own guests."

"Sometimes," Ellen said, "you sound just like a banker."

Ellen and Nancy settled on The Helmsman, a waterfront restaurant overlooking Summertown Harbor. Because it ruled out bare feet and halter tops, young people had not preempted it, but it was not dressy enough to make them uncomfortable. Nancy and Ellen also agreed it would be just drinks after Anthony got off work, not a dinner. Ellen would meet them there. Just before leaving the house, Nancy gave her a quick hug and said, "Thanks. I hope you like him."

At Ellen's insistence, Nancy had not told Anthony about Ah-boo's veto. It made Nancy very uneasy. She said it left her in a devious position, but Ellen thought it was better to try to solve the problem quietly. Anthony might never have to know that his invitation had been in jeopardy. If worst came to worst, time enough to tell him then. This left Nancy feeling shifty and dishonest.

Ellen gave them fifteen minutes' head start before driving down State Road into Summertown. Fitting her belly under the steering wheel was awkward now, but comfortable enough once she got settled. Until quite close to town, the two-lane macadam road had no houses visible on the left—they were all down by the water—but many houses on the right, as close to the ocean as they could be. These had beach rights through paths or driveways leading down to the water, but no one had beach rights through the Winderman property. That was the advantage, Lawrence said, of being the first summer people in the neighborhood.

Near town the lots grew smaller, and all the houses on both sides hugged the road. Ellen had to drive through Main Street, where traffic was always heavy and slow, every car looking for a nonexistent parking place. When a space opened, it was even worse: traffic stopped in both directions while the driver parked. Any driver who failed to back into his space on the first try was subjected to horn blasts and verbal abuse, as Ellen had once learned. Now she always parked on a side street. Off-season the traffic and parking weren't so bad, but August was impossible.

She turned off at the drugstore and drove a block to the Congregational Church, where, as usual, she found a space. She and Old Seventeen wriggled out and walked back to Main Street, then another block down to the harbor. The Helmsman was only a few doors from the ferry slip. Customers near the windows could see the mainland ferry arrive and leave every hour.

The large, high-gabled room had open beams and rafters stained the soft gray of weathered shingles. Globe lamps of clear glass hung from the beams by chains, now turned on to

dim merely for decoration, since late-afternoon daylight
flooded in through the far wall of glass. She gave her name to
the perky hostess and followed her across the room, squeezing between tables. Several men shifted their chairs to make
way for her bulk.

Nancy waved from a booth next to the window wall. The
black-haired man next to her slid from his seat and stood,
waiting for Ellen to reach them.

"There we are," said the hostess, sounding like a hospital
nurse. "Your waitress will be right here."

"You looked like the ferry coming in to dock," Nancy said.
"Ellen, this is Anthony."

"Hello, Mrs. Winderman."

My goodness, Ellen thought as they shook hands, no wonder Nancy is all asquiggle. Anthony Balto was about twenty-
five and several inches taller than Ellen, perhaps five-ten. He
had long, straight black hair, clean and neatly combed, that
fell across his forehead. Eyes full of mischief. His skin was
dark, deeply tanned. His handshake was firm and friendly,
not too hard. He wore a tan linen jacket and an open-necked
pale yellow shirt. Wide, curved mouth, wide shoulders. He
was, to use Nancy's playful phrase, yums.

She sat down and ordered a vodka and tonic. Nancy and
Anthony sipped piña coladas, a drink Ellen considered suit-
able only for the young milkshake crowd. She made chitchat
about the pleasant afternoon, the light on the harbor, the August crowds, while she watched Nancy and Anthony together. They did not touch, but each was attentive to what
the other said, always turning to watch the other speak. Anthony lighted Nancy's cigarettes but apparently did not
smoke himself. Ellen realized it was Nancy's lighter he was
carrying in his jacket pocket. His voice had a rich Italian
warmth. He kidded Nancy, who reveled in it, but was polite
to Ellen without being diffident. He seemed at ease.

When Ellen asked him about his work, Anthony smiled, a

big white smile across his tanned face, and said, "I'm just completing the Grand Tour." Without detail but with nice touches of humor he described his long apprenticeship in Balto & Company. Under "Papa's" direction he had started as a stock boy in the plumbing business while he was still in junior high school. Just when he had finally learned where to lay his hand on every piece of equipment and how soon to order replacements, Papa had decided he was ready for progress. He was "promoted" to digging foundations for houses. Then electrical wiring. Then heating. Then masonry, "which sounds professional, unless you're the one lifting the stones and bricks and cement. Then it's a lot like digging foundations." Then construction work for three years, mostly house-building, and that was hardest of all "because that's where Papa pays the most attention." This year he was assistant manager of the hardware store "under another of my uncles." The hardware store was the last stop on the Grand Tour, and at the end of this year Papa would have to decide "whether or not I've learned anything useful."

Obviously Tony Balto had been teaching his oldest son every aspect of the family business. Anthony had not gone to college, but Ellen could tell he had had the best possible education to run Balto & Company, whenever Papa decided to hand it over. It would be in good hands, she thought.

"You have a wonderful house, Mrs. Winderman," Anthony said, changing the subject.

"I didn't know you had been in it."

"I haven't."

"Anthony's a winter snoop," Nancy explained. "After Labor Day when the summer people have left, he goes around and looks at all the houses."

"Except the ones that are boarded up. It's no fun snooping if you can't see the furniture."

"Would you two like another drink?"

"They *are* kind of sweet," Anthony said, "but Nancy likes them. Yes, please."

Ellen signaled the waitress. "Have you ever worked on our house?"

"No, not yours. But I've worked on the other two, Nancy's aunt's and uncle's houses. It's a beautiful property, the old Benbow place."

"Our family hopes someday it will get to be known as the Winderman place."

"Oh well," Anthony said, the mischief flashing in his eyes, "Mr. Winderman's only had it forty years or so. It takes time for people here to accept change."

"Oh, come on," Nancy said, hitting his arm lightly. It was the first touch, an easy, familiar affection. "You can't be that stodgy."

"You don't know the Island," he said, looking at her with a direct fondness.

The response in Nancy's face was melting. Can't blame her, Ellen thought. I'd probably melt too.

Anthony turned back to Ellen. "I'm really looking forward to the party next week. The big house is always boarded up. I've never seen the inside."

Ellen could sense that Nancy was stricken, but she kept her eyes on Anthony. "Yes," Ellen said firmly to make Nancy accept it, "we're looking forward to it too."

Anthony warmed to the idea. "You know," he said, "Mr. Winderman's quite a figure among the islanders, owning that big beach and all the houses, but I've never met him. It sounds like I picked the right time. Or Nancy did."

A strangled look on Nancy's face. Ellen shot a glance of warning. Then she said, "Yes, a seventieth birthday party is a special event."

"I'll say," Anthony agreed. "I remember when Papa was fifty a few years ago, we had the biggest family party in Balto history. But that's nothing like seventy."

No good. It was coming out. Nancy couldn't hold it back any longer.

"Anthony." Now Nancy put her hand on his. "There's a hitch. I'm sorry, Ellen, this just isn't fair."

"What's not fair?"

"My grandfather—oh, shit. My grandfather doesn't want you to come."

Anthony looked back at Ellen for confirmation. His face held no expression. The warmth was gone.

"He's a very old man," Ellen said, keeping her voice even. "He has to get used to the idea."

"What idea is that?" Anthony's face was cold.

Ellen considered how to answer that, but there was no stopping Nancy.

"You're not one of the summer people, that's what." Nancy was angry and close to tears.

"Not good enough," Anthony translated. He said something fierce in Italian.

"It doesn't mean any such thing," Ellen protested. "It's just an old man's whim. He's going to change his mind."

Anthony did not lose his manners. He drew a deep breath. "Well. I guess I better go." He stood up. "Thanks for the drinks, Mrs. Winderman. I enjoyed meeting you. I mean it. I'll call you, Nancy."

He bowed his head to Ellen, then walked quickly away, his broad shoulders straight and hard.

Nancy put her hand out to Ellen, all the ache of twenty years old in her face. "I love him. I had to tell him."

"I know," Ellen said. "I like him too. We'll work this out."

Nancy shook her head, squeezing Ellen's hand.

Ellen waited impatiently through the next morning and noon because she wanted to catch Bonjy alone, face to face and without interruptions. Tuesday afternoons Ah-boo went to Roger Bernstein's house on the other side of Summertown for their chess and backgammon matches. Tuesdays at Roger's, Thursdays at Ah-boo's. Ah-boo would be absent until dinnertime. Ellen waited until midafternoon, when she was sure to catch Bonjy. Something told her not to telephone first but simply to appear.

She found Bonjy in the kitchen, standing over the big maple worktable, grating onions and carrots. Arranged in neat order on the table were piles of ground beef, pork and veal.

"Hi," Ellen said. "Meat-loaf time, I see."

"Hello, there." Bonjy looked up to smile but continued grating. "Pull a chair and keep me company."

Ellen did so. She loved kitchens and cooking, and she liked to watch Bonjy at work, the soft quick hands making all the motions without waste.

"I get so tired," Bonjy said, "of all the seafood. Oh, I like eating it, but it's boring to cook. Especially the way Mr. Winderman likes it. Broiled swordfish, broiled bluefish, broiled salmon. Then boiled lobster and steamed clams and then around again. It's what he likes in the summer"—she scraped the onion and carrot into the mixing bowl and picked up the ground beef—"but sometimes I just have to get my hands into a good meat loaf. Not too often though, or Mr. Winderman will say, 'Mary, didn't we just have this?' "

"Cold meat-loaf sandwiches are my favorite," Ellen said. "I'll sneak by tomorrow."

"There'll be some left for you, I expect." She added the pork and veal and mixed them vigorously. "There's nothing like getting into raw meat up to your elbows. Like some iced tea? I'm afraid you'll have to get it yourself. My hands are a little busy."

"No, thanks." She paused. "I saw Anthony yesterday. Nancy's young friend."

Bonjy stopped with the bowl of beaten eggs in midair. "I heard you were going to."

"How did you hear that?"

"Oh, you know how word gets around this family. Bryan and his friend Angie stopped in for some cake. What did you think of him?"

"Terrific. Handsome in a very masculine way. About as masculine as you can get at that age. Good manners—excellent manners. He's self-confident, I'd say, but not cocky. He cares about his work, and he sounds expert about it. I liked him a lot."

"Isn't that nice." Bonjy poured the eggs into the bowl and continued mixing. Then she looked up, eyes twinkling behind the rimless spectacles. "Is he sexy?" She blushed.

Ellen laughed and Bonjy joined in. "I'll say. If you and I were twenty, Bonjy . . . But there's nothing macho about it. It's just there. By the way, Nancy told him."

"That he couldn't come to the party?"

Ellen nodded. "I advised her not to, at least not until you had a chance to talk to Ah-boo. Did you get anywhere?"

Bonjy mixed in silence, hands working in and out of the bowl. The silence went on. "No, but I haven't tried yet. It hasn't seemed like the right moment."

Ellen wondered about this. Was Bonjy backing out? She mustn't back out. "There isn't all that much time, you know."

"I certainly do, if anybody does."

"I didn't mean you didn't know. I just meant it can't wait very long. I'm really counting on you to help." And lest that sound too dictatorial, she added, "Nancy is too."

"Poor Nancy. How is she taking this?"

"Not too well. She's very worried about Anthony's feelings. He was quite wounded, I think."

"Are you sure?"

"I was right there. Yes, I'm sure. He has pride."

"Are they in love?"

"Oh, yes. Nancy said so. Besides, I could see it."

"Dear, dear." Bonjy gave her handiwork a final pat of approval before looking at Ellen. "That always makes things more complicated, doesn't it?"

"You will help though?"

"If I can. Yes, if I can."

I think I better get some more help, Ellen said to herself.

"Sure," Martha's husky voice came over the phone. "We're going out for cocktails, but it won't be till seven. Come on over."

"Can we talk alone?"

"Now that sounds interesting. Sure. Richie's playing Scrabble with Amy. I'll keep him at it. Christopher's somewhere, I guess."

The walk to Martha's house was steep enough to make her stop several times for breath. First up the rising land in the direction of State Road, where the oak trees were thicker and taller as she climbed between them on the dirt path. Then the very steep climb up Martha's driveway to the hilltop clearing. The house stood much farther from the water than her own, but because of the height she liked the view even better. From Martha's deck she could see the curve of the state land well past the lighthouse. In the opposite direction she could see Smollett's house and the two houses beyond it and, far down, the bend of Summertown Harbor. Because of careful siting, the other Winderman houses were invisible, all hidden behind the thick foliage of oaks, maples and tall pines.

Martha was stretched out on her deck in the wheeled chaise longue, ignoring the view. She wore a bright blue bathing suit, huge, very dark sunglasses and a straw hat. She held two fashion magazines. "My God," she said when Ellen puffed up the stairs, "you walked up?"

"Good exercise. Maybe too much."

"How about a drink?" This was Martha's first and recommended solution to any given problem. Ellen settled for a Perrier. Martha brought it, along with a tumbler of ice and Scotch for herself. She took off the hat and the glasses because the late afternoon sun had lost its glare.

Ellen settled into a spacious Brown & Jordan deck chair, feeling the comfortable give of the beige netting beneath her weight. "I need an insider's opinion—and maybe some help from the woman of the family."

"The woman? Don't you and Sue count?"

"Maybe not in this." She explained Nancy's predicament, about which Martha had heard nothing. Ellen told about Ah-boo and Anthony and Bonjy while Martha sipped her Scotch. "Everything's mixed up in it," she finished. "Love, sex, pride, youth, age. And a lot of stubbornness."

Martha had listened well, not interrupting with questions. Now she asked, "What does Lawrence think about it?"

"Well, first he says it's a trivial matter. And then he says for me to stay out of it. And then he says it's Ah-boo's birthday party, so it should be up to him. But you know, Martha, sex and love are never trivial to someone Nancy's age."

"Or your and my age."

"Agreed. But how about when you were twenty?"

"Jesus, that was the whole world then. Well, almost. Clothes and music were pretty important, too. But I guess they were important just because they were closely connected with love and sex. What a time!" She shook her head in memory and suddenly looked younger than her forty years. "Ah-boo and Mother were evaluating every boy I went out with. And not just them. Lawrence and Brad were watching too, because I was the youngest and the only girl. I don't know how my dates stood it. I couldn't." She took a big sip from her drink. "Maybe that's why I got married so quick to the first man who passed inspection. That's what the analyst said anyway."

"Did it do any good?"

"Marriage or analysis?" Martha laughed at herself. She had a good laugh, just a little bitter. "No help in either case."

"Well, you can sympathize with Nancy. She's a lovely girl, but very vulnerable. And it's not as though Anthony Balto were some kind of thug. He's quite attractive."

"Are they sleeping together?"

Ellen was practically certain after seeing them with each other, but since she had no direct evidence, this was a duckable question. On the other hand, she wasn't going to get Martha's help if she acted stuffy. "I don't know. Probably."

"Sure. Dumb question. These days it's on with anybody over fourteen. I'm going to get another drink. How's your Perrier? Switch to something else?"

"I'm fine, thanks." She watched Martha swing her bare legs from the chaise longue and get to her feet in a single fluid, sensual motion. I'll be able to do that in about six more weeks, she thought to herself, and my figure will be as good as hers. Maybe not so animal sexy, but better at the hips. She heard Martha inside the house calling something, presumably to Amy and Richie at their Scrabble game, and then she came back outdoors with her fresh drink. Martha was certainly going to be primed for her seven o'clock cocktail party.

"Maybe you could talk to Ah-boo," Ellen said, getting down to business when Martha was back on the chaise. "You've been through all this. Maybe as his own daughter you could get through to him better than I can. Make him understand about Nancy's feelings. He's a naturally kind man, but somehow I'm not getting to him in the right way. In the right words. I'm not sure I know what they are. I'm too new, and he doesn't know me that well."

"Huh. I'm not the most trusted witness about sex, you know. Maybe expert, but not trusted. You're better off without me. Here you are, newest member of the family, eight months pregnant with latest grandchild. And Ah-boo approves of you. Can't say that about myself. I'm pretty far down his approval list."

"I wasn't exactly a goody-goody when I met Lawrence." Ellen was remembering that insane year when she was twenty-nine and was sure she was never going to marry, never going to have anything permanent. The year when she said the hell with her own rules and standards and decided to go to bed with anybody who asked her, as well as with some who didn't. A terrible year. She was ashamed of that time, but, as she often justified it to herself, maybe it cleared the way for Lawrence to happen.

Martha dismissed her comment. "Doesn't matter. It's how you seem to the family. Everybody likes you, you know? Maybe you don't know. That's the kind of thing big brother Lawrence might not tell you." She sighed and stared over the treetops toward the ocean.

Ellen kept quiet. No one except Ah-boo had come out and said the family liked her. Of course, it wasn't true for her own stepsons, and perhaps it wasn't even true for everybody else, but she was very pleased. She wanted to belong. Maybe it meant only that Martha liked her, but if so, she was still very pleased.

Martha's wide, almost lashless blue eyes came back to Ellen. "Some advice, sister-in-law. Drop it. Forget the Nancy thing. Go along with the family, which means go along with Ah-boo. Because if you don't, they'll punish you. They—the Winderman men. Even if you're liked or even loved, that won't count. They'll wind up against you. I'm not talking about this Nancy thing. I mean as a rule, in general. Tell you something, Ellen. I was a shit to my first husband. Nice old Don, who was a sweet, honorable man, and they just drove him out. All my fault, or mostly, and they just drove him out. Just closed ranks behind me. Bye-bye, Donald. Cuff too, Christopher's father. Not so sweet, not so honorable, but tougher and smarter than Don, and they beat him. Bye-bye,

Cuff." She had a big slug of Scotch without taking her eyes from Ellen's. "They—they, my family—could have made a hell of a case against me and in favor of Don. Cuff made a hell of a case for himself. No sale. Bye-bye, Don. Bye-bye, Cuff. Hi there, Martha, good old Martha. Martha wins. I'm one of them, born a Winderman, so I win."

There was something lost and puzzled in her eyes. "Sometimes I wonder if it would have been better the other way. If they had stood up for Don or Cuff and put the pressure on me instead. Made me behave. Who knows. Anyway, if you care as much as I think you do, you better go along. Go along with them. Nancy will survive. We always do. Drop it."

Ellen got to her feet. She wanted to put her arms around Martha but knew she must not. Maybe some other time, some other occasion, when they knew each other better. "Thanks for the talk. And the advice."

"Let Richie drive you down."

"Thanks, but it's good for me to walk. Besides, this way it's all downhill. But I can't drop it, you know."

"Sure you can."

"All right then, I won't. Nancy's my daughter."

"Stepdaughter."

Ellen shrugged. "The principle's the same."

A bitter little laugh. "Principle," said Martha, "will get you nowhere."

Bernstein of the Apes

Roger Bernstein picked up his red bishop and captured Charles Winderman's knight.

"Ka-goda?" he asked, using Tarzan's word for "Do you surrender?"

There was nothing to be done. "Ka-goda," Charles Winderman said.

Roger Bernstein checked his watch. "An hour and thirty-five minutes. You're improving, Charles. Or else playing more slowly." His gnome face, deeply creased, wore a delighted smile. He loved to win.

"Get the backgammon set," Charles said. "As they like to say in the Army, let's play a man's game."

"That was forty years ago. They must be saying something different now, don't you think? All right, you put away the game of reason, and I'll get the game of luck."

He pushed himself to his feet. He was a short man, barely five and a half feet tall. He wore old blue jeans over his pot belly and a loose Madras sport shirt, mostly purple. Since he was in his own home, he was barefoot, his preferred condition. Although he could pull himself together for social occasions, his natural appearance was casual to the point of sloppiness. He was the most unathletic man Charles Winderman knew: large head, narrow shoulders, no chest to speak of, a slouching walk. He looked all his sixty-one years, except for the bright brown eyes dancing with high intelligence. He was Charles Winderman's closest and unlikeliest friend.

While Roger Bernstein was getting the set, Charles Winderman put away the chess pieces in their green velvet pouches. Roger might be sloppy in his own person, but his home and everything in it was as neat and disciplined as his mind. On a day when the cleaning woman, Mrs. Hackett, had been here, Charles Winderman had seen Roger walk in the house and make a series of quick little adjustments in the position of furniture and the placement of objects on tables. Not that Mrs. Hackett was careless. She also cleaned for Charles Winderman, and Bonjy considered her a jewel. But even Mrs. Hackett couldn't be correct to the inch.

It was a small two-bedroom house that Charles had helped Roger find after the trial, when it was plain that Roger was going to have disposable income. Roger's wife had already left him, using his abrupt notoriety as a handy excuse. What had been intended as a vacation house and a modest investment had become Roger's permanent home. He had never written another book, and of course after the trial no self-respecting college would hire him. Roger didn't care. The Winderman Trust had invested his royalties in such a way that he could live cheerfully and modestly without having to work again. This suited Roger, who had become even more an Island devotee than the Windermans. His white clapboard house sat on a side street on the edge of Summertown, close enough so that he could walk down to Main Street for restaurant meals. Its only distinguishing feature was this large screened porch, bigger than the living room and kitchen together.

Roger returned with the brown-and-black leather set that Charles had given him on his sixtieth birthday. "Okay," he said, settling himself in the opposite wicker chair and opening the case. "I have a ten-dollar lead, and you have an hour thirty-five to get it back."

The chess game, which Roger usually won, was worth ten dollars. Each backgammon point was worth one dollar. The length of the backgammon session was determined by the length of the chess game. Because Charles usually won at backgammon, very little money changed hands over the summer. They had kept track the last eleven years, and after hundreds of hours Roger Bernstein was now less than forty dollars ahead. "This is not," Roger said, "a cost-effective competition."

They both rolled a three, doubling the cube.

"Look out," Charles warned. "It's going to be my day."

"In all the jungle," Roger said with a grin, furiously rattling his dice cup, "Bernstein of the Apes fears no one. Not Numa the lion, not Sheeta the leopard, not Dango the hyena, and certainly not Charles Winderman. Mighty is Bernstein, the lithe and sinewy forest giant."

"Come on, roll," Charles Winderman said. Both were smiling at the ancient joke that had first brought them together.

Roger Bernstein had been an obscure, mildly respected assistant professor of anthropology at Harvard when he sat down, at the beginning of the spring reading period, to reread his favorite boyhood books, *Tarzan of the Apes* and *The Return of Tarzan*. Although he knew both books more or less by heart, not only scene by scene but sometimes sentence by sentence, he went back to them every few years, just to remind himself of the wonderful old yarns that had dominated his childhood daydreams. This time something snapped. As he came to the closing pages of *The Return*, he put down the book and opened his portable typewriter.

Over the two weeks of the reading period and the beginning of summer vacation, he rattled off the book that was to change his life. What if Tarzan had been Jewish? What if I had been Tarzan? He wrote *Bernstein of the Apes* purely for fun, out of his own youthful exuberance and his familiar love for the Tarzan characters. All the thinly concealed sexuality of the Edgar Rice Burroughs originals now became rampant. Roger Bernstein chuckled to himself all the way through his book, sometimes writing with tears of laughter at the awful activities of little Bernstein.

It never occurred to him that he might sell the book, but when he showed the manuscript to a colleague in the creative writing department, that man called his own literary agent in New York, who in turn called the unsavory but adventurous publisher Samuel May. May, too, had read the Tarzan books as a boy, and he was as fearless as the Forest God himself. Only a month after he had finished his creative outburst, Roger Bernstein was looking at a contract and a thousand-dollar advance. With some misgivings about his academic career, he signed the contract and cashed the check. He still could not believe that anything more would come of his little joke, but the money was welcome.

Samuel May, whose instinct for controversy was impeccable, realized that his best chance to make real money with a pornographic and racially reprehensible parody was to get it banned. The publisher therefore sent one of the first prepublication copies in a plain manila envelope to the Edgar Rice Burroughs Foundation, whose charter was to protect and defend Tarzan and his author from all intrusions, invasions and incursions against the original books. Just as May had hoped, the Burroughs Foundation took one horrified look at *Bernstein of the Apes* and applied for an injunction to prohibit its distribution and sale. The grounds were extreme obscenity and invasion of copyright.

Samuel May knew how to respond. The publisher called a press conference, invoked the First Amendment and declared that *Bernstein* was in the sacred tradition of *Lady Chatterley's Lover*, *Ulysses* and *Tropic of Cancer*. This preposterous claim made wonderful fodder for newspapers, magazines, radio and television. Roger Bernstein suddenly found himself at the center of a literary, legal and academic controversy. Harvard suspended him. "Don't worry," Samuel May told him. "It will help sales."

Bernstein of the Apes closely followed the plot of the Tarzan books but with two basic changes: the young forest giant was the son of a Jewish peer, Jacob Bernstein, Lord Greatstroke, and every person and every animal in Burroughs's African forest primeval was a sex maniac. After the death of his parents, little Bernstein was raised by a tribe of great apes whose principal preoccupation was sex. Bernstein was introduced, almost as soon as he could swing from the branches of jungle trees, to aerial copulation. Once a month the tribe repaired to its hidden amphitheater where the great apes indulged in a primitive orgy called the Cum-Cum. Little Bernstein was much sought after at the Cum-Cum because of his white skin and his curious circumcised member, an operation that had been performed in the little cabin by his father Lord Greatstroke just before the peer's death. Kala, the great she-ape who was Bernstein's foster mother, basked in her little white ape's popularity and prowess.

Into this sylvan idyll on a gold-seeking expedition came Professor Archimedes Q. Porter, his lovely daughter, Jane, and her faithful black maid, the 280-pound Esmeralda. Jane Porter's experiences in the jungle, although unspeakable, were related at great length. She suffered innumerable sexual indignities, not only from Bernstein but from other tribe members—Kerchak, Tublat, Terkoz, the whole crowd—and from other forest denizens, down to and including Histah the snake. Jane survived them all and then reported them in detailed letters to her friend Hazel Strong back in Baltimore. Each letter began: "Dear Hazel, Today I faced a fate a thousand times worse than death." Jane even survived her capture and abuse by the fifty frightful men of Opar. She was rescued from Opar by Bernstein himself, who confronted the high priestess Oo-La-La in a memorable scene on top of the sacrificial altar.

After many adventures, Bernstein and Jane were reunited and lived happily ever after in great wealth, thanks to the ingenious detective efforts of Bernstein's friend D'Arnot. It was D'Arnot who established Bernstein's right to claim his father's title and vast estates. Faithful to *Tarzan of the Apes*, *Bernstein of the Apes* concluded with the triumphant telegram: FORESKIN PROVES YOU LORD GREATSTROKE. CONGRATULATIONS. D'ARNOT.

Charles Winderman walked into the Bernstein case with eyes not quite wide open. He hated all literary censorship on principle. He admired deft parody as a legitimate form of criticism. And his wide reading had convinced him that artistic sexual description could be a permissible form of literature, though of course not for undergraduates. Besides, as a childhood reader of eight Tarzan books, he was curious to learn what this Bernstein fellow had done with the material. Since the book was under injunction, he could not find out.

He wrote identical letters to Roger Bernstein and to Samuel May, offering his possible support and describing his qualifications as professor of literature at Rutherford College. For years he had taught a popular course in the short novel, which he considered the most underrated form of literary achievement. He had published numerous papers and one book in this field. Among the works he had taught and written about, he cited *Heart of Darkness*, *The Bear*, *The Good Soldier*, *Death in Venice*, *Billy Budd*, *Cakes and Ale*, *A Handful of Dust*, *Appointment in Samarra* and *The Go-Between*. He was prepared to contribute an affidavit or even to give testimony, with the condition that he found *Bernstein of the Apes* worthy of support.

Roger Bernstein, depressed by his suspension from Harvard and still not believing that anything so dramatic as a trial would ever take place, answered Professor Winderman with a brief note thanking him for his kindness. But Samuel May pounced on this stroke of fortune. ARRIVING TOMORROW WITH BERNSTEIN BOOK read his telegram to Rutherford. Indeed, the next evening at home Charles Winderman was reading the adventures of little Bernstein, while Samuel May sat in his room at the nearby Treadway Inn, drinking too many Scotch-and-sodas while waiting for Winderman's phone call. It finally came at eleven-twenty.

"It's brilliant," Professor Winderman said. "Shocking but brilliant. Very funny. What would you like me to do? How can I help?"

Samuel May finished the last half of this particular drink in a single happy gulp. "I'll be right over."

"It's a little late for a conference. I could do it tomorrow morning before my ten o'clock class."

"It's never too late," said Samuel May, "for the defense of literature."

They talked strategy until two in the morning.

In the following weeks Charles Winderman had many talks with May, with the lawyer who would try the case and with the author himself. He found Samuel May an opportunistic rascal, and he did not like the lawyer at all, even though the man was shrewd and icily competent. Perhaps because of these two unappealing partners in litigation, he was quite taken with young Roger Bernstein. The man was bewildered and worried. Having no tenure at Harvard, he thought his suspension would never be lifted, and that no good college or university would want him after all the publicity. Not publicity, really. Notoriety. For an anthropologist to be caught up with, of all things, Tarzan and that preposterous tribe of carnivorous "great apes" was the last word in academic hara-kiri.

In spite of this, Bernstein maintained a sense of humor about himself and his situation. As Charles Winderman got to know him better through their many pretrial conversations, he liked him more and more. Physically, Bernstein was unprepossessing. He would make a poor impression on the court. He was rather ugly and had no presence. Samuel May and the lawyer understandably did not count on him for much help. And yet the man behind the dim façade was extraordinary. He was as far above average intelligence as Tarzan was above the great apes and, of course, amusing and witty, not just on paper but in person. By the time the trial opened, Charles Winderman was determined to help him when it was all over.

It was not over quickly. Because of the injunction, the press had not been able to read the book, but once the trial began, many delightfully obnoxious details became available. Under questioning by the Burroughs Foundation lawyers, Roger Bernstein was forced to confess his dastardly inventions.

"Mr. Bernstein, how many instances of sodomy does your manuscript contain?"

"I don't know."

"Well, can you give some estimate?"

"I don't know. Quite a few, I guess."

"Quite a few. Does it surprise you to hear that there are thirty-seven separate mentions and descriptions of sodomy?"

"Thirty-seven? You must be counting the animals."

The judge: "Order! Order!"

The problem the news media faced was to convey the scandalous content of the trial without using language that would offend readers and listeners of the fifties. Interviews were a difficulty. The pious Burroughs Foundation team would discuss the affair only in platitudes. Bernstein himself was useless to the press because his lawyer had ordered him to keep his mouth shut. Samuel May could be counted on for regular tidbits, but he was so self-serving the press tired of him. He seemed able to speak only when cloaked in First Amendment raiment.

After a week devoted to establishing the obscenity of *Bernstein of the Apes*, the Burroughs team went after copyright infringement and what it called "the improper appropriation of proprietary characters." Roger Bernstein was forced to admit on the stand that he had not invented a single character that did not exist in the Edgar Rice Burroughs original works. Yes, Jacob Bernstein, Lord Greatstroke, was modeled after John Clayton, Lord Greystoke, and of course Tarzan was Bernstein. Yes, Oo-La-La, the high priestess of Opar, was obviously modeled after La, the high priestess of Opar. All the other characters—even such minor walk-on apes as Mungo and Gunto, even lesser creatures of the forest such as Pamba the rat and Pisah the fish—were straight out of Burroughs. As for major figures—Jane Porter, Esmeralda, the really "meaningful" apes such as Kerchak, Tublat and Kala—there could be no doubt.

"You even stole language directly from the Burroughs books?"

"Well, I don't know about 'stole.' "

"Did you or did you not take directly from Mr. Burroughs the description of Jane Porter's attitude as she watched the fight between Tarzan and the ape Terkoz? I quote, 'The veil of centuries of civilization and culture were swept from the blurred vision of the Baltimore girl.' "

"Yes, but for a different purpose. I—"

"Yes is sufficient. In reference to Tarzan's scar on his forehead, did you or did you not take directly from Mr. Burroughs the phrases, I quote, 'The vivid scarlet band upon his forehead,' and, again I quote, 'A bar of inflamed crimson against his tawny hide'?"

"I made it a signal of Bernstein's sexual excitement."

"I didn't ask your motive. Did you or did you not lift those quotes directly from Mr. Burroughs?"

"Sure."

"Did you or did you not take directly from Mr. Burroughs the maid Esmeralda's use of the word 'Terrifical'?"

"Only to describe her reaction to intercourse with Bolgani the gorilla."

The judge: "Order! Order!"

Headline in the New York *Post*: ESMERALDA TO GORILLA: "TERRIFICAL!" ULTIMATE BERNSTEIN INSULT TO NEGRO WOMANHOOD.

Samuel May enjoyed testifying but contributed little to the defense. He disgorged more First Amendment blather, but it was tarnished by his track record as a book publisher. The Burroughs team established that many of May's books were not even reviewed by critics and that for all his protestations about publishing freedom, he was in business to make money from sensational works, most of them sleazy. The Burroughs Foundation had guessed that Samuel May himself had mailed them the prepublication copy of *Bernstein*. May not only had to admit that he had done this but had done it to provoke a legal response—in short, this very trial. The judge's face was grim with distaste when Samuel May was allowed to step down.

Charles Winderman brought the first note of respectability to the Bernstein defense. He made an impression of dignity by the way he walked to the witness stand, took the oath and seated himself for what May's lawyer had warned him would be a lengthy ordeal. As they had planned, the lawyer led him item by item through his academic career and personal life, both impeccable. Several times the Burroughs lawyers volunteered to stipulate that Charles Winderman was a qualified expert witness, but May's lawyer persuaded the judge that it was essential for the court to hear every detail from Professor Winderman himself.

During the long first day of testimony, *Bernstein of the Apes* was not mentioned. Instead, Charles Winderman responded to questions about his undergraduate and graduate work, his grades, his Phi Beta Kappa, his *summa*, his M.A., his doctoral thesis, his teaching, his promotions and his published work by individual title, date and source. The lawyer devoted half an hour to a discussion of Charles Winderman's course on The Short Novel, English 40. How many years had he taught it? What novels and authors were included in the course? Altogether, how many students had taken the course? Would it be fair to say that it was the most popular English course at Rutherford College? Had he published a book based on this popular course? Was this book now used as a textbook at other colleges?

At the end of the first day the press tried to get him to comment on the Bernstein book, but he refused to discuss it until he had testified. The press let him off—for the last time.

The next day he was asked to give his views on parody and obscenity.

"Parody of fiction is an ancient tradition, as old as the novel itself. Scholars and critics disagree about what is the first true novel, but many, including myself, would argue for Samuel Richardson's *Pamela*, published in 1740. It was a popular success, and it immediately attracted burlesques and parodies. Easily the best and wittiest is *Shamela Andrews*, which is also the bawdiest. The universal assumption is that *Shamela* was written by Henry Fielding, whom many consider the greatest English novelist. So we have a two-hundred-year tradition of parody following in the wake of a successful novel. And of bawdy parody being written by a great novelist. I think it is important to recognize that exaggerated sexuality is one of the parodist's most effective weapons. A description of excessive virtue in the original work lends itself to—in fact, almost invites—mockery in the parody."

Although the lawyer and Charles had agreed not to discuss *Bernstein* at this stage, the implications were obvious to the press. Charles Winderman went on to relate the history of parody, emphasizing its frequent sexual content and the necessity for the parodist to build upon the characters, the style and even the language of the original work. "If the reader cannot appreciate the explicit references to the original," Charles testified, "then both the humor and the implied criticism are lost."

The press was delighted with Charles Winderman, but Charles was even more delighted with the press. Although the lawyer had advised him not to give interviews, Charles decided independently that Roger Bernstein needed respectable public support. As General Cummings had once advised him, if you are competent to be in charge, then always take charge. He was not on trial himself, and he did not like the lawyer. Besides, it was a glorious, irresistible opportunity to shine on a national stage. He was the final authority. He was the last word.

He talked freely to reporters and cooperated on television interviews. He turned out to be excellent on camera. This did not surprise him, for he knew that he photographed well, and years of teaching had given him unlimited confidence in his speaking ability. What did surprise him was his intense enjoyment of the results. He and Anne loved watching him on television. The newspaper pictures were a delight. They read the stories aloud to each other. They liked the phone calls from friends, colleagues and acquaintances that usually began, "Charles, I just saw you on TV." He also got phone calls and letters attacking his support of pornography. These were less pleasant but could be endured as the price of fame. Fame, and the authority that came with it, was delicious.

The attention increased when at last he testified about Roger Bernstein's book.

"In your expert opinion, is *Bernstein of the Apes* a fair parody of *Tarzan of the Apes?*"

"Very fair. It is a comic imitation and exaggeration of a

well-known literary work. Almost anyone would accept that as a fair definition of parody."

"What about the charge that Mr. Bernstein 'stole' the plot and characters from the original?"

"That depends on the author's intent. Shakespeare, as we know, 'stole' the plot and characters for almost every play he wrote. Mr. Bernstein's intent clearly was not to plagiarize. That would be reprehensible. Plagiarism is theft, the intent to pass off as one's own work the work of another writer. But here the intent is to hold the original work up to ridicule and, in the process, to amuse the reader. I was certainly amused."

"What about the charge that Mr. Bernstein's work is obscene?"

"Well, in the very narrowest sense—that is, in the use of certain words, in the depiction of certain actions—it is obscene. Obviously. But in the same narrow sense, that would be just as true of many famous works, both ancient and modern, that we all accept as literature. I'm not referring to the classic court cases such as *Lady Chatterley* and *Ulysses* but to everything from Shakespeare and Restoration comedy and Henry Fielding's novels down to William Faulkner today. In this narrowest sense, we would have to brand hundreds of literary monuments obscene. But I don't think we should ever judge writing in this very narrow sense. What is the author's purpose? What is he trying to achieve? It's obvious that *Bernstein of the Apes* was not written to arouse lust or sexual excitement, as is the case with genuine pornography. The purpose here is to arouse laughter, and in this purpose it succeeds brilliantly."

"You said a moment ago that Mr. Bernstein's purpose was to hold the original work up to ridicule. Doesn't that imply he despised the Tarzan books?"

"On the contrary. Nobody ever bothers to parody an unknown, insignificant work. Mr. Bernstein has read the Tarzan books many times for pleasure. Actually, so have I.

The parody is successful for the very reason that Mr. Bernstein knows the original works so well and has enjoyed them so often."

"What about the charge that Mr. Bernstein's book is anti-Semitic and anti-Negro?"

"This is nonsense. Mr. Bernstein himself is Jewish and extremely sensitive to the personal experience of anti-Semitism. As to the other charge, if you want to read a book that truly is anti-Negro, that holds the Negro up to 'hush-my-mouth' mockery, try *Tarzan of the Apes*—or *Gone With the Wind.*"

Charles Winderman calculated that in this single week, through the press and television and radio, he taught far more people his views about writing and literature and censorship than he would ever be able to reach in a lifelong career of teaching at Rutherford. He gave fourteen interviews on *Gone With the Wind* alone, including a three-hour call-in show with an Atlanta radio station. Everyone hung on his words, on his opinions.

Samuel May, fielding phone calls from bookstores, took the biggest gamble in all his years of publishing. He ordered a huge second printing of a book whose first printing he might never be allowed to distribute. He made the decision even before cross-examination.

The Burroughs Foundation team went after Charles Winderman with righteous determination. For three days they counterattacked, drawing on passages of arcane literary criticism to refute his testimony. But Charles Winderman was on his own territory. It was, Roger Bernstein said, like trying to challenge Tarzan in his own jungle. Charles had never had a more marvelous time. To have been an English professor in an excellent but small college, to have been respected in his narrow academic world, to have fenced and jousted only with students and faculty colleagues, and then to be given this national stage and be asked to play a role that he could not possibly have invented for himself. A lot better, as he told

Anne, than being senior vice-president of the Winderman Trust, even though his father refused to concede this. His was the finest role in all the world: to be king, to be undisputed king, and to know all the answers. This was joy—and revelation.

In the late afternoon of the third day of cross-examination, the judge asked the Burroughs lawyers how much more time they would need to question this witness. Although it appeared to be an innocent procedural question, it indicated that the judge thought the Burroughs team was getting nowhere. Gleefully Samuel May slapped his hand on the defense table, drawing a glare from the judge.

The Burroughs lawyers conferred, then admitted that they could probably finish in another fifteen minutes. They were slinking away, Roger Bernstein said that evening over celebratory martinis with Charles Winderman, "with their tail between their legs—like Histah the snake."

The judge's eventual ruling confirmed Samuel May's gamble with his printers. The temporary injunction was vacated, and May was free to publish. The hardcover sales and, later, the perennial paperback sales combined with the careful investment advice of the Winderman Trust to make Roger Bernstein modestly independent for the rest of his life. His wife had divorced him too soon: it was all his. His only regret, he always said, was that there was no movie sale.

At Rutherford College, The Short Novel, English 40, had to be moved to the auditorium because the largest classroom on campus could not contain it. After complicated negotiations over rights, The Book-of-the-Month Club published a handsome boxed set of *The Great Short Novels*, selected and with an introduction to each by Charles Winderman. He was often asked in jest why he had not included *Bernstein of the Apes*. He was also asked, both in jest and seriously, why he did not include *Tarzan* and *Bernstein* in his course. Although tempted, he decided against it. Enough was enough. Besides, every student in the course read both books voluntarily without having to be assigned to read them. Surely this was an ideal result. Charles Winderman's chief regret about the Bernstein trial was that he had made Samuel May an almost respectable publisher. He also regretted that the most important event of his professional career could not have gone on forever. On the other hand, he had gained Roger Bernstein as a friend. A fair trade. More than a fair trade.

"Time," Roger said. "Ten for me on the chess and fourteen for you on the backgammon. I owe you four."

"All luck."

"Yeah, I know. I can hear irony when I hear it. Son of a bitch."

"I don't understand why anybody so 'logical' and 'reasonable' can't learn how to use the cube better."

"Bosh. It's luck. How's your birthday party coming?"

"Short of a hurricane, it will happen. From here on, it's mostly Bonjy's show anyway. All I have to do is act noble and give an appropriate speech of thanks."

"You're getting pretty old, Charles."

"I always intended to. My tenth grandchild will arrive in about a month."

"Too bad it won't be born at the Island. That would be nice. How's—what's her name—Ellen?"

"Fine. Write down the four dollars, will you? She's very good, and I don't mean just her health. I couldn't ask for a better daughter-in-law. It's not easy, you know, marrying into a household with three grown children. One slight bother. She's a bit too feisty, too independent. I think she's been too used to having her own way as a single woman with a good job. For instance, she's trying to persuade me to have somebody to the party that I don't want."

"Who's that?"

"The son of our foremost selectman, Tony Balto."

"Which son? Anthony? Carlo?"

"Anthony, I'm told. How do you know who they are?"

"Charles, if you spend the winter on the Island, you get to know everybody. Anthony's a terrific young guy. Everybody says he's going to inherit the empire. Besides, I think Ellen's pretty terrific, too—what I know of her. But why is she asking him?"

"It's not Ellen. It's Nancy. Ellen is merely prosecuting the case."

"And you don't want him? So whose party is it anyway?"

"Exactly. How about writing down that four dollars?"

"Ka-goda."

Clearing
the Quatchum

At this stage of her pregnancy Ellen was useless for clearing the stream. She could not bend down to snip the vines and bushes close to the ground. She could not drag the debris from the banks of the stream deep into the brush where it could decompose out of sight. She did not have the strength to wield the three-foot-long loppers on the overhanging branches of trees. And, thank God, she was not allowed to use the chain saw. Chain saws terrified her. All she could contribute was the pruning of light brush with her orange-handled clippers, and even that was restricted to what she could comfortably reach at a height between head and hip. Fortunately, the entire Winderman army was at work, so the size of her contribution did not matter.

Her group—her own family plus Martha's children, Amy and Christopher, and Bryan's friend Angie, a volunteer—had started this morning at the ocean and worked its way inland. The other group—Brad and Sue's family and Martha and her friend Richie—had started at the State Road boundary and would be cutting and clearing the upper half of the stream. Ellen's group had to work uphill, but Brad and Sue's group had the area with the heavier brush, so it came out approximately even, as it usually did when Ah-boo set up a system. The groups were even working in the territory of their own houses, all except Amy and Christopher, who had to help down here in order to make the teams even.

The work went quickly, even though they were clearing paths on both sides of the Quatchum. Not only were there many hands, but all they had to clear was what had grown up or fallen down over the winter and spring. The basic paths had been created long ago after years of effort. Now it was merely annual maintenance, easily done in a single day.

This day was gray and cool. Unlike Deck Day, which had to be clear and sunny so that the decks would dry quickly and not be spotted by rain, Stream Day—or Scotchum Quatchum, as it was also known—was always selected for poor weather so that the family would not lose a day of beach and tennis. Poor but not raining. Ah-boo would not permit the use of the chain saws in wet, slippery weather.

Nancy and Amy shared the clipping with Ellen. Howard, through seniority, wielded the loppers. The other boys, Bryan and Angie and Christopher, had the hard, heavy work, dragging the brush out of sight behind trees and bushes. Bryan and Angie worked together in perpetual conversation and horseplay. Christopher, predictably, worked alone—silent, relentless. Lawrence was also using clippers, but whenever they came to a fallen tree or an extra-thick branch, he stuck the clippers in his hip pocket and, to Ellen's dismay, switched on the bright yellow chain saw and pulled the cord to fire the motor. All the boys would join him to hold the tree trunk so that it did not roll as he cut it into firewood length with the screaming saw. Ellen hated to watch, even though Lawrence assured her there had never been an accident or even a close call. Only Lawrence and Brad were allowed to run the saws, much to the frustration of Howard, who had been told by Ah-boo that he would have to be twenty-five before he got permission. Ellen could only be grateful that much less fallen timber lay on this lower part of the stream. On the upper half Brad would be using his chain saw almost constantly. Sue didn't mind. When Ellen had mentioned her concern, Sue looked as though she didn't understand what Ellen was talking about.

Ah-boo came down the stream toward them, dressed like the rest in a long-sleeved work shirt and long pants and work gloves, protection against the bull-vine thorns.

"How's it going?" he asked as he reached them. "Are you all scotching away?"

They stopped work for a moment.

"Good," Lawrence said. "As usual, the right side is worse than the left, I still can't figure out why. But not too bad this year. How are they doing upstream?"

"Moving along. The brush isn't bad. We lost only two big trees, an oak and a pine. The pine fell the right way, away from the stream, but the oak fell across. It took them an hour, but there'll be plenty of firewood. And then it's fairly light brush work down to Picnic Rock."

"What do we have ahead?"

"Nothing big. A four-inch maple. And the usual bull-vine crop just this side of the Rock. We'll finish early. All right, I will let you get back to it. One o'clock at Picnic Rock."

He waved to them all and started the long walk back uphill toward Brad's group. Ellen could see him snipping here and there as he walked. Her last glimpse was of his white hair against the green foliage. "He's the only one," Ellen had observed last summer, "who has the pleasure of visiting both working groups." "Well, it's his stream," Lawrence had explained.

Yes, Ellen thought now. His stream. His birthday party. His family. His land. And his way—always his way. She conceded that he always thought about what was best for everyone in the family. The blue notebooks made this clear. But she could not help asking, especially now with Nancy's problem: Who gave him the right to know what was best for everyone? Oh yes, he was the paterfamilias, and it was his stream and all the rest of it, but that did not confer infallibility. Different opinions, different needs, different wishes—there seemed no room for them. And as she was now learning, Ah-boo was hard to persuade.

Then the idea jumped into her mind. I wonder, she thought suddenly, if it is really all good judgment and kindness, all wisdom and generosity. I wonder if it couldn't also be something else. I wonder if he just *likes* to have everything his way.

She had stopped clipping, thinking about Ah-boo. When she turned back to work, she was startled to find Christopher standing right beside her. He was constantly appearing from nowhere, unannounced and unexpected, and always alone. One might be anywhere on the property, even on one's own deck, and suddenly he would appear—tall, silent, expressionless. She found him unnerving, even though she realized it was probably because he had nothing to do and no one to be with. He had come up to her so silently and was now standing so close that she actually raised her hands in a surprised little gesture of self-protection.

"I need to talk to you," he said in a low voice. He never addressed her by name, never called her "Ellen" or "Aunt Ellen" like the other grandchildren. But for once his nicely shaped mouth was not twisting as it usually did, mocking either himself or others. His long, bony face was serious, the blue eyes direct. A good-looking boy when he was like this.

"You scared me," she admitted. "What about?"

He looked across the stream where Nancy was clipping and nodded his head in that direction. "About Nancy."

"Fine," Ellen said, but now began to worry. She had

enough concerns about Nancy without any fresh contribution from Christopher. It was unlike Christopher to take anything but a negative, destructive interest in people. Yet Nancy always stood up for Christopher and got along with him much better than the other children did. So perhaps this time . . . "What about Nancy?"

Christopher shook his head, his long blond hair moving with the gesture. "Not now. Maybe during the picnic. Or after?"

Ellen gave a little laugh that she did not quite feel. "Don't keep me in suspense, Christopher."

"I know all about it," he said. His face was still serious, his mouth still straight. "I could help persuade Ah-boo to invite Anthony."

"You mean about the party?" Ellen said in relief.

"Hey, you two," Lawrence called across the stream. "Let's see some action."

Christopher's mouth twisted at the reprimand. Ellen had watched him work hard all morning, without any of the pleasure and companionship that Bryan and Angie shared but with dogged concentration, dragging away load after load of brush and branches. Ellen felt a flash of sympathy for him. Christopher turned away without speaking.

They made excellent progress. When they reached the fallen maple, Lawrence stopped to calculate how much time it would take them. Not a big tree, but it had fallen sometime after its spring foliage had appeared, so all the branches carried a full crop of dead leaves, making it a longer, messier job.

"Let's save it till after lunch," Lawrence decided. "We don't have that much time left. We'll move on and come back to it."

Just before the one o'clock break, Ah-boo visited them again. "The fires are about ready," he said. "Is everybody hungry?"

"You bet," Bryan said. "Can we stop?"

Ah-boo looked at his watch. Keeping everyone waiting just a little longer than necessary, Ellen noticed. Holding their attention. His way.

"Yes, I think so. Remember to put all the tools and gloves together in one spot."

A chorus of approval from the grandchildren. Gloves, clippers, loppers were all quickly piled in an open space around the chain saw.

Ellen had thought to walk up to Picnic Rock with Christopher, but Lawrence came across the stream to be with her. Nancy and Angie and Bryan took running jumps across the Quatchum at the same narrow spot, but Lawrence, always prudent, found a place where he could walk across on two stepping-stones in the stream bed. They walked up together, the grandchildren hurrying ahead with Ah-boo.

"How are you holding up?" Lawrence asked. "Had about enough for one day?"

She appreciated how solicitous he had been all these months. "I'm fine," she said. "I haven't done much work, but I'm fine."

"You might want to go home and take a nap after the picnic. We don't have all that much left to do." His hand was tucked under her arm so that she would not trip in this uncleared stretch of the path.

"After a hamburger I'll be as strong as an ox. And just as big. By the way, Christopher said he wanted to talk to me."

"That's a first." He smiled down at her. "Christopher doesn't want t⸢ talk to anybody. What's he done now?"

"Nothing as far as I know. He wants to talk about Nancy."

"Huh. Well, if it's Christopher, it's some kind of trouble."

"He worked very hard this morning, Lawrence. You probably didn't notice. He wasn't playing around like Bryan and Angie. He didn't stop once except that time he was talking to me and you yelled at us. I think you hurt his feelings."

"If he has any," Lawrence said. "Besides, I didn't yell."

"All right, called." She looked at him with affection. "You probably haven't yelled since you were ten."

He acknowledged the joke with a tiny smile, not quite sure that he liked it but willing to let her tease him. "Well," he said, "here we are."

The path opened into a wide glade. Here the stream curved around a huge, flat boulder the size of a dining room. It was by far the largest rock on the property, a good twenty feet long but never more than a foot above the ground except at the far end where it rose into a knob, like the hump of a whale. Gray and smooth and broad, bare of lichen, the dark slab served both as a picnic table and as a sitting place for the whole family. No one knew, no one would ever know, how deep and how broad the rock ran underground.

When Ah-boo bought the property, he and Anne did not know the rock existed because trees and dense brush had been growing all around it, hiding it from sight. Only when the stream was cleared for the first time was the rock discovered. Lawrence and Brad, children then, still remembered the day when, as the tangle of brush was cut away, the rock began to emerge. Ah-boo had written in the notebooks how their wonder and excitement rose as he kept cutting brush and the great flat boulder kept stretching on and on until its full extent lay revealed. He had sent Lawrence running back to the house to tell Anne and Martha about the discovery— and to tell Anne to bring sandwiches because they were going to have a celebratory picnic right here, this very day. Picnic Rock was christened that afternoon.

Now the two fire pits—the round one for grilling hamburgers and hot dogs, the long narrow trench for corn—held thick beds of glowing coals, ready for cooking. Bonjy had stripped four dozen ears of corn down to a single layer of husks so they could be laid directly on the coals. The pale yellow-green ears lay neatly stacked like mortar shells beside the fire. Platters of hamburgers and hot dogs, covered with plastic wrap, waited beside the round pit next to the long-handled cast-iron grills and the tongs for turning the corn.

Ah-boo had resisted all proposals for picnic furniture. No tables, no benches. He would not even permit the installation of a permanent grill over the round pit. When a picnic was over, the rock and glade must return to their pure state.

Bonjy, wearing a dress even on a picnic, had done all the preparations with the help of Mrs. Hackett, the cleaning woman, but now her work was done. Outdoor cooking, she told Ellen, was the province of men. It was the only cooking they could be trusted to perform competently, and since it always made them feel powerful, why not leave it to them. "When it comes to picnics," Bonjy said, "they all turn into little cavemen."

"Cooking time," Lawrence announced. He and Brad picked up the grills with the hamburgers, relegating the hot-dog grill to Richie.

Richie did not seem offended at being assigned a lesser task. One of the attributes of a personnel consultant was, apparently, to be a damned good sport. Richie Miller, whom Ellen could not bring herself to like very much, was a damned good sport about everything. Scrabble with Amy, tennis with anyone, bridge, yard work, boat tag, running on the beach, or getting the hot-dog grill instead of a more esteemed hamburger grill, he did everything cheerfully and heartily but without ever quite seeming to fit in. Thanks to coconut oil, he was more deeply tanned than anyone else. His dark, flat hair was combed straight back from his wide, somewhat knobby forehead.

The three cavemen squatted around the pit with their grills. After some minutes Ah-boo walked over and said to Richie, "Those hot dogs look just about done."

"Yes, sir," Richie agreed. He lifted his grill from the fire. He was ready to play any game if you just told him the rules.

Well, Ellen thought, if you like rules, you've come to the right family.

A small but shrill altercation broke out on the rock where Sue and Martha and several of the children had been laying out the ketchup, mustard, relish, tomatoes, onions and the sticks of butter for the corn. Sue had been issuing instructions. Now came Martha's voice.

"How about knocking off the orders?"

"Everything has to be ready," Sue said, annoyed at this interruption.

"It will be. Just stop bossing."

"I'm not bossing. I'm trying to—"

"Listen, I was picnicking on this rock twenty years before you even got here. I can figure out where to put the onions without a whole lot of advice."

"Now then," Ah-boo said, "everything seems just fine." Ellen had watched him turn away from the corn fire the instant he heard raised voices, and now he was on the rock beside Martha and Sue, spreading his soothing approval over both women. "Just in time for the hamburgers."

The squabble died away as it was meant to. Most of the time Martha and Sue got along because Martha paid no attention, but every once in a while Sue pushed too hard with her energy and enthusiasm, provoking Martha to object. Ellen had noticed that when Ah-boo was around, nothing ever came of it. She herself tended to side with Martha, because Sue's zealotry could become overbearing. However, Martha ought to be used to it by now and be able to ignore it. Perhaps Martha was missing her noontime Scotch. Ah-boo did not permit any alcohol, not even beer, when the chain saws were in use.

Ellen was leaning against the knob at the far end of the rock, munching her hamburger, when Brad came up to her.

"How's your hamburger? How are you feeling?" he asked.

"Fine and fine," she said, knowing at once that this was not why he was here. Brad had no guile. As Lawrence said, what made Brad such a success in advertising was his total sincerity in an insincere profession.

"That's good," he said, which was plainly the end of his introductory small talk. "I heard about Nancy inviting that Balto boy." His rugged face showed honest concern. The tallest of all the Windermans, with the widest, heaviest shoulders, he loomed over her without being at all threatening. He was too nice for that, too well-meaning.

"Then you probably heard that Ah-boo has said no," Ellen guessed. Brad was a poor prospect for help, but why not sound him out? "I'm trying to persuade him to change his mind."

"I heard that too," Brad said, showing still more concern, "but I wasn't sure it was true. I don't like to interfere, but it doesn't seem like a good idea."

Although Brad was ten years older than Ellen, she often thought that he seemed younger. Perhaps it was the simplicity, the transparency of his approach. It was always easy to know where Brad stood. And Sue as well.

"I don't like to see Nancy hurt," she said, although that was far from the complete answer.

"Well, I know, but she'll get over it."

Ellen could not get angry with Brad, but she was already tired of this comment. "How do you know? Young women have very tender feelings."

"Oh, I know. My Anne's like that."

"Anne's only fifteen. And she's not in love, is she?"

"I hope not," Brad said with his first smile. "Just the same . . ."

"Just the same," Ellen repeated, "I hope Ah-boo will change his mind."

"I doubt that." He wanted to say something more but could not find the words. "Well, back to the grill, I suppose." He turned away, but then turned back for a second. "I still don't think it's a good idea. Sue doesn't either. She thought I should tell you."

Well, Ellen thought, that's no great surprise. No help would be coming from Brad and Sue, but then she had not expected any.

She was not surprised that Christopher joined her almost as soon as Brad moved off. He looked around to make sure that no one else was close to them.

"About Ah-boo's birthday," he said. He took another look over his shoulder. All the others were busy helping themselves to more food. "Nancy should have her friend. That Anthony."

"I'm glad you think so. We don't have too much support. You like him then?"

"Not really. But it isn't fair. Not fair to her. We've always been allowed to pick our own guest."

"By the way, why don't you ever ask a guest?"

Christopher's face shut down, bleak as stone. "I don't want anybody."

What a sad thing for a sixteen-year-old boy to say, Ellen thought. Better not pursue that. "I don't think it's fair, either. What did you mean back there at the stream that you knew all about it? Did Nancy tell you?"

Christopher took another bite of hamburger, obviously thinking about how much to say. What he finally settled for was, "I find out about a lot of things." Not boasting. Just a statement of fact.

"You mean Nancy didn't tell you?"

Apparently this opening was more than he could resist. "No, you did."

"We've never talked about it, Christopher. You know that isn't true."

He finished his hamburger and then stood in front of her, tall, slightly awkward, clasping one wrist with his other hand. "I heard you telling my mother. That afternoon on the deck."

Ellen thought back. She and Martha had sat alone, no one near them, no nearby open window. Why was he lying to her? "I'm sorry, I can't believe you."

He looked down at his hands, long, bony hands like his face. When he looked up again, his blue eyes were defiant, but he was somehow pleased with himself. "I was under the deck."

"Under? What were you doing under the deck?"

"Listening."

Ellen finished her own hamburger. "Do you spend a lot of time under your deck?"

"Of course not," he said scornfully. "Only when it's useful."

Another look over his shoulder, this time at Martha to make sure his mother wasn't listening. She certainly wasn't. Martha was wrapped in conversation with Richie, whose handsome, slightly younger face was smiling at her with a certain degree of physical possession.

"I heard you on the phone. You asked my mother if you could talk to her alone." A rather unpleasant grin. "That sounded interesting."

"You mean," Ellen said, feeling less friendly, "that you listen on phone extensions to people's private conversations?"

He shrugged at her criticism. "I like to know what's going on."

"The corn is born!" Ah-boo called, using the family phrase. "Everybody over for the corn."

Howard and Bryan and Angie, using tongs and forks, were plucking the ears from the trench and tossing them onto the flat surface of the rock where Sue kept them from rolling off. The quarter-pound sticks of butter had been unwrapped and placed at intervals on the rock so that several people at once could roll their ears without getting in each other's way. Salt-shakers were beside each butter stick.

"Let's get our corn," Ellen said, not liking the tone of this conversation.

When they had all finally finished eating, Ah-boo walked up to Ellen. "Ellen, my dear, are you still with us for the rest of the work? Or wouldn't you rather go home and take a rest? We don't have that much left to do."

But Ellen refused to accept special treatment, nor was she in a mood for special kindness. "I'm here till the finish," she said.

So Ellen was there for the accident. She saw it happen.

Lawrence and Howard, one with the chain saw and one with the loppers, had stripped the fallen maple of all its side branches, which the boys dragged away. With the tree diminished to its long main trunk, Lawrence began to cut it into eighteen-inch lengths, starting at the top.

Bryan took the first length as it came off, and then Angie took the second. Instead of dropping them to the ground, the two boys began a mock fencing duel, aping the musketeer movies. Ellen marveled that they still had energy for fun after all the food and the long morning's work.

Lawrence and Christopher stuck to the job, Christopher holding the trunk steady while Lawrence's loud saw continued to bite off sections.

Bryan made a thrust at Angie, who parried with his own stick of wood. Then Angie jumped forward with his own attack, yelling a raucous "Yah-h-h-h!"

To avoid the attack, Bryan made an exaggerated leap backward—and banged into Christopher from behind. Christopher lost his grip on the trunk and was slammed toward Lawrence.

Lawrence, who was just bringing the chain saw down for another cut, saw Christopher falling toward him and yanked the screaming saw high in the air. Ellen thought it had been a narrow miss. Then she saw the sudden dark blood against Christopher's pale blue work shirt. The saw had hit his right arm, both above and below the elbow.

"Oh, Jesus!"

One of the girls screamed.

Lawrence switched off the saw and almost flung it away. He was dragging at his belt, trying to pull it out of the loops, pulling so hard that it would not come free. Christopher, stunned, was staring at his arm.

Lawrence got the belt free and wrapped it around Christopher's arm, just below the shoulder, and pulled it tight. Where did he learn that, Ellen wondered.

"Bryan!" Lawrence said. No panic in his voice, but Ellen had never heard him speak with such force. "Tell the others. Run! Howard. Get Brad's truck. Drive as close to here as you can get. Give me shirts, somebody. Hurry up."

Bryan, after one more horrified look, sped away up the path after Howard. Angie pulled his T-shirt over his head and handed it to Lawrence, who wrapped it around Christopher's arm.

"More," Lawrence said. "More. And belts, anybody, quick."

Christopher sank to the ground. He had not fainted. He just went down. Lawrence hovered over him. Amy and Nancy and Ellen handed their shirts and belts to Angie. Amy and Ellen were now in their bras. Nancy was bare-breasted and not even thinking about it. Lawrence wrapped all the clothing around Christopher's arm and fastened it with belts.

It began to rain. Cold rain. Ellen shivered.

Howard was the first to come back, Sue right behind him.

"Is he all right?" Sue asked.

"Where's the fucking truck?" Lawrence said. Ellen had never heard him use the word except when making love.

"The other side of the old stone wall. I left the motor running. Can he walk?"

"Good work," Lawrence said to both of them. "We better carry him. All right, Howard, Angie. Lift him under his back and under his legs. I'll watch his arm. Sue, get back and turn the truck around."

"I backed it in," Sue said.

"Damn good," Lawrence said. He looked around and seemed to notice Ellen and the girls for the first time. "You stay here."

"I want to come," Ellen said.

They were lifting Christopher carefully, Lawrence trying to make sure his heavily bandaged arm was not jostled. Blood was soaking through the shirts.

"Stay here," Lawrence repeated. "Tell Ah-boo and the others when they get here. Tell them we've left for the hospital." He took one moment for kindness. "There won't be room in the truck," he explained to Ellen.

When the men and Sue had left, moving as quickly as they dared, Nancy came up to Ellen and burst into tears. "God, how awful," she said. "Poor Christopher. Is he—is he going to die?"

This was so extreme that Ellen almost laughed. There had been a good deal of blood, but it hadn't gushed. She knew nothing major had been hit. "Of course not," she said. She patted Nancy's bare shoulder, cold and wet from the rain. "Run get some clothes," she said, giving Nancy something to do. "Bring some for me too. Hurry now. Oh, and Nancy. Call the hospital the second you get in the house. The emergency room. Tell them to have a surgeon there immediately. Don't forget. Now run."

"Aunt Ellen," Amy said. Her face was white. "Is my brother—?"

"Go find your mother," Ellen said. "Tell her they're on their way to the hospital, so that's where she should go. It will make her feel better." Ellen doubted her own words, but perhaps they would make Amy herself feel better.

Ellen was left alone in the light cold rain. She rubbed her shoulders to warm them. Her bra was soaked through, and her breasts were cold. Cold breasts felt like statue marble. She looked at the trunk of the maple, flat on the damp ground where Lawrence and Christopher had dropped it. Nearby lay the yellow chain saw. There had never been an accident, Lawrence said, not even a close call. She knew Christopher was safe unless he lost too much blood. But what about his arm? She had no way of knowing how deep the cuts were. What would it be like to be sixteen years old and lose your arm? And because your own cousin was playing D'Artagnan.

She felt suddenly exhausted as well as chilled. In spite of that, she walked over to the chain saw, bent down with some difficulty, picked it up by the handle—it was lighter than she had expected—and dropped it into the Quatchum. Then there was nothing to do but wait for the others.

It was an hour before Ellen reached the hospital. She had made Nancy stay home, explaining that hospital emergencies lasted forever and that there was no point in the whole family sitting around the waiting room.

"Then why are you going?" Nancy asked.

"Because your father will need someone to talk to."

Actually she could not bear to stay at home, waiting for news. She wanted to be where the news was. Howard had presumably gone to the hospital in the truck with Lawrence, but where was Bryan? She thought he should come with her. It had been his fault. When she had changed to dry clothes and drunk the cup of hot coffee she had asked Nancy to make, the exhaustion vanished. She drove to the Island hospital, a large two-story frame building on the far outskirts of Summertown. It had stopped raining. She left her car in the parking lot outside the Emergency entrance. The truck was there, and Ah-boo's blue Buick and Martha's jaunty Mustang. Another Winderman rally. She braced herself for whatever news she was about to hear but, pulling open the big glass entrance door, she made up her mind that it was going to be all right. Lawrence had been very quick to pull away that saw.

When she introduced herself at the Emergency desk, the nurse asked, "Are you in labor?" When Ellen explained, the nurse pointed her down the corridor to the waiting room.

"How is the boy?" Ellen asked.

"Oh, I wouldn't know about that. You'd have to ask the doctor, but I think he's still in the operating room."

Just like every other hospital, Ellen thought as she walked down the tiled corridor. Only the doctor has information, and the doctor is not available.

But it turned out otherwise. They were all in the waiting room, sitting around on bright, cheerfully flowered chairs and couches: Lawrence, Sue, Howard, Martha and Richie, Ah-boo. Ah-boo was the first to see her. He got to his feet and walked toward her before anyone else realized she was in the room. He was smiling.

"Christopher's going to be all right," he said.

"Thank God."

Lawrence also came over.

"A very nasty cut," Ah-boo said. "In the deltoid muscle. Very messy, the doctor says, but not too deep and no bone damage. Christopher was lucky. And another cut in the lower arm, but the doctor says that one is 'little more than a bad graze.' "

"You mean it's all over?"

"Oh no, they're still working on him. Cleaning it all out and sewing him up. You must be tired. Here, sit down."

And indeed she was tired. Lawrence guided her into a green-and-orange plastic-covered armchair. "How do you know all this? The nurse at the desk didn't know anything."

An almost merry look came into Ah-boo's bright blue eyes.

"If you contribute regularly to the hospital fund," he said, "they tell you everything."

"He lost a lot of blood," Lawrence said, "but even that's all right. He's going to be bandaged up for a good while, but all the muscle is supposed to come back. He can even go home in a few days."

"In time for the party," Ah-boo said. He nodded his head at Ellen's questioning look. "I already asked, and the doctor said why not, if Christopher feels up to it."

Oh well, then, Ellen thought, of course everything's all right. The party is what counts. No, that's not being fair. It's not just for Ah-boo, it's for the whole family.

Ah-boo continued to look at her, standing over her chair. "Tell me, my dear," he said in his courteous voice, "why did you throw the chain saw in the stream? It wasn't the chain saw's fault, you know."

"Oh, I know," Ellen said, hearing the weariness in her own voice. "And I've also heard that guns don't kill people. People kill people. Just the same."

A long moment of silence before Ah-boo spoke again. He seemed to be considering her carefully from several different angles. Then he shrugged and smiled. "Well, the important thing is that Christopher is going to be all right. And as a matter of fact, the chain saw will be all right, too."

When Ellen visited the hospital next day, she was surprised to find that Christopher already had two visitors, Nancy and Anthony Balto. Nancy had said nothing at breakfast about going to see Christopher—or about Anthony, either. Perhaps, like many of Nancy's actions, it had been spontaneous. *Hey, Anthony, let's go see my cousin Christopher.*

Christopher lay in his hospital bed, looking frail and uncomfortable in his short-sleeved muslin hospital gown. People would recover more quickly, Ellen was convinced, if hospitals didn't insist on those horrible gowns with the nasty string ties. In a garment like that, how could you feel anything but sick? Christopher's right arm was heavily bandaged, a huge, bulging bandage near his shoulder, a smaller one on his forearm.

Nancy was sitting on the foot of the bed, and Anthony was on a low arm chair beside it. He got to his feet as soon as he saw Ellen.

"Good morning, Mrs. Winderman."

Polite but with no particular warmth. I guess I'm part of the enemy, Ellen thought. "Hello, Anthony." She shook hands with him and accepted the chair he pulled up for her. He wore a pale yellow shirt and slacks as black as his hair. She wanted him to smile so that she could see that wide flash of white against his dark-tanned skin, but he was sober this morning. "So, Christopher, how are you feeling?" she asked.

Christopher wriggled carefully, trying to make his arm comfortable. "All right, I guess." His voice was a little drowsy. Still on medication, no doubt.

"I thought you'd bring Bryan," Nancy said.

Ellen had thought so too. She had had quite an argument about it with Lawrence. When Bryan refused her suggestion, she had told Lawrence in private that he should order Bryan to go. After all, the accident would never have happened if Bryan and Angie had not been horsing around. But this time Lawrence would not support her. "I should have stopped Bryan and Angie," he said. "It was my responsibility, not theirs. Bryan doesn't like Christopher, as you know." "Then maybe *you* should go," Ellen had suggested. Lawrence just looked at her, sometimes his way of dealing with a suggestion he didn't approve. She did not press it. Lawrence had done everything right yesterday afternoon. Even the surgeon had said that getting Christopher to the hospital so promptly and with a good tourniquet in place had been a great help. Besides, Lawrence didn't think much of Christopher either.

No point in saying all this. "Bryan will probably come later," she said vaguely. "He's very sorry."

"Shit," Nancy said. She had a gift for seeing things without confusion.

Anthony stood up. "I have to get back to the store, Nancy." He turned to Christopher. "I have to tell you," he said, "that nobody comes out of a chain saw better than you did. We get a lot of them on the Island, and they're usually pretty bad. Get well. Nice to see you again, Mrs. Winderman."

Nancy squeezed Christopher's leg under the sheets, then hopped off the bed. "Hurry home," she said.

For just a moment Christopher seemed almost tearful. "Thanks for coming."

When Nancy and Anthony had gone, Ellen said, "I won't stay long. You probably feel like sleeping."

Christopher shook his head but did not answer. Again he tried to move his bandaged arm to a different position.

"Your mother's coming over this afternoon. And Ah-boo will be over too."

"You know what my mother said last night? I mean, once she knew I was going to be okay? She thought it must have been my fault."

"Well, it wasn't," Ellen said in a brisk voice. God damn Martha. Probably too many drinks, too much excitement— and too much experience with all the times when it really had been Christopher's fault. "And she knows it wasn't. I saw the whole thing, and I told her exactly how it happened. She was just upset."

Christopher's mouth twisted. "It's the thought that counts." Then his face brightened. "But how about that Nancy? The first one to come over today?"

He was so obviously pleased that Ellen made a note to tell Nancy. "And nice of Anthony to come too, to take time off from work."

"Yeah," Christopher admitted. "He's not so bad."

A nurse came in to tell Ellen that she must leave now because some things had to be done for "our patient." With heavy pressure on the arm rests, Ellen heaved herself out of the low chair. "You'll be home soon, but I'll see you again before then." Like Nancy, she patted Christopher's leg. "When you're better, let's talk about your idea for getting Anthony invited to the birthday party."

The nurse bustled in with a cart of hospital oddments, paper cups with pills, a thermometer, a blood-pressure gauge.

"Oh, that's simple," Christopher said, almost cheerfully. "Blackmail."

Summer Visitors,
Island Folks

Charles Winderman was working the grounds around his
house. He never thought of it as gardening, because that implied flowers—roses, tulips, peonies. He did not believe in
having such flowers, although others could grow them without offending him. Brad and Sue's house was surrounded by
tame flowers that came and went all summer long. He could
walk right past them without an opprobrious glance. But
here at his own home close to the beach he tolerated only
what grew wild: beach plum, daisies, goldenrod, Indian
paintbrush, bearberry, huckleberry. He had had this out with
Anne at the very beginning, Anne who loved all flowers. The
compromise was that the grounds would be his way but that
Anne could buy as many cut flowers as she wanted. The
house used to be full of geraniums all summer long. He still
asked Bonjy to buy geraniums whenever he thought of it.

Nor did Charles Winderman believe in lawns, and here
Anne had agreed. They both liked wild grass. It required no
attention. It had a lovely light straw color, and one could see

every breath of wind moving through it, changing the color as light struck it from different angles.

When Charles was working the grounds, he was pulling up sumac and weeds and blackberry vines, and occasionally trimming back the wild grass where it threatened to engulf a stand of wildflowers. On a sunny but cool morning with the light bouncing off the waves, it was easy and pleasant work, nothing like the heavy duty of clearing the Quatchum paths two days ago. By the time he finished this morning, he would have no more than two or three armfuls of sumac and other trash to remove.

He had thought seriously of calling a Family Meeting the evening of the Quatchum. If Christopher had been more seriously hurt, if he had lost the arm or the use of it, he would certainly have done it. While they were all at the hospital, waiting for the surgeon's report on Christopher, he had thought about it.

There had been only three Family Meetings, so designated. The first had been at the time of Anne's death, when he felt he owed everyone all the information he had, including how he felt and what would happen next and how things would have to be different, but especially how some things would remain the same. There had been a Family Meeting at the time of Martha's first divorce to explain this extraordinary event, but none on the occasion of her second divorce, which he had considered less extraordinary, perhaps not even quite an event—except, of course, to Christopher. And then the very brief, painful Family Meeting when Lawrence's first wife, Barbara, absconded. That was how he still thought of it: absconded. Lawrence, with his profound sense of privacy, had not wanted the meeting at all, but Charles Winderman knew it must take place and had insisted. He could still remember Lawrence's face at the meeting—icy, formal. Lawrence had not avoided anyone's eyes, he had not ducked his head. He simply had seemed not to be present, not saying a

word, and as soon as Charles had made the short announcement, Lawrence had raised his eyebrows—is that the end?—
and walked out of the house, never having spoken.

When the chain-saw accident happened, Charles Winderman had had to think, waiting there at the hospital, about
what would actually happen, what would actually have to be
said, if he called a Family Meeting that night. He could not
hold the meeting without assigning blame. And the blame
was clear. Lawrence had failed to stop the horseplay that
caused the accident. Bryan, Lawrence's son, and Angie, Bryan's best friend and a guest besides, had created the accident,
in violation of every rule about the chain saws. And then
Ellen, Lawrence's wife and eight months pregnant, had committed the minor, feminine stupidity of throwing the chain
saw into the Quatchum. Everything in a single branch of the
family. Even after Charles Winderman heard that Christopher was going to be all right, he still gave it some thought
before deciding that he would not call a Family Meeting. Instead, he had a private, fairly satisfactory talk with Lawrence.
Lawrence accepted the responsibility, and did so much more
readily than either Brad or Martha would have done. But
there it was again: Lawrence's strange detachment. How
could someone like that take over control of the family when
Charles himself was no longer here?

He was working at the corner of the house next to the
driveway when he saw the blue pickup truck come down the
road, stirring up puffs of dust. He stood, holding the shears,
to see who it was. The truck came to a stop twenty feet away.
He had time to read the sign in white letters on the blue door
panel, Balto & Co., Summertown, before the heavyset figure
emerged from the cab.

Charles Winderman put down his shears on the veranda
railing and laid his work gloves beside them. This much acknowledgment but no more. He stayed where he was and let
Tony Balto come to him.

But the selectman was in no hurry either. "Morning," he said, nodding his head, but then instead of walking up to Charles he took half-a-dozen steps through the wild grass to look down at the beach. "Beautiful day," he said. "Beautiful place you have. The old Benbow place." Reminding Charles Winderman that he was, of course, a newcomer. "I remember when old Hester Benbow used to live here. Long time ago." But not a recent newcomer.

He stood looking out to sea, arms folded across his big barrel chest. Tony Balto was several inches under six feet, but his wide shoulders and thick body gave an impression of size and strength. His arms and torso filled his faded blue work shirt, the cuffs rolled back from his big brown hands and thick wrists, and his sturdy thighs filled his blue jeans. He was bareheaded as always, a man obviously proud of his wild shock of iron-gray hair. One could recognize that shock of hair half a block away on Main Street, a useful feature both for a politician and a businessman. One always knew when Tony Balto was within hailing distance.

Apparently he had completed his study of the ocean because he turned now to look at Charles. His face, deeply sunburned and windburned from long days outdoors, was dominated by shaggy black eyebrows and a powerful Roman nose. Wide forehead, wide straight mouth, strong jaw with just the beginning of wattles underneath. The tough brown eyes were almost lost beneath the brows. A strong, handsome man in his fifties with the strength far outweighing the handsomeness. Not a Roman emperor, not with that peasant face, but perhaps a legion commander or else the hardest centurion in the legion.

As a summer visitor, even one owning 49.3 acres of waterfront property and paying one of the highest tax bills on the Island, Charles Winderman did not have the right to vote in local elections, but if he had, he would have voted against Tony Balto every year. Tony Circulari.

"Hope you don't mind me dropping in. I thought we might have a talk."

"It's customary," Charles Winderman said, "to telephone first."

Tony Balto stared for a moment, ran a hand through his wild shock of hair, rubbed his cheek with one palm and then smiled. His smile was open, cheerful. "Yeah," he said, "it's customary with my folks, too. But if I'd called you, what d'you think you'd say? Maybe too busy, ha?"

Charles had to grant a small smile in return. "Maybe."

"Yeah, so I figured I'd just take the chance. I heard about your kid, your grandson, in the hospital. Lucky it wasn't no worse."

"Very lucky."

A pause while they looked at each other, standing two steps apart.

"What did you want to see me about, Mr. Balto?"

Tony Balto fished in his shirt pocket and brought out a box of Marlboros. He put a cigarette in his mouth, then offered the box.

"No, thank you. I gave them up years ago."

"Yeah. I try that now and then. To please my wife, ha? Not very serious, though." He pulled a blue-tip kitchen match from the same pocket and flipped it alight with his thumbnail, a trick Charles Winderman had never been able to master. After lighting his cigarette, Tony Balto blew out the match and stuck it back in his pocket. No littering.

"My kid Anthony says you have a big birthday coming."

"Yes, that's right."

"Seventy. A big one. Congratulations."

"Thank you."

Balto looked out at the ocean, took a long drag of smoke, then faced Charles again.

"I remember when you bought this place, you and your wife. Hardly any summer people out this way then. This far out of town. No city water, no electricity." He shook his head, not in disapproval but in wonder.

Charles Winderman did not know where the selectman was headed, or rather he thought he knew where he was headed—what other reason could there be for this visit?—but he did not know how Tony Balto was going to get there. Curious, he kept silent, waiting to see.

Tony Balto seemed in no hurry. At the height of the summer season, he had a plumbing and heating and electrical and hardware and building empire to run, no doubt a hundred summer visitors were waiting to talk to him about installations or repairs, anxious or impatient and some of them surely angry, but Tony Balto maintained his slow, conversational tone.

"You know what they thought? Everybody in the building trades? They heard about you buying this place, and they thought bonanza." He threw his arms wide and laughed. "Bonanza! They knew what a wreck it was, what it would take to fix it up, ha? Course they didn't think you'd stick it out. They figured you'd quit when you found out how long it would take the electricity and water to get out here. Rich Easterners not going to like it out here in the woods with no light bulbs. But first you'd spend a lot of money before you quit. They all wanted to get a piece of it, just a little share, not too greedy." Suddenly he winked. "My father too. Sure, I'll take some, long as they're passing it out. But you know what I thought, Mr. Winderman? I thought you had a beautiful piece of land, nice as anything on the Island, with all this beach. Fifty acres of beautiful land."

"Forty-nine point three," Charles corrected him.

Tony Balto waved a big hand, dismissing it. "And I knew if I had this land, here I'd stay. And I figured here you'd stay. And here you are." Almost as though he, Tony Balto, had brought this to pass.

His face turned more serious. "Some hard times, I expect."

"Yes," Charles said, also serious. "And some of the hardest were caused by Island workmen."

Balto took no offense. He nodded his head. "That can happen. Specially when you build three new houses. And fix up an old one. That's a lot of opportunity for things to go wrong."

"On a grand scale."

They were still standing a few steps apart in the wild grass, in the sunlight, with the sound of waves coming to them from the beach. Charles Winderman had no intention of inviting his visitor to sit down on the veranda, not even on the front steps, or to go inside or to have a cup of coffee. Balto did not seem to expect any of these amenities. He stubbed out his cigarette against the sole of his work boot, then put the butt in the same shirt pocket.

"They say you were pretty tough yourself. About contracts. Any work to be done, everything just so. Write it all down on paper. Even the price."

Charles Winderman gave Tony Balto a grim smile. "Only after I learned what could be done to me if I didn't protect myself. The delays. Substitute materials. And some very surprising prices when the work was finally finished. If it was finished."

Balto nodded agreement. "Yeah. Different days when you came here. Just getting started then myself. Place wasn't really settled down as a summer resort. Oh sure, lots of summer people, but just July and August. Nobody here in June or September. Mostly rental properties, ha? And folks that lived here had a lot of other things on their minds. Fishing, farming, swapping lies. Oh, sure, it was amateur times then. Man who could hammer a nail in straight or saw a piece of wood within couple inches of the right length, he was a carpenter— at least in July and August. It wasn't what you call organized." He waved his big hands to indicate general confusion. "But some of us thought we could see what was coming.

More summer people. Folks wanting to own their own homes, maybe spend more time here. Not going to happen though if they couldn't get good work done at a fair price." This was too much for Charles Winderman. All politicians such as Selectman Balto were entitled to tell a few lies to their constituency, but there was a limit. "Good work at a fair price," he repeated. "Like the Tony Circulari copper basement."

"Ha!" Balto threw back his head with a great laugh. The man had a fierce vitality that was hard not to like. "You heard about that one."

"Difficult not to," Charles said.

"Yeah. Guess I couldn't be more famous if I built a pyramid. But you know, Mr. Winderman"—he put his hands on his hips and leaned forward, suddenly intense—"I wish you'd known that fella I did it to. Son of a bitch, he was asking for it. 'Do this, do that, do it yesterday.' And mean—he was dead mean. I don't like 'em mean." He leaned back now, the anger gone, and once again he was cheerful. "Oh, there's something to be said on both sides. Good summer people, good islanders, lots of both. But lots of the other kind too, both sides. You be a selectman here, you run into everything. But what I was saying—"

The screen door opened behind them, and Charles looked around to see Mary Benjamin coming to his rescue. "Excuse me," she said, "but there's a phone call, Mr. Winderman."

He could tell from the look on her face and by the fact that she did not say who it was that the call was imaginary. If he wanted to escape, here it was. But while he could not claim to be enjoying himself, he was not bored. Besides, Tony Balto still had not got to his point. Perhaps he never would. "If you'll take the message, Mary, I'll call back."

She nodded, satisfied that she had done her part, and went back into the house.

"Taking up too much of your time," Balto said, and then

proceeded to take up some more. He ran his hand over his shock of hair. It was like brushing a hand over wild grass, which sprang up again as soon as the pressure had passed. "I was saying. You know, when I was just starting business, back about the time you came here, it was all one thing or other. Summer people, Island folks. One or other. Even when I got elected the first time, all the voters were folks I'd known my whole life. Born here like me. I grew up with them, most everybody. Not many like your friend Mr. Bernstein. Roger, he needed some guts back then to move in here full time with us natives. But not today." He shook his head for emphasis. "Not today. I go to town meeting in the winter, and me and the other selectmen, we're looking out at all kinds of folks didn't used to be here. Summer people who retire here. Maybe a little tough for them the first winter or two, have to run off to Florida or Bermuda or somewhere in February when there's snow and it gets dark at four o'clock in the afternoon. But then first thing you know they're here all the time. And young folks, maybe used to visit here as teenage summer hippies, but now they get married and decide this is where to live. I got three or four of them working for me— carpenter, plumber, salesman in the hardware store. I tell you, town meeting is something different. Used to be we just voted to pave a couple of roads and maybe buy a new fire engine every ten years. Then time to adjourn. But now, but now—"

Tony Balto stretched his arms wide, showing the extent, the breadth of this new world. "Now we got retired lawyers, a doctor used to run a big-city hospital, even some kind of woman chicken expert who's trying to improve the oyster beds. Chickens, oysters, I don't see the connection, but she does. And then the young people from off-Island, all with their own ideas about the good life. And they all get to vote. It's something. It's all mixed up, summer people and Island folks, and there's going to be more of it. Not like what you and I remember from back then. Different days."

Tony Balto had finally, almost, got where he was going. Charles Winderman decided to give him a hand before the morning was over. "Oh yes," he said, "I know it's getting all mixed up, as you put it. My granddaughter Nancy, a summer visitor since the year she was born, going out with your son Anthony, born an islander. That would never have happened when my wife and I first came here." There, is that what you meant? He looked straight in Tony Balto's eyes, almost hidden underneath the shaggy eyebrows. "Frankly, as you may know from your son, I don't think it's a very good idea."

Tony Balto nodded several times, returning the stare. At last he said, his voice hard for the first time, "Frankly, as you may not know, I don't think so either. Lots of ways, I liked it better when it was simple. Summer people knew who they were, Island folks the same. But that isn't the way it is, Mr. Winderman, not anymore. So everybody tells me, including my son, but I can see for myself. I wasn't happy when your kid, granddaughter, invited Anthony to your birthday party. But *he* was."

Charles nodded. "I'm glad to hear you say that. I wasn't happy about it either. That's why I said no. I hope you accept that."

"Accept it!" Tony Balto snorted. The voice stayed hard. "You got to understand something, Mr. Winderman. I don't give a shit if Anthony comes to your party. I got my own friends, mostly Italian like me but all of them islanders. Natives. That's how I grew up."

"So did I," Charles Winderman said. "So we both understand."

"Yeah." Tony Balto looked straight at him, nodding his large head. "Yeah, we understand. And I'm comfortable about it, too, real easy. Thing is, not everybody sees it our way. The newer folks, the kids. If you're in politics like me, or Island business like me, you got to listen close to some them other views, because all those folks got votes. And checkbooks."

"I don't have a vote."

"Yeah, that's right. Lucky for me, ha? Just the same, I always found it pays to listen, hear what's rustling around under your feet. Know what's going on, even in your own family, you know?"

Charles Winderman found himself in such complete agreement with the selectman that he had to answer. "I think the most important thing the head of a large family can do is, as you say, listen to what's rustling around. I have nine grandchildren, and I spend a good deal of my time paying close attention to them." Perhaps this sounded too forthcoming. "Not that I always agree with them," he added.

"Me, I just got into the grandchildren business couple of years ago. My oldest daughter, two kids so far, but up to now they aren't telling me much, mostly crying or laughing." He stared out at the ocean again. His heavy voice did not soften, no sentimentality here. "My experience is all with my own kids, but lots of that. Six of them, so I'm liable to collect my share of grandchildren somewhere down the line. Maybe even pass you, I wouldn't be surprised. Anthony, he's the oldest and the smartest, so maybe I listen to him the most. He's the one always saying, 'Papa, it's all changing.'"

Charles Winderman could think of nothing to say to this.

The selectman sounded as though he were about to add something more about Anthony, but after a moment he shrugged his wide shoulders. "Got some work to do," was all he said.

"So do I," Charles Winderman said. He picked up his shears.

By the time Tony Balto climbed back in his truck and started the motor, Charles Winderman was again working his grounds.

The Old Indian Scout

"It's no use," Nancy said, stabbing out her cigarette as though trying to punch a hole in the ashtray.

Nancy and Ellen perched on stools at the kitchen counter while Nancy drank a beer and Ellen thought about how she could possibly help her stepdaughter.

"You know what happened this morning?" Nancy's wide blue eyes seemed on the verge of tears, as they frequently did these past few days. "Papa Balto went to see Ah-boo and had a long talk with him. About Anthony and me and the party. It didn't make the slightest difference." Nancy gave Ellen one of those sudden fake smiles that young women use when pretending that something doesn't matter, even though it matters desperately. "But he tried. Anthony says he just went there on his own. He didn't even tell Anthony until afterward. Anthony was touched. I'm touched. He doesn't even really know me."

"I'm surprised he went," Ellen said. "What was Ah-boo like?"

"Polite, Anthony says, but firm." She finished her beer and got off the stool. "I have to shower. We're going on a beach binge."

"Who with?"

"I don't know. Some of Anthony's friends. Sort of a picnic, so I won't be home for dinner."

"Have fun."

"You know something?" Nancy said suddenly. The tears were so close that Ellen thought they would break. Nancy gulped to hold them back. "That's part of the problem. Things just aren't quite as much fun. Even with Anthony. I mean, this party, this damn party has just—just screwed up everything." Nancy looked helpless. "I wish—" She stopped. "I guess I have to go."

God damn it, Ellen thought, as she watched Nancy walk away. She seldom swore in conversation with herself, but Ah-boo was being so stubborn. So dictatorial. And over nothing. Yes, Lawrence was right in theory that it was a trivial matter, but not trivial to Nancy, a young woman in love, and therefore not trivial to Ellen. She did not think Bonjy had been much help, perhaps had not even tried. No help from Martha. And Brad and Sue saw it Ah-boo's way.

Ellen could not let it go at that. She certainly intended to talk to Ah-boo's nice friend, Roger Bernstein. She had liked him the few times they had talked, and instinct told her that he was, behind that façade, a kind and sensitive man. He would see it Ah-boo's way too, no doubt, but he might be able to give her good advice. After all, he knew Ah-boo better than anyone. Well worth a try. Who else could be enlisted?

Christopher. She couldn't help smiling. Christopher lying there in his hospital bed promising his "simple" solution: blackmail. Only a perverse sixteen-year-old would come up with such a notion. But she had better find out what he had in mind.

He probably hadn't even had any visitors today. He was due home from the hospital tomorrow, and Ellen would bet anything that Martha hadn't bothered to go today, since he would soon be home anyway. It must be hard to be unpopular even with your own mother.

Ellen put her hands on the counter to steady herself while she got off the stool. She must leave a note for Lawrence, who was down playing doubles with Brad and Sue and Ah-boo. Grudgingly, she admired Ah-boo, still playing competitive tennis the week of his seventieth birthday. "Gone to visit Christopher," she wrote, leaving the pad in the usual message spot on the counter, and went to get the car keys.

Christopher was out of his hospital bed, sitting in a chair by the window, reading a paperback that he held in his left hand. The right arm, bandaged in two places, was now in a sling, white sling against the white hospital gown. She could tell he was surprised to see her, but if he was also pleased, he did not let it show. But he did put down his book.

Ellen lowered herself into the other chair, a straight-backed bentwood piece that seemed a bit rickety for her bulk. Old Seventeen was beginning to make even the simplest maneuver a cumbersome engineering feat.

"So you're going home tomorrow," she said cheerfully, hearing the hospital visit note in her own voice.

Christopher nodded. He looked slightly pale beneath his summer tan. Even sitting down his body was long and lanky, his bare feet stretched out in front of him.

"How does the arm feel?"

"Sore," he said. He shifted it in the sling. "But I get a lot of aspirin. It's not too bad. I guess I won't be doing much the rest of the summer."

"That goes for both of us," Ellen said, drawing a slight smile from him. "Neither one of us is going to win the family tennis tournament."

Christopher actually laughed. The tennis tournament seemed to appeal to his bitter sense of humor. "I almost won it one summer," he said. "The handicaps make it all kind of flaky."

"I bet my handicap is bigger than yours."

This made him laugh again. He was quite nice when he laughed.

"Christopher," she said, getting to business, "I'm still working on your grandfather. To let Nancy bring Anthony to the birthday party. I'm not getting anywhere."

"Nancy and Anthony came to see me."

"I know. I was here."

"I know you were here. I just mentioned it."

Ellen had to be careful. She knew Christopher's pleasure in their visit was so fragile that if she said anything too kind or too friendly, he would twist away from her. She said nothing.

Christopher said nothing. They looked at each other. Ellen tried to keep her expression pleasant and inviting. Christopher turned his head to make sure no one else was in the room.

"Do you want me to shut the door?" Ellen asked, still pleasant, still not pushing.

"I'll do it." He got up from his chair, careful with the bandaged arm, and walked in his too-short hospital gown to close the door. Long, long bare legs. He returned to his chair, committed now to saying something. She waited for him.

Christopher looked out the window. In profile his long, bony Winderman face seemed even longer. His long, loose blond hair hung straight. Plainly he was thinking about what to say. He turned back to her.

"I'm telling you this just for Nancy."

Ellen nodded. "I know."

He shook his head, correcting her. "I mean I never tell secrets."

"I don't either," Ellen said, not knowing what was coming but giving her promise in any case. She wondered if Christopher was a bit in love with his cousin Nancy. Or did he just like her because she was nicer to him than any of the rest of the family?

Christopher looked down at his free left hand, making a fist and then opening the fingers wide. He did it several times. "I had a deer once," he said in a long-ago voice. "The summer I was five years old. A doe. A young doe, I'm pretty sure. Everybody said there weren't any deer on the property anymore. Ah-boo and Uncle Lawrence and Uncle Brad would tell how they used to see deer all the time in the early years, but now they were all gone. Too many houses and everything built up. All the deer had gone away to the other end of the Island. Grandfather said there hadn't been deer on our place in a long time.

"I don't know how she got here. My deer. I liked to get up real early then. I'd wake up when it just started turning light and get dressed and go out and just walk around. When it was really early and I got away from the house, out in the woods, I could pretend it was all woods. Like nobody lived here, no houses or anything, no people. Just me and the woods. I'd be very quiet. I'd see if I could move like an Indian. You know, not stepping on sticks or twigs. An Indian scout."

Christopher was not looking at her. He was still staring down at his hand, still making a fist, then spreading wide his long fingers. Ellen knew she must not speak.

"That's how I found her. I was sitting near the stream, the deep woodsy part at the upper end. Still kind of spooky dark in the woods but the sky was already light. And then she just walked out of the woods, real slow, and stood there on the path. So still, listening, looking. Wonderful big ears standing out straight. I kept as still as she did. I tried to breathe real shallow so she wouldn't hear me. She stood there a long time, and then finally she walked to the stream on those thin, graceful legs and then bent her head down and drank out of the stream. I couldn't believe it. She was so pretty. I could see the white spots on her hide, and she was all white underneath. When she finished her morning drink, she lifted up her head and looked around some more. I could tell she thought she was all alone, nobody near her. Then she turned and walked back into the brush. I sat there a long time after she was gone. I didn't know how far back she was. I didn't want her to hear me and get scared."

Christopher finally looked at Ellen. Then she knew she could comment. "How wonderful," Ellen said. "Did you ever see her again?"

He nodded. "Lots of times. I got up early all that summer so I could go down to the stream. Get there before she did and get in place. I always wore dark clothes, never anything white to catch her eye. Sometimes she didn't come. Maybe she could smell me on some mornings, or maybe she just went to another part of the Quatchum. But most mornings she was there for her drink. I thought of leaving food for her, but I decided I better not change anything. Just keep it the way it was."

Ellen had been trying to figure out why Christopher was telling her this obviously private, personal story. And now she thought she knew. The little five-year-old boy, solitary even then, his father and mother already divorced, doing things by himself, the secret Indian scout. And then—his very own deer. Her heart went out to the young Christopher, and to the sixteen-year-old boy sitting across from her, still lonely today but never admitting it. "And you didn't tell anybody," she guessed.

He nodded again. "That's right. I didn't want anybody to spoil it. Only at the end, when summer was almost over. I told Ah-boo I had something important to show him, but only if he promised to keep it a secret. Not tell anybody, not put it in the notebooks. And he kept his word, just the way I knew he would. I didn't tell him it was a deer. I wanted to surprise him. He got up at five o'clock that morning, and he met me at the lower bridge, and I took him to the hiding place. I'd told him how quiet we had to be, no talking, and he was wearing dark clothes just like I told him to. We waited and waited, but she didn't come. He didn't blame me or anything. You know what he did? He got up the next morning and did it all over again. And this time she came, so he got to see her after all."

"That," said Ellen, "is how to be a good grandfather."

"And he never told," Christopher said with pride. "But once when a lot of us were down on the beach, Uncle Brad said something about how there used to be a lot of deer on the property but there weren't any now, I looked over at my grandfather, and he was looking at me too, and he winked. Just this terrific wink."

"Was the deer there the next summer?"

"No, just that one year. I went out every morning the first week I was on the Island, but she didn't come. Maybe she moved off to join the rest of the deer. Or maybe somebody shot her over the winter. There's a deer season. They aren't supposed to shoot does, but I bet they do."

"Well, I hope they didn't shoot yours. I don't want to believe that. What was her name?"

Christopher's eyes went wide with surprise. "How did you know I gave her a name?"

"Because I would have. What did you call her?"

But Christopher would not go that far. It must have been a very romantic or sentimental name. He shook his head. "It doesn't matter," he said. "I just wanted you to know I can really keep a secret. I haven't told anybody else about the deer since Grandfather. Until right now."

"I'm honored," Ellen said, and she was. "Thank you for trusting me."

"I know a lot of things," he said, boasting now. "I find out lots of things, but I don't tell anybody. Except when it's useful."

"How do you mean, 'useful'? Useful for what?"

"Like now. Nancy and Anthony. We can make Ah-boo invite Anthony. We can force him."

There was a strange expression on Christopher's face. He had been almost sweet telling the story of his deer, but now his face was fierce. Not meanness, quite, but more a look of— Ellen groped for it—yes, power. He was proud of his power, or at least what he construed as power. She was not sure she was going to like this. "How are we going to make him do something he doesn't want to do?"

Christopher got up from his chair, restless, perhaps at the last moment not quite sure what he wanted to say. He carefully shifted his arm in the sling, as though he had just discovered the sling was there. He walked past her, walked around his hospital bed to the far side, then walked back to her side and leaned back against the bed. That expression, power or whatever it was, grew even stronger. He was almost righteous.

"I can threaten to expose him. He's screwing Bonjy. Also he still smokes, but he lies about it."

Ellen had to make an effort not to laugh at him. "I'm sorry," she said rather coldly, "that's a bit preposterous."

Christopher nodded his head as though that was just what he had expected. "It's true, though."

"Now listen to me, Christopher. Your grandfather is seventy years old. Men of that age are not very active sexually. And certainly he wouldn't do that with Bonjy. You mustn't go around saying such things."

A flash of anger in Christopher's eyes, and the twist of the mouth. "I don't go around saying such things. I haven't said it to anybody at all."

"You just said it to me."

"I thought you wanted to help Nancy." Sarcastic. Superior.

Ellen sighed. "Of course, I do. But this isn't going to help."

"Why not? I've thought about it. He can't afford to have the whole family know about Bonjy. And the smoking. He couldn't stand it. You don't know him."

"Christopher, you can't lie about him. He doesn't deserve that."

"I'm not lying." Very angry now. "I told you I find out a lot of things. I've heard him and Bonjy. And it's true about the cigarettes."

"I'm sorry, but I don't believe you. You're making it up." He flung himself back in his chair, forgetting about his arm, and then squeezed his eyes tight shut at the sudden pain. He kept them shut for a long moment. Then he opened them, and that expression of power was back.

"Will you believe me if I tell you something that you know is true? About you and Uncle Lawrence?"

Ellen felt both a chill and at the same time an abrupt curiosity. What did this strange boy know, or think he knew? "I don't know what you mean, and I'm not sure I want to hear anything about this. Well, all right, what?"

Christopher measured her. His voice came out factual, cool, scientific: "In bed you like to be the one on top. And you also like the bowling ball, whatever that means. I don't know what it is, but you like it."

Ellen could feel the flush hit her face.

"You absolute bastard," she said.

She got to her feet and without looking at him, without saying good-bye, she walked out of the room, out of the hospital to the parking lot, the flush still burning her face.

Her first thought, when she was calm enough to think, was to wonder how he knew. Neither she nor Lawrence would ever discuss their sexual life with anyone else. The thought of Lawrence, the reserved banker deeply protective of his personal privacy, talking about what went on in his own bedroom was ludicrous. So Christopher simply had to find out by spying. Yes indeed, the old Indian scout rides again. But that didn't explain how.

What was he doing? Hiding under beds? In closets? They all left their houses open at all times, locking up only for the winter. Any of the family could and did walk into each other's house at any time without even knocking. She had done it herself, walking into Ah-boo's or Martha's or Brad and Sue's unoccupied house to leave a note or return a book. Yes, Christopher could easily get in when no one was home and then hide under the bed or in a bedroom closet. Possible but not likely. It would mean a very long wait, even for the old scout. And then waiting afterward—all night long until the house cleared in the morning, or else sneaking out during the night, running a high risk of being discovered. Not really very likely.

But that left a much worse possibility. Suppose Christopher was taping. Ellen could feel her face grow hot again. She and Lawrence talked to each other while making love, and not for publication. She knew little about electronics, but she did know there were long-running tapes used in divorce cases and wiretaps. Could a sixteen-year-old boy get hold of such sophisticated equipment? Was it available only to the FBI and other law enforcement agencies? Actually she had no idea how sophisticated it had to be. For all she knew one could buy it at one's local electronics center, right between the video cassettes and the computer games. Not on the Island, of course, but perhaps in New York? A microphone and a reel of tape and a couple of batteries, complete kit for only $19.95, surprise all your friends and family. Could it be as simple as that?

She tried to remember if Christopher had ever said or done anything that indicated an interest in the electronic world, but she came up with nothing. Of course, that didn't prove much. Until the last several days she had spent little time with Christopher, scarcely ever had any private conversation with him. Had Martha ever said anything? No, when Martha spoke of her son, it was invariably some form of criticism.

Had Christopher's sister, Amy, said anything? Again nothing.

There was a third possibility that Ellen found more plausible, perhaps because it was also slightly more attractive. He was always skulking around the property, turning up unexpectedly. As she had learned today, Christopher from his earliest years had taken to wandering around the property by himself. At dawn when he was five years old, but perhaps now he had turned into a nighttime wanderer, quietly visiting other houses, listening at doors and windows, picking up bits and pieces of conversations, storing them away in his strange mind. Thank God she and Lawrence kept their bedroom window shades drawn, not for privacy—until now—but against the early morning sunlight.

But however he was getting his information about her and Lawrence, it was unfortunately accurate. Yes, she did enjoy making love on top, and not just because it was more convenient during the later months of pregnancy. She had always enjoyed it: the greater freedom of movement, the better chance to control and time her own pleasure and to give more pleasure. Yes indeed, guilty as charged. True, Christopher could simply have guessed at this because of her advanced pregnancy, but she very much doubted that he had anything like that amount of sexual knowledge or understanding. But even if she were mistaken, even if it had been only an inspired guess, that still did not account for . . . the other. Come on, Ellen. As Hortense always told her, you have to face up to things. That still did not account for the bowling ball.

She could remember the first time it had happened, although as with so many aspects of good lovemaking, it was not possible to say whose idea it had been. She and Lawrence had just finished a completely happy and satisfying session of love, and as they were lying still, not quite ready yet to go to sleep, his thumb and finger were slipped deep inside her. The effect on both of them was intense. Within a few moments they were making love all over again, even more elaborately this time. And when they had finished and were now ready for exhausted sleep, both of them wanted his thumb and finger inside her again, and they had gone to sleep in that deep, erotic intimacy.

It soon became their signature gesture at the end of special lovemaking, a lovely way to go to sleep. And sometimes a fiercely arousing act in the midst of love. Neither of them could remember who had christened it the bowling ball, a rather obvious jest, but they both called it that, with affection and excitement. Do the bowling ball. I want the bowling ball.

And now Christopher had said it. She supposed she should be grateful that he had no idea what it meant, but she felt nothing but resentment. Outrage. What a wicked thing to do.

She was not going to tell Lawrence. She did not feel restrained, not in this matter, by her promise to Christopher to "keep a secret," but she knew Lawrence could not handle it. She did not know what form his reaction would take—violence? pain? icy withdrawal? She only knew it was more than he could manage, strong though he was. His privacy went too deep to absorb this kind of assault. She could live with it because she had to. But by God, she certainly had to deal with Christopher.

And then there was the corollary to her own concern. Could it really be that Ah-boo was sleeping with Bonjy? And still smoking secretly after all that righteous guff he gave Nancy and the other smokers in the family? If Christopher's information was right about her and Lawrence, what did it say about Ah-boo? How about that, Ah-boo?

She cornered Christopher the morning he came home from the hospital. It was easy enough to do. Getting dressed in his own clothes, going through the release procedures, taking the trip home with Martha and Richie—all this so soon after the accident and the loss of blood and the surgery had worn him down. She found him on the deck on the chaise longue. He had a small orange throw blanket across his legs, even though the day was warm and sunny. An old brown tweed jacket over his shoulders covered the arm in the sling. He wasn't doing anything, just lying there staring out at the long view down to Summertown Harbor.

"Where is everybody?" she said. She pulled up a director's chair, not close enough to crowd him but close enough so that it would be difficult for him to avoid looking at her.

"I don't know," he said in a tired voice. "They went to town for something."

Well, she thought, welcome home, Christopher. Sometimes Martha was just too much. "Nobody to take care of you?"

No expression on his face. "I'm glad to be alone. I don't need anybody."

The hell you don't, Ellen thought. You need people as much as any young man I ever met. "I'm glad you're alone too. That gives us a chance to talk."

"What's to talk about? You called me a bastard."

Ellen had given a lot of thought to what she wanted to accomplish, but she had realized she would have to play it by ear, depending on Christopher's attitude. This was not a promising start, but at least neither of them had to pretend that nothing had happened. She intended to be very straight with him, and this was the moment to begin.

"Well," she said, with no false friendliness, "don't you think you were a bastard? Spying on your own family?"

He looked away and did not answer. He fiddled with the blanket, smoothing it out with his left hand.

"How do you think it feels to learn that my private life has been spied on?"

"I don't know," he said. After a moment he asked, "How does it feel?"

All right, give it to him. "Shitty," she said. "That's the only word for it. Shitty. You ought to be ashamed."

He seemed to appreciate the direct talk. At any rate, he did not pull away from her. And he did not flinch from the criticism. She reminded herself that Christopher had had a lot of experience with criticism.

"What makes you do it?"

"I don't know."

"Yes, you do. You know what I think it is? I think you're bored. I think you don't know what to do with yourself, so you take it out on everybody else. Sneaking around at night, hiding under people's windows. Is that what you do?"

He made a fist again with his left hand, held it a long time before spreading the fingers wide. "I'm not hurting anybody," he said, more to himself than to her.

"That's what you think."

"I never told anything about anybody until yesterday."

"Swell," Ellen said. "That makes it all right, does it? Let me tell you something. You hurt everybody you spy on, whether they know it or not. You find out things about them that you were never meant to know. You demean them. But most of all you demean yourself. You make yourself cheap."

He pulled the blanket around him.

"Are you cold?" she said. "Can I get you anything?"

"Could I have some coffee?" he asked, shy to be asking any favor. "It's all made."

"Sure. I'll have some with you." She pushed herself to her feet. "What do you like in it?"

"Cream and sugar. Please."

The please had come as an afterthought, but it was there.

Ellen waddled into the kitchen, which was neater than she had expected, no breakfast dishes anywhere in sight, the beige Formica counters wiped clean. Richie's work? She didn't think Martha would be this neat on a morning when she had had to make an early trip to the hospital. Ellen found two mugs in the cabinet above the coffeemaker. On her way back through the living room she saw another throw blanket on the couch and brought that along.

"Here you are," she said, handing Christopher his mug. "And another blanket in case the coffee doesn't warm you up."

"Thanks. Aunt Ellen."

Well, well. He had actually used her name. "Call me Ellen if that's any easier," she said as casually as possible, not wanting to make anything of it. She lowered herself into the director's chair.

"Now, Christopher. I want to say something serious. As a friend. I want you to cut this out. Right now and for good. You are much too smart not to see that it's wicked. Find some other way to entertain yourself."

He shook his head. "It's not entertainment. I like knowing things. I like finding them out."

"That's not an excuse."

"Yes, it is."

"Then it's not good enough. Leave your family alone."

"What about Ah-boo and Bonjy?"

"Leave them alone too."

"No, I mean about making Ah-boo let Anthony come."

"Oh." Then she could not resist asking. "Is it really true?" Christopher only nodded.

"Then that's between you and me, and I'm going to try to forget it. Although," she added, seeing the perverse humor, "I doubt that I will. But nothing—nothing I can think of— would ever drive me to use that in any way. Your grandfather can be a difficult man, or at least a stubborn one, but he's a good man. A good father and a good grandfather. Remember how he treated you about your deer. He's made this whole place possible, all our houses, this house of yours. Now I'm going to beat him on this Anthony thing if I can, but I won't beat him your way. And you mustn't think about it either.

It's not fair. Even Nancy would hate it if we did that to Ah-boo."

"Nancy wouldn't have to know."

"Christopher, you haven't been listening to me."

"Yes, I have. I'm just saying Nancy wouldn't have to be involved."

"Well, I'm not going to be involved either. Nor are you." Then before she thought about it, she heard herself asking, "How did you find out?"

"I climbed up on the roof. It's easy to do from the veranda."

"What—?" Ellen stopped herself. She was letting herself get entirely too curious. "Now, Christopher, I mean it. I want you to stop this. All this sneaking around at night."

"I don't know," he said.

At least he was wavering. She smiled at him, not quite knowing why she felt this sudden conspiratorial affection. Perhaps because he was so alone, even on the day he came home from the hospital. "How can I make love to my husband if I know you might be outside the window?"

To her surprise, they both laughed at what, only yesterday, had been such a frightful thought. It was still frightful, but somehow . . .

"All right," he said, still laughing.

"Is that a promise? Are you as good at keeping promises as keeping secrets?"

Now his face was solemn. "Yes," he said.

She had been wondering what had driven him to it. Certainly boredom, as she had said, and certainly "wanting to know things," as he had said. But surely something more. Living in that house with his mother, Martha bringing home all those "friends" and "houseguests," a situation impossible for this boy to ignore or to avoid. Or to tolerate. Had he been spying on other homes and other families to bring them down to the level of his own household, his own mother?

Easy to speculate, impossible to know. Probably impossible even for Christopher to know.

She thought of pressing him further but decided that was enough. "Good," she said. "Then I'll take your promise. You know, I've been thinking about the story you told me. About your deer. Please tell me what you named her."

A very long pause, and she thought he was going to refuse again. But something had happened between them this morning.

"I called her Beauty," he said.

The Curve
in the Road

Charles Winderman lay on his side, propped on one elbow so that he could look out his bedroom window. The broken moonlight dusted the tops of the little waves that he could hear landing softly on his beach. He was, with great pleasure, smoking his postcoital cigarette. Mary Benjamin lay beside him, now sound asleep and breathing deeply.

Charles Winderman had always stayed awake for a while after making love, and not just for the cigarette. He often wished, more and more often in these later years, that he had made a different pact with himself about smoking. Many different times in earlier days he had tried to give up smoking altogether, never successfully, or at least not for long. His best effort had come when he created the warning acronym BLETCH, which he quickly said to himself every time he thought of having a cigarette. BLETCH stood for everything bad about cigarettes: Blood pressure, Lungs, Emphysema, Throat, Cancer, Heart. This had worked well for two months but then he got used to it. BLETCH no longer frightened him. He tried other devices, including a brief but absurd bout with hypnotism, but nothing worked. And as he grew older, the health statistics diminished in their power to alarm him, because giving up smoking meant less and less potential contribution to his longevity.

What finally worked was the acknowledgment that he did not really want to stop smoking forever and ever. He only wanted to give it up most of the time. So he would give it up except for certain occasions. And then had come the painful choice: which occasions? When was a cigarette most enjoyable? He had narrowed it to four possibilities: after tennis, after swimming, after sex, with a martini. Easily the most treasured moments. But tennis, swimming and cocktails were all public occasions, and he did hope to set an example for his children and grandchildren. He wanted them all to see that it was possible to stop, and then perhaps they would be encouraged to do the same.

So finally he had settled on after sex. And since he had indeed been able to quit after years of frustration, he could not complain. In fact, he was very pleased with his accomplishment. But he could not help realizing, especially in these last five years, how many more cigarettes he would have been entitled to if he had chosen any of the other three occasions, which he still enjoyed almost daily. At his present age his smoking opportunities were severely limited. A man of seventy was, after all, fighting a rather squalid rearguard action against impotence.

On the other hand, it was certainly possible that the happy combination prospect of sex and cigarettes was doing wonders for his aging libido. They still went very well together, as they always had.

He put out his cigarette in the windowsill ashtray, then reached across Mary to get her pack and lighter from the night table. The first cigarette after a period of abstinence always made him briefly dizzy, but the second was an unmixed delight. Mary did not move, not even when he patted her shoulder in passing affection.

Mary, too, was an unmixed delight—as housekeeper, companion, cook, manager, family counselor and bed partner. Their curious relationship worked well for both. They were not close enough to be friends in the sense that he and Roger Bernstein were. And in spite of their sporadic meetings in bed, however pleasant these might be, they were not lovers. She still thought of herself, even after these twenty years, as his employee. With the solitary exception of bed, she never called him anything except "Mr. Winderman," even though he had suggested long ago that she call him Ah-boo, as everyone else did. And in bed he never called her or thought of her as anything but Mary. One could not, they both agreed, get sexually excited with a woman named Bonjy.

None of this was likely to change. They got along perfectly together. Oh, sometimes she talked too much, but it was seldom idle babble. She would join him in bed whenever he asked her to, and they enjoyed each other in an undemanding way. She was very much a member of the family, not only in his eyes but in everyone else's. Her advice in family matters was always worth listening to. He might not take the advice, but whatever Mary said was unselfish and well-informed. But she still worked for him and always made sure to keep it that way, perhaps for her own independence. That was fine with him.

Tonight, when they had finished, she had come at him with some family advice. "Are you in a good mood?" she began.

"Of course. You want another raise, is that it?" This was an old bedroom joke between them: was it better to ask for a raise just before or just after the granting of favors?

"No, I'm serious. It's about Ellen."

His first thought was that Mary had picked up some information that he didn't know. This happened occasionally. Perhaps some difficulty about Ellen's pregnancy. Having her first baby at thirty-two might cause problems, although she certainly looked and sounded as healthy as one could ask. Or perhaps some trouble between Ellen and Lawrence, or between Ellen and Lawrence's children. If it was the children, it would be Bryan. Charles Winderman had seen and felt that tension all month.

But it turned out that the only thing on Mary's mind was the familiar matter of that Balto boy not being allowed to attend his birthday party. This annoyed him, since he had already been through this with Nancy and then with Ellen and now, most recently, with Selectman Balto. Enough. The decision had been made. He had learned long ago not to rethink decisions. Decide whatever you have to decide and then move on to something else—unless, of course, important new information came to light. That was not the case here. Mary simply gave her own opinion that this invitation to Anthony Balto was somehow more important to Ellen than it was to Nancy herself. That made no sense to him. Ellen had scarcely met the young man. And she had attended only one of his birthday parties, the one last August, so how could she fully appreciate its significance? What it represented, not so much to him as to the entire family. But he heard Mary out. She wanted him to reconsider. It was clear to him that Ellen had been doing some lobbying work, and it annoyed him. His decision had been made, and she should accept it. Ellen was entirely too independent.

"I'll think about it," he said. "Now I'm going to have my cigarette, and you're going to sleep."

"Are you really going to think about it? Or just pretend to?" Her voice was already a little drowsy.

"Go to sleep," he said. There were disadvantages to a long, close relationship, such as knowing the other person's methods too well. Mary had guessed that he didn't plan to think about it at all. There was no need to, since no new information existed. But the advantages of closeness far outweighed the disadvantages.

It was painful to remember those years just before Mary Benjamin came to work for him. Those years after Anne's death when Lawrence and Bradford and Martha banded together in an effort to reorganize his life. They tried to persuade him to marry again. They took turns inviting him to dinner, either here on the Island or at their homes in New York, always with a widow or a divorcee as the surprise guest —until he ordered them to stop. They insisted that, pending his hoped-for remarriage, he must have a live-in housekeeper, preferably one who could take care of him both at Rutherford College and at his New York apartment and during his summers on the Island.

Oh, those housekeeper candidates! He could no longer remember the full parade of women who were submitted to him for approval. Brad and Sue, recently married, had been especially active on the housekeeper front. Indeed, Sue had been indefatigable. Never a week passed without a letter or a visit from Sue, pressing upon him with all her extraordinary energy and enthusiasm the latest nominee. Sue adopted the housekeeper question as a burning personal issue, more personal to her than to him. Well, that was what one got with Sue, along with her good will, her hard work, her efficiency in managing her household and her children. Sue did not enjoy life; she overcame it. All four of Brad and Sue's children—Charlie, Anne, Brad Junior, even nine-year-old Alice —were programmed to achieve. They might be lacking in imagination or any sense of the poetry of life, but they all worked hard and followed orders. Perhaps he would make an exception of Alice. As the youngest grandchild, she had a difficult role, and perhaps that difficulty drove her to more independence, more feistiness, than the others had. It was strange that the only two grandchildren named after himself and his wife bore the least resemblance to him and Anne.

Charlie and Anne, eighteen and fifteen, were already pretty straight arrow. But they were all good family members, Brad and Sue and their four children, and they all profited from their membership in the Winderman tribe. He gave Sue as much of the credit as he gave Bradford, even though when it came to such undertakings as searching for a good housekeeper, Sue could wear him down.

The Island had been easier to manage than Rutherford. Here he had been able to hire a series of Island women to come in and cook, clean, shop and launder. Twenty years ago it had been much easier to hire summer help because the Island had not yet exploded as a summer resort. But Rutherford had been difficult. In that small town, dominated by the college, few people were available for part-time jobs. He had been forced, against his instincts, to try out several imported housekeepers. They had worked out as badly as he anticipated. None of them earned tenure.

Charles Winderman was not helpless. After his experience in the Army and his early years on the Island, he could do most things around the house for himself. Anne had always cooked, so his background at the stove was weak, but he could manage. He could have managed it all, but it took too much time away from his teaching and writing and responsibilities as chairman of the English Department. Reluctantly he agreed with his children that something must be done.

Roger Bernstein did not find Mary Benjamin, but he pointed the way. "What you need, Charles, is an army or navy widow. They're used to working their ass off. They know how to run a household on a tight budget, and most of them need money. Lots of spit and polish around the house in case they have to impress the colonel and the colonel's wife. Don't get a colonel's wife. And they've learned how to move from one place to another with no fuss. Rutherford, New York, the Island—an army widow could switch you back and forth five times a year. You can't miss."

And indeed he did not miss. There was even, he discovered, an organization for service widows to make his search easy. Mary Benjamin's letter was the best of the six he received, and in person she was even better than her letter. She was the widow of an army captain who had been killed tragically at the end of the Korean War. No children. Said she loved cooking and was proud of her skill. Said she liked housekeeping and was good at it. Said she came from a large family herself and would enjoy being part of one again. Said she liked dogs and didn't like cats. Charles Winderman hired her on faith, but everything she had promised turned out to be true. One might quibble only about her husband's "tragic death." He had actually died, Mary Benjamin admitted some years later, when he was run over by a Jeep in the parking lot of the Fort Benning officers club at the end of a raucous party. Charles Winderman did not hold this misleading representation against Mary. After all, it was presumably tragic for Captain Benjamin.

He often wondered, if Mary had not turned up to become housekeeper supreme, would he have married again? The children, even though devoted to Anne and shaken by her loss, had urged it for a long time, though not during the last ten years. They said it was what Anne would have wanted. Since no evidence existed as to what Anne would have wanted or not wanted, anyone was entitled to speculate. Charles himself was dubious. At the time of her death they had three grown children and had had twenty-five years of marriage and a very good life together, including the inspired creation of their Island world. Charles wasn't so sure that Anne would have wanted him to share this achievement or repeat it with someone else. Probably not. She would have wanted him looked after, taken care of, perhaps even pampered on occasion, but not necessarily cherished, loved, adored by some other woman. She would not have wanted anyone to take her place emotionally, but of course there had never been any danger of that.

It was not true, as Charles and Anne Winderman sometimes liked to pretend in later years, that they had been childhood sweethearts. They had been childhood enemies.

Most of the boys and girls forced by their parents to attend Miss Haversham's Wednesday afternoon dancing classes became antagonists. The twelve- and thirteen-year-old boys, compelled to give up afternoon sports in favor of dark suits (only navy blue, dark gray or black were permissible) and white shirts and well-shined black shoes, arrived at Miss Haversham's studio in a state of barely suppressed anger. The girls, slightly younger, wore short white dresses, short white gloves, long white stockings and black Mary Janes. Although most of the girls found some pleasure in the fact that they were engaged in their first grown-up social experience, they soon realized that their male partners resented every moment of every Wednesday afternoon.

Only Miss Haversham's discipline kept the boys under control. A tall, regal woman with the eyes and voice of a master sergeant and the beak of a falcon, she was prepared to expel anyone who disobeyed. Since parents had to sign up for her classes several years in advance, and since social standing was a prerequisite for admission, every boy risked parental damnation if Miss Haversham found him unsuitable. And so, to the measured piano accompaniment of her assistant, the boys dutifully danced their assigned partners around and around the polished hardwood floor, carefully disguising their hatred of Miss Haversham, the lessons and whatever young girl they happened to be holding at the moment.

Anne Linton's attitude was similar to that of the boys. She was an outdoors girl. She despised the horrid little white gloves with their round white buttons, the nasty, itchy cotton stockings, the repulsively shiny Mary Janes and every boy in the class, very much including Charles Winderman. Tall for her age, easily the tallest girl in her class, she was assigned by Miss Haversham to dance only with the three tallest boys, of whom she found Charles Winderman the most obnoxious. His appearance was pleasant enough, but he had nothing to say to her, he resented being stuck with her over and over again, and his dancing ranged from indifferent to shoddy. Just to get through it all, she found herself trying to lead him, which he would not accept. Each session together was a quiet, sustained struggle for mastery, carefully hidden from Miss Haversham's sharp eye by a blandness of expression that neither of them felt. Both were relieved when, at the end of their long season of misery, Charles was sent away to boarding school. Neither of them could have endured a second season. They gratefully lost track of each other for the better part of a decade.

He did not see her again until a large Saturday night party when she was a junior at Wellesley. He recognized her first. She was still tall, perhaps five-eight, but she no longer stuck out because of her height. She had the same long, blond, almost taffy-colored hair, but it was now worn piled high on her head instead of hanging to her shoulders as in the Miss Haversham days. She was graceful, standing easily, but with a definite, almost athletic confidence in herself. She was handsome rather than pretty or beautiful. Big gray eyes with a nice hint of humor, although as he watched her, she was laughing far less than the noisy crowd around her. A long, sculptured face with good bones, reserved but softened by a roundness in her cheeks and a generous mouth, a good deal nicer than he remembered it. Now she smiled suddenly and the reserve vanished, but then it returned as soon as the smile ended. He had recognized her at once and had come up with her name in ten seconds. He wondered if she would know him.

He pushed his way through the college crowd and the smoke, trying not to spill his glass of punch as he dodged jostling elbows. When he reached her, he tapped her shoulder to get her attention. When she turned, he said, as he had been taught by Miss Haversham long ago, "Excuse me, Miss Linton. May I have the honor of this dance?"

Since there was no dancing and in fact no music, her first expression was puzzlement. He watched her face change: first, curiosity, raised eyebrows, then acknowledgment that, yes, this was a familiar face. Close study, the big gray eyes looking him over in search of the right clues. He did not have to help her. Now she had placed him somewhere in their past, and then suddenly she knew. Her eyes went wide, and she actually laughed with pleasure. "My God," she said, "Charles!" And then with the quickness that he would come to know well she added, "But I promised myself never to dance with you again."

They found a slightly less crowded corner to talk in. With delight they exchanged fond recollections of how much and in how many different ways they had hated each other. Later they left the party to walk through the wooded Wellesley campus, and later still, as soon as she graduated, they were married with the intense approval of both the Winderman and Linton clans. "It just shows," Anne had joked, "that if children are exposed to a very proper dancing school at the right age, good will surely come of it."

And good certainly came of it, Charles agreed. They had had twenty-five years of marriage. This year it would have been forty-six. The three children and the nine grandchildren —now about to be ten. And of course he and Anne had created this gathering place on the Island that did so much to cement the family together, even through divorces and other mishaps. He did not expect all his family to realize explicitly what this coming together every August in the same spot meant to them, individually and collectively. He tried to convey it in the blue notebooks and in everything he said, but he did not expect everyone to understand that message. No matter. The important thing was for all of them to experience it.

Whatever each of them did during the year in their different homes and jobs and schools, all of them returned to this Island each August to renew their membership in something larger than themselves and to do familiar things together. He knew it gave them a dimension that was missing in many other families. That was what he and Anne had founded.

Anne had missed most of the grandchildren—Martha had not even been married for the first time when she died—but Anne had lived long enough to help establish the pattern. Anne was serious, adventurous, ambitious, and she had as strong a sense of family as he did. There was humor behind the seriousness that made her a great pleasure to live with, but in most matters the seriousness came first. In public she was proper, calm, a bit reserved.

Within the family she was less restrained. She could make the children laugh as often and as heartily as he could. She was inventive about family undertakings—parties, picnics, treasure hunts, surprise treats, unexpected games during the car trips to and from the Island. He had learned a lot from Anne that he had never experienced in his own growing up. In his father's household the focal point of family enterprise and concern had always been the Winderman Trust Company. In the Linton family the emphasis had been on public service. Anne's father had served on many civic commissions, always without pay, and her mother had been active in hospitals, libraries and other community services. Anne had been raised to be Useful, and she did her best to instill this sense of purpose in her children. Charles was not absolutely sure she would have married him if, as his father had always intended, he had gone to work for the Winderman Trust. His decision to teach instead had impressed her. So had his decision to enlist in the Army. Anne was a woman of many convictions.

This had passed through to their two sons. Lawrence in his thoughtful, dispassionate way took part in New York City community affairs, not as a leader or drumbeater but as an adviser and arranger. He also gave to Island charities, although he reserved all his time here for himself and his family. Bradford and Sue were uncontrollable activists. In their home community of Glen Cove scarcely a public cause existed in which they were not involved. Schools, clubs, fundraising drives, local committees of every kind. Anne would have been proud of them, although Charles found it a bit excessive.

But as for Martha—well, Martha. Hard to say just what Martha did with herself. Oh, various *pro bono* activities from time to time, but always on a part-time basis so as not to interfere with tennis and bridge. Charles had to concede that of all the things he and Anne had tried to teach their children, their greatest success with Martha had been games. She was good at them, she enjoyed them, and she gave them much of her time. When he retired from Rutherford and moved to New York City permanently, he had been amazed by the number of well-to-do women who could be spotted in apartment house lobbies each morning, dressed in their tennis whites and bound for the courts. Martha played almost every morning.

No question that Martha had been the child most deeply wounded by Anne's death. She would have been a problem anyway, even if Anne had lived. The youngest child by four years, the only daughter, rebellious by instinct, Martha had already become, in Anne's word, "difficult." Talented and intelligent, in certain ways even brighter than Lawrence, she made little practical use of her abilities. The sad truth was that she was captivated by men. And captivating to them. It wasn't just sex, just animal magnetism, although there was plenty of that. It was something beyond mere chemistry, beyond the physical. And yet Martha invariably had trouble with her men, not just the two marriages but all the others in between. Men and alcohol, tennis and bridge.

Would Anne have been able to guide Martha into more useful pursuits? He did not know, but surely, surely things would have been better. What he did know was that Anne's death removed Martha's strongest anchor. Downhill from there, no matter what Charles had tried. He had finally settled, for want of a more successful approach, on cautious leniency. He did not want to drive her away from the Island and the family. What would Anne have done? Perhaps the same. But could Anne have prevented Martha's two divorces? Would Anne have permitted Martha to have summer "house guests," like the current Richie? Would Anne have succeeded in doing anything about Martha's drinking? Or did the house guests and the drinking grow out of Anne's death? One would never know.

All Charles Winderman could claim with certainty was that Martha was still here, still part of the family, still part of the Island. He was determined to preserve that state for every member of his tribe, from Lawrence down to his soon-to-be youngest grandchild. Yes, "grapple them to thy soul with hoops of steel"—but always take care not to let the steel show. He wondered if that would continue after his own death. It would depend on how the family functioned after he was gone. Would Martha still be here every August, with or without house guest? Lawrence was more lenient with Martha, although perhaps from indifference rather than affection. Lawrence could keep his distance from almost anyone. Bradford was closer to his sister if more critical of her, but Sue and Martha did not fit together at all. Only the other day at Picnic Rock he had had to step between them and make peace.

Now Ellen and Martha were much better together. Perhaps something helpful to Martha would grow out of that new relationship, although he was not sure he still believed anything could help Martha. He would do what he could to encourage Ellen and Martha—a word here, a compliment there. He knew how it was done, but he wasn't sure how much good he could accomplish, at least for Martha. Perhaps maintenance of the status quo was the best he could hope for. He did not know who besides himself would provide that maintenance.

Charles Winderman was left where he always was on the future of his family: uncertain. If only Anne had lived.

That final night had had nothing unusual about it. No portents, no warnings of any kind. No one had said anything that would later seem freighted with significance because of what was about to happen. Just an ordinary summer night at the end of an ordinary August day.

After dinner had been cleared away, Anne went upstairs to get her purse and her yellow cardigan sweater in case the night turned cool. She was going to a meeting of the Island Conservation Society, of which she had been a founding member. Charles, who was rereading his way through Henry Fielding with considerable pleasure, planned to stay up until she came home.

"Back around ten," Anne said as she went out the door. Her last words to him. Hardly memorable.

After a minute Charles heard her start the car, and then the sound of the motor faded away as she headed out the driveway toward Summertown. His last touch of her.

He read quietly until some time after ten when he heard a car coming down the driveway. At first he thought it was Anne returning but then realized from the sound of the motor it was not their car. He got up to see who could be visiting at this time of night, so he was standing at the door when the police car stopped, and the chubby young officer with apology written all over his face got out to tell him that Anne had been killed in an accident.

He rode back in the police car to the curve where it had

happened. A second police car was there and a tow truck that was about to drag his Buick away from the broken pine tree against which it had crashed. Anne's body had already been carried away in an ambulance, but an officer told him—with a genuine effort at kindness—that she must have died instantly, her neck broken on impact.

He did not learn until the next day what had happened. A summer visitor whose house was on the curve, a man out walking his dog before going to bed, had seen it and described it to the police. A car coming from the other direction—"really fast," the man said—had swung wide going around the curve just at the moment that Anne's car was entering the curve from the other end. No time for brakes. She had swerved to avoid collision, gone off the road and hit the tree head on. The other car had slowed briefly, long enough for the summer visitor to see the familiar "76" at the beginning of the license plate, and then sped on in the direction of Summertown. The man could not describe the car beyond the fact that it was "some dark color, maybe black, maybe blue," and he did not see the rest of the license number.

They never learned anything more about the car or its driver or occupants. Just the "76" number that was the prefix for the license plate of every car owned and registered on the Island. So Charles Winderman knew that his wife had been killed by some islander, not by a summer visitor.

He had always preached—and still did, to the fond amusement of his family—that "Love is the key." A worthy and salutary sentiment, but after that night he had not really believed it. He knew from then on that death is the key.

WASPs Don't Cry

"Ellen? It's Bonjy. How are you feeling this pretty morning? I just wanted you to know that I did have a talk with Mr. Winderman. About Nancy's young man and the birthday party. I know you were beginning to think I wasn't going to talk to him at all, but it was just a matter of catching him at the right time. In the right mood. He promised to think about it, but if you want my opinion, I'm afraid he's made up his mind. I really don't think he's going to change. I'm sorry for Nancy, of course. And I know it was important to you, too. Anyway, we tried."

So. Ellen had indeed thought that Bonjy was reneging on her promise to make an effort in Nancy's behalf. Well, now Bonjy had, and nothing had changed. Ellen was willing to accept Bonjy's assessment of Ah-boo's state of mind, especially after what Christopher had told her.

She looked up Roger Bernstein in the Island phone book. Even though she didn't know him well, she had always found him easy and delightful.

"Mr. Bernstein? This is Ellen Winderman, Lawrence's wife."

"Sure, Ellen. How's the young mother?"

"Not all that young, but fine, thank you. I wonder if I could come talk to you about something? About Ah-boo's party. It won't take very long."

A pause, then a friendly response. "I've got a couple of things to do in town, but after that I'm always good for a cup of coffee. Why don't you meet me at Ellihew's? Up by the bank."

"Yes, I know where it is."

"In about an hour? Quarter of eleven?"

"I'll be there. Thanks very much, Mr. Bernstein."

"I'm Roger to all the Windermans."

"Then thank you, Roger."

She did not know him at all well. Although he was invited to various family functions, like the birthday party and the tennis tournament, he was really Ah-boo's friend, not the family's. But what she knew of him she liked. He had a cynical—no, that was the wrong word—a skeptical, sardonic view of life that appealed to her. It was not her own view of life, but Roger Bernstein was amusing, almost affectionate in his way of mocking pretension. An ugly little man, but a nice ugliness, a charming homeliness. He could not be expected to help her in any way against his closest friend, but perhaps some advice, some useful insight . . .

Why am I going through all this? Everybody else thinks it's silly or hopeless or, worst of all, trivial. Well, perhaps not quite everybody. The selectman, Anthony's father, seemed to think it was worth an unusual effort. And Anthony, who was at least angry about it. And of course Christopher. Nancy herself was one of those who considered it hopeless, as no doubt it was.

But Ellen knew why she was committed to trying every possibility. Ah-boo did not have the right to push everyone

around, to have everything his way. Not fair to all these people who had their own lives, their own homes, their own
loves and marriages. Oh, Charles Winderman was unques-
tionably benevolent. Nothing malicious or cruel. And she
knew enough history to be aware that the benevolent despot
was often the most effective ruler, his people basking in the
glow of his kindly wisdom and total authority. But suppose
one didn't happen to agree with all the decisions? People
should have the right to decide some things for themselves,
even if they made mistakes.

This was more than Nancy's happiness or unhappiness on
a given occasion. That would pass. Ah-boo's reign would en-
dure.

Ellihew's, a cross between a coffee shop and a restaurant,
was on Summertown's Main Street two doors above the
bank. Except for the installation of a picture window, it had
not changed in twenty years. No need for it to change. Convenient to both the bank and the post office and within walking distance of every shop on Main Street, it had a large natural constituency. Ellen seldom came here, but she knew it had
a reputation for good strong coffee and fresh pastry. A long
wooden counter with leather stools stretched in front of the
kitchen area. The rest of the room was filled with high-
backed wooden booths. It was fiercely old-fashioned.

Ellihew's was crowded when Ellen walked in at exactly
quarter to eleven. Because of the high-backed booths, she had
to walk through the room peering at customers before she
could be sure Roger Bernstein was not there. When she asked
a waitress, the girl told her that Mr. Bernstein always came in
for a coffee and would surely be along in a few minutes.

"That's his booth, next to the corner," she said. "He won't
mind you sitting in it till he comes."

Always grateful for resting places, Ellen started to slide
into the seat facing the entrance, but the waitress stopped

her. "That's his seat," she said. "But you can take the other one."

In New York City Ellen had had a dozen years' experience in restaurantism. She knew how difficult it was, even after steady patronage and tips to headwaiters, to be treated as a special customer, to get a good table even on short notice, to be greeted cheerfully by name, to be told on arrival—most gratifying of all—"I have two orders left of soft-shell crabs. Shall I save one for you?" In her working days at Bendel's, she had been able to achieve this kind of clout only at Le Printemps—and then she had lost it when Gustave retired. At Ellihew's, Roger Bernstein plainly had the clout.

He came in a few minutes later, bustling a bit, his arms filled with paper bag packages. "Sorry to be late," he said. "Got trapped by one of those Main Street conversationalists. How are you?" He put his packages on the floor under his seat and sat down opposite her. "You certainly look blooming," he said with a smile.

The waitress was quickly beside him.

"Morning, Jenny. What do you have to make us fat and happy?"

"Good croissants," she said. "And a terrific Danish with grape jelly and sprinkled almonds."

"What would you like, Ellen?"

"Just coffee for me, I'm afraid. I had all the breakfast I'm supposed to eat."

"Protein toast, right? Without butter. And a small glass of juice?"

He spoke with such eager disapproval that she laughed with him. "And skim milk," she said.

"Ugh. Well, if you're supposed to have milk, how about a cappuccino? It's very good. I get them to make it with double cinnamon. And whipped cream on top."

"Oh, I *can't*," Ellen said. She looked up at the waitress. "Just plain coffee for me, thanks."

"Sad," Roger said, shaking his head. "Well, I'm not pregnant this summer, and this is my breakfast. So I think I'll have cappuccino à la Bernstein. Do you mind if I have a Danish?"

"No," Ellen lied.

"Okay, Jenny, your grape-and-almond Danish." Apparently someone came in that he recognized, for he waved in the direction of the entrance, then looked quickly back to her. He lowered his voice to a conspiratorial whisper and leaned across the table. "If you look at them too long, they come right over to the booth. You have to do a very quick hello."

He looked impish in this mood. Very bright brown eyes full of rather wicked fun. His brown-gray hair was receding in two V-shaped spots that added to his demonic look. But a nice demon.

"How did you get to be such a big hit here?" she asked. "The waitress wouldn't let me sit on your side of the booth. She said that was your seat."

"Oh, I come here pretty much every day, whenever I've finished whatever I have to do in town. After a couple of years they began to notice me. Especially in the winter, when there weren't so many people to look at. Besides, Lew Ellihew, the owner, he and I are in the cribbage club. You know, you'd think that if you were a woman named Ellihew, and you had nine months of pregnancy to think about it, you could pick some other name than Lew. Lew Ellihew. Have you picked out a name yet?"

"We're all set on a boy's name, but there's a big argument about a girl's name."

"Then it's sure to be a girl. What's the boy's name, Ah-boo Two? Ah, Jenny. In the very nick of time. That looks pretty good. Sure you won't change your mind, Ellen?"

It looked better than pretty good. It looked glorious. The cappuccino was in a big brown mug and on top was a thick cloud of whipped cream. The Danish was large, thick and drooling with grape jelly. Ellen's plain mug of coffee squatted in front of her, stark and loathsome. Her stomach lurched in protest.

"I can't stand it. Could I please have a Danish too?"

Both Roger and Jenny beamed. "Coming right up," Jenny said.

And sure enough, in a single minute she was back to place the incredible treat in front of Ellen. Ellen took a large bite and closed her eyes so that she could concentrate on the soft satin sweetness of the grape jelly. "Wurra, wurra, wurra," she said at last. "That's what Tiggers like."

"Everybody needs to misbehave once in a while," Roger said. "That's what life is for." He put a spoonful of whipped cream in his mouth, then licked his lips in appreciation. His mouth was small. His face came down from a very broad forehead and bright eyes to thin cheeks and the small mouth and finally a small sharp chin. All the content of his face was in his eyes. "Now that I've seduced you, which is what men of my age and disposition are supposed to do, what did you want to talk to me about?"

"Well, first, this isn't private. I mean, I know what close friends you and Ah-boo are. I'm not asking you to keep this to yourself."

"Okay. Stipulated. I'm to be as loose-lipped as I like." He grinned at her. "What's the problem?"

"My daughter Nancy. Stepdaughter, I should say. She wants to invite her boyfriend to the birthday party—has already invited him, actually—and Ah-boo said no."

"Yeah, I heard about it. From Charles himself. Too bad."

"You know Ah-boo's rule? That every member of the family can invite one guest?"

"Know it? I've been his designated guest ever since I moved here." He bent forward to take a big bite of Danish and another dollop of whipped cream, then looked up at her.

"You left out the part about the boy being an islander. And not just an islander but Tony Balto's son."

Ellen was trying not to gobble. She had hoped to leave half the Danish on her plate, but she already knew that would be impossible. At least she put it down now and wiped her hands clean, just as though she were finished. A false, temporizing gesture. "The family tells me that Ah-boo has never vetoed anyone's guest. Never. This is the first time."

"That so? Well, you know, Ellen, it really is his birthday and his party. He ought to have it his way, don't you think?"

"Roger, that's what everybody in the family says all the time. It's his this or his that, so shouldn't it be his way? Can I say one sentence off the record? One you won't repeat?"

"Sure."

Ellen could tell he was interested. And also that he liked her. It made her feel certain she could trust him. "I think it would do Ah-boo a lot of good," she said, "if he didn't get his way all the time. Maybe he should lose a couple."

Roger Bernstein threw back his head and whooped. "Great," he said. "Wonderful. I won't tell, but you ought to let me. Charles would enjoy it."

"Anyway, Ah-boo has never even met Nancy's friend, Anthony Balto. I have, and he's very attractive and has nice manners. Better than some of the Winderman grandchildren, to be honest. But Ah-boo just said no. Anthony is an islander and an Italian and in the building business. It's nothing but prejudice."

Roger put the heels of his hands on his forehead and rubbed them back over the two balding spots. "Yes, I know Anthony too. A good kid. Better than his old man. Straighter, anyway."

He looked at her, considering whether or not to say something. He finally decided yes.

"Listen, Ellen. 'Nothing but prejudice,' you say. Prejudice is a very tricky business. Not too easy to get it just right. I'm about twice as old as you, I'd guess, and I'm not sure I've got it right. Even though I've been a kike all my life. I'm not one of those Jews who was eighteen years old before he found out what it meant to be Jewish. No sir, I got into that early. Four years old I knew what a kike was. Me. And not just a kike. There are lots of them. An ugly little kike. You can pick up a lot about prejudice if you're an ugly little kike and keep your ears open. I had big ears." He pulled on his right earlobe and smiled at Ellen. "Still do. You know, if I hadn't been what I was, grown up what I was, I could never have written that book about Tarzan. The book gave me everything I wanted. Enough money to live on the rest of my life. Time to read everything I wanted to, time to talk to people and listen to people without having to hurry on to something else. Time to play all the games I enjoy playing and eat good food. This good cappuccino. That tasty Danish I just demolished. And to live here on this beautiful Island and find out what all my friends and enemies and neighbors are up to. All from that book about a handsome, tall, powerful, brave, sexually attractive Jew who wins everything. I still read it once a year on my birthday, and I have to admit I think it's a very good, very funny book. I'm proud of it. But I know I couldn't have done that unless I'd been an ugly little kike. I have to ask myself though, a real question: If I could have been someone else— say, a rich good-looking WASP—and not have written *Bernstein of the Apes,* what would I pick?" Roger Bernstein shook his head. "I have to ask the question, but I don't have to answer it." He gave an elaborate shrug of his thin shoulders. "A good thing," he whispered, his eyes twinkling, "because I'm not sure what I'd say!

"It was very interesting when I first came here, when I bought the house and decided to live here all year around. Not many people did that then. Those days you were either born an islander and lived here, or you were a summer visitor and didn't live here. Well, that first winter I lived here, I couldn't *buy* a good morning from anybody on Main Street. Funny, nobody seemed to notice me. I knew I was short but not *that* short."

Although he was laughing at himself, enjoying the story, Ellen could imagine how grim that first winter must have been. Grim and lonely. "How did you stand it?"

"Oh, I just pretended I didn't notice they weren't noticing me. I'd go on saying good morning to anybody I recognized. I joined everything I could, the cribbage club, the pinochle club, anything that didn't have admission standards. I attended every town meeting or open hearing, keeping my mouth shut but listening to every speaker with rapt attention. Bernstein was a first-class listener, but he never stuck in his own nosy opinions. And I used the library a lot, and I bought everything I needed from the Island stores. Never ordered anything from the mainland. I was one of the most frequent shoppers you ever saw. If I needed a hammer and nails, I'd buy a hammer the first day, but only after asking a lot of questions about which one to pick, and then I'd come back the next day and go through the questions all over again for the nails. People love to give advice. They began to get used to me. I got all my meals at the few Island restaurants that stayed open for the winter. I was a very good customer. And eventually it all worked out. It just took time."

"Like this reserved booth," Ellen said.

"Yeah. In July and August it's pretty busy here. Of course, in the winter it's not so crowded, but they save it for me anyway from ten-thirty to noon. And you know something?" He leaned forward again with conspiratorial glee. "I like it."

"You mean so much for prejudice?"

"Oh, I won't go that far. I still have my many detractors and always will. That's all right. I'll defend to the death your right to hate me, once you get to know me. And vice versa. It's only the strangers that get to you. But most people on the

Island accept me now. Or"—he waved one hand—"at least tolerate me. We get along."

He used his hands when he talked. Quite graceful hands, considering the rest of his appearance. Long, thin fingers, very clean hands.

"Well, Anthony Balto is a complete stranger to Ah-boo."

"Charles is something different. This is going to be a bit complicated. I suppose you know how Charles and I got together. My book would never have been published without him. His testimony not only saved the book. It helped make the book a big success. And he didn't stop there. He, or at least his family's bank, made good investments for me, and Charles introduced me to the Island and then helped me find my house. Oh, I owe Charles a lot, although that isn't why we're friends. You can be grateful to someone without liking him. In fact"—he lowered his voice again and leaned forward —"that's usually the way it is with gratitude."

He had a way of imparting his opinions as though they were secrets being shared only with her. This gave their talk a coziness that Ellen found very enjoyable.

"Now Charles and prejudice. Charles doesn't hate Anthony sight unseen, which is my idea of prejudice. And certainly not because he's Italian. Charles is much too civilized, much too educated for that. I mean, a man who has a Jew for his best friend isn't going to go around hating somebody who is only an Italian." He smiled with delight at his own comment and repeated, "Only an Italian. My guess is that Charles doesn't have any emotion about Anthony personally at all. He just doesn't want to invite him to his house."

Ellen shook her head. "But isn't that like not wanting a Jew in your country club? Or not wanting a black to eat in your restaurant?"

"No, not at all. Well, I don't know, maybe it is, but that isn't what I mean. It has nothing to do with Anthony being Italian or anything about Anthony as a person. But it's got a

lot to do with his being in the Balto clan, the biggest construction gang on the Island. You know those blue notebooks
Charles keeps, his sort of house history?"

"Of course. I read them as soon as I joined the family.
Before, actually, while Lawrence and I were engaged."

"Then you know all the trouble Charles had getting work
done on his house, especially in the earliest years when he
and his wife were knocking themselves out trying to fix up
that old wreck of a place. Charles's account is, let us say, one-
sided. He wrote down a lot about his frustrations, all the
delays, the shoddy work, the high costs, but he didn't write
anything about how demanding he may have been, or how
impatient. These people here, they don't take too kindly to
summer visitors trying to push them around or hurry them
along. And also the Island was relatively primitive then. The
building trades weren't as organized or as skilled as they are
today, but you don't read anything about that in Charles's
notebooks. And he himself wasn't as tolerant then. To say
nothing of Anne, who was a very determined woman. Oh,
the notebooks are heartfelt all right, but I doubt that they
provide what you and I could call a rounded picture. But all
of that really got to Charles, and it stayed with him. So now
that he's seventy, he's not about to treat the son of Tony
Balto, the shogun of all the builders and head selectman besides, as an honored guest. Especially not at the celebration of
his seventieth birthday. For him, this is much more than a
special birthday. This is a great big important *family* event.
He may not show it or talk about it"—Roger leaned forward
to deliver another significant opinion—"WASPs don't talk
about these things, you know—but it's there.

"And then there's another thing. Or at least I think there
is. I don't have any proof. You know about Anne's death?"

"Of course. She was killed in a car accident. Twenty years
ago or so."

Roger shook his head emphatically. "No, Ellen. No, she

was killed in an accident caused by an Island car. Forced off the road by a car driven and occupied by a person or persons unknown but living on this Island. And whoever it was didn't even stop. Yeah, it was twenty years ago, but as far as Charles is concerned, it's yesterday. He remembers."

"And you think he holds that against all islanders?"

"I don't know. As I say, I haven't any proof. It was very hard to help Charles after Anne's death. He just closed up and wouldn't talk about it, wouldn't let anything out. WASPs don't cry, you know."

"But even if—Roger, even if you're right and it still— haunts him, what does that have to do with the Balto family? Anthony must have been—what? Four or five years old at the time."

"He's an islander. One of them did it."

"But that doesn't make any sense. It's not reasonable."

"My dear Ellen. You're a sensible, lovely woman and a delightful addition to the Winderman family. You're not going to sit there and insult my intelligence, as well as your own, by suggesting that in matters of the human heart, you expect anybody to be reasonable?"

"But that really is prejudice."

"Sure it is. Don't you have any prejudices?"

"Of course. I guess everybody does. But in this case my prejudice is all in favor of Nancy and Anthony. What can I do?"

"You're asking for advice?" Roger Bernstein finished his coffee and leaned back in his seat. "What can anybody do? All you can do is play your own cards, whatever you were dealt. Just as Charles Winderman is going to play his."

"I really hurt for Nancy. She's being treated unfairly. But there's something else I have to say. Anthony Balto is a very handsome, charming young man who happens to be of Italian extraction. But right now he's being treated"—on impulse she put her hand on Roger Bernstein's arm—"just like an ugly little kike."

Roger Bernstein stared at her. She could not read his face, but she knew he was not offended. After a while he put his hand over hers and patted it twice. "You're quite something," he said. "Lawrence is very lucky."

"Yes, and Ah-boo is very lucky to have you as his friend."

He sustained the seriousness for another moment. Then he laughed and said, "Well, I suppose that's enough mutual admiration for one morning. If you're not going to eat the rest of that Danish, I'm not going to let it go to waste." He reached over and took it from her plate.

Okay, Ellen thought, you deserve it.

A Man Around
the House

"God damn it," Lawrence said as soon as Martha left. He
hated change, whether in business affairs or family matters
because it always brought uncertainty. And this event was
worse because the change had not yet actually happened,
which meant that even the uncertainty was uncertain. "She
could at least have waited till the summer was over. Only
another week."

"Maybe she wanted to announce it while we were all here
together," Ellen suggested. "And while Richie was here too."

"Yes, well it's still inconsiderate. Now there will be a big
fuss. Not just Ah-boo but Brad and Sue, too. Brad's going to
be furious, and Sue will egg him on."

"I think it's her own private business," Ellen said. "After
all, she's forty. She can make up her own mind."

"Nothing is ever private business in this family," Lawrence said.

He told the children that evening.

They were all having cocktails on the deck while the

swordfish was cooking on the charcoal grill. Lawrence carefully worked his two spatulas under the five-pound slab of fish so that he could lift it from the grate and turn it over without tearing the meat apart. He had been grilling swordfish ever since he first moved into his own house. It was one task he never delegated to Howard or Bryan. Ellen watched him smoothly flip the fish.

At first, last summer, she had allowed three quarters of a pound per person, but that had proved to be not nearly enough for Howard and Bryan, so now she allowed a pound each. Even so, they always finished the full five pounds. Bryan argued that she should get six or seven pounds, even if it meant having leftover swordfish. Cold swordfish was delicious, he insisted. "Listen," Ellen said, "cold swordfish was what Lizzie Borden had for breakfast the morning of the murders."

The upper side was now a deep golden brown with white stripes from the bars of the grate. Lawrence put evenly spaced butter slices on the fish, closed the lid of the grill and looked at his watch. He could ignore the grill for ten minutes.

He picked up his martini, took a swallow and looked around at his children. "There's some important family news," he said in an even voice. "Your Aunt Martha is going to get married."

Bryan got there first. "Oh no, not *again.*"

"Is it Richie?" Nancy asked.

"Who else?" Bryan said with scorn. "Is she going to marry somebody else after shacking up with him all summer?"

When Lawrence said nothing, Ellen stepped in. "Bryan, that will do."

"What will do?" Bryan asked innocently.

"Where will the wedding be?" Howard asked, in what for him was considerable alarm. "It isn't going to be here, is it? Sam's coming this week." His college roommate's visit would, clearly, be spoiled by a family wedding.

"I doubt it," Lawrence said. "Unless she thinks Richie is about to escape."

All the children laughed, as they were meant to, but Ellen thought it too cruel for laughter.

They discussed Martha and Richie until the swordfish was done. Ellen had to go inside to cook the corn Nancy had stripped for her and to get the platter of sliced tomatoes from the refrigerator, but she still could hear the chatter on the deck. Aunt Martha was not getting a particularly good shake from her nephews and niece, or from her older brother.

When the corn water came back to a boil, she turned off the flame and set the timer for five minutes. She never minded coordinating her kitchen with the grill when it was sword-fish, because she knew she always had exactly twenty-five minutes from the moment Lawrence put the fish on the fire. Timing was far more hazardous when Lawrence was grilling steak or chicken or butterflied lamb, but since everyone liked the charcoal flavor, she acquiesced. But on those occasions, especially with chicken, she made sure to have dishes that she could cook and then keep warm in the oven until Lawrence was ready, which might be five or ten minutes either side of his original pronouncement. She did not know why a man capable of running a good-sized bank was so consistently un-able to predict when a piece of chicken would be cooked through.

After five minutes she poured out the corn water, and sure enough, here was Lawrence coming through the sliding screen door with his platter. She put half-a-dozen ears in the long wooden bowl, spread a clean dish towel over them to keep them warm and handed the bowl to Nancy.

"What I want to know," Nancy said, as they sat down and Howard began pouring wine, "is how does Christopher feel about all this?"

"Who cares?" Bryan said.

Considering Bryan's contribution to the chain-saw accident and the fact that Christopher was still in bandages, Ellen thought this excessive, but she decided to leave this one to Lawrence. Lawrence said nothing.

"No, I mean it," Nancy said. "I don't worry about Amy. She's more peaceful about everything, and she's off at college anyway and has a lot of friends. But Christopher's different. Maybe it will be good for him to have a man around the house."

"Well," Lawrence said dryly, "it's not as though there wasn't usually a man around Martha's house."

"Just the same, I hope they get along," Nancy said.

Ellen hoped so too, although she had no reason to expect it. She could not see Christopher and Richie becoming buddies. In fact, Christopher was capable of taking away from Bryan the title of most difficult Winderman stepchild.

After dinner Brad and Sue came over for their scheduled bridge game and coffee. As Lawrence had foreseen, general disapproval was firmly expressed.

"It's not that I have anything against Richie personally," Brad said with clear distaste, "except that maybe he's five years younger."

"*And* a fortune hunter," said Sue, brandishing a term that Ellen had not heard used seriously in years.

"We can't be sure of that," Brad said in a tone indicating that it was, however, almost certainly true. Brad and Sue had their positions established in advance, as they usually did. "What we do know is that Martha can't handle marriage, at least not for long. It'll just be another mess, like with Don and with Cuff. Lawrence, we really have to protect her from this. And you too, Ellen," he added politely.

He was always nice about including her, although usually a few seconds late. She looked at his concerned face. He meant well, more consistently and sincerely than perhaps anyone else in the family.

"Come on," Lawrence said, hoping to derail this family discussion, "let's get down to bridge."

Ellen had learned to play bridge in college and had kept up with it because she enjoyed it, but playing with Lawrence had required learning a whole new set of conventions. He was very precise and expected her to be equally accurate in bidding and play. He never forgot what cards had already been played in a hand, and his knowledge of odds and probabilities was extensive. Because Ellen was a good learner, they usually won, although she had enjoyed bridge more when she had played with less fierce concentration.

Her favorite partner in the family was Martha, not because she was the best (although she was) but because she was the most imaginative and unpredictable. Three or four times a night Martha would double because she didn't like the "smell" of the bidding, and most of the time she collected. Martha also bluffed and usually got away with it because of her reputation, and she could sense the chance for a slam even when the point count said it wasn't there. Playing with her or against her was a challenge. Lawrence was so meticulous that there was little opportunity for Ellen to be daring. Brad was much more slapdash than Lawrence. His real game, as to be expected in the advertising world, was gin rummy, at which he was unbeatable in the Winderman family. Sue's bridge game was earnest and sound but unimaginative. She played by the book, so one never had to wonder if she was making a deceptive play. All four of them liked to win, but so did all the Windermans.

Ah-boo had started early with each of the grandchildren, patiently teaching them hearts and concentration until he thought them ready to graduate to bridge. And it was not just the regular card games. He was willing to teach backgammon or chess or cribbage to anyone who was interested. If you were a Winderman, you were sure to learn about competition at an early age.

Tonight Brad was willing to stick to bridge during the course of each hand, but during shuffling and dealing he kept returning to Martha and Richie. "Personnel," he said angrily at one point. "Personnel departments are necessary, I admit, to keep track of payroll and benefits and employee grievances and all that, but who needs a personnel consultant? They're always expensive, and half of what they tell you you already know, and the other half probably doesn't apply to your company."

"Deal," Lawrence said.

After another hand Brad said, "Has anyone talked to Ah-boo? He must be in shock. We tried to call him, but Bonjy said he was at the Pearsons' dinner party at the club. Poor Ah-boo."

"One no trump," Lawrence said.

Still later in the evening Brad said, "What gets me is that Martha never seems to learn. What the hell is she doing even thinking about getting married again? She ought to realize she isn't cut out for it."

Sue agreed. "Marriage has to be worked at," she said with the confidence of a woman who has married only once and who has four children to show for it.

An hour's further discussion produced neither fresh ideas nor additional information. Brad lost his temper twice while talking about Martha's poor judgment. When Ellen excused herself to go to bed, they were still at it.

Ah-boo was heard from early the next morning. He summoned a council with Lawrence and Brad at his house, the daughters-in-law not invited. Just the battleships this time, no light cruisers. Ellen would have liked to attend, just to hear Ah-boo's position, but Lawrence would tell her the gist of it.

Such a beautiful day, sunny and quiet. The air was still warming up from the night, although later it would be hot because there was no breeze. She decided to go to the beach before it got too warm. This late in pregnancy she seemed to feel the heat more, although she wasn't sure there was any biological basis for this. Perhaps it was just that everything now started from a higher base of discomfort. She would be glad when it was over and there was a real baby to show for it.

In the bedroom she took off her clothes and looked at herself before putting on her suit. She had loved looking at her bare body all through the pregnancy, and still did. At the very beginning, she had been pleased that nothing showed and her figure was still good. She had nice long legs, an only slightly rounded belly (just enough to be sexy, Lawrence said) and good healthy breasts that, thanks to exercise and good luck, had not begun to sag. Then after a few more weeks she became impatient for it to show and was very pleased when she could tell by sight that her breasts were a little bigger, her belly a little rounder. To friends, to colleagues at work, she probably looked as though she were just putting on a little weight, but she could walk around saying to herself, it's not weight, folks, it's a baby. The middle months were, visually, less exciting. While she enjoyed the swelling progress, it went slowly, and of course then the whole world could see she was pregnant—but not very pregnant.

This past month or so all the excitement had come back. When she looked at herself now, she could see that she was grotesque. Her arms and legs were still slim, almost normal, but in between came this huge naked bulge extending from her hair—almost hiding it, in fact—all the way up to her chest. And right in the middle came her now protuberant navel. Her breasts were markedly bigger and heavier. She wouldn't want them to be this big all the time, but it was lovely for the time being. Even her nipples were bigger. Her body was so unabashedly, so insistently grotesque that she found it exciting. Thank God Lawrence did too. Her face was fuller, too, especially in the cheeks, and the glow of her skin— part summer tan and part sheer good health—went well with her soft, deep brown hair. As Roger Bernstein had said yesterday, she was certainly blooming. As soon as the baby was born, she intended to cut her hair short. She wanted to be thin and trim everywhere. Lawrence would object, but he would just have to indulge her. Eventually she would grow it back for him, but for a while she wanted to become the ever-so-sleek-and-slim Ellen Winderman.

Reluctantly she got into her pink-and-green flowered suit, the silly tie-on pants and the big, floating, cover-up dress. She much preferred herself naked. She wished for the fiftieth time in the last few months that Bendel's carried maternity clothes. Style would have made pregnancy so much simpler. She left a note for Lawrence on the kitchen counter, and got her paperback and her folding aluminum chair. She had never sat on a beach chair in her life until a few weeks ago when Nancy, seeing her stretched out on her back on the sand, called "Whale ahoy!" Everybody laughed, including Ellen, but next day she brought the chair.

She walked down the sandy path that led to the tennis court, where Nancy and Bryan were playing brother-sister doubles against Charlie and Anne. The grandchildren usually preferred singles, dismissing doubles as an old folks' game, but this close to the tennis tournament, everybody wanted to get in last-minute practice, so the court was in too much demand for singles. She watched them for a few minutes because these were the best players among the grandchildren. Bryan and Charlie, both bare-chested, were outstanding, although Bryan was steadier. It was early in the morning for Bryan to be playing, but he hoped to win this year. Of course, the handicap system was designed so that the best player didn't necessarily win. Besides, Brad was still the best in the family, although, since he was forty-four and Bryan eighteen, that wouldn't be true for more than a year or two longer. Anne, at fifteen, was already better than Nancy. She had her father's height and strength, and Ellen knew she had been taking lessons all winter long. Often when the court was not in use for a game, Anne could be found here, banging balls against the backboard in solitary concentration, her long brown ponytail flying behind her. Anne had inherited the bony Winderman face, but it never seemed to bother her that she was not as pretty as Nancy or Amy or even her little sister Alice. Anne had Sue's energy and determination, but somehow with Anne the effect was nicer. Doubles was not her game. She was better at singles, where her long legs and speed could carry her all over the court. Nancy was playing well, Ellen noticed with pleasure, but the game did not mean as much to her as it did to Anne and the boys.

Ellen watched till the end of the game, and then, when the players changed courts, she walked down to the beach. As she had expected, she had it to herself this early in the morning. Most of the family did not swim until eleven o'clock. She set her chair in the firm sand at the water's edge so that the tail end of the waves could wash over her feet. The surf was mild, as it usually was on such a windless morning. The sailboat and the Whaler bobbed gently at their offshore moorings, their white hulls bright against the blue sea. She found her place in her book and sat back to read.

She had fifteen minutes to herself before the arrival of Richie, her new brother-in-law-to-be. She was not aware of him until she felt a tap on her shoulder, and he said, "Hi, there," in his cheerful personnel voice.

Instead of bathing trunks he wore running shorts, bright blue with gold stripes down the sides and gold piping on the edges. He was deeply tanned, the result of many hours of marinating himself in the sun while bathed in coconut oil.

"Hello," Ellen said. She took off her sunglasses to look at him. "Congratulations."

"Thanks. I haven't heard too much of that." He grinned to show that he didn't care. "Our news doesn't seem to be exactly popular."

Ellen didn't know what to say to that, so she ignored it.

"Are you here for running or swimming?"

"Both," Richie said, "but first the morning run, before it gets too hot. Although I don't really mind the heat too much." He slapped his flat, tanned stomach, making a healthy sound. "Talk to you when I've done my mileage." He looked up and down the beach, choosing his path. "Guess it'll be the lighthouse today. Well, off we go." And he ran briskly away, keeping to the firm sand at the water's edge.

Ellen returned to her book and had twenty minutes to herself before Richie came pounding back. He was sweating when he stopped beside her, but he was not breathing heavily. "Whoo," he said. "That felt good." He slapped his now sweaty stomach, producing the wet smack of a large bluefish flopping against the floorboards of a boat.

"That's what all joggers say. I've never heard anyone say, 'That felt boring.' "

"Aha! An antijogger. Now to cool off."

She watched him plunge into the ocean with the same exuberance. He swam hard through the waves, straight out, as though headed for Europe. When he finally stopped, he turned and waved a distant arm to her. Look, Mommy, how far I swam. Ellen smiled to herself and returned to her book. She wondered if Richie was like that as a lover. If so, he would be a bit tiresome, though perhaps not to Martha. Then the wicked thought occurred to her: if she really wanted a reading on Richie in bed, she could probably get it from Christopher. Or would he spy on his own mother? Yes or no, Ellen hoped he was cutting that out. Something told her that she just might have persuaded him. She felt positive that he would now leave her and Lawrence alone. She had not seen Christopher in a day or so. She wondered how his arm was— and how he was.

Richie took his time swimming back to shore. Ellen finished a chapter before he was once again beside her, now dripping water.

"Feels great," he said. "Aren't you going in?"

"Sure, later. This feels pretty good too. Where's Martha?"

"She said she'd be right behind me, so I guess she'll be along." He moved to one side of her and sat down in the sand above the reach of the waves to dry off.

Ellen closed her book and, to be polite, turned her chair to face him. "When's the wedding going to be?"

"Who knows? We might just run off and do it. After all, we've both been married before." His voice had sounded casual, but now it turned more serious. "Tell me something. You're the most recent person to join this family. What's it like to be an outsider here?"

"Compared to what?"

"Witness is unresponsive." He shrugged and gave an empty smile that quickly vanished.

"I don't mean to be," Ellen said, somewhat annoyed. "It's just that it's a very large subject." She thought a moment. "At first, it was hard for me to keep things straight. Even names and faces. I'd never been in a big family before. I didn't know what was expected. Sometimes I still don't. But on the whole, I was made to feel very welcome. Especially by Ah-boo."

"He's certainly the high muckamuck, isn't he? What he says goes. I can't say he makes me feel very welcome."

No good answer occurred to Ellen.

"How do you get along with your stepchildren?"

"Fine," Ellen said. What is this, a personnel interview? She was not about to discuss the stepchild problem.

But Richie was. "Amy's a cinch, takes everything in stride. But that Christopher, he's a can of worms. I've never seen such a screwed-up kid. Martha doesn't know what to do about him, and at the moment I don't either." The implication was that with more time, the old personnel consultant would surely know what to do.

You might try talking to him, Ellen thought, but she did not say it.

Martha came over the rim of the dune. She had on the salmon-colored bathing suit that fitted her very well and a light cotton beach jacket, striped gray-blue and white. Big, very dark sunglasses. A pale blue beach towel slung over one shoulder.

"Hi," she said. "It's hot. Anybody for a swim?"

Richie scrambled to his feet. Martha dropped towel, jacket and glasses on the sand, and they both went straight into the water.

Martha dressed better than the rest of the Windermans, Ellen thought. Whether it was a bathing suit with just the right accompanying jacket, or a summer dress for an Island dinner party, or a suit for lunch in a good New York restaurant, Martha had good instincts about what would work best for her. This usually meant emphasizing legs and breasts while minimizing neck and, most recently, hips. But she did it with taste. She didn't have to be blatant, because the physical appeal came through anyway. Lucky woman, but she knew how to make the most of it. Martha didn't like to talk about clothes the way Ellen did; she just chose them well and wore them well.

Lawrence and Brad dressed for their professions, banking and advertising, which required Brad to be far more imaginative—even reckless. Lawrence and Brad paid about the same for their business suits and custom shirts, but Lawrence's suits were intended to disappear from view, leaving behind an aura of grave responsibility and judgment, while Brad's suits called attention to themselves: here is a snappy, up-to-the-minute dresser. Ellen did not care for either effect.

But an even greater difference between the brothers was revealed in their informal clothes. For Brad, who led a sportsman's country-club life, it was all bright colors—pink slacks, yellow slacks, fire-engine-red slacks, and green linen jackets as bright as new grass. Flamboyant ties and ascots. Bermuda shorts and socks to dazzle the eyes. Brad had been shattered when Madras jackets went out of style because he owned one of the great collections. However, it would have been fatal for him, at the top of the advertising world, to continue wearing them. He still kept them in a back closet here on the Island, hoping that someday they, like Russian wolfhounds, would return to favor. Even within the almost infinite boundaries of the ad community's standards, Brad's clothes were too flashy for Ellen, but his height and good looks enabled him to carry them off.

Oh dear, and then there was Lawrence. Lawrence was imprisoned by banker gray and banker blue, or at least imprisoned by that mentality. A brown suit, he explained to her, would be a signal to his clients of fiscal irresponsibility. A tweed suit would connote an unsound policy toward investments. Ellen argued that we are now in the 1980s and that bankers didn't have to think that way or dress that way anymore. Maybe not at Citicorp, Lawrence conceded, but the Winderman Trust Company was not a go-go bank. It was a stay-stay bank. "Our customers already *have* their money," Lawrence said. In fact, if they really had their druthers, he would be wearing a frock coat and starched collar. "Well," Ellen suggested, "at least you could wear a bright tie." "Bright ties," Lawrence said, with his banker's smile, "are worn only by Bolsheviks, and you know their attitude toward asset management."

It was not that Lawrence liked conservative clothes. He endured them as a uniform that came with his profession, like a surgeon's mask and gown. Away from the bank, either at home or on the Island, he relished clothes that he characterized as "informal" or "comfortable" or "country style." The correct word was sloppy. Unpressed slacks, corduroy in winter and khaki in summer, sports shirts that he liked because they were "familiar" (old) and loafers or sneakers that had been "broken in" (old).

It was not indifference. He appreciated Ellen's own clothes. He was quick to praise a new dress, and she always sought his vote when she was uncertain which of two outfits worked better for her. But it was almost impossible to make him buy, or even accept as a gift, any new clothes for himself. The one area where Ellen felt she had had some influence was weekend clothes for going out to dinner, either to a restaurant or to the home of friends. On these occasions he would have looked ridiculous in his banking uniform and contemptible in corduroys, and he knew it. He had a few sports jackets and slacks, but they did nothing for him. She went to work and, after six months of his stubborn and sometimes irritated resistance, finally persuaded him into a perfectly plain—and perfect—navy blue blazer. He insisted on changing the buttons because he refused to wear buttons with anchors on them, but he did accept it. He looked wonderful in it, but now she could never get him to wear anything else. She had plans, however. One must consider the long term of marriage and husbands and what husbands should wear. She looked forward to the project, even though she knew there would be areas of total intransigence.

Nancy, on the other hand, was easy. She loved clothes, and although her taste was sometimes shaky, as was to be expected in a twenty-year-old girl, she was eager to hear advice and usually took it. They had fun together with clothes. Too bad that Ellen was too tall for Nancy to wear most of her clothes. Sweaters and shoes and jewelry were about all that Nancy could borrow.

Ellen wondered if she and Sue would ever be close enough for her to give Sue advice. Sue could use it, but Ellen wouldn't dare offer it, and she doubted that Sue would accept it. Sue spent enough money on clothes, but she had a tendency to go overboard, both on color and on drama, probably under the influence of Brad's advertising world. Shorter than both Ellen and Martha and with a decent but slightly chunky-looking figure, Sue should have concentrated on simple clothes that did not draw too much attention to themselves. Instead, she chose bright colors and too much adornment. She was at her worst in evening clothes and at her best in casual Island dress. Ellen had the impression that Brad didn't care much about women's clothes and simply wanted Sue to be happy, provided she wore the right labels.

Sue should learn from Ah-boo, not from Brad. Now there was Ellen's idea of perfect taste, at least for a man. Of course, it helped to be handsome and distinguished to begin with, but that was only a beginning. Nothing Ah-boo wore, here or in New York, was obtrusive. Unless one was in the clothing business and used to paying attention, one would never notice what Ah-boo was wearing. He just looked right. The occasion didn't matter, from working clothes on Deck Day to black tie and dinner jacket at a formal party in New York. Everything was simple, of excellent quality, perfectly fitted and worn with an air of never giving his clothes a thought, even though Ellen knew that no one could dress so harmoniously without thinking about it.

And I think about clothes too much, Ellen told herself, but that's my profession. She knew she wanted to go back to work after the baby. Not right away, even though Gerry had said she was welcome back at Bendel's the day she got out of the hospital. This was going to be her one and only baby, and she was not going to miss that experience, as so many of her working friends had done. But after the first year she would certainly return, though perhaps less than full time. She had hated to stop two months ago, although a visibly pregnant buyer scarcely fitted Bendel's image. She missed the excitement of the marketplace, the thrill of discovery, the gambles and risks that she constantly had to take to be successful. She could not give that up. Lawrence was very good about her working. He didn't just permit it or approve it, he was proud of her success. Their home might not run as well as it had in Cecilia's day, but Cecilia's replacement was more than satisfactory, and Lawrence took more pleasure in Ellen's career than he did in household perfection. What a splendid husband in so many ways—if only he would be sensible about his damned clothes.

By the time Martha and Richie finished their swim, the four tennis players arrived on the beach, and a few minutes later, Alice and Brad Junior. Alice came bouncing across the sand to tell Ellen good morning. She had almost adopted Ellen since Deck Day, when Ellen had let her use the roller. Then came Sue, wearing her tangerine suit, which was cut low in the back, revealing lots of skin without being sexy (Sue, we *must* have a talk). And then the rest of the children except for Christopher. No one else was missing but Bonjy and the three battleships. This kind of hot, still August day brought the entire clan to the beach. It must be a pretty heavy conference at Ah-boo's house.

"Hey," Martha said, "you haven't had your exercise. I'll walk you up the beach."

"Sure, come on, Ellen," Richie said.

"Now, Richie," Martha said, eliminating him smoothly, "you've had your exercise. I want to talk to Ellen."

Ellen climbed out of her chair and turned toward the lighthouse, but Martha picked up her jacket from the sand and started in the other direction, toward Ah-boo's and Smollett's houses.

"You said 'up the beach.' To me this way is 'down the beach.' "

"Oh no. 'Up the beach' means away from our property in either direction. 'Down the beach' is when you're walking back toward home."

"Well, up or down, you'll have to go a little slower."

"Sorry."

"How is Christopher doing?"

"What? Oh, he's all right, I guess."

"How's his arm?"

"He can't do much of anything, but it's healing, if that's what you mean. Listen, what's going on? I don't like what I hear."

"What do you hear? You mean the family conference?"

"It's not a family conference," Martha explained. "There are three kinds of those, and this one doesn't fit the rules. There's the one with everybody in the whole family, and then there's the one with all adults but no grandchildren, which is always the worst because Sue tries to hog the floor. And then there's the one with native-born Winderman adults only, and it's not that this morning because I'm not there."

"I'm not there either, so I don't know any more than you do."

Martha stopped and got a cigarette and lighter from her jacket pocket. As she lighted, she looked up at Ah-boo's house, which they were now passing. No one was to be seen on the veranda, so maybe the meeting was finished.

"I don't like it," Martha said. "I get the feeling everybody is disapproving of me and Richie. Or worse. What does Lawrence say?"

"I think you really ought to ask Lawrence that," Ellen said after thinking it over for a moment.

Martha faced Ellen, her eyes invisible behind the big, round, very dark sunglasses. "Fuck it," she said in a hard, flat voice. "So don't tell me."

Ellen got angry. She put her hands on her hips. "Why don't you ask me what I think?"

"Okay," Martha said. They were both standing still on the beach in front of Ah-boo's, looking hard at each other. "What do you think?"

"I think it's nobody's business to tell you who you can or can't marry. You're old enough to do whatever you want."

Martha stood there smoking. Because Ellen was down
closer to the water, they were at almost the same eye level.
"Well," Martha finally said, "that's a new one." The mouth
below the big glasses gave Ellen a tiny, almost tender smile.
"I'll tell you what," Ellen said. "If we're going to have a
serious talk, you take off your glasses and I'll take off mine. I
can't see you."
"All right." Martha abruptly removed her glasses and
tucked them in her jacket pocket. "How's that?"
To Ellen's astonishment, Martha's eyes were filled with
tears. Without thinking, Ellen quickly touched her sister-in-
law's shoulder. "What is it?" she asked. "What did I say?"
"You wouldn't understand," Martha said. She shook her
head quickly.
"Try me. Is it because I said you can do what you want?"
"Come on," Martha said. "Let's keep walking."
They walked in silence for several minutes until they
reached the angled stone wall that separated Ah-boo's land
from Smollett's.
"Enough exercise," Ellen said. "You mind turning back?"
"What do you think of Richie?" Martha stopped again.
"What kind of question is that? Does it call for a polite
answer, or am I under oath?"
"Under oath."
"Then no comment."
Martha gave her husky laugh, then was serious. "I mean it.
Go ahead and say what you think."
"All right. I don't think he's any great prize."
"Huh. I'm no great prize myself. I'm forty years old, and I
drink too much for my own damn good. My figure's not what
it used to be. No accomplishments except two divorces and
two children who don't interest me very much. To say noth-
ing of vice-versa. No prize here, kiddo."
Ellen's back was beginning to hurt from walking in sand
and from standing so long with all that weight pulling down

in front of her. She put her hands behind her back at the waist to give herself support. But she could not let Martha go unanswered. She couldn't let Martha run herself down that way, even though what she said was true as far as it went.

"Sure, you drink too much," Ellen said, "but I must say you handle it well. And motherhood isn't your long suit. I don't know that it will turn out to be mine, either. Everybody isn't a born broodmare. But try it another way. You're a ter- rific-looking forty. You have a good face with good bones, and a very sexy body. You can't be in a room without every man being aware of you. You know how many women would kill for that? You dress extremely well. You know instinctively how to look your best any time you feel like it. You have money. You have a good home on the Island and a good apart- ment in New York. You're interesting to talk to. I think so anyway, and there are plenty of women I don't want to talk to at all. And you're a fine tennis player and bridge player. It sounds like a pretty good package to me. Listen, my back is really hurting. Let's walk on back."

"You sure do know how to set a girl up," Martha said, mocking, but she was obviously pleased. "Can I put my glasses back on? This sun is bright. Listen, Ellen. Thank you. It's good to have you in the family. Tell you the truth, I'm not so damn sure about Richie myself. I take it you're not im- pressed."

"I wish I could answer something different."

"The jogging can get on your nerves."

"And the jargon. And the coconut oil."

Martha almost never giggled, but this one was unmistak- able. "And the tummy slap—his own tummy, that is." She tried to imitate Richie but could not get his resonant sound effect of flat palm striking flat stomach. "And then there's the marmalade in his old-fashioneds."

"Marmalade? In a drink?"

"Absolutely. Too much, huh?"

They had returned almost to their starting point. Among the family figures on the beach, Ellen could see her comfortable aluminum chair waiting to receive her.

"You know," Martha said, lowering her husky voice, "I might wind up calling this thing off. Don't say anything. Maybe I'll just put the whole thing down to summer entertainment."

"I've done the same. Women can talk themselves into almost any man. Especially in summer."

"Don't I know. But at least Martha's Caper has stirred up some excitement."

"Do whatever hits you right. Just don't let them tell you what to do."

"I won't. Thanks. God, it's got to be time for a drink."

"With marmalade, of course."

"With marmalade, definitely."

Champagne
Is for Winners

Lawrence was being patient and reasonable. If there was anything Ellen couldn't stand in an argument, it was a patient
and reasonable man.

"It's very simple," Lawrence said. "He isn't a member of
the family, so he can't play in the tournament. It's just like
Angie or Howard's roommate, Sam. They can't play, and
neither can Richie."

"It isn't a bit like Angie and Sam, and you know it. Angie
and Sam are only the boys' friends. Richie is a fiancé. He's
been a guest here all summer. He's been playing family tennis every day."

The pain in her back had gone away, as it usually did when
she sat down. But she was still feeling the heat, so she was
huddled in the one corner of the deck where there was shade
at midday. Lawrence, who never minded hot sun, was slowly
pacing the deck, hands behind his back as he marshaled his
reasons.

"Now, Ellen, it's the Winderman tennis tournament and

always has been. Only the family participates. Only a family member can win."

"Don't 'Now, Ellen' me. I know what the rule is, but it doesn't take fiancés into account. Suppose you and I had been engaged last summer but hadn't married yet. Would I have been allowed to play?"

Lawrence's hesitation went on just long enough to enable Ellen to say "Ha!"

"I don't think so," he finally said, though without great conviction. "But it's entirely hypothetical. Ah-boo is very fond of you and was glad to welcome you into the family. Your question's basically irrelevant. Ah-boo does not want to encourage Richie and Martha. In any way."

"Well, obviously, or you and Ah-boo and Brad wouldn't have spent all morning trying to figure out how to discourage them. Was this the best you could come up with? And besides, how can you say it's irrelevant?"

Lawrence stopped and looked at her with an expression that was not only patient but also considerate. "Aren't you tired after the beach? Isn't it about time for a nap?"

"Don't try to shut me up. I'm not having some kind of pregnancy pout. Look, I'm no fan of Richie or of this marriage, but I think this is flat-out rude. If I were able to play in the tournament, I'd refuse to play because of the way you're treating him. Maybe Martha will drop out."

"Oh, I don't really think so." Judicious voice. "After all, she's played since the very beginning, and she loves it."

Ellen had to admit this. It was hard to imagine Martha dropping out. "If you can stand some advice from someone who is a Winderman only by marriage and not even a man besides, I think the smartest thing you three could do is leave Martha alone."

"What makes you say that?"

She could see she had caught his interest, but she did not want to betray Martha's confidence. "When it comes to her relationship with a man, a woman doesn't like to be pushed around by outsiders."

Lawrence smiled, but it was friendly. "Ah-boo and Brad and I aren't exactly outsiders."

"No, but you are hoping to push her around. I suggest you let her be and see what happens. This business of keeping Richie out of the tournament is silly. Why, it even means that with me and Christopher out, you have thirteen people. How're you going to work with the odd number?"

"It's complicated," Lawrence said, "but arithmetically it can be done."

"Here's the way it works," Lawrence said.

He and Ah-boo and Brad were gathered around her dining room table with the necessary papers, pencils and lists. Lawrence in his favorite ragged yellow sweater, Brad in a chrysoprase crocodile polo shirt, Ah-boo in a quiet blue long-sleeved shirt open at the neck. Ellen had brought them after-dinner coffee, Sanka for Ah-boo, and then sat down at the far end of the table to listen. No one had suggested she leave, so she assumed tacit permission to watch them construct the tournament.

Brad had been observing the family players all month long and keeping track of who was beating whom and by how many games. His job was to recommend the handicaps, which changed from summer to summer as the children grew older and spent more or less time on the tennis court. Brad took his task seriously, always asking who won today, and he made certain that he played each member of the family several times, although his favorite opponent was Lawrence, whom he had been playing every summer for something like thirty-five years. After Brad had made up his own handicap list the day before the tournament, he went over it with Lawrence, just to make sure there were no serious disagreements.

There seldom were. Finally, tonight, they would present the proposal to Ah-boo, who, of course, had the last say. When didn't he have the last say?

Lawrence's assignment was to manage the mechanics of the draw and then to keep the records as the tournament progressed. In the olden days when the tournament first began, this had not been necessary because the total field had consisted of Ah-boo, Anne, Lawrence, Brad and Martha. At the end of each summer they had played normal sets, Ah-boo and Anne spotting the children a few games. The chief purpose was to encourage the children in their annual August progress. But with the addition of more and more grandchildren, with the substitution of nine-point tie-breaker games for sets, with the concept of double elimination and the awarding of the Ah-boo Cup to the winner of the Winderman Open, the keeping of records during the day's matches had become crucial.

"With Ellen and Christopher out, we have thirteen players," Lawrence said. "That means the last name drawn, number thirteen, doesn't play in the first round. In the second round, number twelve gets a by, and so on. If you draw a by, you don't get a win. You just get a delay. None of the four seeds ever gets a by. At the end of the second round, as many as five people *could* be eliminated if they had played two matches and lost them both. By the end of the third round, when ten of the thirteen players have had three matches, five people *must* have been eliminated because five people will have to have lost two matches. I see no reason to change from the nine-point games in the early rounds, and the finals have worked well at fifteen points. But I do have one suggestion, especially with fewer players this year. What would you think of giving the semifinals a little extra importance by making them eleven-pointers?"

"That helps the better players," Brad said. "You can always slip up, hit a couple of bad shots, double-fault once or twice, and you've lost a nine-pointer. A good player is less likely to lose an eleven-pointer."

"That's true," Ah-boo said. "But of course, you're usually down to four good players in the semis."

"But not always," Brad said. "Remember Sue got to the *finals* two summers ago when she had a four handicap."

"Yes, but that's part of the fun," Ah-boo said. "Besides, we changed her to a three last summer. What do you have her down for this year?"

"Three again."

"Let's go over the handicaps," Ah-boo said, "and come back to the semis. Anything else in the way of rules, Lawrence?"

"No. Alice still gets to serve from the service line instead of the baseline. Everything else is straight tennis."

"All right, Bradford. What have you come up with this year? Are you and Lawrence in agreement?" He looked down the table at Ellen, who had thought no one was noticing her presence. "This is my favorite part, Ellen. I find out whether my sons agree with me about my grandchildren's tennis abilities, and"—he winked at her—"I also learn how much older I've grown. I'm afraid my handicap has been increasing the last few years."

"If it was doubles," Brad said, "we wouldn't give you any handicap at all."

"If it *were* doubles," Ah-boo corrected him. "Subjunctive. A condition contrary, unfortunately, to fact."

"Anyway, Lawrence and I agree. We argued about only one, and we'll let you try to guess who it was."

"I hope you argued about me. All right, lay on."

"Okay. Alice gets the maximum, seven points."

This meant that Alice would start each of her nine-point games with seven points and would have to get only two more points to win a match. However, since she was only nine years old and not talented even for that age, she would lose her first two matches and be eliminated, unless someone played carelessly against her. Eight points' handicap would have given her a better chance, but Ah-boo had ruled several years ago that no one could win a match by winning a single point. Everyone thought this was proper—even Alice.

"Brad Junior gets four points," Brad said. "Down one from last year." This meant that if Alice and Brad Junior happened to draw each other, their game would begin with Alice ahead at 7–4.

Ah-boo nodded. "As he should be."

"Now there are a lot of threes. Including, I'm sorry to say, you. But you have plenty of company."

"Yes, but my handicap is getting bigger and theirs are getting smaller. However, I can't in all honesty protest. Who else is three?"

"Sue, as I said. And then most of the other kids: Howard, Nancy, Anne and Amy."

Ah-boo disagreed for the first time. "Howard and Anne are better than Nancy and Amy. Wasn't Howard a three last year, too? Shouldn't he get a promotion?"

"Howard's improved a bit," Lawrence admitted, "but not as much as some of the others. Brad has lowered both Nancy and Amy from four to three, and I agree completely. If we gave half points, then Howard would be two-and-a-half."

"Nancy and Howard play close to even," Brad argued. "Except for his height and reach, they would be dead even."

Ellen listened with amusement. Here were the three Winderman men, all accomplished and successful, one forty-six, one forty-four and the other a few days from seventy, and yet they were treating a family tennis tournament with all the solemnity of a Winderman Trust board meeting. Lawrence and Brad were watching Ah-boo, waiting for his decision to accept or reject their recommendation. Ellen thought she could detect a deliberate delay as Ah-boo thought it over.

"It's a close call," Ah-boo said, and now Ellen was sure

about her hunch. "But I'm afraid I'm going to overrule. It's partly a matter of Howard's pride. Let's make him a two."

"Okay, two it is," Brad conceded, making the change with his pencil. Apparently this sort of thing had happened before, since neither Brad nor Lawrence objected.

"Now what about Anne as a three? She's the most improved player in the family."

"Right," Brad said, proud of his daughter. "She's grown a couple of inches since last summer, and she's got power now. Also she's worked at it, taking lessons all winter and spring. But she had a five handicap last year. We've never lowered a handicap by more than two strokes from one year to another. In fact, a two-stroke drop is very rare."

"That's true," Ah-boo said. "Well, perhaps she shouldn't be punished too much for working so hard. Three for this year."

"Okay," Brad said. "Two for Howard, three for Anne. And Charlie is a two."

"Poor Charles," Charles Winderman said. "I never could stand that diminutive. Even 'Chuck' would be preferable. Yes, two is right. Down from three last year?"

"That's right. And Martha goes up from a one to a two."

"Oho. She won't like that."

"Probably not. She's just as good as ever, serve and ground strokes, but she's definitely slowed down. Anyway, she's still a seed, the fourth seed. Maybe for the last time. And then Bryan gets one point, and Lawrence and I stay at zero. That's it."

"Indeed. All right, I'll make my guess. The one you argued about was Lawrence."

Brad's face broke into a big smile. "You've been keeping your eyes open. I wanted to give Lawrence one point, and he refused to take it."

"I still beat him once in a while," Lawrence said. "That's good enough for a short tournament where anything can happen."

"Fair enough," Ah-boo said. "Or almost fair enough. All right, now about the semifinals. I like Lawrence's idea of an eleven-pointer. Let's try it."

Brad turned to Lawrence. "There goes your chance."

The hot, still weather held. Perfect for tennis.

The Windermans had borrowed a tall green referee's chair and a second long wooden bench from the club, but there still was not enough seating. In addition to the thirteen players and Bonjy, Ellen, Richie and Christopher, there were many guests. Bryan's friend Angie, his constant summer opponent, was now here to root for Bryan. Howard's college roommate, Sam Walsh, another string bean almost as tall as Howard and just as polite and quiet, had arrived for his visit yesterday morning. The Angells, neighbors from across State Road who often played tennis with the older Windermans, were here. Roger Bernstein had never played tennis in his life, but he had not missed the Winderman Open in years. And half a dozen of the grandchildren's friends had come to watch.

Each household had furnished folding chairs or director's chairs in various colors, which were lined up on both sides of the court. There were seats enough for all, although some of the younger spectators preferred to sit on the court surface, leaning their backs against the wire screen. A large water cooler stood at one end of the court. All the players wore sneakers and shorts, except Sue and Martha in tennis skirts, but tops were a matter of free choice. Polo shirts, T-shirts, halters, sports shirts of every kind and color. Bryan and Brad Junior wore no tops at all, a recent concession by Ah-boo.

Just before the tournament began, Richie came up to Ellen. He wore tennis clothes—sneakers and tall white cotton sweat socks with green stripes at the top, green shorts and a white T-shirt—just in case anyone had a last-minute change of mind and allowed him to play. Not a chance, Ellen knew.

"Well," Richie said in what for him was a voice of rare bitterness, "we both seem to be excluded."

Ellen felt embarrassed for him, both for his tennis clothing and for the nakedness of his disappointment. She said, "Next year will be different for both of us."

Richie flashed a wolfish smile with no mirth. "If there is a next year," he said.

At two minutes to ten, Ah-boo, in full tennis whites including his brimmed hat, climbed into the referee's chair, a position he would hold except when he had to play a match, at which time Brad would take his place. Lawrence sat across the court with his clipboard and two ballpoint pens.

Settled in his chair, Ah-boo raised both arms for silence and then declared, "The thirty-second Winderman Open is now open." Clapping of hands around the court. "According to the draw, the first match is Anne, handicap of three, against the top seed Bradford, handicap of zero. The score is three-love, Anne to serve one serve."

Scrambling and scampering, her long brown ponytail flying behind her, Anne gave her father an excellent fight. She was going to be a top player in another year or two, a challenge to everyone. Ellen thought Brad carried her only once when he failed to put a ball away with Anne well out of position. She lost at 9–7, very respectably, and she looked pleased with herself when they shook hands at the net and Brad then hugged her shoulders.

While Martha was trying to warm up Alice with pat balls, Ellen carried her aluminum chair down to the end of the court where Christopher was sitting off by himself. His arm was out of the sling but still had two bandages, smaller now. She put her chair beside him, plainly to his surprise.

"I haven't seen you," she said. "How's the arm?"

He touched the bandages as though he hadn't quite thought about the matter. "All right, I guess."

"Too bad you can't play." When he didn't answer this, she asked, "What would your handicap have been?"

This reached him a little. "I was four last year. I'm sure no more than three this time."

"That's what I think I'd have been if it weren't for this." She patted her stomach. She thought of saying something about Christopher's new stepfather but decided that was not the way to phrase it. "Big news in your family. About your mother and Richie."

He turned to look at her with angry eyes and that familiar twist to his mouth. "Big news. Big deal."

"Yes," Ellen said in a deliberately casual voice, "that's about what I thought you would think. Not too good from your viewpoint. What does Amy think?"

Christopher shrugged, staring at the court where Martha was demolishing Alice as gently as possible. "We don't talk about it."

She wondered if that was possible—and decided that it was. It was also unhealthy. That was one of Christopher's troubles, not talking about things that bothered him. Or even things that didn't bother him. Well, let's have another try at it.

"When do you think the wedding's going to be?"

Silence. He was still staring at the court. Then he said, "Whenever it is, I'm not going."

"Hm. That's pretty extreme. Do you disapprove that much?"

He turned back to her. "Yes."

"I'd think that would hurt your mother's feelings."

There was sudden pain in his eyes that she was sure he would never have chosen to reveal. "I wonder," he said. "Anyway, that's how I feel."

Applause around the court as Martha, who had double-faulted once, finished off Alice at 10–8. Lawrence stood up, giving his clipboard to Howard.

"Oh, my husband's turn. I have to go support him. I'm glad your arm's better." She stood up, smiling at him.

"Thanks. Aunt Ellen."

Practically a burst of friendship.

When Ellen got back to her spot near the net to watch Lawrence play Charlie, Alice almost pounced on her. "Aunt Ellen, did you see? I got a point off Aunt Martha. I almost beat her, and she's the best woman player. It was a deuce match!"

Ellen laughed. "I saw. It was really close."

Indeed, if Martha had made one more mistake in addition to her double fault, Alice would have scored the upset of the summer.

Martha herself came to sit beside Ellen. She leaned over and said quietly, "That's the last time I try to give that little brat a soft serve to hit."

"She's not really a brat."

"Yeah, I know. But any nine-year-old who gets me to ten–eight is a brat. This is going to be a good one."

They both settled back to watch Charlie, a fierce but erratic eighteen-year-old with a two handicap, take on his Uncle Lawrence. To Ellen's dismay, Charlie was not erratic enough in this short match, and he beat Lawrence. He got loud applause, which he deserved, but that left Lawrence only one match away from being eliminated. Lawrence left the court with what Ellen recognized as his strained expression, and he almost snatched the clipboard out of Howard's hand.

Family honor was redeemed in the next match when Bryan, the last of the seeds to play his opening match, destroyed Brad Junior without giving him a single point.

"He's hot," Martha said. "I hope I don't draw him for a couple of rounds."

Ah-boo was now surrendering his referee's chair to Brad, and he came on the court to play his first match, against Howard. The draw had taken place only after the handicaps had been settled, but Ellen was amused that the only handicap Ah-boo had changed, Howard from a three to a two, was an immediate benefit to himself. Ellen was quite sure that Ah-boo appreciated the irony. He did not miss many of those.

"I'm going to watch this one with Roger," she said to Martha, and moved down the court to where Roger Bernstein was sitting with the Angells. She and Roger had said hello when he arrived, exchanging affectionate remarks about Danish pastry. Now he got to his feet to offer her his seat on the wooden bench.

"No, I'm going to stand," Ellen said. "For exercise."

"Okay," Roger said, quick and smiling, "I need exercise, too." He stood beside her, several inches shorter, both of them leaning back against the heavy mesh wire screen. "Look at that old Charles. God, I'd love to see him win the tournament again, although I suppose he never will. He's so bloody wily. I must say, the older I get, the more I appreciate wile. He plays tennis the way he plays backgammon. You think he's giving you something and you reach out for it, and suddenly it isn't there anymore. Oh, look at that."

Ah-boo had barely managed to get to one of Howard's deep shots, and everyone could see him preparing to lob. Howard was already pedaling backward. Then Ah-boo hitched his stroke at the last second and delivered a sliced drop shot just over the net. Howard was still going back when the ball fell in front of him and died. Everyone applauded, including Howard, who patted the face of his racket.

"He won't give you anything," Roger said. "You have to take it from him."

That's right, Ellen thought. He won't give it away. "I was listening to the handicapping last night. Brad said that if this tournament had been doubles, he would have given Ah-boo a zero handicap."

"Well, as they say in the jungle, the legs go first. If Charles can get to the ball, he has all those wicked cuts and slices, but he can't cover the territory. Of course, in my case what went first was the legs and the arms and the shoulders and the belly, if you'll excuse a reference to the belly. Everything went more or less all at once, at about the age of fourteen. In the end, of course, all any of us has left is the brain and the mouth, although age fourteen is a little early to be reduced to that. I heard about Martha and what's-his-name. How's that going down with the family?"

"Terrible, since you ask. Ah-boo and Lawrence and Brad are conspiring to break it up. They wouldn't even let Richie play in the tournament today. Because he's not yet family. And Christopher told me just a few minutes ago that he won't even go to the wedding."

"Well, that's probably the only card Christopher has to play. Oh, Charles!"

Ah-boo had been caught at the net, apparently helpless, but when Howard fired a hard passing shot, Ah-boo anticipated perfectly, took two quick steps, reached way out and tapped the ball in for another winner. Heavy applause for Ah-boo.

Something jogged at Ellen's mind. Something Roger had said at the coffee shop about playing the cards you were dealt.

To everyone's delight, Ah-boo managed to win 9–6. Howard actually seemed proud of his grandfather when they shook hands. And then in the last of the first-round matches Nancy beat Sue, so Ellen's family had split the round, two wins and two losses.

By the end of the second round, after losing for the second time, Alice and Brad Junior were eliminated, as expected, but so was Howard, who had the bad luck to draw his uncle Brad. And by the end of the third round Lawrence was eliminated, along with Sue and Amy, without ever getting a chance to test his zero handicap against his brother. Poor Lawrence, Ellen thought. All he has left now is clipboard duty.

Ah-boo and Nancy were the next to go out, and then finally Martha, who had run up against too many highly mobile teenagers. That left Brad, Bryan, Charlie and Anne for the semifinals. Both Charlie and Anne had lost one match, Charlie to Nancy when he hit a wild streak, and Anne the opener to her father, while Brad and Bryan were unbeaten. But that no longer mattered. For the semifinals all four slates would be wiped clean, and the players would start even, except for their handicaps. Brad's family had done very well with three out of the final four places. The rewards of tennis lessons and country-club life in Glen Cove.

It was after one-thirty by the time they all stopped for sandwiches. This was the one event of the summer where Bonjy drew the line against preparing the food. Making sandwiches for close to thirty people was, she said, too boring, so she had ordered from the Harbor Deli in Summertown. "It's always their biggest order of the year," she told Ellen with pride. "Would you care to guess what thirty roast beef sandwiches cost? In August on the Island? Not to mention thirty white-meat chicken. Of course, they never put in quite enough mayonnaise, no matter what I tell them. Still, for deli food . . ."

Ellen congratulated Nancy, who had played well and had come close to making the semifinals for the first time.

Nancy felt good about herself. "I was okay, wasn't I? I almost had it except for that stupid backhand. I know better than to try to hit a hard backhand when I'm off balance. But I still feel terrific. I just wish Anthony could have been here to see me."

Such a simple wish, so easily granted, but Nancy and Anthony had decided it was impossible for him to come.

Ellen knew she had to say something to Bryan, just to show she was pleased he was in the semifinals. He and Angie Dunlap were sitting cross-legged on the court, wolfing roast beef sandwiches.

"Nice going, Bryan," she said as she came up. "Good luck."

"Hm," he said, making a noncommittal noise through a mouthful of sandwich.

"Don't eat too much," she advised him. "It will slow you down." Immediately she wished she had not tried to be helpful.

"Oh, I think I'll be all right," he said. And then, deliberately, he said, "Hey, Angie, let's try the chicken."

Ellen turned away. She had noticed that Brad, in spite of the long morning's exercise, was eating nothing but a single pickle. The hell with it, Ellen thought.

She ate her own chicken sandwich sitting on the bench with Peggy and Don Angell and Roger Bernstein. It was very hot with almost no breeze. Ellen was glad she had worn her big linen cowboy-style hat to keep off the sun.

Ah-boo joined them. He was cheerful and well pleased with the day. Not only had he won two matches and lost creditably in the other two, but his tournament had gone beautifully. No serious disputes had risen about his line calls as referee, and almost every match had been close enough to be interesting. "That proves that the handicapping was good," he explained with satisfaction.

"I thought after your first match," Roger said, "you were going to make it to the semifinals yourself."

Ah-boo smiled. "Well, I didn't," he said. "I'd need a four or five handicap to do that, and frankly I'd rather have the honor of being awarded only a three. Besides, if I made the semifinals, I probably wouldn't live through them." He leaned across to the Angells. "I don't know if you've heard," he said, "but we're trying something different this year. The semis will be eleven-pointers. Lawrence's idea," he said with a nod to Ellen.

"Have we heard?" Peggy Angell said. "Have we heard? Only from about seven or eight people. In this tournament any change is front-page news."

"Good," Ah-boo said. "That's the way it should be. First,

there has to be an established tradition. Then when you change it, as all traditions should be changed now and then, it's noticed by everyone. And that actually makes the tradition stronger, not weaker. As Mr. Tennyson says, 'God fulfills himself in many ways, lest one good custom should corrupt the world.'"

"Oh, come on, Charles," Roger said. "You're not that much in favor of change."

Indeed he isn't, Ellen thought. How about letting a nice Italian Island boy into your sacred birthday party?

"Change within tradition," Ah-boo said smugly. "Preferably not revolution. Take this tournament. When it first began, thirty-two years ago now, it was just a game, an end-of-August game. Then when the children seemed to enjoy it, Anne and I made a bit more of it. A bit more structure. We decided, for example, that for the tournament, everyone should wear tennis whites. A little extra touch of significance. We did that for many years. Then with all the grandchildren coming along and taking part, it seemed wise to permit a freer dress code. After all, even the professionals were wearing colors, and many in the family felt that different kinds of clothes on the tennis court were, as the young like to say, 'a form of personal expression.' So we changed. I think I may have gone too far in allowing no tops at all for the men, but it was part of the personal expression. Yes, perhaps too far. Even the pros haven't taken that step. Who knows, maybe some day there will be no tops for the women, although not in my time, I can promise you. And as you can see, I myself am still wearing whites and always will. The old order changeth—but not completely. Well, I think it's time for the semifinals."

He walked over to consult with Lawrence.

It's not God fulfilling himself in many ways, Ellen thought. It's Ah-boo. Or rather, Ah-boo *is* God. A benign deity, to be sure. She wondered if he ever thought of himself in just that way, perhaps in those very words. *Good morning, God. How are we feeling today? Shall we pass a miracle today? Let the players wear colored shirts? Make the semifinals eleven points this year instead of nine? We are, after all, a just God, a kindly God. And when we have finished our day's labors and seen that they are good, we will write it all down in the tablets, the blue notebooks, so that all can see what the hand of God hath wrought. God himself, of course, will continue to wear white.*

I've had about enough. I've had about enough.

Because Anne had already played her father once in the tournament, she did not have to play him again in the semis, but this did not help her. She drew Bryan rather than Charlie, and as Martha had said at the beginning, Bryan was hot. Even though Anne started with her 3–1 handicap lead, Bryan was too much for her.

Ellen sat beside Lawrence, who was still holding his clipboard covered with the results of each match.

"Bryan's really playing," Lawrence said in a whisper, trying not to let too much admiration show through.

Bare-chested, gleaming with sweat, his tangled curly hair wet and matted, Bryan was indeed playing beautifully. He was as fast and full of energy as Anne but much more powerful and very steady. When he went ahead at 6–5, Ellen was sure he would win.

"Do you think he can beat Brad?" Ellen asked while they were changing courts.

"Brad hasn't beaten Charlie yet," Lawrence said with his habitual caution. "Though he probably will. I don't know. Brad has every shot, as well as five different serves. Don't get your hopes up."

"Aren't yours up?"

Lawrence didn't answer. Anne served again. Although she must know she had little chance now, she didn't play like it. Bryan had to treat her with respect, bearing down on each shot, playing hard. He ran her out at 11–7.

As she left the court, Anne was both smiling and crying, which struck Ellen as exactly the right combination. She had had a great tournament, especially after losing her opening match, and she couldn't really have expected to beat Bryan. But oh how she must have wanted to. Brad and Sue gave her huge hugs before Brad went out to tackle his son Charlie.

"Charlie's got one chance," Lawrence said as they were hitting their warmups. "He's got to score right away, build on his handicap, get up on Brad four–zero or five–one so that Brad has to play carefully. And even then Charlie will have to be steadier than I think he can be. He can't afford any of those wild errors."

Charlie played for broke, as usual, always hitting out. His big first serve was more likely to go out than in, and when he attacked for winners, as he did on virtually every stroke, he was capable of missing the line by six inches, and once by two feet. Brad had to lose some points to this style of play, but not enough. It was 11–8.

Lawrence wrote down the score, then handed the clipboard and pen to Ellen. "Hold this a minute. I want to say a word to Bryan."

In spite of Bryan's behavior, Ellen had to root for her own family. She wished it could have been Lawrence going out to play Brad. "Tell him to win," she said.

During the intermission Ellen watched Lawrence and Bryan in earnest conversation, standing off by themselves, Bryan nodding his head from time to time. She had heard Lawrence say that Bryan was going to be college-caliber first team—"and not just the freshman team." Looking at Bryan's earnest face, she thought how much better things could be between him and her if only he would let it happen.

Brad, she noticed, was changing. He stripped off his damp yellow shirt and mopped his big chest and shoulders with the towel Sue gave him. He was the only Winderman male with a hairy chest. He shrugged into a peppermint-striped shirt that

Sue also had ready for him. Then he put on his cap, a white strap with a broad visor, white on top, green underneath. He looked big and solemn.

Finally Ah-boo, in his referee's chair, raised his arms. "And now for the finals," he said. "For the Winderman Open championship, Bradford against Bryan. Fifteen points and the winner must win by two points. Bryan's handicap is one point. Gentlemen, take your places."

When they were both on the court, Ah-boo asked, "Do you want a warmup?"

"No," Brad said.

"Yes," Bryan said.

"The rule is that if either player in the finals requests a warmup, there will be a warmup."

Lawrence sat down beside her and took the clipboard.

"What did you tell him?"

Lawrence did not turn to answer her. He was watching Bryan. "I told him to win."

"Why does he want a warmup? He's been playing all day. And he just had a match."

"No, Brad is the one who just had a match. Bryan had the match before. Besides, Brad's been playing all day, too. It's hot and he's forty-four. It won't help him to have to hit a few more balls."

"That sounds unfair."

"And that sounds naïve. Now hush."

During the warmup Brad was wasting no energy. He smoothly returned every ball that was hit directly to him, merely playing it back, never chasing anything that Bryan hit away from him. Brad still used a wooden racket, as did Lawrence. Both claimed it gave them more touch. Bryan's racket, last year's Christmas present, was an Arthur Ashe graphite model with an elongated head and a strange triangular hole in the throat.

"All right, time," Ah-boo announced. "And new balls."

As they went to their baselines, Brad to serve, a clear voice broke the expectant silence. "Go, Bryan!" That was Nancy. Everyone laughed, and even Brad smiled.

Competing shouts of "Go, Brad!" and "Go, Bryan!" until Ah-boo said, "Order on the court, order on the court." When everyone had quieted down, he said, "Brad to serve one serve. Play."

Bryan hit Brad's first twisting serve into the net. "Damn," Lawrence whispered. "Nerves." So much for Bryan's handicap. They were starting even.

But Bryan settled down, and everyone got to see excellent tennis. Unlike Charlie, Bryan played position tennis, hitting deep, heavy ground strokes from side to side, waiting for an opening. He was steady enough to play this way. Brad, of course, could play this kind of tennis all afternoon, varying between flat strokes, topspins and slices but always keeping the ball deep in Bryan's court. Both were having difficulty getting to the net because of the depth of each other's strokes.

At the end of a long point that Brad won, Lawrence said, "Bryan has to put on more pressure. He can't outwait Brad."

They kept trading points back and forth, Brad inching ahead by two at 7–5 and then being cut back to a lead of one, then up to two again at 8–6. Everyone at courtside was completely still during the points. Perfect tennis manners, as was to be expected in this family.

Bryan couldn't bring it back to even. He was one or two points behind, one or two, always in the game but unable to tie it. And then at 12–10 he double-faulted, the first time for either player. Everyone groaned. Bryan shook his head in anger: 13–10. "That's it," Lawrence said quietly.

But apparently Bryan realized it too. With nothing to gain by going on the same way, he cut loose. He served hard, followed his serve to the net for the first time and, catching Brad by surprise, lunged out and caught Brad's return. A desperate shot but it went in. And then he attacked Brad's serve, crossing the baseline to take the ball on the rise, getting to net and, after two tough volleys, winning the point. Brad didn't give him that chance again. His next serve was his deep topspin which kept Bryan back. It was a furious point, Bryan pressing and hitting and running, and Brad banging everything back. Bryan finally saw what he thought was a chance and took a dangerous crosscourt shot.

"Out!" Ah-boo called.

Bryan was at the referee's chair in a second. Everyone could hear him say in a tense voice, "That was on the line."

Ah-boo shook his head. "Sorry, Bryan."

"But it was in," Bryan said. "That was in."

Then Brad waved his racket. "It was good," he said. "His point."

"Sure?"

Brad nodded. "On the line."

"All right; thirteen–all. Bryan's serve."

"Jesus," Lawrence said. "Three high-risk shots in a row. That's some playing."

"Yes," Ellen said, "and some call by Brad."

But Brad did not panic, and Bryan could not sustain his desperate play without mistakes. They split each other's serves to 14–all and 15–all, Brad having match point both times. Then Brad broke Bryan's first service point once again for 16–15. Bryan's next serve was long.

Brad jumped on the second serve and drove Bryan far into the opposite corner where he had to lob. Not deep enough. Everybody could see it. Brad stepped forward quickly. He got in place, turned sideways and stood there waiting for it, staring up into the afternoon sun, keeping track of Bryan's position. Then he slammed it away beyond Bryan's reach.

Bryan, a fragile eighteen-year-old loser, walked to the net to shake hands with his uncle. Ellen was so proud of the open, pleasant look Bryan managed to maintain that she felt a lump in her throat. She knew how much that look cost.

That evening, when they were having cocktails on the deck, Ellen brought out her surprise, a tray with six glasses and a bottle of iced champagne.

"Sam," she said to Howard's roommate, "would you mind passing these glasses around?" She took the bottle of champagne and handed it to Bryan. "Here. This is for you." Bryan looked flustered and, as he so often was with her, suspicious. He accepted the bottle because he didn't know what else to do. Then he said, "What's this for? Champagne is for winners."

"That's right," Ellen said. "We're all very proud of you."

"Hear hear," Lawrence said.

"Yay, Bryan," Nancy said.

Bryan blushed. He tried to hand the bottle to his father. "I don't know how to open these."

"Then it's time to learn," Lawrence said, refusing to take it. "First, you peel off the foil, then you untwist the little wire. Go ahead. It won't hurt you."

Bryan was awkward and slow, but after some cautious twisting he was at last rewarded by the pop of the cork. When the glasses were filled, Lawrence said, "Do you have a toast, Ellen?"

"Yes," she said. "Yes, I do. Here's to Bryan," she proposed, looking at her blushing, impossible stepson. "Not for winning, but for the way you played when you were behind thirteen–ten."

They all raised their glasses. Ellen could see that Bryan was profoundly embarrassed, as only an eighteen-year-old boy can be when he is subjected to public praise.

"Personally," Bryan said, getting a grip on himself at last, "if nobody minds too much, I'd just as soon have a beer."

They all laughed, and the embarrassment was over.

"Thanks, Dad," Bryan said.

"Don't thank me. This was all Ellen's idea. Thank Ellen."

Bryan turned to her. There was a long moment of in-grained dismay, the kind of look she was accustomed to. Nothing ever seemed to work between her and Bryan.

And then his face changed. With what Ellen thought was the very nicest, most mischievous grin she had received from anyone this entire summer, Bryan said, straight to her, person to person, "Gee, do I have to?"

That night in bed, heaving herself around in a futile effort to get comfortable, Ellen thought about the next inescapable family event. Ah-boo's party, now only two days away. That could not be a success, as today had been. Ah-boo's party would be her failure, the worst this summer. In other ways she had had a successful summer. Her health had stayed good, and she knew that Old Seventeen was moving down the road in good style. Many good things with other members of the family: Martha, Bonjy, Christopher, and now maybe a start with Bryan. And her new friend, Roger Bernstein, who was so promising that she was almost afraid to acknowledge it. And her marriage to Lawrence had grown even stronger. But she had failed Nancy and young Anthony Balto and herself on Ah-boo's party in spite of her trying.

Suddenly she remembered what it was Roger had said in the coffee shop, over that delicious pastry. *All you can do is play your own cards, whatever you were dealt.* That was it.

God knows I've played mine. I've played the Ah-boo card, appealing to him directly. No luck. I've played the Lawrence card, only on this one he refused to help. I've played the Bonjy card, but nothing happened. I've played the Roger Bernstein card, which came out nicely in other ways, but again nothing happened. I've played the Martha card, although I'm not sure there is such a card. I've played the Christopher card. Well, actually I haven't, but I can't do that.

Am I sure of that?—really sure? Yes, I'm afraid so. I can't bring myself to do that to Ah-boo and Bonjy, or to let Christopher do it either. And even Tony Balto, senior selectman, has played the Tony Balto card. Same result: nothing doing. What's left? What other card is left?

The me card. The Ellen card.

What does that amount to? Ah-boo has all the cards. What have I got? Well, I'm the newest member of the family, not counting Richie, who may never make it. And I guess I'm well received, except by my own stepsons, and maybe some sign of improvement there tonight. No, I'm not being fair to myself. It's better than that. I'm really very well received. I even have some genuine fans. I belong. I'm a serious, serious member of this family. And beyond that, I'm Lawrence's wife. I'm the oldest son's second wife, after a disastrous first. That has to count. And most of all, I'm a mother-to-be. Mother of Old Seventeen. Mother of the last grandchild, the very last. I'm carrying it—him or her—the last one. That must count a lot.

All right, I see where this is coming out. It's right, I know it's right. I said it earlier about Richie: if they wouldn't let him in the tournament, I would have refused to play—if I were able to play. And Christopher, poor angry Christopher, only this morning: "I won't go to the wedding." That's the me card.

Okay, Roger, my delightful Bernstein of the Apes, I'll play what I was dealt. Okay, Nancy, my lovely friend and daughter. Okay, Ah-boo. Okay, God, still dressed in white. Somebody has to draw this line. Okay, I call and raise. Ah-boo, I won't go to your birthday party.

Showdown Time

She chose her time, twenty minutes to ten the next morning. Breakfast was out of the way for everyone except Bryan, who, now that the tournament had ended, was once again sleeping late. Howard and Sam had gone sailing, and Nancy was off with Amy on "a girl expedition." Lawrence had had his second cup of coffee, made the bed for her, and was getting ready for his ten o'clock game with Brad, of which he had been deprived yesterday. He sat on the living-room couch, putting on his white sweat socks and battered, formerly white sneakers.

The still, hot weather of the last two days had broken. A nice ocean breeze was coming through the sliding screen doors. Ellen could see, beyond the deck and over the waving wild grass and the sandy beach, that there was surf this morning.

She sat down beside him on the couch. "Lawrence. I've decided something you should know about."

He looked up, friendly. "What's that? New towels?"

"No, serious. I'm not going to go to Ah-boo's party."

Instant concern. "Are you feeling bad? Sick? Is it the baby?"

"I'm feeling perfectly fine. And so's the baby. It's just that
—well, it's Nancy." When he seemed mystified, she added,
"Nancy and her young man, Anthony. Anthony Balto. I can't
go if she can't have her own guest."

"What do you mean, 'can't'? Of course you can."

"All right. Won't, then."

"Now, Ellen." He stopped tying his laces. "I know how
you feel about Nancy, and you know how much that pleases
me. But you're making far too much of this thing. You're
making more of it than Nancy is."

"Lawrence, it's the first time ever that a grandchild has not
been allowed to bring a guest."

"Nancy can bring a guest. She just can't bring that one."

"That's—whatever it's called—specious."

"Well, perhaps. But it was bad judgment on Nancy's part
to settle on this fellow. I'm not saying anything against him,
but he is hardly what I would call a good fit."

"His name is Anthony."

"Don't get sore."

"Actually, if you knew him, you would think he is a very
good fit. But how can you talk about 'bad judgment' when
somebody's in love? Didn't you ever fall in love with the so-
called 'wrong person'?"

Lawrence smiled at her. "Quite recently, in fact."

She couldn't help smiling back. "You're funny. But anyway, I'm not going."

"What are you trying to prove?"

"Nothing. Well, yes, I guess maybe I am. I just don't think
your father should get away with it all the time. Pushing
people around."

"Now, Ellen—"

"Lawrence, you know how I hate that phrase."

"Sorry. But you do realize that this is his birthday party,
not yours or mine or Nancy's. He should be able to invite
whom he wants."

"It's his everything," Ellen said. "That's the trouble."

"I don't know what that means, but anyway you have to come to the party. It's important."

"I know it is. That's why I'm not going."

He thought this over for a moment, studying her. "I better postpone the tennis. Let me call Brad."

To Ellen's surprise, he got Brad on the phone and canceled their game. She heard him say, "No, no, she's fine," so Brad must have asked if this was some kind of medical emergency related to her pregnancy. Indeed, a last-minute tennis cancellation by Lawrence was rare enough to invite speculation.

"I'm sorry," she said when he had hung up and returned to the couch. "I know you were looking forward to this game."

"It doesn't matter, we can play this afternoon. Now let's be serious about this."

What he meant was that he was now taking it seriously, but she let that go.

"This is an all-family event, the last of the summer. Ah-boo's birthday and Christmas Eve are the two most important ones of the whole year. And because this is Ah-boo's seventieth, it's the most important single occasion the family has had in years."

She thought of mentioning their wedding but decided to let that go, too.

"Now you know I think there's sometimes too much family. Too many organized occasions. There are times when I'd rather be alone with just my own family, or just with you. A large family can get to be rather pervasive. True, we have much more independence from it during the rest of the year, but August is special. I think we owe it—all of us owe it—to each other to go along with the traditions, even when they may be inconvenient. There can be exceptions, of course. You could have skipped Deck Day this year, or the stream-clearing. In fact, you remember I suggested that you might not be up to it, and so did Ah-boo. I know he was pleased that you took part in spite of the pregnancy. He said so. He likes you."

"I know he does. That's what makes it hard. And I like him, too. He's a wonderful old man. He's courtly and affectionate, and I know how much he loves the family, and I know he has everyone's best interests at heart. All that. But don't you see how he insists on running everything? That tournament yesterday, you should have heard him talking about change and tradition. As though he were God. We all have to do everything his way. Everything. It's too much. And here he is dictating to Nancy, our daughter. Somebody has to stand up to that. Anyway, I feel that I have to."

"Yes, but not on his birthday."

"Yes, *because* it's his birthday."

"I'm going to ask you as a favor. A favor to me. I want you to come."

"Lawrence, don't. That's not fair."

"Why not? You're my wife. This is my family. He's my father."

He was not pleading. His voice was calm, even, and his face showed no expression of strain. One of the many things she loved about him was that he never pleaded. She shook her head. "I can't." She could barely hear her own voice. "It's my family, too, you know. And Ah-boo is not just your father, he's also Nancy's grandfather. And he's not being fair."

"He's the fairest man I know."

"Not now he isn't. Lawrence, it's no use. I've made up my mind. This has been bothering me ever since it happened. I've tried everything I know, and this is all that's left."

Lawrence studied her in silence. Many things were going on, she suspected, but she could not pierce the mask of his face. Was he figuring out some new line of argument? Was he saying to himself that this was just feminine irrationality? Or the hysteria of pregnancy? If so, was he going to humor her? Was he, perhaps, just angry at her? She thought not.

"All right," he said, finally coming to a decision on whatever he had been thinking. "I know you're not whimsical, so all right. Though I still hope you will change your mind before tomorrow. The best way, I think, will be for me to tell him, and probably the later the better. Just before the party, or perhaps even as it's starting. I'll say you had an awful night . . . no sleep . . . totally exhausted. Something like that, and that I insisted you stay home in bed . . . get some rest. He'll be very disappointed, but—"

"Lawrence," she interrupted. "You're not getting this at all. You can't tell him. I have to tell him. And no pregnancy excuses, either. I have to tell him why."

"What are you talking about?"

"It's not that I can't make the party because of no sleep or having cramps or something. It's because of *him*. Because of Nancy. It's not that I'm unable to come. I refuse to come, and I have to explain that to him."

"Are you crazy? You can't do that."

Ellen felt a tremendous rush, as though she were on some careening vehicle that was now out of control, out of her hands. But she had committed herself. Too late to stop, too late even to correct course in any useful way. She nodded her head. "Yes," she said in a small but clear voice. "Yes, that's it."

"Well, that is too much. Too much." Suddenly he got to his feet, and now he was angry. His face had that tight look of severe self-control, and she could see the flush. He stood at his full height, no slouch now. He stared down at her, his blue eyes sharp and cold. "This is perverse," he said. His carefully flat voice carried none of the emotion he was feeling. "This is betrayal, Ellen. I forbid it. Stay away if you must, but you are not going to wreck my father's seventieth birthday. You hear that?"

He was frightening when he was angry, in part because it was so rare, but his last words made her angry too. Her voice rose. "I hear that perfectly. What you obviously don't care about is your own daughter or your own wife."

This was not only reckless but untrue, and he dismissed it with one abrupt wave of the hand. "Nancy has her whole life ahead," he said. "You know she'll get over it, and you don't see *her* boycotting this event. But who knows how many more great birthdays Ah-boo will live to see, or to enjoy?"

This argument made her even more angry. "He looks pretty healthy to me. Playing tennis every day. He's good for plenty of birthdays. How about seventy-five? How about eighty? How about—"

"Stop it. You can't do this."

"But I will. Just watch me, buster."

" 'Buster,' " he mimicked. "You're absurd when you pretend to be a vulgarian. Now enough of this. I'm willing to have you stay away from the party, even though I think you're wrong. But you're not going to tell Ah-boo what you're up to."

"Want to bet? Want to bet? Today." Ellen hated the sounds her voice was making. Loud and shrill, the whole fishwife bit.

Lawrence stepped away from her, turned his back on her. But even through her anger she could tell he was not walking away from the argument. He was pulling himself together. He stopped, standing still in the middle of the living room, almost exactly centered on the huge woven-straw rug, one tennis shoe still untied. He put both hands up to his forehead and just stood there. She knew something was coming. The expectation cooled her anger. She waited for him.

He put his hands down.

Still not looking at her, he said, "I've told you I never want to talk about my first wife. I don't. You force me to." There was no reproach in his voice. Just stating a fact. He put his hands behind his back and began to pace, slowly, staring down at the patterns in the straw.

"I had nothing to do with the breakup of my marriage. I

don't mean I had no responsibility. I mean I had no choices in the matter. I took no action. It was entirely her choice. Her unilateral act, about which I had virtually nothing to say. She decided to leave, and so she left. My role was passive. I found this repugnant, demeaning—and still do.

"Oh, there was a man. He still comes to the Island, I understand. Over in Bel Harbor. But she herself admitted that he was simply a device. A provocation. A statement. A way of saying, 'I'm through.' I could actually have understood her falling in love with another man. Or even if it had just been passion. Those things happen all the time, as we know. But—" He paused. He even stopped walking for a moment. "This was just—as she said—nothing."

Lawrence looked up for the first time. "Right here in this room. Sitting on the couch where you are, only over in that corner. Completely cool about it. 'Yes, I've been having an affair, but it doesn't matter.' That was what she said: 'It doesn't matter.' And then she went on to say, almost in the same sentence, 'I'm leaving you.' Not saying she wanted a divorce or that she thought we'd been having our troubles. As indeed we had. I wasn't terribly surprised, except by her abruptness. The totality of it. Just that simple 'I'm leaving you.' I don't know what I said. Something or other. I don't think I argued with her, certainly not very much. At some point I asked her what about the children. She was still sitting there in the corner of the couch, very cool, a good-looking woman but always cool. She said the children would be better off with me. Just as cool as that. Bryan was barely a year old. And then she said that even if she wanted them, which she didn't, she knew she could never get them away from the Windermans. That was her phrase: from the Windermans, not from me. And then she said . . . This is why I am telling you this painful story—painful to me, anyway. She said, 'But *I* can get away from the Windermans.

From all of you, your father on down. Nobody is given a
chance to live around here. I'm smothered.' "

Lawrence sighed. He turned to face the deck, looking far
out to the ocean, as well as to that long-ago scene. Seventeen
years now. He was silent for a few moments. Ellen thought
he might be finished speaking. Then, still gazing at the ocean,
he said, "There was more discussion and several more
talks—but not much more. Ah-boo wanted to talk to her, to
try to persuade her, even after I told him about her affair with
the Bel Harbor man. She wouldn't do it. She wouldn't meet
with him. She said she'd had enough of this family. She
wasn't going to take any more orders."

Ellen could see Barbara Winderman sitting there on the
end of the couch. Tall, slim and, as Lawrence described her,
completely cool. There were no snapshots of Barbara in the
family albums or in the carousels of color slides. No doubt
there had been once, as there were many casual shots of everyone else in the family. Ellen had looked. They did not
exist. Barbara on the beach, Barbara playing tennis, Barbara
at a picnic—none of those existed. Ellen wondered who had
seen to that. Lawrence? Ah-boo? Perhaps a family conference
among all the adults? *It is now time to delete Barbara. Bye-bye,*
Barbara. But, of course, there was one place where Barbara
Winderman could not be deleted. Each year at Ah-boo's
birthday party a picture of the entire family was taken, all of
them carefully lined up on the steps of Ah-boo's veranda.
Ellen herself had posed for last year's picture and had thus
appeared for the first time in that annual end-of-summer record. She would be absent this year by her own choice, but
there would be many years to come. Next summer her own
child would be there, probably in her arms and almost a year
old. As Ah-boo said, it was wonderful to watch everyone
grow up through the pictures. In each of her six years as
Lawrence's wife, Barbara had been in that picture. She could

not be removed without eliminating the entire group portrait, which was, of course, unthinkable.

So Ellen knew the face of her predecessor, as she did the faces of Richie's predecessors, Martha's two husbands, Don and Cuff. No one had taken the trouble to expunge Don and Cuff from the snapshot collections. Perhaps Martha didn't care that much. But Barbara was preserved only in the group portraits. Howard and Nancy barely remembered her, Bryan not at all. A tall woman with wide shoulders and a light, well-kept body. According to the pictures, she changed her hairstyle at least once a year. Not the color. That stayed the same, a light brown-blond, just like Howard's. But sometimes it was short, sometimes long, sometimes pageboy, sometimes with bangs. One summer she had even gone for curls, in spite of the fact that her hair was naturally straight. Ellen's experience was that women who repeatedly changed their hairstyle had trouble figuring out who they were, or else they were bored. Possibly both. Barbara Winderman had the kind of face that survived any hairstyle. Almost a model's face but, as with many a model's face, lacking in warmth. From the pictures, Ellen did not think she would have liked her.

"That must have been awful for you," she said, still on the edge of anger but softened by sympathy.

She could see Lawrence slowly return to today. He gave up his long study of the ocean and faced her. Nothing had softened on his face. On the contrary. "Well, it was," he conceded. "And now you are saying many of the same things she said."

Ellen could not believe this. "What? That I'm smothered? I never said any such thing."

"In effect," Lawrence said, nodding his head in agreement with himself. "In effect, that's what you mean. Although you are directing it at my father, while my wife applied it to the whole family."

"*I'm* your wife," Ellen snapped. "That was your *former*

wife. How can you be so wrong? Yes, I think Ah-boo has far too many things his own way. And I think that's exactly how he likes it, regardless of what anybody else wants. Even if the rest of you don't seem to see it. Or maybe it just doesn't bother you. But that's the only resemblance between what I think and what your first wife said. The only. For God's sake, Lawrence, I *like* your family. How many times have I told you that? That I love being part of a big family. How I looked forward to coming up here this summer. Remember? And it wasn't just because of the Island breezes. It's being up here with everybody, the whole family in one place, all of us together. And I love Ah-boo. I admire him. I like him. I love him. Can't you get that through your thick banker's head? But that doesn't mean I want him to run my whole life. All our lives. No, and not you, either. I love you, and I love it that in another month we're going to have a baby together. You can't have any idea how great that is for me. But our child isn't going to grow up being swallowed alive by this family. Or dictated to by Ah-boo."

"Are you finished?"

"What do you mean, am I finished? What am I supposed to do, sign off or something? Weren't you listening to me?"

"I certainly was. That's a refreshing way to think about our baby. Being swallowed alive by the family."

Men were so horrible about extracting a single phrase from an argument. "Oh, Lawrence!"

"I suggest," he said, "that you think this whole thing over very carefully. Now I'm going to the beach."

To her dismay, because of the ice in his voice, she burst into tears. This time he did not comfort her.

When he had left the house and she had herself under control again, she tried to call Roger Bernstein. No answer. She looked at her watch. Almost eleven. She called Ellihew's coffee shop and asked if he had come in. Not yet, but it was close to his usual time.

"Would you mind giving him a message? It's Ellen Winderman, and I'm at home. Would you ask him please to call me? It's urgent."

While she waited, she washed her face in cold water, holding the washcloth pressed to her eyes to keep them from puffing up. She was always annoyed with herself when Lawrence, or any other man, made her cry. She ought to be able to fight without crying.

She sat down on the couch to wait, and to think. Without realizing it, she instinctively chose the opposite corner from the one Barbara Winderman had sat in. When she did realize what she had done, she smiled at herself. I must be recovering, she thought. But I wonder if I will always think of that as Barbara's corner.

She would not back off from her decision. She believed that a decision made in solitude after long marination was likely to be right. Besides, she would not let herself be bullied by Lawrence, or by anyone else. Ordinarily he was not a bully. He was too sensible and thoughtful for that, even too considerate—although being considerate was one of his more flexible virtues. Sometimes he overrode it for another purpose. But this morning he had been not merely inconsiderate but unjust and unkind. She wondered how deep his anger was. In this family, when the subject was the family itself, emotions ran deep. For Lawrence, this event involved both his former wife and his father. I wonder just how alarmed I should be.

When the phone rang and she said hello, Roger's opening words were, "They said it was urgent, but I don't do babies."

That made her feel better. "Roger, I need to talk to you about something, and I don't want to do it over the phone."

"Well now," he said. "The jungle giant's charms must be getting to you. It happens to every woman sooner or later. Want to join me for a Danish? I'll stall till you get here."

"No Danish, but I'll be right there."

When she walked into Ellihew's, Roger was in his booth, wearing horn-rimmed half glasses way down on the tip of his nose as he read the *Island Chronicle*, their weekly local newspaper. A cup of coffee was beside him. She reached the booth and slid into the seat opposite before he noticed her.

"Well, good morning," he said with what she could see was genuine pleasure. He folded the paper, took off his glasses and tucked them in the breast pocket of his short-sleeved plaid shirt. And then to the waitress who had already scampered up to him, "Jenny, a coffee for Mrs. Winderman, and then your two juiciest Danish."

"Not for me, thanks," Ellen said.

"Yeah, that's what you said last time. Okay, Jenny, two Danish for me then and a knife and an extra plate. So what are you up to?"

She told him about her decision, why she had made it and why she had to tell Ah-boo the truth about it. Then about her fight with Lawrence. Roger Bernstein sat leaning forward with his arms flat on the table, his graceful hands folded with fingers interlaced. His eyes held steady on hers, even when Jenny set down their order.

When she finished, she said, "You knew Lawrence's first wife. Tell me I'm not acting the same."

"Oh, don't worry about that. People who get divorced are supposed to turn around and marry the same kind of person all over again. But Lawrence is smarter than that—or else just a lot luckier. No, Ellen, you wouldn't even know how to think like Barbara, much less act like her. You have something called principle, which is an extremely inconvenient affliction. Barbara wouldn't have known a principle if it fell on her. Not my favorite lady, as you may have guessed."

"I told you, Lawrence said I was being crazy. About this party. What do you think? Am I?"

"Sure, in his terms. You're rocking the boat." She must

have looked miserable, because he said, "Hey, there's nothing wrong with that. Some boats need rocking."

"Lawrence doesn't even seem to see what I'm talking about."

"Ellen, your husband is a very smart man. But he's a master of equanimity. He's wonderful at pretending that some awkward event simply has not happened. You know the Durante scene where he's stealing a circus elephant, and a cop catches him and asks 'What are you doing with that elephant?' And Durante says, 'What elephant?' Lawrence can do that: 'What elephant?' But don't think he doesn't know. He'd just rather not know."

"Yes, but here it's his own daughter who's being hurt."

"Well, forgive me, but I wonder if that's really what all the fuss is about. I'm sure that's how it started out, but it sounds to me as though this isn't just Nancy anymore. It's you and Charles, isn't it?"

Ellen thought about that. After she had thought about it, she sighed. "I guess so. Although Nancy's still very much in it for me. But yes, it's more than Nancy. Only that makes it sound as though I didn't like Ah-boo. Actually, I like him and admire him a great deal. I said that to Lawrence. Look at what he's built, this whole family, all of us coming back every August."

Roger nodded. "Which only makes it more difficult. He'll be hurt."

"You think I shouldn't do it?"

He laughed. "Don't expect me to stick my neck out on that one. It's what you think. You're a grown-up girl. You have to decide." He bit off some Danish and chewed it while he thought something over. "I used to be an anthropologist, you know. I still read in the field now and then, just to remind myself that I don't really have to study it anymore. But you don't have to go to Samoa or Tashkent to study tribal customs. It's all right here." He tapped his forefinger on the table top. "Right here, at the Winderman property. It has everything." He smiled, getting ready to build his case. "You have the big hut, full of tribal lore and artifacts, and then you have the satellite huts. You have the big chief, Charles, and then the subchiefs and then all the spear-carrying tribesmen. You have the traditions and the customs and the taboos and the quasi-religious rituals, like the chief's birthday party. You could write a thesis."

"And what's your role? Are you the historian?"

"Me?" Roger laughed. "No, I'm the medicine man. Sort of on the edge of the tribe, not quite a member but still accepted because I'm the chief's friend, and because I know how to throw the mumbo-jumbo, even though I don't altogether believe it."

"The medicine man is supposed to give advice. What should I do?"

Roger shook his head. "Not on this one, Ellen. You have to decide."

Ellen squared her shoulders. "If you put it that way, then it's easy. I think everybody has to decide—or at least get a chance to decide. Every tender, lovely, easily wounded Nancy. Every charming young Anthony who just happens to come from the wrong tribe. Yes, and Martha, who has the right to choose her own poison. Or Lawrence, or Brad, or whoever. Everybody. Including me."

"You're a romantic, Ellen—and I couldn't agree with you more. This matters, doesn't it? This really matters."

She nodded her head.

He kept looking at her. Then he said, "I think I may have a word with Charles."

"That would be wonderful. It might help him understand better and not be hurt. But me first. I have to speak to him first."

She had learned in business that if there is going to be an announcement or a promotion or an important action of any kind, you have to make sure that the key people are told in advance. Whether the news is welcome or not, you must not blind-side the people who are most involved.

From the beginning she had had only one full supporter. She wanted him to know before this became public.

"Christopher? It's Ellen."

"Hi. Ellen."

Good, she thought. That's his first "Ellen." No doubt she had caught him by surprise. Because it was Christopher, she tried to sound more casual and relaxed than she felt. "Are you where you can talk? I'm going to do something that I want you to know about in advance. Because you were the only other person who really wanted to help Nancy. But you have to keep it a secret for a couple of hours. Agreed?"

"Okay. Sure."

Even in those two words she could hear his interest, his voice up a notch from normal. "I'm not going to Ah-boo's birthday party tomorrow. Because of Nancy. I'm going to tell him that as soon as I can see him."

Long pause at the other end of the phone as Christopher thought it over, taking it in, figuring out what it meant. "Wow."

"Yeah, wow. Wish me luck. And listen, Christopher, a secret, right? Because he has to hear it from me."

"Right." Another long pause. "Me too."

"Me too what?"

"Me too I won't go either."

Now wait, let's not get a sixteen-year-old boy in more family trouble than he's already in. But at the same time it meant that she had a partner, an ally. She would not have to be completely alone. Hard to resist. She compromised. "Christopher, you don't have to join me. Although I'm pleased that you want to. This is my call. I'm not asking you for help. In fact, it'll just get you in trouble."

"Trouble," he said, with a heavy weight of irony for his age, "doesn't especially bother me. You're doing it for Nancy."

After her conversation with Roger and after all her own thoughts, this was at the very least a moot point. But it was not untrue. "Yes," she said.

"Count me in." He gave a short laugh. "Or out."

"Christopher, I don't want to—"

"—get me in trouble," he finished. "Is Nancy going to skip it too?"

"Oh, I hardly think so. Nancy is such a good soldier when it comes to the family."

He did not answer this.

Ellen said, "Do you want me to say anything to Ah-boo about you? Do you want to think about it?"

"Whatever you say. No, go ahead."

Okay, Ellen thought, there's one card I've been dealt that I can play or not play. "Christopher, thanks. Lots of thanks."

She could feel the glow over the phone, a true glow. "Don't mention it," he said with pride.

She had no sooner hung up the phone than another thought occurred to her. It was a reach, but worth a try. She dialed Christopher again.

"Is your mother there?"

"She's down at the beach."

Ellen found Martha and Richie sunbathing side by side. She said good morning to Richie, just to be polite to a man who looked as though he could use some kindness, and then she asked Martha to join her for a few minutes' walk.

When they were out of earshot, Ellen told Martha what she was going to do.

"Jesus," Martha said.

"Yes, exactly. Now how about joining me?"

"You mean not go to the party?" Martha shook her head, definitely. "I can't do that."

"It's the same for you as it is for Nancy," Ellen said. "No Richie, no Anthony. It's just the same."

"Maybe," Martha said. "Even so, that's just not possible. Not for me."

"Okay. I didn't really think so. But I had to ask. I thought you might be on my side."

"I am. I am on your side."

"Can I say so? Can I tell Ah-boo that?"

Martha looked at her a long time—ten, fifteen seconds in silence. Then her chin went up in an abrupt little move. "Sure," she said. "Sure. And you know why, Ellen? Because I think you're on my side. But I can't miss the party."

Ellen smiled. "Thanks. Now I have to make a phone call before I lose my nerve."

Back at her house she called Ah-boo's number. Bonjy answered the phone, a rare note of exasperation in her voice because of all the party preparations.

"It's Ellen, Bonjy. I'd like to come over and see Ah-boo."

"Ellen, goodness sakes, it's the *party* tomorrow. We're in a dither over here. The truck with the tables just arrived."

"I know, but it's important. It's about the party, in fact."

"I don't know. Mr. Winderman just got up from his nap."

"Bonjy, I have to see him."

"Well, I'll ask." She actually banged the phone on the table. She was back in a minute. "He says all right," she said with clear disapproval. "In fifteen minutes. Now, Ellen, I simply must go. Good-bye."

Fifteen minutes. How am I going to say it? You should have thought of that before. She went to the bedroom to brush her hair and check her appearance. Her blouse didn't look fresh enough. Too many wrinkles. She took it off and grabbed a pink one from her bureau drawer, but when she put it on, it looked too festive. Her fingers were trembling as she tried quickly to unbutton it. What about the gray and white? She held it up to her shoulders. Yes, all right with the denim maternity skirt. She managed to get into it and button it, leaving the tail outside the skirt. I look like a tent. I wish I looked better. She brushed her hair again. It would have to do.

As she walked down the path to the tennis court, she tried to put words in order. A game was going on, Lawrence and Brad, in fact, but she went by without speaking or being noticed. Over the footbridge, careful to keep her balance, and past the blue spruce, silvery in the afternoon sun. There was the barn and the looming presence of Ah-boo's huge old house. She stopped to get her breath. Perhaps she should have driven over? Come on, Ellen, this is just stalling. Stalling never helps, Hortense always said.

As she came around the corner of the house to the front facing the water, she saw Ah-boo directing two workmen who were carrying wooden trestles and planked table tops down to the beach. A fine-looking old man in his white shirt and khaki trousers, he stood straight and tall in the pleasant sunshine, bareheaded, his white hair blowing a little in the breeze.

He waved when he noticed her and called, "I'll just be a minute. Have a seat on the veranda."

She walked to the steps where tomorrow they would be taking the family picture without her and then onto the veranda where she lowered herself into a comfortable canvas chair. No escape now.

She looked between the veranda pillars that framed her view of the beach and the ocean. In the center of the frame Ah-boo was directing the two men as they set up the tables on the sand. When they were placed to his satisfaction, he came back toward the house, the men following. When they stopped, still in the center of her frame, she heard him say that they should pick up the tables the first thing in the morning the day after tomorrow. Then he was coming toward her through the frame, smiling to her.

"Lots of excitement," he said cheerfully as he sat down facing her. "I must say, I don't feel a day under seventy." He chuckled at his little joke. "Well, my dear, Bonjy says you have some kind of problem. I hope it's nothing serious."

"I'm afraid it is," Ellen said.

His face turned serious to match her tone. "I'm sorry to hear that. Tell me what it is."

"You remember our talk about Nancy and her friend Anthony?"

He nodded. "Of course, I do. Yes, you wanted her to bring him to the party. Nancy and I talked, too. But I'm afraid I'm too old and set in my ways."

Ellen drew a deep breath and said what everybody else had been saying all month long. "It's your party, of course. I respect that. But I also feel strongly—very strongly—that it isn't right. Please, I'm not putting that properly. I'm not saying you're wrong and I'm right. It's just that—under the circumstances, I don't think I can come to the party."

There. Out at last.

His eyes as he stared back at her were grave, a calm blue, not pale and watery like old men's eyes. He did not argue with her, did not say anything at all. He just sat there, one leg crossed over the other, his arms resting quietly on the sides of his chair.

Had he not taken it in? Had he failed to understand her? "I've thought about it a lot," Ellen went on, knowing that she was rushing but unable to slow down. She had to get it all said. "Lawrence and I even had a bad fight about it this morning. But I have to do what seems right to me, so I won't be coming tomorrow. I just can't. And that's true for Christopher, too. For the same reason, because of Nancy. He said I could tell you he's not coming. I also think you'll be hearing from Roger. Roger Bernstein. But I told him it was important for me to speak to you first. And Martha. She agrees with me. She's coming, of course, but she's on my side. Anyway, I'm sorry."

She had finished.

And then as she watched, to her dismay, to her horror, Ahboo's bright blue eyes filled with tears. Then the tears rolled down his cheeks. The sight was terrible, heartbreaking for her. She didn't know what to say. She felt this was the cruelest thing she had ever done. And she had done it to this wonderful old man on the very eve of his seventieth birthday. She hated herself. Lawrence had been right.

At first he made no move to cope with his tears. Then at last, mercifully, he reached into a pocket, brought out a handkerchief and wiped his eyes and his cheeks. "You'll have to forgive me," he said. His voice was unnaturally husky. He cleared his throat. "I'm afraid old people cry too easily. Yes, one more sign of age." He wiped his face once more, then returned the handkerchief to his pocket. He sat still. Ellen did not know what to say.

"Actually, I don't cry very often," he said. "As a matter of fact, not at all. But I was so moved by you. My dear Ellen, I never realized—never guessed—how much this meant to you. And to Nancy. I wouldn't hurt you for the world. And especially you, in your condition, about to present me with another grandchild." He shook his head, as though surprised by his own lack of understanding. "Of course Nancy can bring the young man. Now you go home and tell her. I wish we could talk longer, but Mrs. Benjamin will have my hide if I don't get to work on my party."

He stood up and then—courtly, almost gallant—helped her to her feet. "At which I will be happy to see you."

A hard walk home. She felt no elation. She could not recall ever having won such an empty victory. Nice for Nancy, to be sure, but at what a cost. Ellen felt the flush of shame on her face for making Ah-boo cry. Roger had said that WASPs don't cry, but he hadn't allowed for Ellen's skills. And for Ah-boo to cry in her behalf, that made it even more unforgivable.

The dark green surface of the tennis court was blank and silent now as she passed it. The breeze had died down as it often did in the late afternoon—every sailor's excuse for being late to dinner. As she started up the path to her house, she could feel the slight difficulty in breathing, even though the rising ground was not steep. I'll be glad when this baby is out in the open, she thought, and I can be myself again. She had enjoyed her pregnancy, but enough was enough.

By the time she reached the house, she was almost panting. She stopped to get her breath before climbing the four open plank steps to the deck. No one was in the living room, and when she called hello, no one answered. At her bedroom door she could hear the sound of the shower, so that accounted for Lawrence, cleaning up after tennis. Ordinarily she would have gone in to ask him about his game. Not today.

Back across the living room to the children's wing of the house. Since there was no music, there were probably no children, but she checked anyway. All bedrooms were empty, and so was what was still called the playroom, even though it had long ago become the children's separate living room. Nobody home.

She had better tell her colleagues what had happened. She called Christopher. Not there. She called Roger. No answer. Well, she thought, here we are flushed with triumph and nobody to report to. She was tired, drained. She went out on the deck again, just to sit peacefully in the late sunshine. Somebody else could get dinner tonight.

But it was better when Nancy came home a few minutes later, bouncing onto the deck to say hello. When Ellen told her, Nancy gave one loud, happy whoop and then flung her

arms around Ellen's neck. "Terrific!" she said. "Zowie! You
did it! My God, I've got to call Anthony." She literally ran off
the deck to get to the phone.

"What's all the fuss?" Lawrence asked, coming out on deck.
His voice was unfriendly, which was all right with her. He
was wearing gray slacks and the blue plaid shirt that she had
told him she particularly disliked. Had he chosen it on purpose? His hair, wet from the shower, was slicked back against
his head, a style that did not become him. When you've been
fighting, all the little details seem worse than usual.

"I talked to Ah-boo," she said. "Anthony's coming to the
party."

"What? Why did he do that?"

"He's *your* father, as you pointed out this morning. Why
don't you ask him?"

He looked at her, weighing things in his mind. "I'd rather
ask you."

"He said he hadn't realized how much it meant to me. He
was very sweet."

"Did you tell him you weren't going to the party?"

"Yes."

"Even after I told you not to? What did he say?"

"He cried."

"I don't believe it. He never cries."

"Suit yourself. I'm tired, Lawrence, and I'd rather not have
an argument. What I'd like to have is a drink."

Nancy joined them again, full of smiles. "Let me get it for
you," she said. "Anthony says *molte grazie* and so do I."

However, as they learned that evening, that was not what
Tony Balto Senior had said. As Nancy reported in despair, he
forbade his son to attend.

"But Anthony is twenty-five years old," Ellen said. "He
can decide for himself."

"No he can't. It's all very Italian."

Ellen had spent part of the evening on the phone already,

short talks with Christopher and Martha and a long talk with
Roger to tell them the surprising news. Now she would have
one more call to make. To Ah-boo. Ah-boo, you win after all.

She dialed his number. "Ah-boo? It's Ellen. I want to thank
you again, very much, for changing your mind about Anthony Balto. But I'm afraid it turns out to be no use. His
father says he can't come."

She waited for a response, but none came. Had they been
disconnected? "Ah-boo? Hello? Are you still there?"

A dry chuckle reached her. "Oh yes, still very much here.
At least through tomorrow. So the selectman says no, does
he? Well, let's see."

Happy Birthday, Dear Ah-boo

Clear day.

A gentle ocean breeze tempered the late August heat. Ellen knew that various fallback provisions insured that the party could take place under any weather conditions, as it had even during the driving rainstorm of 1978. But good weather was more cheerful. She herself did not feel cheerful about facing Ah-boo after what she had done yesterday.

The heavy work for the party had all been completed this morning. The ancient metal washtub that Anne Winderman had bought long ago for fifteen dollars at the Bel Harbor antique store was exhumed from Ah-boo's barn, along with its wrought-iron stand, and carried to the beach where it was filled with seawater for boiling the corn. It had survived all these years because it was used only once or twice a summer and then dried thoroughly before it was stored away. The fifty-five-gallon drums for lobster shells and corncobs were in much worse condition, almost rusted through in places, but Ah-boo would not replace these honorable receptacles as long as they still served. Small pieces of firewood in a huge jumbled pile had been placed where sparks from the fire could not reach them.

Under Ah-boo's direction the boys had strung the beach lights on their aluminum stands and run the heavy-duty yellow extension cable all the way back to the electric outlet on Ah-boo's veranda. That way there would still be light no matter how late the party continued. "Somebody always wants to eat a last lobster," Ah-boo said, "and that's difficult in the dark."

Blueberry picking had gone on for days at the nineteen known bushes on the property. Even though the family had wanted to get the number up to an even twenty and had searched especially hard, no one had discovered a new bush this year. The Island berries were much smaller and darker than the monsters sold in the supermarkets, so it took many more of them to make a pie. Bonjy would not use commercial berries because of their feeble flavor. She allowed six generous slices to a pie, so one might have thought that five pies would be enough for the sixteen Windermans and their eleven guests. But since blueberry appetites were hearty— Bryan and Angie had been known to eat an entire pie each— Bonjy wanted ten pies, just to be safe. Lots of berry picking.

For once in her pregnancy, Ellen had no trouble with the dress code. Everyone was expected to wear a brightly colored shirt or blouse for the group portrait, but this was, after all, a beach picnic as well as a birthday party. Old shorts, old slacks or casual skirts would do, and almost everyone would be barefoot. Ellen chose her light blue denim skirt, which was both comfortable and capacious, and the shocking pink blouse she had rejected yesterday as being too festive for her talk with Ah-boo. Lawrence wore the checked yellow shirt she had bought him for last year's party. He had resisted it then, but now that it was a year old and broken in, he accepted it. Nancy had tried out half-a-dozen different tops in front of Ellen before settling on a strapless red-and-orange blouse. She had both the shoulders and the breasts for it. And her tattered short blue jean shorts, for which she had the legs. She was eager to impress Anthony, who was coming after all. No one knew what Ah-boo had said to persuade Tony Balto to change his mind, but Anthony had called today to say he was coming. Nancy's excitement and pleasure were delightful to see, but Ellen wished she herself could feel better about the way it had come about.

Four o'clock in Ah-boo's front yard was the moment for the picture, but as Lawrence had explained last year, "If you're just on time, you're late." Angie came to their house at three-thirty. Nancy bounced off a few minutes later to meet Anthony so that they could arrive at Ah-boo's together. The rest of the family, with Angie and Sam, piled into the car and drove to Ah-boo's so that they wouldn't have to walk home in the dark when everyone was stuffed and weary.

When they reached the crowded parking area in front of the barn (seven cars, Ellen counted, including Roger's ancient black Volkswagen), Ah-boo was standing at the corner of his house, ready to greet them. Bareheaded, white hair gleaming in the afternoon sun, he had a warm smile for them all. Although everyone else was in the required colorful party shirt for the picture, Ellen noted that Ah-boo remained in his customary white cotton shirt. *Droit de seigneur.* It also occurred to her that in a sea of colors, the single white shirt was bound to stand out in the picture. Oh well, you're only seventy once.

"Thank you, thank you," he answered the chorus of happy birthdays. "We're all here, I think"—he looked straight at Ellen—"including Nancy's young man." If he held anything against her for yesterday, he did not show it. "How are you, my dear?" He took her arm and led them around the house to where everyone was gathered in front of the veranda steps. All the family and all their guests. There was Roger, mauve shirt and yellow slacks. Her eyes went quickly to Nancy's red-and-orange blouse, and yes, there was Anthony. Well, regardless of cost, that's some milestone.

She did not have a chance to say hello to anyone because Ah-boo was already organizing the picture, "while the light is perfect." Brad had his camera set up on a tripod in front of the steps. He had a cable release attached so that there could be no question of shaky hands spoiling the picture.

"All right now," Ah-boo said. "We'll do the family first, and then we'll do one of the family and guests together." The family picture was the important one, but each of the guests would get a color print of the second picture as a memento of the day. "The grandchildren will all be seated on the first step as usual. In ascending order of age, of course, starting with Alice on the far left."

Everyone already knew it. The picture had been taken exactly the same way for the last eighteen years, ever since Howard, Nancy and Amy first sat on the bottom step.

To Ellen's astonishment, Ah-boo said, "Now Ellen, I want you beside me on the second step, right here in the middle." When she demurred, he said, "No, no, come on now. After all, we want the next grandchild prominently displayed. Next summer, he or she will be in full view."

She could not understand why he was being so nice to her, after yesterday, but that was how the picture was taken, with all the guests watching. She and Ah-boo stood together in the center. When they were all in their designated places on the three lowest steps, Brad came out of the group to check the focus, the framing, the speed and the *f.* stop. Angie, who was a fine amateur photographer, could have done this perfectly well, but it was Brad's responsibility to make sure that the picture came out right. When he was satisfied, he returned to his place on the steps and let Angie take over.

Angie shot a full roll, encouraging good smiles with a steady line of patter and checking the meter every four or five frames to make certain the light had not changed. With this large a group, and with sixteen different facial expressions at stake, he wanted to be sure that at least one frame had everyone looking his best. When Angie was satisfied, Brad put in another roll of film while Ah-boo arranged the guests on the steps for the second picture. Bonjy was impatient because she insisted she still had things to do in the kitchen, but Ah-boo shushed her. "Mrs. Hackett has everything under control, I'm sure."

"Now," Brad said when all was ready, "this has to be taken with the timer, and we have to reset it for each picture. So everybody give us big smiles right away, and then we can all have a drink."

"Yay!" Martha said, without shame.

Brad checked the light and focus, set the timer and then scrambled to his spot on the steps. "Big smiles," he reminded everyone as he stepped over Alice and whirled to face the camera.

On this picture, five frames were deemed sufficient, partly because Bonjy announced that she was now leaving to get the clams, finished or not.

"Okay, that's it," Brad said. "Ah-boo, is the bar open?"

"The bar is open."

It was a long table in the wide space at the corner of the veranda. While Bonjy and Mrs. Hackett carried out platter after platter of opened cherrystone clams covered with sheets of plastic wrap, Lawrence and Brad mixed drinks and Sue poured white wine. Howard and Sam handed out beers and Cokes from a big tub filled with ice.

Ellen did not have to seek out Anthony. He came up to her at once, with his pleasant handshake, the good manners, the very direct look, the shock of straight black hair falling across his forehead. "I just want to thank you," he said. "Nancy says it's all your doing."

"I'm glad you're here. I mean it. But it wasn't just me, Anthony. Mr. Winderman is the one to thank."

That bright wide smile spread across his dark-tanned face. "Oh, I have. But just the same, Nancy and I know. Can I get you something to drink?"

She was not sure, with the long evening ahead, that such an early drink was wise, but she did not want to say no to him. "A glass of white wine would be perfect."

Roger Bernstein came over to see her. "So," he said. "Congratulations."

"I guess so. I don't know. Roger, I hurt Ah-boo's feelings very badly."

"If you did, it doesn't show. Besides, the thing to remember is that you got him to change his mind. That doesn't happen very often. Are you going to say anything during the speeches?"

"Of course. I have to. Nothing very much, though."

Roger leaned forward and lowered his voice in the conspiratorial way she enjoyed, letting a friend in on something good. "I've got a poem," he said. "A work of genius."

"I can't wait," she laughed.

"You'll have to. Family speaks first, guests second, oldest guest last. You better have a drink."

"Anthony's getting me one. What I'm going to need is a chair."

Roger looked around and told Brad Junior to bring her one from the veranda. Anthony came back with her glass of wine and a small paper plate with three cherrystones and a slice of lemon. Nancy must have told him. Seafood sauce and horseradish and lemon were always available, especially for guests, but it was almost a point of honor in the Winderman family that if you really appreciated clams, you didn't spoil them with what Nancy called gunk. Ellen had eliminated everything but the lemon and was working on that.

Everyone seemed to have a drink, so it must be time to start, and indeed, just then Lawrence leaned over the veranda railing and clapped his hands loudly.

"It's time for a few words," he said. General laughter, because everyone knew that the words would be more than a few. "If you all have your drinks, let's get started. Alice, where are you? What do you have to say?"

Not everyone had to speak, especially not the guests, but every member of the family would have something to say on this seventieth birthday. In a random group, some of them still up on the veranda with Lawrence, they all faced Ah-boo, who stood casually in the wild grass, his hands folded in front of him. He seemed not the least embarrassed by the attention he was about to be paid. Ellen moved her chair so that she could see better.

Alice was nervous, being the first to speak, but they always started with the youngest and worked upward in age. She unfolded a piece of paper. "Mine isn't—"

"Can't hear you, Alice," Lawrence spoke from his master-of-ceremonies post on the veranda. "Speak up, honey."

Alice raised her voice. "Mine isn't quite a poem," she said. "Dear Ah-boo, happy birthday. I love you being my grandfather. Love, signed Alice."

Everyone clapped and Alice blushed. Ah-boo patted her head, and then Lawrence called on Brad Junior, the second youngest. Alice scooted across the grass to Ellen's chair. She bent down and whispered, "Was I all right, Aunt Ellen?"

Ellen was touched by Alice's newfound devotion. "You were perfect," she whispered back. "Just the right words."

Each grandchild had something brief to say, mostly unmemorable except for the obvious affection and the sense of an important occasion. Memorable or not, each speech was written down so that Ah-boo could save them. Howard was also taping the speeches so that the record would be complete.

When it was Christopher's turn, he began solemnly, "Ah-boo Ben Adam," but of course everyone interrupted him with laughter. Even the guests knew the story of how Chris-

topher had given Ah-boo his name. Ellen was pleased to see
that Christopher himself managed a small smile. Then he began again:

> "Ah-boo Ben Adam (may his tribe increase)
> Awoke one night from a deep dream of peace
> And saw an angel writing in a blue notebook.
> What writest thou? old Ah-boo said.
> I writest family history, the angel said.
> And am I in the book? old Ah-boo sighed.
> *In* the book? You *are* the book, the angel cried."

Laughter and much applause. Oh, Christopher, Ellen
thought, what a nice success for you. But of course he did not
show that it mattered. Never mind, Christopher. I'm going to
teach you that, even if you don't want to learn.

She also thought Howard did well.

Howard walked out of the crowd, the oldest grandchild,
already the tallest member of the family except for Brad, and
stood close to his grandfather. "Ah-boo," he said, "you beat
me in the tennis tournament. Okay, Ah-boo, but wait till
you're eighty."

Then it was her turn as the youngest member of the older
generation. She pushed herself out of her chair and faced the
group. "This," she said, patting her vast stomach, "is a message from the future. From Old Seventeen to a very Young
Seventy, happy birthday to you both."

And, during the friendly clapping, Ah-boo walked over to
her and kissed her on the cheek. I don't understand this, she
thought. He's going out of his way to be especially nice to me.
She knew him too well. Why is he doing this? First, the family picture and now this.

When all the family had been heard from and it was time
for the guests, she was surprised by Anthony. She and Nancy
had agreed that Anthony's proper role was silence. But An-

thony must have spoken to Lawrence, because Lawrence
called on him.

Anthony kept his place back in the crowd, but his voice,
tinged with the familiar Italian flavor, was clear. "I'm an islander, not a summer visitor. I just want to say how nice it is
to be here with you. *Felice compleanno*, Mr. Winderman."
Ellen caught the look on Nancy's face as she stood next to
Anthony and applauded, smiling up at him.

And finally, at the very end, came Roger Bernstein, who
walked up to stand next to his old friend. "I have here,"
Roger said, "a small hymn to backgammon and wine, two
substances of which Charles and I are extremely fond." He
unfolded a large sheet of paper, slipped a small, pleased smile
to Ah-boo, then took his horn-rimmed glasses out of his shirt
pocket and settled them in their usual position, far down on
his nose.

"I'm not sure," Ah-boo said, "that backgammon qualifies as
a 'substance.'"

"Yeah, well the way you play it, it does. In any case:

"Rowley powley, backgammon and spinach,
Sing heigh-ho and hoo-hoo
For Ah-boo,
A man with the flow
Of Château Margaux,
A man with the tone
Of Château Ausone,
As loose
As a goose
Shot full of Pétrus,
With the sweet elite
And the heat
And the beat
And the meat
Of Lafite,

And the wonderful sheen
Of Prieuré Lichine,
And the glorious smack
Of a Brane-Cantenac,
And the delicate nose
Of Gruaud-Larose,
And the hearty hello
Of a Clos de Vougeot,
And the swell
And the smell
Of Cos d'Estournel,
And the swing and the sway
Of a La Romanée,
With a heart just as pure
As Calon Ségur,
With the confident air
Of La Gaffelière,
With the boop-boop-dee-doo
Of Ducru-Beaucaillou,
And the grand afterglow
Of Grands Échézeaux,
And the dash
And the splash
And the flash
And panache
Of La Tâche,
But with none of the phlegm
Of Château d'Yquem.
Rowley powley, backgammon and spinach,
Sing heigh-ho and hoo-hoo
For Ah-boo."

The smile had been growing on Ah-boo's face all through
Roger's recital, and when the applause had stopped, he said
fondly, "That's your best, Roger, since *Bernstein of the Apes.*"

"You know something, Charles? I think so too. For inspiration, it's you and Tarzan."

Ellen felt sure that Ah-boo would never have initiated the gesture, but when Roger suddenly turned to embrace him, Ah-boo responded. She thought to herself, few things in life are better than an old, close friendship between two men. She wished Lawrence had one.

Roger had been the final speaker. When he stepped back, Lawrence said from the veranda, "That concludes our birthday greetings. Just by any chance, Ah-boo, might you have anything to say?"

Ellen joined in the laughter and cheering.

Ah-boo smiled around at them all. He took his time, waiting for all sound to die down. And then he waited a good bit longer, as though wondering what to say. Ellen put her hand over her mouth to hide her grin. The prospect of Ah-boo at a loss for words was too preposterous to be considered. This long pause was nothing but showmanship.

"I suppose," he said at last in the clear, slightly high-pitched voice that had once carried through lecture halls filled with several hundred students, "that at this unseemly age of three score years and ten, it is incumbent on me to deliver some kind of homily."

Howard, with his tape recorder, had moved close and crouched down directly in front of his grandfather. Ah-boo pretended not to notice.

"This is such a happy occasion for me, perhaps for us all. To be surrounded by one's family and by so many welcome guests, and to hear so many charming, and creative, and undeserved tributes is very touching. Very touching." He shook his head, almost to himself. He was speaking slowly, thoughtfully, but without hesitation. "I only wish that my wife, Anne, the mother of this large and special family, could have shared this day. Yes," he nodded to himself, "I would like to have heard from Anne today. I wish she could have been one of you, one of this group. I would have loved that—and so would she. She loved all the occasions when the family and its friends came together in celebration."

Ellen felt tears in her eyes. Of course, it was sentimental, but she could not help herself. A quick glance at Lawrence on the veranda showed that he was plainly moved in spite of his enormous capacity for reserve in public places. And Nancy, holding Anthony's hand, quickly wiped her eyes. So it's not just me.

"I think Anne would have reminded us all that it wasn't always like this." He waved his hand gently across the group. "I believe there are twenty-seven of us here today, family and guests. Twenty-eight, counting Lawrence and Ellen's welcome addition, soon to join us. We used to be so few. Lawrence and Bradford can remember how it was in those early days on this property, even though they were very small, and even Martha can remember some of it, though she was so small as to be tiny. My goodness, what a jungle we used to have here! Just this one dilapidated old house, with everything in it falling down or broken. I know some of you grandchildren still think this house is dilapidated, but you should have seen it then. And the bull vine! We owned more bull vine than you can possibly imagine. Alice, you've done your share of clipping bull vine, as have all the others here, and you know how awful a job that is, but you wouldn't believe how plentiful it used to be. Why, if there had been any market for bull vine, we would all have been as wealthy as Texas oil barons."

Alice, standing with a friendly hand on Ellen's shoulder, squirmed with pleasure at being mentioned.

"But I don't want to reminisce too much, a common disease that attacks gentlemen of a certain age. I do think Anne would have reminded us all that once upon a time, long ago, we had a very small family with a lot of work to do. And I think she would have told us today, be thankful.

"Well, I am thankful. I feel that I have been blessed. Christopher, I suspect from your speech today that you have had a recent occasion to look up Leigh Hunt's poem, and you'll remember that on the second night the angel 'showed the names whom love of God had blessed, and lo! Ben Adhem's name led all the rest.' That is how I feel this perfect August evening. That is how I truly feel.

"Because here today, on this biblical birthday of threescore years and ten, I can look around me and see the houses of my three children, all within walking distance, even for an elderly gentleman. And I can see all my grandchildren. All of us are here. No one is away, no one is absent for sickness. Christopher is out of the hospital, and Ellen isn't yet in it. We're all here.

"And our beloved guests as well, each of you chosen, personally selected by a member of this family as the one person to be invited. For myself, of course, my very old friend and fierce competitor, Roger Bernstein, who obviously knows much more about wine than I do—though perhaps not as much about backgammon. And Bryan's friend Angie, who, next to Roger, has been present for more of these birthday parties than any other guest. What is it, Angie, thirteen now? And I want to say something about a brand-new guest, Anthony Balto, invited by Nancy. Anthony? Yes, there you are. You come from one of the most distinguished Island families, and since I happen to think that the Windermans are one of the most distinguished off-Island families, I think it is high time we got together. *Benvenuto*, Anthony."

My God, Ellen thought. What *is* he up to? Three weeks of intransigence, and now the soul of hospitality.

"Now before we move down to the beach for another of Mary Benjamin's ultimate picnics, I want to say a brief last word about being seventy. I have had a wonderful life, chiefly because of all of you. Oh, there has been sadness and some disappointments, but not excessive, considering how long I have lived. 'Yet all experience is an arch wherethrough gleams that untraveled world, whose margin fades forever and forever when I move.' I wish I had written that, but I can only subscribe to it. And to cite one other writer, whose work I used to teach and who may have written the finest last paragraph in that suspect world of the novel, I, too, 'believe in the green light, the orgiastic future that year by year recedes before us.' I'm not, perhaps, as good at orgies as I used to be, though I intend to eat my share of lobster tonight. So in tribute both to the untraveled world and to the green light, let's all move down to the beach for lobster and corn and Mrs. Benjamin's blueberry pie. All grandchildren report to Bonjy to help carry. And it just may be," he ended with a wink, "that in tribute to the orgiastic future, later on there might even be a bit of moonlight skinny-dipping."

The final applause went on and on, but Ah-boo waved a hand, dismissing it, and walked straight to Bonjy to give the necessary orders.

"Come on, Ellen," Roger said. "You and I are excused from this part. We'll help each other to the beach."

Ellen got up from her chair. "I loved your poem," she said. "Is there really a wine called Ducru-Beaucaillou?"

"Indeed there is. A fine St. Julien. I'm glad you liked it. I thought it was pretty good myself."

"A work of genius, as you predicted."

"Well, if you say so. Wait, I'm going to take a second martini with me. Want some more wine?"

"No, thanks. I'll wait for you."

Roger came back with a full glass, stirring the ice cubes with his finger. "I used to know an English professor, Dick Fogle, who taught Romantic poetry—Keats and Shelley and all that. He finally distilled all his scholarship into a single couplet. 'Truth is beauty, beauty is truth; vermouth is gin, gin is vermouth.' Lot of wisdom in that."

"That's perfect. Lawrence will love it."

"Most martini drinkers do. Should we take your chair?"

"No, my folding chair's down at the beach. Wasn't Ah-boo terrific?"

They started down to the beach, Ellen balancing herself carefully, Roger balancing his drink.

"Not only Charles but the whole show. I always enjoy this shindig of his, but of course his being seventy puts a little extra spin on it."

"He's up to something, you know."

"What do you mean?"

They were out of the grass now and down on the sand. The big plank tables held only plastic utensils, a stack of oval-shaped white cardboard plates and a large box of napkins. The food would be coming right behind them. Off to one side the washtub squatted on its stand over the fire, the steam rising from the boiling seawater.

"I don't know, but it's something. He's being too nice to me. And what did you think of his comment about Anthony? 'A distinguished Island family. *Benvenuto*, Anthony.' *Benvenuto!* You know what he thinks about Tony Balto."

"I wouldn't read too much into it. You finally persuaded him, and now he's just being the good host."

"No, it's more than that. By the way, what do you suppose he said to Tony Balto?"

"Who knows? He told me they just had a little talk, and the selectman changed his mind."

"I don't believe it. Look, here comes the parade."

Angie was first, backing toward them on the beach as he snapped pictures of the procession. Ah-boo led the way, like a white explorer at the head of a file of native bearers. All he needed was a swagger stick. Jungle drums should be throbbing in the background.

Howard was the lead bearer, carrying a platter of bright red lobsters. Right behind came Charlie and Bryan, each also laden with lobsters. Bonjy had cooked the entire lot yesterday

because she did not trust anyone else to provide perfect timing, long enough to firm the gurry and turn the roe from
black to red but not long enough to toughen the meat. The
cooked lobsters had then been parceled out to each of the
houses because even Ah-boo's refrigerator was not big
enough to hold them all. Forty lobsters, two to two-and-a-half
pounds each, ordered two weeks ago, a six-hundred-dollar
summer's-end bonanza for Squire's Fish Market.

Then came Nancy and Christopher and Anthony, each
with a gunnysack of corn. Ellen knew that Bonjy and Mrs.
Hackett had stripped only half the ears just before the party
began, leaving the rest in their shucks to keep them fresh for
later cooking. Anne and Brad Junior had the wooden bowls
of melted butter, and Howard's friend Sam carried two white
cardboard painter's buckets filled with mayonnaise. Alice at
the tail end was entrusted with the lobster forks and nut-
crackers, the one burden that could be spilled on the sand
without disaster.

"Hollywood," Roger said. "Or Gatsby. I love it."

Trailing behind the food safari came the rest of the family
and the other guests. Angie made the bearers stand still for a
final picture before they placed their loads on the plank tables. The biggest boys were sent back to the house to bring
the tubs of beer and white wine.

"All right, then," Ah-boo said. "Now, where are my lobster
surgeons? Lawrence? Brad? You brought your weapons?"

Brad waved the two long, black-handled carving knives and
the duck shears for scissoring through the back of the shell.
Last summer Ellen had suggested that it might be simpler
and more efficient to split the lobsters in the kitchen before-
hand, but Bonjy said this would dry out the meat. "Besides,
Mr. Winderman thinks it's more fun on the beach."

"And let's see who will be the nurses," Ah-boo said. "I
think Amy can assist Lawrence, and"—he appeared to pause

and look around the group for inspiration—"what about it, Alice? Ready to be a nurse?"

Ellen could see that Alice was thrilled. Very skillful, Ellen thought. The nurse's job was not too difficult for Alice. She just had to hold the claws stretched out flat on the table so that the lobster did not slip around when the surgeon cut down with his carving knife. Alice could do it, but Ah-boo had given her a signal honor. This was her first time as a nurse.

Nancy volunteered herself and Anthony for corn duty. This was less glamorous, simply feeding the fire, taking corn orders and then boiling the corn four-and-a-half minutes before lifting out the ears with wooden tongs and placing them on one of the tables. It was, however, companionable.

Ellen decided she had been carrying her weight long enough in the soft sand. She got her folding chair and placed it carefully: not too close to the smoke and heat of the fire, not too close to the plank tables where she would be in people's way, and yet near enough to be a member of the party. She sat down facing the ocean. The sunset light was lovely on the white tips of the waves. The two boats bobbed pleasantly on their moorings. She felt a little tired and very heavy. Old Seventeen kicked her a couple of times and then settled down.

"Christopher," she said when she could catch his attention, "would you mind getting me another glass of wine?"

"Sure, Ellen," he said. He had learned to use her name easily.

When he brought her wine, she said, "I liked your poem. It's both funny and nice. Say it again, will you?"

He paused and she thought he was going to refuse, but then he recited it to her, not loud enough for anyone else to hear. When he finished, she laughed and clapped her hands lightly. No question about it: Christopher was pleased by her approval.

" 'What writest thou?' is in the original poem," he said. "Pretty silly, huh?"

"It certainly is. Do you know why Abou Ben Adhem's name led all the rest?" she said, fishing an old joke from her memory. "The angel was just doing it alphabetically. Adhem, Abou Ben."

Christopher was delighted. He looked so good when he was caught smiling. "Would you like a lobster?" he asked. "Or a corn?"

She shook her head. "Not yet, thanks. I'll finish my wine first. Old Seventeen and I are pacing ourselves."

Christopher nodded in the direction of Nancy and Anthony, tending the corn pot. "So he's here. You really did it."

"No," she said, *"we* did it. I got the idea from you—and some from Roger. We did it. So I'll treat you to a lobster. Go get yourself some food."

Perhaps because she was sitting down, perhaps because she wasn't moving around like everyone else, she had quite a succession of visitors. Ah-boo came over to make sure she was comfortable. (Whatever it is, he's overdoing it, she thought.) When Nancy and Anthony dropped in another half-dozen ears and Anthony checked his watch, Nancy came to see her.

"You okay, Ellen? Can we cook you an ear on the next round?"

"Not yet. Having fun?"

Great big smile. "Am I ever. Are we ever." She bent over and gave Ellen a sudden hug. "Thanks. Really thanks."

Richie sat down beside her on the sand, chewing on an ear of corn. "How come you aren't eating?"

"I will. I'm working up to it."

"Listen," he said, "tell me how you do it. I saw Ah-boo picking you out to pose beside him in the picture. How'd you get to be so in?"

Richie had a talent for asking questions that could not be answered. "Clean living, I guess."

"I live pretty clean," Richie said. "But you know? I have a feeling I'm never going to be in. Not in this family."

I'm afraid that's true, Ellen thought.

Sue's visit, when it came, was far from friendly. Seeing her approach, Ellen could tell Sue had something on her mind and was determined to speak it. Sue was wearing what Ellen thought of as her Ethel Kennedy look: energetic accomplishment is about to be performed. Duty came strong with Sue. No preamble. "I hear," Sue said, "that you forced Ah-boo to invite this Balto boy to the party."

"He's not a boy. He's twenty-five."

Sue ignored the correction. "Don't you think it's a bit much, especially on Ah-boo's seventieth birthday?"

Although Ellen had felt miserable precisely because of that, Sue's manner restored her to full strength. "I think Ah-boo's old enough to take care of himself. You heard him welcome Anthony."

"He was just being polite," Sue said, the daughter-in-law of twenty years explaining family matters to the daughter-in-law of one year. "You know he didn't want to invite him. He said so. We all heard about it. I'm sorry to say, Ellen, that I think you were trading on your pregnancy to get him to do something. Against all his instincts. I think it was mean."

Ellen did not get up, but her hand tightened on the arm of her chair. She reminded herself not to lose her temper. It's all right to be angry, but don't let it show. This was a moment to gamble on Ah-boo, on the way he had been behaving all afternoon—and also to gamble on her knowledge of Sue. If she let Sue get away with this, something would. be established between them that Ellen did not want.

"I'll tell you what, Sue." She could hear the ice crystals in her own voice. "Ah-boo's standing right over there. Now you go over and tell him what you just said. Tell him exactly. That I traded on my pregnancy, I made him do something against his will, and you think it's mean. And then you just trot back here and report what he says. Go on, I'll wait."

Ellen could see the effect. Without saying anything, Sue began to back off. Sue didn't like head-on challenge. She preferred to be safely in the right, and with a substantial majority behind her.

Now Ellen stood up, not as smoothly as she would have liked, and looked down on Sue's nervous face. "Or would you like to do it together?" She gave Sue what she hoped was a smile of total confidence. Malicious confidence. I have a straight flush, what do you have? "I'd kind of enjoy hearing him myself. Let's go."

"Look," Sue said, "I didn't mean—"

"Oh yes you did. You were very clear. And you were so wrong that you deserve to have your nose rubbed in it. Are you coming? Or"—as though this alternative had just occurred to her—"would you rather apologize?"

Sue took a step backward. "Listen, Ellen—"

"Oh, the hell with it," Ellen said, deliberately letting her disgust show, "you probably don't know how to apologize."

"I really didn't mean . . ."

"Fine," Ellen snapped. "Now excuse me. I'm going to get my lobster." She walked away.

At the nearest plank table she helped herself to a whole split lobster and a hearty spoonful of mayonnaise. No diet tonight. She picked up a lobster fork and several napkins. As she returned to her chair, she passed the corn pot where Nancy and Anthony were eating their lobsters while waiting for more orders.

"Include me in the next round," she told them.

"Coming right up, Mrs. Winderman," Anthony said. He looked and sounded wonderfully cheerful.

Martha was beside her before she could sit down. Her eyes were bright with pleasure. "I saw it," she whispered. "You really stuck it to Sue. What was all that about?"

"Oh, nothing. Sue trying to give me a lesson."

"I want to hear every word. Every word. Promise you'll tell me?"

Ellen laughed and lowered herself into her chair. "You're a snoop, Martha."

"Of course. Promise?"

"All right, I'll think about it. But not during lobster."

"If you don't tell me, I won't tell you."

"Tell me what?" Ellen liked to begin on the little tail pieces. Very small portions of flavor, just enough to whet the appetite before starting the immoral gorge on the tail meat. Like Pooh taking a tiny preliminary lick, just to make sure it really was honey.

"Richie is sulking. He says he can't get with this party."

"That's not very big news."

"I know, but it's all I've got. You don't think I should marry him, do you?"

"I'm smart enough not to answer that one."

"Yeah, I don't really think so, either. He was more fun when we were just thinking about it."

Now, Ellen thought, if her father and brothers will just leave her alone. She lifted out the tail meat, pulled it in half lengthwise and dipped one end into the mayonnaise.

"Hold it," Angie said, hurrying up to take her picture. "Just have to focus. Okay, go ahead."

She smiled and took an obscene bite for him. He was a definite asset, not just to Bryan but to the whole family. And besides, he took good pictures. He looked charming with his red hair and freckles. Was she imagining it, or was he being nicer to her since her champagne gift to Bryan?

"I had everybody else," Angie said. "I was afraid you weren't going to eat one."

"When are you going to have some?"

"I've already had mine. And since that's the end of the lobster pictures, I'm going to have another."

Anthony brought her ear of corn, already rolled in butter and salted. He held it delicately at the two ends and put it on her plate.

"Four-and-a-half minutes?"

"To the dot," he said. "In my family it's four minutes."

"How is your family? How's your father?"

Anthony was very quick. "They're fine," he said, and then with a grin, "I don't know what my father and Mr. Winderman talked about, either. All I know is, here I am. And having a wonderful time. Thanks again."

"Take good care of Nancy. I'm very fond of her."

"Me, too. I wish you all didn't have to leave so soon."

"So do I. Nancy's not a good letter writer, I'm afraid."

"Nobody writes letters anymore, Mrs. Winderman. But look out for your phone bill." He gave her his million-dollar smile.

She had finished her tail meat and was just starting on the trickier part at the base of the legs when Brad walked over to see her. His honest, rugged face showed his concern. His face always revealed what was going on. He had none of Lawrence's natural privacy.

"I'm very sorry to hear about your and Sue's fight. She says you were very tough on her."

Ellen held nothing against Brad, but she didn't want this to come out one-sided. "Did she tell you she was tough on me?"

Brad nodded. "I'd thought the same thing about you and Ah-boo. I just want to tell you I'm glad we were both wrong."

"Thank you," Ellen said. They had not been all that wrong.

"No hard feelings, I hope. We all need to stick together in this family."

"Agreed. I agree completely. And, Brad, listen. Let me suggest something, just as part of sticking together. I think Martha's coming to her own conclusions about her—engagement. The marriage. I think if we *all* just leave her alone for a while . . ."

This was obviously news to Brad. He took time to think it over. "No kidding," he finally said. "That would be a break. Well, enjoy your lobster. Blueberry pie coming up."

Ellen did not look at her watch. She was much more interested in breaking off the lobster knuckles without cutting her fingers on the shell. But it could not have taken much more than five minutes for Brad to talk to Lawrence, and for Lawrence to decide that he had better check out the Martha advice with its source. Ellen did not notice him until he was standing beside her.

"Well," he said, announcing his presence in the most neutral possible way.

They had scarcely spoken since their argument yesterday afternoon. She had gone to bed first, by herself, and he had been careful not to touch her when he came to bed an hour later. In the morning he had said nothing. Of course, he seldom spoke before finishing his coffee, but this was different. Unlike Richie, Lawrence did not sulk during or after an argument. He simply unplugged himself. He might be physically present, but he just wasn't there. When he felt like it, he could do this for several days at a stretch. He could go to the office, come home in the evening at the usual time, read his banking reports or a book and then go to bed and to sleep, all without being there as far as she was concerned. Ellen felt it was a most irritating way to conduct marital warfare. She much preferred to talk things out, fight them out if necessary, and get it all over with so that life could go on. But she had learned it was pointless to try this on Lawrence. He would not respond. All she could do was wait and sort of pretend she wasn't married until Lawrence returned to the world from wherever he had been.

"Hello," she said, being careful to make nothing special of

it. Not too cheerful but not sullen, either, and above all not indicating any surprise that he had come to talk.

Lawrence looked over at Nancy and Anthony, who were standing beside the corn pot and talking with Ah-boo. "That seems to have worked out all right," he said. "After all."

"A great relief to me," Ellen said. "And to Nancy."

"Yes. Well."

It was dark now, but the beach lights had been turned on, so she could see his expression. Or, rather, his lack of expression. But she knew him well enough to realize that he was conceding she had done no real harm. Not that she had been right, mind you, but maybe—just maybe—she might not have been wrong. One would never know for sure. However, she found this acceptable.

"I can't break this claw," she said. "Would you mind getting me a nutcracker?" If you want a man to know that he has returned to grace, ask him to do you a favor. If he really has returned, he will do it.

"Sure," Lawrence said.

He stepped over to the nearest plank table, found a nutcracker and brought it to her. He did not offer to crack the claw for her. That would have been excessive. Any woman who can't manage her own lobster doesn't deserve one.

"Uh, Brad said you said something about Martha. Something or other."

Oh, come on now, Lawrence, you can do better than that. "When was that?" she asked innocently.

"Just now."

"You mean here? At the picnic?"

Lawrence glared at her. Then he smiled. "Yes, here at the picnic. In fact, right on this very beach. You were sitting here in this chair, and Brad must have been standing approximately where I'm standing right now. Give or take maybe a foot closer or even possibly a foot farther away. He spoke and you spoke. As a matter of fact, you were speaking to each other. I would say the time of this conversation was not less than five minutes ago but not more than fifteen minutes ago. The night was warm and the sky was dark because the moon had not yet risen. Now, does that refresh your recollection?"

"Yes," she said, matching his mock solemnity, "now that you describe it, I do begin to remember. In fact, I think it's all coming back to me. But would you repeat the question please?"

"You're a very funny woman," Lawrence said. "Okay. What's all this about Martha having second thoughts on Richie?"

"Oh, *that* conversation. Well, that's really all there is to it. She is. But my point to Brad was for all of you to lay off Martha. And lay off Richie, too. Just leave her alone and let it be up to her. She's not your baby sister. She's a forty-year-old woman. If you go after her, you may wind up forcing her in the wrong direction."

"How do you know all this?"

"I just do. Trust me. And I forgot to say this to Brad. You should tell Ah-boo, of course, but I suggest you keep Sue out of it. She'll find some way to screw it up, like telling Martha she's glad it's all over between her and Richie."

"I heard about your fight with Sue."

"There's a lot of gossip on this beach."

"What happened?"

"Nothing. I just stood up and crushed her with my giant pelvis. There was hardly a struggle."

"About Martha, why didn't you tell me instead of Brad?"

"We weren't speaking, remember?"

"Hm. If you've finished that lobster, Bonjy's almost ready with the pies."

"I don't suppose I should have any."

"Sure you should. It's a celebration."

Yes, Ellen thought, and not just for Ah-boo. "Sold. Give me a hand."

Half the pies had been brought down hot from the kitchen and were already sliced. The rest were keeping warm in the oven. Bonjy was lifting out the slices with a pie-server and placing them on small cardboard plates. Her hands moved with the deft speed of one long accustomed to dealing with food. No sense of haste but within minutes everyone had a plate of juicy pie.

Ellen could not believe how good it tasted. She would gladly accept heartburn tonight and a disturbing report tomorrow morning from the bathroom scales.

"Bonjy," Bryan said, "you want Angie and me to bring down some more pies?"

"Now I wonder," Bonjy said, "whatever made you volunteer?" She was beaming with the pleasure she always showed when people enjoyed what she cooked. "Yes, bring three more. Leave the other two in the oven. In case of emergency."

"I'm an emergency," Bryan said. "Best pie ever. Come on, Angie."

Ellen had to draw the line somewhere tonight, and a second helping of pie seemed the place to draw it. This was no great act of virtue, since Bonjy's slices were generous, and the first piece had really been enough. None of the grandchildren felt that way. When Bryan and Angie returned with the reinforcements, almost all the children and their guests had seconds. These were the last blueberry pies of the summer, for all the bushes had been stripped clean.

As Ellen was going back to her chair, Ah-boo took her arm. "Well," he said, "are you having a nice time? Did you get enough to eat?"

"I'm having a lovely time, thank you, and I'm stuffed. As perhaps you can see."

"I had a chat with Nancy and Anthony. He seems like a very nice young man."

"I'm glad. And also, Ah-boo, I'm very grateful to you."

He patted her arm. "Nonsense. Nothing to be grateful for. As I say, he's good company. And he has excellent manners. I believe very strongly in good manners."

"So do I. Maybe," Ellen added cautiously, "he's part of your 'untraveled world.'"

"Everything is. That was Ulysses's point. Now I expect we'll be having some fireside singing. Why don't we move your chair a little closer to the fire? And there comes the moon, just on time. Moonlight's the right setting for song."

"Ah-boo, thank you." She kissed his cheek. "I hope you had a perfect birthday."

"One of the best. One of the very best. And thank *you*, my dear."

After the second round of pie had been finished, Howard and Sam put on the thick asbestos gloves so that they could lift the washtub away from the fire. They poured the water on the sand. Then Howard picked up the wrought-iron stand and put it inside the empty pot. Nancy and Anthony piled more wood on the fire. The family and their guests gathered around the fire, a huge ring of twenty-seven people, some standing, most sitting cross-legged on the sand. Many had grabbed new cans of beer. The big orange August moon floated clear above the horizon.

"Now then," Ah-boo said. "Can anyone think of a song?"

Happy laughter, because everyone knew what most of the songs would be.

"I know one," Alice said eagerly.

"No doubt," Ah-boo said. "However, I think the first song should be selected by the person most responsible for our great feast. Bonjy, what will it be?"

"Pooh," Bonjy said, though clearly pleased. "I'm glad I'm not responsible for the lobster bill."

"Me, too," said Martha. "Let's hear it for Ah-boo's lobsters."

After the applause, Bonjy said, "All right. I'll pick *For Me and My Gal.*"

For Me and My Gal. Snowball. A Man Without a Woman. In the Evening by the Moonlight. Sweet Adeline. Don't Send My Boy to Harvard. Old Buttermilk Sky. Down by the Riverside. Minnie the Mermaid. In Old New York. Aura Lee. Heart of My Heart. That Old Gang of Mine. Considering that all the grandchildren had grown up in a world of totally different music, Ellen was still surprised that none of them ever tried to introduce a modern song. All the fireside songs were at least twenty years old, many of them fifty, some probably one hundred.

At last, when a pause indicated that all the old family standards had been honored, Lawrence said, "I think, now that we're warmed up and while we're all still in good voice, it's time to salute our host, our father, our grandfather and, for the first time on this day, our septuagenarian. 'Happy birthday to you . . .' "

Every voice was suddenly louder, stronger. Every face turned toward Ah-boo. Damn it, Ellen told herself, I've got to stop feeling tearful at every obvious moment. Look at Ah-boo, he's not crying.

"Happy birthday, dear Ah-boo, happy birthday to you."

Whistles, applause.

They will all remember this, Ellen thought. They will remember this day all their lives. The ceremony, the celebration, the happiness of all being together on an important occasion. As she looked around the fire at the smiling faces, young and old, from Alice to Ah-boo, spanning sixty years' difference in age, she knew they were all sharing something larger than themselves, larger than any one individual or any one branch of the family. Yes, as Roger would say, this was a tribal memory, and everyone would be richer for it.

"Thank you all," Ah-boo said. "You'll be happy to hear that I have nothing to say. Except, maybe some of you would like to go for a moonlight swim."

Nancy was instantly on her feet, unzipping her shorts in the firelight. All the grandchildren jumped up to take off their clothes. Shorts and shirts were dropping on the sand all around the fire. Beautiful young, naked bodies ran toward the water with yells of delight.

Alice, her slim little bare body showing no protuberances anywhere, stopped in front of Ellen, wild with excitement. "Hey, Aunt Ellen, are you going skinny-dipping?"

Ellen laughed. "I'm afraid I'm not the right shape for it just now. But next year I will."

Alice's eyes grew wide. Only the grandchildren went skinny-dipping, never the adults. "You mean it? Next summer you'll go *skinny-dipping* with us?"

"Guaranteed."

"Hey!" Alice cried, as she ran toward the water. "Hey!" she called to the other grandchildren. "Next year Aunt Ellen's going skinny-dipping with us. Guaranteed!"

Next in Line

A splendid party, Charles Winderman thought. Alone at last in his living room, with Bonjy and Mrs. Hackett in the kitchen washing up and putting away the leftover lobster and blueberry pie, he could review in peace. He would not write in the blue notebook tonight. He knew he could better describe the occasion if he waited until tomorrow, when all his busy recollections would fall into proper order.

Everything had worked out as he had wanted. Except, of course, for Anthony Balto, but that could not be helped. Ellen had certainly beaten him on that one. It had been a clear, definite defeat, but he had learned long ago to accept inescapable losses, not to brood over them. When you lost, you lost. In theory, Selectman Tony Balto had given him a reprieve by forbidding his son to attend the party, but Charles Winderman did not see it that way. Once Ellen had forced him to change his position, once Anthony had been invited, Charles could not permit a refusal. A refusal combined the worst of everything: an insult to the family, disappointment for Ellen and Nancy, a personal affront to Charles himself, and all this coming on top of his defeat by Ellen. It made that defeat doubly painful because it would have no value, not even to the winner. No, no, it couldn't be left like that.

So last evening, after an early dinner but while it was still light outside, he had put on his beige linen jacket over his white polo shirt. The jacket would show respect for the occasion, an indication that this was a visit of importance, but a tie would have been going too far. A tie would have announced that this was a formal event, rather than a conversation between two men of substance. Besides, Tony Balto would not be wearing a tie, and that fact would emphasize the difference between islander and summer visitor. That was not the effect Charles was seeking. But he did change his slacks from khaki to gabardine.

As he drove through Summertown and out the far side, he hoped that his timing was right. Most islanders ate dinner early, went to bed early and got up early, at least on weekdays. He hoped to catch Tony Balto right after family dinner.

The long, low-lying shingle house had been built some ten years ago on what used to be farmland. Tony Balto could have afforded any kind of house he wanted—all teak and glass and great stone chimneys, if he had so desired—but he had chosen the Island style, although on a large scale. The windows were standard six-over-six with white trim set into gray, weathered shingle walls. A pea-gravel circular driveway curved around a grass parking area that now held two cars and Balto's blue pickup truck. All was nicely done, although Charles would have preferred wild grass to the more formal lawn, its rich greenness broken up by low stone walls and a host of rosebushes. The broad front door was painted white, matching the trim. It had an elaborate brass knocker and a huge brass handle. There was also a doorbell for those not bold enough to use the knocker.

Charles struck firmly three times, admiring the resonant *chunk* of the solid brass. After a few moments the door opened to reveal a teenage Balto daughter with long black hair in pigtails.

"Good evening," Charles said. "If I'm not disturbing your father at dinner, I'd like to see him. My name is Winderman."

"Just a minute," she said, politely enough, although she did not invite him in.

While he waited, he looked out at the property, the green grass darkening in the twilight. Off to one side stood a straight row of tall pines, obviously planted as a windbreak. In the distance stood three grand oaks that had certainly been here before Tony Balto was born. Fine trees, good for climbing although a little far from the house. It must be quite a chore to keep this land mowed. No doubt a tractor and mower were hidden away somewhere.

"Evening," said the heavy, familiar voice behind him.

Tony Balto wore a long-sleeved white shirt, open at the neck but buttoned at his thick wrists, and dark blue slacks with a decorative silver belt buckle that was at least four inches long. Yet it did not seem too large for his sturdy body.

"Good evening," Charles said. He was determined not to hurry the conversation. He would be as leisurely as Tony Balto had been last week at Charles's house. "It's customary to telephone," he said, deliberately reminding Balto of their original exchange on this topic, "but I thought if I called, you might not see me."

"Ha!" Balto said with a laugh. So he remembered.

"Did I catch you at dinner?"

Balto looked him over from beneath the shaggy black eyebrows and the big shock of hair. "Nope. Want some coffee?"

"Thanks, not at night." Charles gazed around the landscape. "This is a beautiful place. Those oaks are special. I'm very fond of old oaks, but there's nothing like those on my place."

"Too much saltwater wind, probably. I had to clear a lot of brush and smaller trees around them so you could see them.

They like space. My wife thinks a tree is a tree. What she likes is flowers, as you can see." He gestured toward the rosebushes. "Want to come inside?"

Charles had to make a snap guess as to what would work best. "I wonder if you'd show me around outside. I've never been here before."

"Sure. Getting a little dark to see much."

He stalked off along the front of the house, Charles walking beside him. "Living room in there," he waved at the curtained windows they were passing. "Now what I like out this side," he said as they turned the corner of the house, "is the old farm pond and that stand of sassafras trees." The clump of trees at the edge of the pond seemed to have a single curving dark umbrella of foliage but with many different slim trunks outlined against the western sky.

"Did you plant those?"

"Nah, they're old ones. Didn't plant the pond either, but I like the way it looks. Pain in the ass to keep it clean."

"You swim in it?"

Balto stopped, hands on hips, staring at the pond and the trees. "It's only a couple of feet deep. I figure if you live on this Island with all these beaches, you want to swim, you go to the beach. No offense, you don't have a pool, do you?"

"Certainly not. For the same reason."

"Yeah, well I didn't think so. More and more pools on the Island, though. We put one in most every summer now."

"Changing times."

Balto turned to look at him, but it was getting a little dark to read expressions. "Yeah, changing times."

"That's why I came to see you tonight. You gave me a little talk the other day about changing times. I wasn't very responsive. On the other hand, I'm older than you and probably more set in my ways."

"Mr. Winderman, nobody is more set in his ways than an islander."

"Be that as it may, I've thought it over and changed my mind. I'd like to have your son at my party tomorrow. I hope you'll change your mind, too."

Long silence in the falling light. Charles waited.

"What made you change your mind?"

Charles paused long enough to make sure Tony Balto was curious about what was coming. Then he gave him what he felt sure the selectman was least expecting, the truth. "Pressure," he said. "Family pressure."

Balto hooted, a joyful burst of laughter. "Pressure. That's something a politician can understand."

"Or the head of a family."

Charles saw the hand come up to rub the big jaw and then move back over the shock of hair. "I got to say something, Mr. Winderman. It wasn't the easiest thing to drop in on you the other morning. And I can't say I felt too damn welcome, either."

Charles decided to surprise him again with the same weapon, truth. He thought Tony Balto would find truth both surprising and refreshing. "You weren't," he admitted. "I'm asking you to be more considerate than I was. Or at least more modern. As you said, times are different."

"Let me ask you something. If I understand you, you're asking me a favor. Lots of people ask me favors. That's what a selectman is for. And so I do a favor. And then later on I may say, hey, remember that little thing I helped you with. How about supporting me in the election? Suppose I asked you. Would I get your vote?"

The heavy voice was more curious than calculating. Charles thought he knew his man. At any rate, he had gone this far in one direction. Now for one more shot in the same style. "As you know, I don't even have a vote on this Island. But if I did, I wouldn't give it to you because I'd be running for office myself. On a reform ticket."

Tony Balto laughed with genuine pleasure. "Mr. Winderman, I got to warn you. You'd get your ass whipped. They don't want reform around here, they want favors."

Time to make his request. No, what was the advertising term that Bradford used? Time to ask for the order. "So can we expect Anthony at four o'clock tomorrow? As a favor."

"*Per favore.* Well, what the hell? You got it. Now how about some coffee?"

"How about a glass of wine instead?"

"You got it."

The next twenty minutes were surprisingly pleasant. He had suggested the glass of wine only because, by saying no thanks to coffee, he did not want to reject a second offer of Italian hospitality—and perhaps make the selectman change his mind a second time. Tony Balto introduced Charles to his wife and two of his children, then poured two large glasses of Barolo and led him away to the den "to discuss business." The den was lush compared to Charles's own office: two squashy leather chairs, an ornately carved desk with matching armchair, a television set, thick carpeting.

"I never work here," Balto said, waving him to one of the deep leather chairs. "I get enough of that all day at business."

The wine was excellent, as good as a fine Burgundy. That was fortunate because Charles knew he was expected to drink the whole glass. When he complimented the selectman on his house, Tony Balto said that of all the houses he had ever built, he had enjoyed building this one the least. "Every stud, every damn nail, every little improvement my wife thought up along the way was costing me money instead of making me money. Never had that happen before."

While Charles sipped his wine, Balto talked about Island building. His host was a charming storyteller, making fun of himself as well as his competitors. By the time Charles had finished his wine and said good night, he had picked up three good building anecdotes to share with Roger Bernstein, who collected examples of Island mischief.

He had driven home in a good mood, fueled only in part by the Barolo. He had the order in his pocket. And he had not had to be too humble.

Now Mrs. Hackett interrupted Charles's thoughts. "I be saying good night now, Mr. Winderman." She had her sweater thrown over her shoulders, even though the night was warm. She had lived on the Island all her life but had never trusted its weather. "A nice, nice party. Well, happy birthday again."

Charles had once tried to tip Mrs. Hackett after a busy birthday party, but she had been hurt. He had then tried to conceal the tip in her next check, but she knew exactly how many hours she had worked and exactly how much she was owed. For such a small woman, she could be quite fierce.

He thanked her and saw her to the door, then put his head in the kitchen. "How's it going?" he asked.

"Nearly done," Mary Benjamin said cheerfully. She did not sound the least bit weary.

He did not feel tired himself, in spite of the long day and the length of the party. He had always claimed that the eating of lobster renewed one's vigor, and he half believed it. But of course tonight was much more than that. Vigor was one thing, but excitement—genuine excitement—was something else. At his age and with his long experience in family affairs, it did not occur too often.

He went out to his veranda to sit in the dark, looking at the moon and the water, listening to the waves breaking on his beach. He once used to sit here with Anne, holding hands, sometimes talking about important things, sometimes sitting silent. Dear Anne, I wish I could tell you about tonight.

Look at Ellen on the beach this evening. Sitting in that flimsy aluminum chair, displaying all the unwieldiness of late pregnancy, forced by physical discomfort to be somewhat removed from the high sociability of all the family and guests who were moving around the beach, changing groups, chang-

ing partners in conversation. Poor Ellen! Or as Tony Balto
would put it, poor Ellen—ha!
He had kept an eye on her, sitting there, theoretically just a
bit out of things. But she hadn't been out of things at all. He
had seen the parade, all those people, family members or
guests, one after another going to see her. As though she were
holding court, that flimsy chair her throne. He could not be
close enough to overhear the conversation that she had with
each supplicant, but he could see each conversation taking
place. And they were not idle talks, not mere genuflections of
sympathy. No, they were matters of substance. Well, *supplicant* was too strong a term. As he had so often pointed out to
his classes, a metaphor cannot be carried very far before it
collapses under its own burden. No, they were not suppli-
cants. They were just people who had some particular reason
to talk to or to consult with Ellen. And of course, however it
might have appeared to him, Ellen herself had no idea that
she was holding court. She was too young, too inexperienced,
to recognize that it might look that way to anyone else, much
less to have done it deliberately. The metaphor collapses.
Nevertheless, to an interested and admiring observer, it remained basically accurate.   -
He went back to that extraordinary moment yesterday afternoon. He had to admit, and this was a confession of failure,
that he had not had the slightest notion why she wanted to
see him. In most cases, when some member of the family
asked to see him, he knew what it was about. That was just
part of keeping on top of the family. But when Ellen had
asked, in the very teeth of the party preparations, to see him,
he had not been able to guess why. So he had said yes, come
on over, much to Mary Benjamin's annoyance. But whatever
the inconvenience, each family mystery must be unraveled.
She had been sitting right here, just a few yards down the
veranda. He could see as he approached her that she was nervous. She had little of Lawrence's ability to conceal the state

of her mind, but that could be learned. Her voice had been nervous, too, as she started to speak. But he still could not tell what was coming until she actually uttered the words:

"Under the circumstances, I don't think I can come to the party."

He had not answered right away, another device that could be learned. Instead, he sat quietly, absorbing this remarkable statement. He knew it required great courage to go up against him like this, and he always admired that. But it was also a beautiful tactic. She could not have chosen better. Here was the mother of what might well be his last grandchild, a woman who was a personal favorite of his in spite of her somewhat thorny independence, and she was going to boycott his seventieth birthday party. Marvelous! Really quite ingenious. He would not have thought she could bring herself to such an act. He was not only impressed but moved. Courage and political skill always moved him.

But then came the stunning rest of it:

"Lawrence and I even had a bad fight about it this morning. But I have to do what seems right to me, so I won't be coming tomorrow. I just can't. And that's true for Christopher, too. For the same reason, because of Nancy. He said I could tell you he's not coming. I also think you'll be hearing from Roger. Roger Bernstein. But I told him it was important for me to speak to you first. And Martha. She agrees with me. She's coming, of course, but she's on my side."

Extraordinary. First, she had told Lawrence her intention and then held her own against him. That would have been real trench warfare, for Lawrence, when aroused, was a formidable opponent—articulate, icy and ruthless. Think of Ellen standing up to that and sticking to her decision. Tremendous courage. But best of all was this coalition she had somehow put together. An almost incredible coalition. Christopher—nobody could get along with Christopher these days. Charles had pretty much decided that nothing could be done with him at this stage. He was too isolated, too angry at life, too wounded. All that could be done with Christopher was to treat him with measured kindness and be patient, wait for him to grow out of it, however long that might take. And yet somehow Ellen had managed to enlist this supremely difficult boy. How had she done it? And had she realized Christopher's special place in this birthday occasion? For today it would be Ah-boo, Ah-boo, Ah-boo all day long, and Christopher had been the originator, the name-giver. For him to be absent would have been especially inappropriate.

And Roger. That, in a different way, was just as amazing. For Roger was his totally loyal friend. Complete loyalty, annealed over thirty years. Charles had not even been aware that Roger and Ellen knew each other in anything but the most peripheral way. True, Roger admired lovely women, and that meant that he would admire Ellen. But it would take far more than loveliness to attract Roger's serious attention. It would take intelligence, warmth, humor. Well, yes, Ellen had all those, but even so? How did she ever collect him? He doubted that Roger would go so far as to boycott the party, but Ellen had the most important ally she could have chosen, his oldest, closest friend.

Martha was a decided surprise. She was so caught up in her own affairs and difficulties that she never joined anyone else's team. It just wasn't like her to give her proxy—"She's on my side"—to another member of the family. However, if Charles had been in Ellen's place, he would have left Martha out of the coalition. If Martha was unwilling to take a stronger stand, she did not add much weight to the equation. Still, Ellen had achieved something remarkable even to win that much from Martha.

Yesterday afternoon, it was only from the horrified look on Ellen's face that he realized the foolish tears were running down his cheeks. Well, let them run. They were tears of admiration—and of joy. Yes, true joy. For now he knew that at last he had found his successor. It would not, after all, have to be some awkward combination of Lawrence and Bradford. Not at all. It was this wonderful young woman with the courage to defy both him and her own powerful husband, with the skill and the political instinct to win over to her cause both the impossible Christopher and the loyal Roger and the uncooperative Martha. Yet Ellen also had the kindness and affection that he had recognized in her from the very start.

Well, he must do something to spare her from his tears. Her face was torn with sympathy for him. Sympathy and guilt. He pulled out his handkerchief and, while he wiped his face, thought about what he had best say to her.

He was beaten, no question about that. A birthday party without Ellen and Christopher and perhaps even without Roger could not be contemplated. It was time to retreat with honor from the lost battlefield, making certain, however, not to lose the regimental colors.

And so he had told her that he simply had not realized how much this meant to her and Nancy, and that of course Anthony Balto could come to the party. He had tried his best to seem sincere and kindly. He thought it had gone down quite well. And when he had helped her to her feet, she seemed grateful. Yes, given the impossible circumstances, it had gone quite well.

He had loved being nice to her today at the party. Taking her arm when she arrived. Giving her the place of honor beside him for the family picture. Kissing her on the cheek after she made her little birthday speech. Moving her chair closer to the fire when it was time for the singing. He had enjoyed it in part because Ellen herself noticed that he was being particularly nice to her. He could tell from her pleased but puzzled expression. She had excellent antennae. Good antennae were an important factor in family management.

He had even taken a certain pleasure in being nice to Anthony Balto because this was another gift to Ellen. An attractive young man. It was easy to see why Nancy was smitten with him. However, that was one of the good things about summer romances. They tended to end with the summer. With Nancy going back to college, he doubted that the romance would survive both the separation and the winter. If it did, next summer would be time enough to worry about that. Some day he would have the satisfaction of telling Ellen what had really happened yesterday and today. They would look at the picture of her standing beside him, and he would explain that this had been his first public recognition of the new role he expected her to play. If he told her now, it would only confuse her. She was not yet ready.

He stood up on his darkened veranda, because he was too excited to sit still. What a marvelous prospect lay before him and Ellen. He would be a teacher once again, and she would be his student, his favorite among all the students he had ever taught, because their subject would be this family. She had already read all the blue notebooks, so she was well grounded, but the notebooks, being public documents, did not tell everything. There was so much more to tell her. At first, she must not even realize that she was taking a course. He would make sure of that.

And teaching was never a one-way street. He had always learned as much as he had taught. He was curious about Ellen and Christopher and would have to learn all about this from her. And Martha. He had noticed this summer that Martha and Ellen were forming some kind of bond, something more than just being sisters-in-law. Martha's support for Ellen, however limited, had shown this yesterday. Tonight he had been even more sure of it, both from the way Martha had rushed over to Ellen right after that obvious argument between Ellen and Sue, and from the fact that Ellen had handed out such firm advice about how to handle the Martha-Richie situation. Bradford had told him what Ellen had recommended, and he was inclined to follow that advice, but he hoped to learn from Ellen what it was based on. Martha, who had been his serious concern for many years, was developing some kind of special connection with Ellen. Well, he supposed it was good for Martha to have a woman friend to aid her against her menfolk. As long as that didn't get out of hand, Ellen might be able to help Martha more than he could. He had always believed in salvage.

Ellen's child would be another source of strength. From the way she had behaved and talked during her pregnancy, he knew that Ellen would soon be tied even more closely to all the Winderman family. And she would have her cub to protect against all the older, stronger grandchildren. Charles Winderman smiled to himself in the darkness. That child would lead an interesting life.

Of course, Ellen could never become the formal head of the family. To the extent that anyone would be the head after him, it would be Lawrence. But Lawrence, as Charles Winderman had recognized for years, did not enjoy exercising authority in family matters. Strange, since Lawrence had no such reluctance about running the Winderman Trust, which he did with vigor and success. It could only be, Charles had decided, because the family involved people and the bank involved money. When it came to people, Lawrence guarded his own privacy. Charles was not sure how much the humiliation of Lawrence's first marriage had contributed to his deliberate detachment from the larger family, but surely it must be considerable. Oh, Lawrence played his part when the occasion demanded it. He had been a worthy master of ceremonies during the speeches this afternoon. But everyday interest and involvement and caring? And taking the right steps, the right action, whenever action was necessary? Above all, being open and alert to every nuance of family life and family politics? No, that was not Lawrence. That was Ellen.

He did not care that Ellen could never become the official leader. Titles were unnecessary. Leadership grew out of performance. Already, after little more than a year, she was not only accepted by the family but had become a complete member. She was liked and listened to. Look at that extraordinary little incident this evening when Ellen had promised Alice to go skinny-dipping at next summer's party. It was just the kind of unexpected act, surprising and delightful, that a born leader occasionally pulls out of the hat. Fortunately, Ellen had the figure—or would have the figure next summer—to make good on her promise without seeming ridiculous.

Ellen did not convey aggression, as Sue did, but as she had shown him yesterday here on this veranda, Ellen was prepared to take a strong position, to stand and win. All she needed was more experience. He was so ready to help her. Oh, Ellen, he thought, what a wonderful time you and I are going to have over these next years!

He realized that he was clasping his hands tightly together out of sheer pleasure. When had he last felt so confident and so happy about his family? And when, in that curious, old-fashioned phrase, had he felt so full of beans? In fact, in fact—

The screen door opened behind him. "What are you doing out here all alone in the dark?" Mary Benjamin said.

"Enjoying myself, Mary. Making plans."

"I thought you'd gone to bed."

"I was just thinking about it."

"I should think so. You must be worn out."

"As a matter of fact," he said, "I'm not tired at all." He smiled at her with great fondness. "How could I possibly be tired on a day like this? Come on, Mary, let's go upstairs. And bring the cigarettes."